DEBBIE MACOMBER

Falling for Christmas

featuring
A Cedar Cove Christmas and
Call Me Mrs Miracle

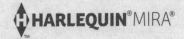

This edition published in Great Britain 2014
by Harlequin MIRA, an imprint of Harlequin (UK) Limited,
Eton House, 18-24 Paradise Road,
Richmond, Surrey, TW9 1SR

FALLING FOR CHRISTMAS © 2010 Harlequin Books S.A.

The publisher acknowledges the copyright holder of the individual works as follows:

A Cedar Cove Christmas © 2008 Debbie Macomber
Call Me Mrs. Miracle © 2010 Debbie Macomber

ISBN 978-0-7783-0394-7

59-1110

Harlequin (UK) Limited's policy is to use papers that are natural, renewable and recyclable products and made from wood grown in sustainable forests. The logging and manufacturing processes conform to the legal environmental regulations of the country of origin.

Printed and bound by
CPI Group (UK) Ltd, Croydon, CR0 4YY

Debbie Macomber is a number one *New York Times* bestselling author. Her recent books include *44 Cranberry Point, 50 Harbor Way, 6 Rainier Drive* and *Hannah's List*. She has become a leading voice in women's fiction worldwide and her work has appeared on every major bestseller list. There are more than one hundred million copies of her books in print. For more information on Debbie and her books, visit www.DebbieMacomber.com.

A Cedar Cove Christmas

To our dear friends
Rhett Palmer
and
Claudia Faye Johnson
plus
Beni
The cutest dog in the universe

Prologue

"I can't believe Grace is willing to do this on Christmas Eve," Mary Jo said, slipping the frilly red dress over Noelle's head. The one-year-old fussed, objecting to the fact that her face was momentarily covered.

"It's Noelle's birthday," Mack reminded her.

Not that Mary Jo needed reminding…

"A year ago today you stepped off the foot ferry to Cedar Cove…"

"And met you," she finished for him.

"At the library…"

"Because Grace thought I needed medical attention."

"Which you did," Mac continued, smiling at their exchange, "because you were about to give birth."

"Only I didn't know that at the time."

"No one did."

Noelle squealed.

"Except Noelle," Mary Jo said. "Right, sweetie?" She nuzzled her daughter's face. "Happy birthday, baby girl."

"Ma Ma."

"That's right, sweetie. That's me."

"Ma Ma," Noelle repeated and gleefully clapped her hands.

"Are my two girls ready to party?" Mack asked. He had his coat on and a big collection of birthday and Christmas gifts tied up in a large bag that made Mary Jo think of something Santa would haul around. "We don't want to keep everyone waiting."

Grace had invited half of Cedar Cove—or so it seemed to Mary Jo—to her Christmas Eve bash, which was also Noelle's birthday party. All three of Mary Jo's brothers planned to attend, which was only fitting since they'd lost out on the chance to welcome their niece into the world a year ago. Mary Jo still had to grin whenever she thought about her brothers racing around the county like Keystone Kops frantically searching for their missing sister.

Grace's two daughters and their families would be at the ranch as well, along with Grace's dear friend Olivia and Olivia's husband, Jack. And Charlotte and Ben Rhodes were on the invitation list, too, as well they should be.

Then, of course, there were Mack's parents, Roy and Corrie McAfee. His oldest sister, Gloria, had sent her regrets. She was a sheriff's deputy and unfortunately she'd pulled the Christmas Eve shift. His other sister, Linnette, who lived in North Dakota, was a new mom herself and had mailed a gift Noelle had cheerfully ripped open that morning. It was a pull toy that made popping sounds with every step. Mack had laughed and promised revenge. Mary Jo could see a toy drum set in little Wade Mason's future.

Oh, yes, this was going to be quite the party and one Mary Jo had never expected. But then, she hadn't expected *any* of this. That day exactly a year ago—when she'd come from Seattle with the desperate, and misguided, idea of finding Noelle's birth father—had changed her life.

What she'd found was love, friends, a home, a whole new family. Not that there was anything wrong with her old one, but the people of Cedar Cove had expanded her family above and beyond anything she could ever have dreamed of.

"I'll get the car warmed up and then come back and help you and Noelle," Mack said.

"Okay, darling."

"Darling?" Mack's eyebrows rose ever so slightly, giving him a sexy, enticing look. "I have to say I prefer that to the nickname the guys at the firehouse have for me."

"And what's that?"

"You think I'm going to tell you? Not on your life."

"Loverboy?"

He laughed, shook his head and disappeared out the front door. Mack returned a couple of minutes later to carry Noelle to the car. "You ready?"

"Ready."

Noelle, bundled up in her winter coat with the faux-fur hem and edging around the hood, raised her tiny arms up to Mack. Her daughter had reached out to Mack a year ago, too. And Mack had responded—to both of them.

Love, family, friends—a place to belong. Her first Christmas in Cedar Cove had given her all that. And this, her second one, was a celebration of the first.

Christmas Eve. It was a night for remembering and rejoicing in *two* birthdays, wasn't it?

Chapter One

A year ago

Even though she was listening to Christmas carols on her iPod, Mary Jo Wyse could hear her brothers arguing. How could she not? Individually, the three of them had voices that were usually described as booming; together they sounded like an entire football stadium full of fans. All three worked as mechanics in the family-owned car repair business and stood well over six feet. Their size alone was intimidating. Add to that their voices, and they'd put the fear of God into the most hardened criminal.

"It's nearly Christmas," Linc was saying. He was the oldest and, if possible, loudest of the bunch.

"Mary Jo said he'd call her before now," Mel said.

Ned, her youngest brother, remained suspiciously quiet. He was the sensitive one. Translated, that meant he'd apologize after he broke David Rhodes's fingers for getting his little sister pregnant and then abandoning her.

"We've got to do *something*," Linc insisted.

The determination in his voice gave her pause. Mary Jo's situation was complicated enough without the involvement of her loving but meddlesome older brothers. However, it wasn't *their* fault that she was about to have a baby and the father was nowhere in sight.

"I say we find David Rhodes and string him up until he agrees to marry our sister."

Mary Jo gasped. She couldn't help it. Knowing Linc, he'd have no qualms about doing exactly that.

"I think we should, too—if only we knew where he was," she heard Mel say.

Unable to sit still any longer, Mary Jo tore off her earphones and burst out of her bedroom. She marched into the living room, where her brothers stood around the Christmas tree, beers in hand, as its lights blinked cheerfully. Ever since their parents had been killed in a car accident six years earlier, her older brothers had considered themselves her guardians. Which was ridiculous, since she was over twenty-one. Twenty-three, to be precise. She hadn't been legally of age at the time of their deaths, but her brothers seemed to forget she was now an adult.

All four of them still lived in the family home. Mel and Ned were currently seeing women, but neither relationship seemed all that serious. Linc had recently broken up with someone. Mary Jo was the only one eager to leave, chafing as she did at her brothers' attempts to decree how she should live her life.

Admittedly she'd made a mess of things; she couldn't

deny it. But she was trying to deal with the consequences, to act like the adult she was. Yes, she'd made a massive error in judgment, falling for an attractive older man and doing what came all too naturally. And no, she didn't need her brothers' assistance.

"Would you guys mind your own business," she demanded, hands on her hips. At five-three she stared up at her brothers, who towered above her.

She probably looked a sight, although at the moment her appearance was the least of her problems. She was dressed in her old flannel nightgown, the one with the Christmas angels on it, her belly stretched out so far it looked like she'd swallowed a giant snow globe. Her long dark hair fell in tangles, and her feet were bare.

Linc frowned back at her. "You're our sister and that makes you our business."

"We're worried about you," Ned said, speaking for the first time. "You're gonna have that baby any day."

"I don't know nothin' about birthing no babies," Mel added in a falsetto voice.

If he was trying to add humor to the situation, Mary Jo wasn't amused. She glared at him angrily. "You don't have to worry about delivering my baby. This child is my concern and mine alone."

"No, he isn't."

From the very minute she'd tearfully announced her pregnancy four months ago, her brothers had decided the baby was a boy. For some reason, the alternative never seemed to occur to them, no matter how often she suggested it.

"You're depriving this baby of his father," Linc said stubbornly. It was a lament he'd voiced a hundred times over the past months. "A baby *needs* a father."

"I agree," Mary Jo told him. "However, I haven't seen David in weeks."

Mel stepped forward, his disapproval obvious. "What about Christmas? Didn't he tell you he'd be in touch before Christmas?"

"He did." But then David Rhodes had made a lot of promises, none of which he'd kept. "He said he'd be visiting his family in the area."

"Where?" Ned asked.

"Cedar Cove," she supplied and wondered if she should've told her three hotheaded brothers that much.

"Let's go there and find him," Linc said.

Mary Jo held up both hands. "Don't be crazy!"

"Crazy," Linc echoed with a snort of indignation. "I refuse to let you have this baby alone."

"I'm not alone," Mary Jo said. She gestured toward them. "I have the three of you, don't I?"

Her brothers went pale before her eyes. "You…you want us in the delivery room?" Mel asked in weak tones. He swallowed visibly. "You're joking, right?"

Mary Jo had delayed registering for birthing classes because David had promised to attend them with her. Only he hadn't managed to show up for the first session or the one after that or the following one, either. Giving up on him, Mary Jo had begun a session that week—a lot later in the pregnancy than she should have. She'd gone by herself and left the class in tears. Although she'd considered asking Ned if he'd be her birthing partner, she hadn't found the courage to do it yet. And she wasn't sure he'd be the best choice, anyway. Her other options were her girlfriends Casey and Chloe; however, Casey was terrified by the idea and Chloe, married last year, was expecting her own baby.

"Right." She struggled to maintain her composure. "That was a joke."

They released a collective sigh.

"You're distracting us from what's important here." Obviously, Linc wasn't going to be put off. "I want to talk to David Rhodes, just him and me, man to man." He clenched his hands at his sides.

"And when Linc's finished, I want a turn," Mel said, plowing his fist into his open palm.

Mary Jo rolled her eyes. She'd defended David to her brothers countless times. She'd defended him to Casey and Chloe—the only other people who knew David was her baby's father. Casey worked with her at the insurance company in Seattle, so she'd met David, since he'd come to their office for meetings every few weeks, representing corporate headquarters in California. David had charmed just about everybody—with the possible exception of Casey.

He'd always had such good excuses for missing the birthing classes, and she'd believed him. It was easy to do because she so badly wanted to trust him. He claimed to love her and while the pregnancy certainly hadn't been planned, he'd seemed genuinely pleased when she'd told him. There were a few legal and financial matters that needed to be cleared up, he'd explained, but as soon as they were dealt with, he'd marry her.

For a number of months Mary Jo had convinced her brothers that David's intentions were honorable. Now, though, she had to resign herself to the fact that David wasn't willing or able to marry her. She realized she didn't know as much about him as she should. Granted, he was older by at least twenty years, but her infatuation had led her to dismiss the significance of that. Now Mary Jo had to doubt his sincerity. She hadn't heard from him in more than two weeks and he wasn't answering his cell phone, and even during their last conversation, he'd been preoccupied and abrupt. He'd mentioned that he'd be in Cedar Cove for Christmas with his father and stepmother and would call her then.

"Do you *want* to marry David?" Ned asked. He was the only brother to take her feelings into consideration.

"Of course she wants to marry him," Linc answered, scowling at him. "She's about to have his baby, isn't she?"

"I believe I can answer for myself." Mary Jo calmly turned toward her oldest brother. "Actually—"

"You're getting married," Linc broke in.

"I won't have you holding a gun on David!"

Linc shook his head, expression puzzled. "I don't own a gun."

She sighed; her brothers could be so literal sometimes. "I was speaking figuratively," she said loftily.

"Oh." Linc frowned. "Well, I'm not talking figures, I'm talking facts." He raised one finger. "You're having a baby."

He raised a second. "The father of that baby needs to accept his responsibilities."

"He will," Mary Jo murmured, although any hope that David would take care of her and the baby had long since been dashed.

"Yes, he will," Mel said firmly, "because we're going to make sure he does."

"And that includes putting a wedding band on your finger," Linc informed her, giving her a look that said he wouldn't tolerate any argument.

The baby kicked as though in protest and Mary Jo echoed the child's feelings. She no longer knew what she wanted. In the beginning she'd been head-over-heels in love with David. He was the most exciting man she'd ever met, and without even trying, he'd swept her off her feet. Mary Jo had been thrilled when he paid attention to her, a lowly accounting clerk. Compared to the boyfriends she'd had—as naive and inexperienced as she'd been herself—David was a romantic hero. An older man, confident, witty, indulgent.

"Mary Josephine," Mel said loudly. "Are you listening?"

Blinking to clear her thoughts, Mary Jo focused on her middle brother. "I guess not, sorry."

"Sorry?" Mel stormed. "We're talking about your future here and the future of your son."

Despite the seriousness of the situation, Mary Jo yawned. She couldn't help it. She covered her mouth with one hand and placed the other on her protruding belly. "I'm going to bed," she declared.

"Mary Jo!" Linc shouted after her as if she were a marine

recruit and he was her drill instructor. "We need to decide what to do *here* and *now*."

"Can't we talk about it in the morning?" She was too exhausted to continue this argument with her brothers at—she glanced toward the antique clock—almost midnight.

"No."

"Linc, be reasonable."

"We have to get this settled." Mel joined forces with his older brother.

Again Ned didn't speak. He cast her a look of quiet sympathy but he wasn't taking sides. Mary Jo could see that he felt Linc and Mel were right—not about becoming Mrs. Rhodes but about the need to make some kind of decision.

"Okay, okay, but we've already said everything there is to say." She sagged onto the sofa and tried to keep her eyes open.

Linc glanced at the clock, too. "As of about one minute ago, it's officially Christmas Eve. Rhodes promised to be in touch *before* Christmas."

Exhaling a deep sigh, Mary Jo shrugged. "He might've said *on* Christmas. I've forgotten."

"Well, I haven't." Mel's feet were braced wide apart, his arms folded across his chest.

"I haven't forgotten, either." Linc, too, crossed his arms. They looked like bouncers at a tough bar, but Mary Jo feared the person they'd toss out on his ear would be David Rhodes.

And he'd deserve it; she knew that. He'd deceived her not once, not twice, but a dozen times or more. Still, some of the responsibility was hers. Even though she was aware that he'd abused her trust, she'd foolishly believed him, giving him chance after chance. Now her brothers were trying to save her from him—and from herself.

"David said he'd contact you *before* Christmas," Linc reminded her. "That gives him less than twenty-four hours."

"Yes, it does." Her agreeing with him was sure to confuse her well-meaning brothers.

Apparently shocked by her unaccustomed meekness, Linc narrowed his eyes, then checked the clock again. "Yup, less than twenty-four hours. It's time you realized he has no intention of doing the proper thing."

Mary Jo couldn't argue with that. She was just tired of discussing it. "You never know," she said, forcing a note of optimism into her voice.

"Then you're living in a dream world, little sister," Mel said through gritted teeth.

Ned sat down next to Mary Jo and reached for her hand. "Linc and Mel are right," he told her gently.

"About what?" She was so exhausted, her vision had started to blur.

"Someone needs to get in touch with David. If we can't find him, then one of his family members. He has to be held accountable."

Linc snorted again. "David Rhodes has to make an honest woman of you."

If Mary Jo heard that one more time she was going to scream. "I *am* an honest woman! I don't need David or any man to validate what each of you should already know."

"Yeah, yeah," Linc muttered. "Don't get your knickers in a knot. It's only an expression."

"What we all want," Mel began, as if to clarify their thoughts, "is for you to be happy—*with* the father of your baby."

Mary Jo doubted that was even possible. She'd lost faith in David and as much as she wanted to believe he loved her and cared about their child, the evidence stated otherwise.

"He's not giving us any choice," Linc said, his dark eyes menacing. "We're going to find him and—"

"Linc, please. Hold off for a few days. Please." She hated to plead but it was Christmas and she didn't want to see the holiday ruined for any of them. She was protecting David—again—and the irony didn't escape her. Despite all these months of intermittent contact and broken promises, Mary Jo still felt the urge to shield him from her brothers.

But her real concern was for Linc, Mel and Ned. She didn't want *them* ending up in jail because of David.

"We're not waiting another minute!" Mel boomed. "If David's in Cedar Cove, we're going to track him down."

"No. Please," she said shakily.

"You don't have a say in this anymore."

"Linc, it's my life! Listen to me. I—"

"We've listened to you enough," her oldest brother said matter-of-factly. "Now the three of us have decided to take matters into our own hands."

Mary Jo couldn't let her brothers get involved. She shuddered as she imagined them charging into Cedar Cove on Christmas Eve, bent on forcing David to marry her.

No, she couldn't allow that to happen. Resolute, she stood up and started for her bedroom. "We'll finish discussing this in the morning," she said in as dignified a voice as she could manage.

Linc seemed about to argue, but her fatigue must have shown because he hesitated, then nodded reluctantly. "There'll be no avoiding it, understand?"

"Perfectly."

"Night, sweetie." He threw his arms around her in a quick hug, as did Mel and then Ned.

Mary Jo slept soundly for six hours and woke in a cold sweat. She knew she'd never be able to stop her interfering brothers from invading Cedar Cove, embarrassing her and possibly doing bodily harm to David. The only solution she could think of was to get there first and warn David and/or his family.

With that in mind, Mary Jo left her brothers a note and slipped quietly out of the house.

Chapter Two

Cedar Cove was a festive little town, Mary Jo thought when she stepped off the ferry. It was a place that took Christmas seriously. Even the terminal was decorated, with bells hanging from the ceiling and large snowflakes in the windows. She'd never been here before and was pleasantly surprised by its charm. After taking the Washington State ferry from downtown Seattle to Bremerton, she'd caught the foot ferry across Sinclair Inlet to the small town David had mentioned.

He'd only talked about it that one time. She'd had the impression he didn't like it much, but she hadn't understood why.

She looked around.

A lighthouse stood off in the distance, picturesque against the backdrop of fir trees and the green waters of the cove. Waves rhythmically splashed the large rocks that marked the beach. Adjusting her purse strap on her shoulder and getting a tighter grip on her bag, Mary Jo walked down the pier into town.

Large evergreen boughs stretched across the main street of Cedar Cove—Harbor Street, according to the sign—and from the center of each hung a huge ornament. There were alternating wreaths, angels and candles. The lightposts were festooned with holly. The effect of all these decorations was delightful and it raised her spirits—until she remembered why she was in Cedar Cove.

It was ten in the morning on Christmas Eve, and everyone seemed to have places to go. So did Mary Jo, except that she was in no hurry to get there, and who could blame her? This was likely to be a painful confrontation.

Not sure where to start searching for David's family and desperate to collect her thoughts, Mary Jo stopped at a coffee house called Mocha Mama's about a block from the waterfront. This, too, was decorated and redolent of Christmas scents—fir, cinnamon, peppermint. And the rich, strong aroma of fresh coffee. The place was nearly empty. The only other person there was a young man who stood behind the counter; he was writing or drawing something in a sketchbook and appeared to be immersed in his task, whatever it was.

"Merry Christmas," Mary Jo said cheerfully, wondering if her words sounded as forced as they felt. She pulled off her wool hat and gloves, cramming them in her pockets.

Her presence startled the young man, who wore a name tag that identified him as Shaw. He glanced up, blinked in apparent confusion, then suddenly smiled. "Sorry. Didn't see you come in. What can I get you?"

"I'd like one of your decaf candy cane mochas, Shaw."

"What size?"

"Oh, grande—is that what you call it here? Medium. One of those." She pointed at a stack of cups.

His eyes went to her stomach, which protruded from the opening of her wool coat. She could no longer fasten more than the top three buttons.

"You're gonna have a baby," Shaw said, as if this information should be a surprise to her.

"Yes, I am." She rested a protective hand on her belly.

Shaw began to prepare her mocha, chatting as he did. "It's been pretty quiet this morning. Maybe 'cause it's Christmas Eve," he commented.

Mary Jo nodded, then took a chair by the window and watched people walk briskly past. The town seemed to be busy and prosperous, with people popping in and out of stores along the street. The bakery had quite a few customers and so did a nearby framing shop.

"I haven't seen you around here before," Shaw said. He added whipped topping and a candy cane to her cup and handed it to her.

"I'm visiting," Mary Jo explained as she got up to pay for her drink. Shaw seemed to be full of information; he might be just the person to ask about David. She poked a folded dollar bill into the tip jar. "Would you know any people named Rhodes in this area?" she asked speculatively, holding her drink with both hands.

"Rhodes, Rhodes," Shaw repeated carefully. He mulled it over for a moment, then shook his head. "The name's familiar but I can't put a face to it."

"Oh." She couldn't quite hide her disappointment. Carrying her mocha, she returned to the table by the window and gazed out at the street again. Her biggest fear was that her three brothers would come rolling into town in their huge pickup, looking like vigilantes out of some old western. Or worse, a bunch of hillbillies. Mary Jo decided she *had* to get to David and his family first.

"Just a minute," Shaw said. "There *is* a Rhodes family in Cedar Cove." He reached behind the counter and pulled out a telephone directory.

Mary Jo wanted to slap her forehead. Of course! How stupid. She should've checked the phone book immediately. That was certainly what her brothers would do.

"Here," Shaw said, flipping the directory around so she could read the listings. As it happened, there was a B. Rhodes, a Kevin Rhodes and three others—and Mary Jo had no way of knowing which of these people were related to David. The only thing to do was to call every one of them and find out.

"Would you mind if I borrowed this for a few minutes?" she asked.

"Sure, go ahead. Tell me if there's anything I can do to help."

"Thanks."

"Consider it a random act of kindness."

"Not so random." Mary Jo smiled as she brought the phone

book back to her table. She rummaged for her cell phone; she hadn't remembered to charge it before she left and was relieved to see that she had nearly a full battery. She dialed the number for B. Rhodes and waited through several rings before a greeting came on, telling her that Ben and Charlotte weren't available and inviting her to leave a message. She didn't. She actually spoke to the next Rhodes, who sounded young and didn't know anyone named David. Of the last three, the first had a disconnected phone line and the other two didn't answer.

Mary Jo had assumed it would be easy to find David in a town as small as Cedar Cove. Walking down Harbor Street, she'd seen a sign for Roy McAfee, a private investigator. She hadn't expected to need one, and even if she could afford to pay someone else to search for David Rhodes, it wasn't likely that Mr. McAfee would accept a case this close to Christmas.

"Any luck?" Shaw asked.

"None." Without knowing the name of David's father, she couldn't figure out what her next step should be. There were three, possibly four, potential candidates, since she'd managed to rule out just one. Her only consolation was the fact that if *she* was having trouble, so would her brothers.

"I can think of one person who might be able to help you," Shaw said thoughtfully.

"Who?"

"Grace Harding. She's the head librarian and she knows practically everyone in town. I'm not sure if she's working this morning but it wouldn't do any harm to go there and see."

"The library is where?" Being on foot and pregnant definitely imposed some limitations, especially now that it had started to snow.

"How'd you get here?" Shaw asked.

"Foot ferry."

He grinned. "Then you walked right past it when you got off. It's the building with the large mural on the front. You won't have any trouble finding it."

Mary Jo had noticed two such murals. She supposed it wouldn't be difficult to distinguish which one was the library. Eager to talk to Grace Harding, she left the remainder of her drink behind. She put the wool hat back on her head and pulled on her gloves. It was cold and the few snowflakes that had begun to drift down seemed persistent, like a harbinger of more to come. The Seattle area rarely experienced a white Christmas, and under other circumstances Mary Jo would've been thrilled at the prospect of snow.

As Shaw had predicted, she didn't have a problem locating the library. The mural of a frontier family was striking, and the library doors were decorated with Christmas wreaths. When she stepped inside, she saw dozens of cut-out snowflakes suspended from the ceiling in the children's area, as well as a display of seasonal picture books, some of which—like *A Snowy Day*—she remembered from her own childhood. A large Christmas tree with book-size wrapped gifts underneath stood just inside the small lobby. One look told Mary Jo that this was a much-used and much-loved place.

She welcomed the warmth, both emotional and physical. There was a woman at the counter, which held a sign stating that the library would close at noon. Glancing at the clock on the wall, Mary Jo was surprised to see that it was already ten-forty-five.

She approached the front counter. "Excuse me. Are you Grace Harding?" she asked in a pleasant voice.

"Afraid not. Should I get her for you?"

"Yes, please."

The woman disappeared into a nearby office. A few minutes later, she reappeared with another middle-aged woman, who greeted Mary Jo with a friendly smile. She wore a bright red turtleneck sweater under a festive holly-green jumper. Her right arm seemed to be thickly bandaged beneath her long sleeve.

"I'm Grace Harding," she announced. "How can I help you?"

Mary Jo gave the woman a strained smile. "Hello, my name is Mary Jo Wyse and—" The baby kicked—hard—and Mary Jo's eyes widened with shock. She placed her hands against her stomach and slowly exhaled.

"Are you okay?" Grace asked, looking concerned.

"I…think so."

"Perhaps you should sit down."

Numbly Mary Jo nodded. This was all so…unseemly. She hated making a fuss, but she suspected the librarian was right and she did need to sit. Thankfully, Ms. Harding came around the counter and led her to a chair. She left for a moment and returned with a glass of water.

"Here, drink this."

"Thank you." Mary Jo felt embarrassed, since almost everyone in the library was staring at her. No doubt she made quite a spectacle and people probably thought she'd give birth any second. Actually, her due date wasn't for another two weeks; she didn't think there was any danger the baby would arrive early, but this was her first pregnancy and she couldn't really tell. She could only hope….

Grace took the chair beside hers. "How can I help you?" she asked again.

Mary Jo gulped down all the water, then put the glass down beside her.

Taking a deep breath, she clasped her hands together. "I'm looking for a man by the name of David Rhodes."

Right away Mary Jo saw that the other woman stiffened.

"You know him?" she asked excitedly, ignoring any misgivings over Grace's reaction. "Is he here? He said he'd be visiting his father and stepmother in Cedar Cove. It's important that I talk to him as soon as possible."

Grace sagged in her chair. "Oh, dear."

"Oh, dear," Mary Jo repeated. "What does that mean?"

"Well…"

"Is David in town?"

Grace shook her head, but her expression was sympathetic. "I'm afraid not."

Mary Jo's heart sank. She should've known not to trust David. This was obviously another lie.

"What about his father and stepmother? Are they available?" If she didn't tell David's family about the baby, then her brothers surely would. The information would be better coming from her. The image of her brothers barging into these people's home lent a sense of urgency to her question.

"Unfortunately," Grace went on, "Ben and Charlotte have taken a Christmas cruise."

"They're gone, then," Mary Jo said in a flat voice. She recalled the message on their phone; ironically, Ben had been the first Rhodes she'd called. Maybe she should be relieved they were out of town, but she wasn't. Instead, a deep sadness settled over her. The uncertainty would continue. Whatever happened, she accepted the likelihood of being a single mother, but her brothers would do their best to prevent it.

"According to a friend of mine, they're coming back sometime tomorrow," Grace told her.

"On Christmas Day?"

"Yes, that's what I understand, at any rate. I can find out for sure if you'd like."

"Yes, please."

Grace looked tentative. "Before I phone Olivia—she's the friend I mentioned—I should tell you that her mother is married to Ben Rhodes."

"I see."

"Would you mind if I asked you a question?"

"Of course not." Although she already knew what that question would be…

"Is your baby…is David Rhodes—"

Rather than respond, Mary Jo closed her eyes and hung her head.

Grace touched her arm gently. "Don't be upset, dear," she murmured. "None of that matters now."

The answer to Grace's question was obvious. Why else would someone in an advanced state of pregnancy come looking for David and his family—especially on Christmas Eve?

As she opened her eyes, Grace squeezed her hand reassuringly.

"I haven't seen or heard from David in weeks," Mary Jo admitted. "He occasionally calls and the last time he did, he said he was coming here to spend Christmas with his family. My brothers want to make him marry me, but…but that isn't what *I* want."

"Of course you don't."

At least Grace shared her point of view. "I've got to talk to Mr. and Mrs. Rhodes as soon as I can and explain that even if David offered to marry me, I don't think it's the right thing for me or my baby."

"I don't either," Grace said. "David isn't to be trusted."

Mary Jo grinned weakly. "I'm afraid I have to agree with you. But this is their grandchild. Or…or Ben's, anyway. Maybe they'll be interested in knowing the baby. Maybe David'll want some kind of relationship." She turned to Grace and said earnestly, "Shouldn't I give them that choice?"

"Yes, that's exactly what you should do." Grace squeezed her hand again. "I'll go call Olivia and get right back to you. She'll know Charlotte and Ben's travel schedule. However, it does seem to me that they're due home on the twenty-fifth."

"Thank you," Mary Jo murmured. She was feeling light-headed and a bit queasy, so she intended to stay where she was until Grace came back. It didn't take long.

Grace sat down next to her again. "I spoke with Olivia and she confirmed that Charlotte and Ben will indeed be home tomorrow afternoon."

"Oh…good." Still, Mary Jo wasn't sure what she should do next. If she went home, her brothers would be impossible. They'd be furious that she'd left with no warning other than a brief note. In any case, they were probably on their way to Cedar Cove now. And with some effort, they'd uncover the same information Mary Jo had.

"What would you like to do?" Grace asked.

"I think I'd better spend the night here," Mary Jo said. She hadn't packed a bag, but her requirements were simple. All she needed was a decent hotel. "Can you recommend a place to stay?"

"Oh, yes, there are several, including a lovely B-and-B. I'm just wondering if there'll be a problem getting a room for tonight."

"A problem?" This wasn't something Mary Jo had considered.

"Let's see if there's anything at the Comfort Inn. It's close by and clean."

"That would be great. Thank you so much," Mary Jo said.

Here it was, Christmas Eve, and she felt as if she'd found an angel to help her. An angel fittingly named Grace…

Chapter Three

Grace Harding studied the young pregnant woman beside her. So David Rhodes was the father of her baby. Not a surprise, she supposed, but it made her think even less of him. Certainly Olivia had told her plenty—about his deceit, his loans that were more like theft, since he never seemed to have any intention of repaying his father, the rumors of women he'd cheated on.… That Ben Rhodes, who was one of the most decent and honorable men she'd ever met, could have a son like David defied explanation. Not only had David fathered this child, which she didn't doubt for a minute, he'd also lied to Mary Jo.

Well, Grace decided, she'd do what she could to give the poor girl a hand. And she knew Charlotte and Ben would, too.

"I'll get that list of places for you," Grace told Mary Jo, rising to her feet. The library had a sheet with phone numbers of the local bed-and-breakfasts, plus all the motels in the area. The best place in town was Thyme and Tide Bed

& Breakfast, run by Bob and Peggy Beldon. However, she recalled, the couple was away for the holidays. So staying there wasn't an option. But there were several chain hotels out by the freeway.

"I'll need to be within walking distance of the Rhodes home," Mary Jo said as Grace handed her the list. "I didn't drive over."

"Don't worry. If there's a vacancy a few miles out of town I'll take you there myself and I can drop you off at Charlotte's tomorrow evening."

Mary Jo glanced up at her, brown eyes wide with astonishment. "You'd do that?"

"Of course. It wouldn't be any problem. I'm going that way myself."

"Thank you."

Grace shrugged lightly. "I'm happy to do it," she said. The offer was a small thing and yet Mary Jo seemed so grateful. "If you'll excuse me, I need to make another phone call."

"Of course." Mary Jo had taken out her cell phone, clearly ready to start her search for a room. Normally, cell phone use in the library was discouraged but in this case Grace couldn't object.

Grace returned to her office. She'd promised to call Olivia back as soon as she could. Although they spoke almost every day, their conversations over the past week had been brief. With so much to do before Christmas, there hadn't been time to chat.

Sitting at her desk, Grace picked up the receiver and punched in Olivia's number. Her dearest friend was at home today, but unfortunately not because it was Christmas Eve. Judge Olivia Griffin had been diagnosed with breast cancer and had undergone surgery; she'd begin chemotherapy and radiation treatments early in the new year. She'd taken a leave of absence from the bench. The last month had been frightening, especially when Olivia developed a life-threatening infection. Grace got chills just thinking about how close they'd all come to losing her.

Olivia answered on the first ring. "It took you forever to call back," she said. "Is the girl still at the library?"

"Yes. She's staying the night and then meeting with Ben and Charlotte tomorrow afternoon."

"Oh, no…"

"Should I tell her it might be better to wait?" Grace asked. Like Olivia, she hated the thought of hitting Ben with this news the minute he and Charlotte got home.

"I don't know," Olivia said. "I mean, they're going to be tired…" Her voice faded away.

"The thing is," Grace went on to say, "I really don't think it *should* wait. Mary Jo's obviously due very soon." She hesitated, unsure how much to tell Olivia. She didn't want to burden her friend. Because of her illness, Olivia was uncharacteristically fragile these days.

"I heard that hesitation in your voice, Grace Harding," Olivia scolded. "There's more to this and you're wondering if you should tell me."

There were times Grace swore Olivia could read her mind. She took a breath. "It seems David told Mary Jo he'd be spending the holidays with Ben and Charlotte."

"I knew it! That's a lie. This cruise has been planned for months and David was well aware of it. Why would he do something like this?"

Grace didn't have an answer—although she had her own opinion on David and his motives.

"He probably used the lie as another tactic to put the poor girl off," Olivia said. "The way David manipulates people and then discards them like so much garbage infuriates me." Outrage echoed in every word.

"It appears that's exactly what he did," Grace murmured. She remembered how David had tried to swindle Charlotte out of several thousand dollars a few years ago. The man was without conscience.

"This poor girl! All alone at Christmas. It's appalling. If I could, I'd wring David's neck myself."

"I have the feeling we'd need to stand in line for that," Grace said wryly.

"No kidding," Olivia agreed. "Okay, now that I know what this Mary Jo business is all about, tell me what happened to your arm."

Instinctively Grace's hand moved to her upper right arm. "You're gonna laugh," she said, smiling herself, though at the time it'd been no laughing matter.

"Grace, from what I heard, you were in a lot of pain."

"And who told you that?"

"Justine. She ran into Cliff at the pharmacy when he was picking up your prescription."

"Oh, right." Small towns were like this. Everything was news and nothing was private. That could be beneficial—and it could be embarrassing. Olivia's daughter, Justine, knew, so Olivia's husband—the local newspaper editor—did, too. It wouldn't surprise her if Jack wrote a humorous piece on her misadventure.

"So, what happened?" Olivia repeated.

Grace saw no reason to hide the truth. "I got bitten by the camel."

"*What?* The *camel?* What camel?"

Grace had to smile again. Olivia's reaction was the same as that of Dr. Timmons. According to the young physician, this was the first time he'd ever treated anyone for a camel bite.

"Cliff and I are housing the animals for the live Nativity scene," she said. "Remember?" The local Methodist church had brought in animals for the display. Grace wasn't sure where the camel had come from but as far as she was concerned it could go back there anytime. And it would. Yesterday had been the final day of the animals' appearances; they'd be returning to their individual homes just after Christmas. True, she'd miss the donkey, since she'd grown fond of him. But the camel? Goodbye, Sleeping Beauty! Grace almost snorted at the animal's unlikely name.

"Of course," Olivia said, "the live Nativity scene. I didn't get a chance to see it. So *that's* how you encountered the camel."

"Yes, I went out to feed the dastardly beast. Cliff warned me that camels can be cantankerous and I *thought* I was being careful."

"Apparently not careful enough." Olivia sputtered with laughter.

"Hey, it isn't that funny," Grace said, slightly miffed that her friend hadn't offered her the requisite amount of sympathy. "I'll have you know it *hurt*."

"Did he break the skin?"

"He's a she, and yes, she did." Grace's arm ached at the memory. "Sleeping Beauty—" she said the name sarcastically "—bit me through two layers of clothing."

"Did you need stitches?" The amusement had left Olivia's voice.

"No, but Dr. Timmons gave me a prescription for antibiotics and then bandaged my arm. From the bandage, you'd think it had nearly been amputated. This morning I had trouble finding a sweater that would go over the dressing."

"Poor Grace."

"That's more like it," she said in a satisfied tone.

"Let Cliff feed the camel from now on."

"You bet I will."

"Good."

"That's not all." Grace figured she might as well go for broke on the sympathy factor.

"What—the donkey bit you, too?"

"No, but the sheep stepped on my foot."

"Poor Grace."

"Thank you."

"A sheep can't weigh *that* much."

"This one did. I've got an unsightly bruise on the top of my foot." She thrust out her leg and gazed down on it.

Her panty hose didn't hide the spectacularly colored bruise at all.

"Oh, poor, poor Gracie."

"You don't sound like you mean that."

"Oh, I do, I do."

"Hmph. We haven't had much of a chance to talk in the last few days, so tell me what you're doing for Christmas," Grace said.

"We're keeping it pretty low-key," Olivia told her. "Justine, Seth and Leif are coming over tonight for dinner and gifts, then we're going to church at eight. What about you and Cliff?"

"Same. Maryellen, Kelly and all the grandkids are coming for dinner and then we're heading to the Christmas Eve service. Cliff's daughter, Lisa, and her family are here as well. Tomorrow we're all going over to Maryellen and Jon's for dinner."

"Jack and I are having Christmas dinner alone. He's let on to everyone that he's cooking but between you and me, D.D.'s on the Cove is catering." Olivia laughed, clearly amused by her husband's resourcefulness. "Justine invited us," she added, "but we declined. Next year," Olivia said, and it sounded like a promise.

Everything would be back to normal by this time next year. Olivia would be finished with her treatments this spring. Seeing what her friend had already endured, and her quiet bravery in the face of what was still to come, had given Grace a deeper understanding of Olivia. Her strength and courage impressed Grace and humbled her. Like all women their age, they'd suffered—and survived—their share of tragedy and grief. And now Olivia was coping with cancer.

Grace stood and looked out the small window that offered a view of the interior of the library. Mary Jo sat with her shoulders hunched forward, cell phone dangling from one hand.

"I have to go."

"Problems?"

"I should get back to Mary Jo."

"You'll keep me updated, won't you?" Olivia said.

"As much as I can."

"Okay, thanks. And listen, Grace, stay away from that camel!" She laughed, and then the line was disconnected.

The next time they met at the Pancake Palace, Grace intended to make Olivia pay for her coconut cream pie.

Grace called her husband quickly, then stepped out of her office and slipped into the chair next to Mary Jo. "How's it going?" she asked.

"Not so well, I'm afraid. I tried to call David. I have his cell phone number and I thought he'd answer. It's Christmas Eve and he *has* to know I'm waiting to hear from him."

Grace took Mary Jo's hand in hers. "He didn't answer?"

"Oh, it's more than that. He…he had his number changed. Last week—" she struggled to speak "—I tried to reach him at his office in California and learned that he's quit his job. We both work—worked—for the same insurance company, which is how we met."

"Oh, dear."

"I don't dare let my brothers know."

Mary Jo had mentioned them earlier.

"How many brothers?"

"Three, all of them older." She sighed. "I'd hoped David would be here with his parents, but I knew the odds that he'd told me the truth weren't good."

Grace nodded, encouraging her to continue.

"I think I told you my brothers want to make David marry me—or at least pay for all the lies he's told. They decided they were going to come and confront him, and if not David, then his family."

Grace could only imagine how distressing it would be for Ben and Charlotte to return from the vacation of a lifetime to find Mary Jo's three angry brothers waiting for them. On Christmas Day, yet.

"That's why it's important for me to talk to Ben and Charlotte first," Mary Jo concluded.

"I think you should," Grace said.

"Except…"

"Yes?" she prompted.

"Except it looks like I'll have to go back to Seattle this afternoon."

"Why?"

"I called all the places on the sheet you gave me and there aren't any vacancies."

"Nowhere? Not in the entire town? What about the Comfort Inn?"

She shook her head. "Nothing."

"You mean everything's already reserved?"

"Yes. There's no room at the Inn."

Chapter Four

"Linc," Mel shouted from the kitchen. Three Wyse Men Automotive had closed early due to the holiday.

"In a minute," Linc shouted back. "Where's Mary Jo?" He'd searched half the house and hadn't found her. He knew she'd taken the day off. Had she gone to the store, perhaps? Or to visit her friend Chloe?

"If you come to the kitchen you'll find out!"

Linc followed his brother's voice and with Ned at his heels, entered the kitchen. As soon as Mel saw him, his brother thrust a sheet of paper into his hands. "Here. This was behind the coffeemaker. Must've fallen off."

Before he'd read two words, Linc's face started to heat up. His stubborn, strong-willed, hardheaded, obstinate little sister had gone to Cedar Cove. Without her family, because she felt she knew best. Tossing the note to the ground, Linc clenched both his fists. "Of all the stupid, idiotic things to do."

"What?" Ned asked.

"Mary Jo's decided to go to Cedar Cove on her own," Mel said.

"By herself?"

"Isn't that what I said?" Mel snapped.

"It's true," Linc informed his youngest brother. "I can't believe she'd do anything this crazy."

"We drove her to it." Ned sank into a kitchen chair and splayed his fingers through his thick dark hair.

"What do you mean?" Mel challenged.

"Explain yourself," Linc ordered.

"Don't you see?" Ned gazed up at them. "All that talk about confronting David and forcing him to do the *honorable* thing. The man hasn't got an honorable bone in his body. What were we thinking?"

"What we were thinking," Linc said irritably, "is that David Rhodes is going to pay for what he did to our little sister." He looked his brothers in the eye and made sure they understood.

When their parents were killed, Mary Jo had only been seventeen. Linc, as the oldest, had been made her legal guardian, since there was no other family in the area. At the time, the responsibility had weighed heavily on his shoulders. He'd gone to his two brothers and asked for their help in raising their sister. Or at least finishing the job their parents had begun.

Both brothers had been equally committed to taking care of Mary Jo. Everything had gone smoothly, too. Mary Jo had graduated from high school the following May, and all three brothers had attended the ceremony. They'd even thrown her a party.

That autumn he'd gone with Mary Jo to the community college and signed her up for classes. She hadn't taken kindly to his accompanying her, but Linc wasn't about to let her walk around campus on her own. Not at first, anyway. Cute little girl like her? With all those lecherous college guys who couldn't keep their hands to themselves? Oh, yeah, he knew what eighteen-year-old boys were like. And he'd insisted she choose solid, practical courses, not that fluffy fun stuff they taught now.

All the brothers were proud of how well Mary Jo had done in her studies. They'd all disapproved when she'd dropped out of school and gone to work at that insurance company. More than once Linc had to bite his tongue. He'd told her no good would come of this job.

The problem with Mary Jo was that she was too eager to move out. She no longer wanted to live in the family home. For the past year, she'd talked incessantly about getting her own place.

Linc didn't understand that either. This was their *home*. Linc saw to it that Mary Jo wasn't stuck with all the cleaning, cooking and laundry. They all did their part of the up-keep—maybe not quite to her standards but well enough. That wasn't the reason she was so determined to live some-where else.

No, Mary Jo had an intense desire for independence. From them.

Okay, maybe they'd gone overboard when it came to dating. Frankly, Linc didn't think there was a man this side of Mars who was good enough for his little sister. Mary Jo was special.

Then she'd met David Rhodes. Linc had never found out precisely when that had happened. Not once in the six months she'd been dating him had she mentioned this guy. What Linc had noticed was how happy Mary Jo seemed all of a sudden—and then, just as suddenly, she'd been depressed. That was when her mood swings started. She'd be happy and then sad and then happy again. It made no sense until he learned there was a man involved.

Even now that Mary Jo was pregnant with this man's baby, Linc still hadn't met him. In retrospect, that was probably for the best because Linc would take real pleasure in ripping his face off.

"What are we going to do?" Mel asked.

His younger brothers were clearly worried.

Linc's hand was already in his pants pocket, fingering his truck keys. "What can we do other than follow her to Cedar Cove?"

"Let's talk this through," Ned suggested, coming to his feet.

"What's there to talk about?" Mel asked. "Mary Jo's going to have a baby. She's alone and pregnant and we all know Rhodes isn't in Cedar Cove. He's lied to her from the beginning. There's no way he's telling the truth now."

"Yes, but…"

Linc looked squarely into his youngest brother's eyes. "What do you think Mom and Dad would have us do?" he asked, allowing time between each word to make sure the message sank in.

Ned sighed. "They'd want us to find her."

"Exactly my point." Linc headed for the back door.

"Wait a minute." Ned raised his hand.

"Now what?" Mel said impatiently.

"Mary Jo left because she's mad."

"Well, let her be mad. By the time we arrive, she'll be singing a different tune. My guess is she'll be mighty glad to see us."

"Maybe," Ned agreed. "But say she isn't. Then what?"

Linc frowned. "We'll bring her home anyway."

"She might not want to come."

"She'll come." Linc wasn't about to leave his little sister with strangers over Christmas.

"If we make demands, she'll only be more determined to stay," Ned told them.

"Do you have any other bright ideas?" Mel asked.

Ned ignored the sarcasm. "Bring her gifts," he said.

"Why?" Linc didn't understand. They all had gifts for her and the baby that she could open Christmas morning, the way she was supposed to.

"She needs to know we love her and welcome the baby."

"Of course we welcome the baby," Linc said. "He's our flesh and blood, our *nephew*."

"Hang on a minute." Mel looked pensive. "Ned has a point."

It wasn't often that Mel agreed with Ned. "What do you mean?"

"Mary Jo's pregnant, right?"

That question didn't require a response.

"And everyone knows how unreasonable women can get when they're in, uh, a delicate condition."

Linc scratched his head. "Mary Jo was like that long before she got pregnant."

"True, but she's been even more unreasonable lately, don't you think?"

Mel wasn't wrong there.

"Maybe we should bring her a gift just so she'll know how concerned we are about her and the baby. How much we care. We want her with us for Christmas, don't we?"

"What woman doesn't like gifts?" Linc said, thinking out loud.

"Yup," Ned said, smiling at Mel. "It couldn't hurt."

Linc conceded. "Okay, then, we'll each bring her a gift."

They returned to their individual bedrooms, planning to meet in the kitchen five minutes later. Linc had gone online a few weeks ago and ordered a miniature football, basketball and soccer ball for his yet-to-be-born nephew. He couldn't speak for the others, but he suspected they too had chosen gifts that were geared toward sports. At first he figured he'd bring the football, but then he reconsidered. He'd been after Mary Jo to save money and in an effort to encourage her, he'd purchased a gold coin that he planned to present on her birthday in February. Perfect. He pocketed the coin and hurried to the kitchen.

"You ready?" he asked.

"Ready," Mel echoed.

"Me, too," Ned confirmed.

The three brothers hurried out to the four-door pickup Linc drove. Mel automatically climbed into the front passenger seat and Ned sat directly behind him.

"You got your gift?" Linc asked Mel.

"Yeah. I'm bringing her perfume."

"Good idea," Linc said approvingly. "Where'd you get it?"

"I actually bought it for Annie, but I'll get her something else...."

"Ned?" Linc asked.

"Incense," his youngest brother mumbled.

"You brought her *what?*"

"Incense. She likes that stuff. It was gonna be part of her Christmas gift anyway."

"Okay..." Linc shook his head rather than ask any further questions. Whatever his brothers chose to bring Mary Jo was up to them.

He turned his key in the ignition, then rested his arm over the back of the seat and angled his head so he could see behind him as he reversed out of the driveway. He'd reached the stop sign at the end of the block before it occurred to him to ask.

"Which way?"

"North," Mel said.

"Cedar Cove is south," Ned contradicted.

"For crying out loud." Linc pulled over to the curb. Leaning across his brother, he opened the glove box and shuffled through a pile of junk until he found the Washington State map he was looking for. Dropping it on Mel's lap, he said, "Find me Cedar Cove."

Mel immediately tossed it into the backseat. "Here, Ned. You seem to think you know where it is."

"It was just a guess," Ned protested. Nevertheless he started to unfold the map.

"Well, we don't have time for guessing. Look it up." Linc put the truck back in gear and drove toward the freeway on-ramp. He assumed Ned would find Cedar Cove before he had to decide which lane to get into—north or south.

He was nearly at the ramp before Ned cried out triumphantly. "Found it!"

"Great. Which way should I go?"

Linc watched his brother through the rearview mirror as he turned the map around.

No answer.

"Which way?" Linc asked impatiently.

"South."

"You don't sound too sure."

"South," Ned said again, this time with more conviction.

Linc entered the lane that would take him in that direction. "How far is it?" he asked.

Ned stared down at the map again. "A ways."

"That doesn't tell me a darn thing. An hour or what?"

"All right, all right, give me a minute." Ned balanced the map on his knees and studied it intently. After carefully walking his fingers along the edge of the map, Ned had the answer. "I'd say...ninety minutes."

"Ninety minutes." Linc hadn't realized it was that far.

"Maybe longer."

Linc groaned silently. Traffic was heavy, which was to be expected at noon on Christmas Eve. At the rate they were crawling, it would be hours before they got there, which made their mission that much more urgent.

"Should we confront the Rhodes family first thing?" Mel asked.

"Damn straight. They need to know what he's done."

Ned cleared his throat. "Don't you think we should find Mary Jo first?"

Linc nodded slowly. "Yeah, I suppose we should."

They rode in silence for several minutes.

"Hey." Ned leaned forward and thrust his face between the two of them.

"What now?" Linc said, frustrated by the heavy traffic, which was guaranteed to be even worse once they hit Tacoma.

"How did Mary Jo get to Cedar Cove?" Mel asked.

"Good question." Linc hadn't stopped to consider her means of transportation. Mary Jo had a driver's license but didn't need a vehicle of her own, living in the city as they did. Each of the brothers owned a car and she could borrow any one of them whenever she wanted.

Ned sat back and studied the map again and after a few minutes announced, "Cedar Cove is on the Kitsap Peninsula."

"So?" Mel muttered sarcastically. The traffic was apparently making him cranky, too.

"So she took the ferry over."

That explained it. "Which ferry?" Linc asked.

"She probably caught the one from downtown Seattle to Bremerton."

"Or she might have gotten a ride," Mel said.

"Who from?" Ned asked.

"She wouldn't bother a friend on Christmas Eve." Ned seemed confident of that.

"Why not?" Mel demanded.

"Mary Jo isn't the type to call someone at the last minute and ask that kind of favor," Ned told them. "Not even Chloe or Casey—especially on Christmas Eve."

Linc agreed with his brother.

They drove in silence for another fifteen minutes before anyone spoke.

"Do you think she's okay?" Ned asked tentatively.

"Sure she is. She's a Wyse, isn't she? We're made of stern stuff."

"I mean physically," Ned clarified. "Last night she seemed so…" He didn't finish the sentence.

"Seemed what?" Linc prompted.

Ned shrugged. "Ready."

"For what?" Mel asked.

Mel could be obtuse, which was only one of his character flaws, in Linc's opinion. He was also argumentative.

"To have the baby, of course," Linc said, casting his brother a dirty look.

"Hey, there's no reason to talk to me like that." Mel shifted his weight and stared out the side window. "I've never been around a pregnant woman before. Besides, what makes *you* such experts on pregnancy and birth?"

"I read a book," Ned told them.

"No way." Linc could hardly believe it.

"I did," Ned insisted. "I figured one of us should. For Mary Jo's sake."

"So one book makes you an expert," Mel teased.

"It makes me smarter than you, anyway."

"No, it doesn't," Mel argued.

"Quit it, you two." Linc spent half his life settling squabbles between his brothers. "You." He gestured over his shoulder. "Call her cell."

Ned did, using his own. "Went right into voice mail," he said. "Must be off."

"Leave her a message, then." Linc wondered if he had to spell *everything* out for them.

"Okay. Who knows if she'll get it, though."

After that they drove in blessed silence for maybe five minutes.

"Hey, I just thought of something." Mel groaned in frustration. "If Mary Jo took the ferry, shouldn't we have done the same thing?"

Good point—except it was too late now. They were stuck in the notorious Seattle traffic, going nowhere fast.

Chapter Five

Mary Jo hated the idea of returning to Seattle having failed in her attempt to find either David or his family. He wasn't in Cedar Cove the way he'd promised; not only that, his parents weren't here, either. Ben and Charlotte Rhodes would show up the next afternoon or evening, but in the meantime…

The thought of her brothers approaching the elderly couple, shocking them with the news and their outrageous demands, made the blood rush to her face. Her situation was uncomfortable enough without her brothers riding to the rescue like the superheroes they weren't.

The fact that Mary Jo had left on Christmas Eve was only going to rile them even more. Linc, Mel and Ned were probably home from the garage by now. Or maybe they'd skipped work when they found her note on the coffeemaker and immediately set out in search of her. Maybe they were already driving up and down the streets of Cedar Cove.…

Looking around, Mary Jo could see that the library was

about to close. People were putting on coats and checking out their books. She wondered how an hour had disappeared so quickly. Now what? There wasn't a single vacant room in the vicinity, which meant the only thing to do was thank Grace Harding for her help and quietly leave.

She waited until the librarian stepped out of her office. The least she could do was let Grace know how much she appreciated her kindness. As she approached, Mary Jo rose from her chair.

All of a sudden the room started to sway. She'd been dizzy before but never like this. Her head swam, and for an instant she seemed about to faint. Blindly Mary Jo reached out, hoping to catch herself before she fell.

"Mary Jo!" Grace gasped and rushed to her side.

If the other woman hadn't caught her when she did, Mary Jo was convinced she would've collapsed onto the floor.

Slowly, Grace eased her into the chair. "Laurie!" she shouted. "Call 9-1-1."

"Please…no," Mary Jo protested. "I'm fine. Really, I am."

"No, you're not."

A moment later, the assistant behind the front counter hurried over to join Grace and Mary Jo. "The fire department's on the way."

Mortified beyond words, Mary Jo leaned her head back and closed her eyes. Needless to say, she'd become the library's main attraction, of far greater interest than any of the Christmas displays. Everyone was staring at her.

"Here, drink this," Grace said.

Mary Jo opened her eyes to find someone holding out a glass of water—again. Her mouth had gone completely dry and she took it gratefully. Sirens could be heard roaring toward the library, and Mary Jo would've given anything to simply disappear.

A few minutes later, two firefighters entered the library, carrying their emergency medical equipment. One of the men moved toward her and knelt down.

"Hi, there." The firefighter's voice was calm.

"Hi," Mary Jo said weakly.

"Can you tell me what happened?"

"I just got a bit light-headed. I wish they hadn't called you. I'm perfectly okay."

He ignored her comment. "You stood up?"

She nodded. "The room began to sway and I thought I was going to faint."

"I think she did faint," Grace added, kneeling down next to the firefighter. "I somehow got her back into the chair. Otherwise I'm sure she would've crumpled to the floor."

The firefighter kept his gaze on Mary Jo. He had kind eyes and, despite everything, she noticed that he was attractive in a craggy, very masculine way. He was in his late twenties, she guessed, a few years older than she was.

"My name's Mack McAfee," he said. "And that guy—" he pointed to the other firefighter "—is Brandon Hutton."

"I'm Mary Jo Wyse."

Mack smiled, maintaining eye contact. "When's your baby due?"

"January seventh."

"In about two weeks then."

"Yes."

"Have you had any other spells like this?"

Mary Jo was reluctant to confess that she had. After a moment she nodded.

"Recently?"

"Yes…"

"That's not uncommon, you know. Your body's under a lot of strain because of the baby. Have you been experiencing any additional stress?"

She bit her lip. "A little."

"The holidays?"

"Not really."

"I'm new to town. I guess that's why I haven't seen you around," Mack said. He opened a response kit he'd brought into the library.

"Mary Jo lives in Seattle," Grace said, now standing behind Mack as the other firefighter hovered close by.

"Do you have relatives in the area?" he asked next.

"No…" She figured she might as well admit the truth. "I was hoping to see the father of my baby…only he isn't here."

"Navy?"

"No… I understood his family was from Cedar Cove, but apparently they're out of town, too."

"Ben and Charlotte Rhodes," Grace murmured.

Mack twisted around to look up at Grace. "The judge's mother, right? And her husband. Retired Navy."

"Right."

"David Rhodes is the baby's father," Mary Jo said. "We're not…together anymore." David had told her one too many lies. She knew intuitively that he'd have no desire to be part of the baby's life.

Mack didn't speak as he removed the blood pressure cuff and wrapped it around her upper arm. "How are you feeling now?" he asked.

"You mean other than mortified?"

He grinned up at her. "Other than that."

"Better," she said.

"Good." He took her blood pressure, a look of concentration on his face.

"How high is it?" Grace asked, sounding worried.

"Not bad," Mack told them both. "It's slightly elevated." He turned back to Mary Jo. "It would probably be best if you relaxed for the rest of the day. It wouldn't hurt to stay off your feet, either. Don't do anything strenuous."

"I'll…I'll try."

"Perhaps she should see a physician?" Grace said. "I'd be happy to take her to the clinic."

"No, that isn't necessary!" Mary Jo objected. "I'm so sorry to cause all this fuss. I feel fine."

Mack met her gaze and seemed to read the distress in her eyes. "As long as you rest and stay calm, I don't think you need to see a doctor."

"Thank you," she breathed.

Although the library was closing, the doors suddenly opened and a tall, regal woman walked in. She was bundled up in a wool coat with a red knit scarf around her neck and a matching knit cap and gloves.

"Olivia," Grace said. "What are you doing here?"

"Why's the aid car out front?" the other woman asked. She immediately turned to Mary Jo, and a stricken look came over her. "Are you in labor?"

"No, no, I'm just…a little light-headed," Mary Jo assured her.

The woman smiled. "I already know who this must be. Mary Jo. Are you all right?"

"This is Olivia, Charlotte Rhodes's daughter." Grace gestured at her. "She's the woman I called to get the information about Ben and Charlotte."

"Oh." Mary Jo shrank back in her chair.

"David Rhodes is my stepbrother," Olivia explained. She smiled sympathetically at Mary Jo. "Although so far, he's been nothing but an embarrassment to the family. And I can see that trend's continuing. But don't assume," she said to Mary Jo, "that I'm blaming you. I know David *far* too well."

Mary Jo nodded mutely but couldn't prevent a surge of guilt that must have reddened her face, judging by her heated cheeks. She *was* to blame, for being naive in falling for a man like David, for being careless enough to get pregnant, for letting the situation ever reach this point.

"What are you doing here?" Grace asked her friend a second time.

"I'm meeting Will at the gallery. We're going to lunch. I saw the aid car outside the library as I drove by." Olivia turned to Mary Jo again. "I was afraid something like this had happened. Thank goodness for young Mack—" they exchanged a smile "—and his partner over there." Brandon was helping an older couple with their bags of groceries and stack of books.

Mary Jo felt no less humiliated. "I should never have come," she moaned.

"I'm glad you did," Olivia said firmly. "Ben would want to know about his grandchild."

Mary Jo hadn't expected everyone to be so…nice. So friendly and willing to accept her—and her dilemma. "It's just that my brothers are upset and determined to defend my honor. I felt I should be the one to tell David's family."

"Of course you should," Olivia said in what appeared to be complete agreement.

Mack finished packing up his equipment. He placed his hand on Mary Jo's knee to gain her attention. When she looked back at him, she was struck by the caring in his gaze.

"You'll do as I suggested and rest? Don't get over-excited."

Mary Jo nodded.

"If you have any other problems, call 9-1-1. I'm on duty all day."

"I will," she promised. "Thank you so much."

Mack stood. "My pleasure." He hesitated for a moment and looked directly into her eyes. "You're going to be a good mom."

Mary Jo blinked back tears. More than anything, that was what she wanted. To be the best mother she could. Her child was coming into the world with one disadvantage already—the baby's father had no interest in him. Or her. It was all up to Mary Jo.

"Thank you," she whispered.

"Merry Christmas," Mack said before he turned to leave.

"Merry Christmas," she called after him.

"You need to rest," Olivia said with an authority few would question. "When's the last time you ate?"

"I had a decaf latte at Mocha Mama's before I came to the library."

"You need lunch."

"I'll eat," Mary Jo said, "as soon as I get back to Seattle." There was the issue of her brothers, but she'd call Linc's cell phone and let them know she was on her way home.

"You drove?" Grace asked.

"No, I took the ferry across."

Grace and Olivia glanced at each other.

"It might be a good idea if you came home with me," Olivia began. "It won't be any inconvenience and we'd enjoy having you."

Mary Jo shook her head. "I…couldn't." Although Olivia was related to David, by marriage anyway, she didn't want to intrude on their Christmas. Olivia and her family certainly didn't need unexpected company. Olivia had stated that David was an embarrassment to the family, and Mary Jo's presence only made things worse. Bad enough that she'd arrived without any warning, but it was beyond the call of duty for Olivia to take her in, and on Christmas Eve of all nights. Olivia must have plans and Mary Jo refused to ruin them.

"No," Grace said emphatically. "You're coming home with me. It's all arranged."

This invitation was just as endearing and just as unnecessary. "Thank you both." She struggled to her feet, cradling her belly with protective hands. "I can't let either of you do that. I appreciate everything, but I'm going back to Seattle."

"Nonsense," Grace said. "I've spoken to my husband and he agrees with me."

"But—"

Grace cut her off, obviously unwilling to listen. "You won't be intruding, I promise."

Mary Jo was about to argue again, but Grace talked right over her.

"We have my stepdaughter and her family visiting us, but we've got an apartment above our barn that's completely furnished. It's empty at the moment and you'd be welcome to stay there for the night."

The invitation was tempting. Still, Mary Jo hesitated.

"Didn't you hear what Mack said?" Grace reminded her. "He said it was important for you to remain calm and relaxed."

"Yes, I know, but—"

"Are you sure?" Olivia asked Grace. "Because I can easily make up the sofa bed in the den."

"Of course I'm sure."

"I don't want to interfere with your Christmas," Mary Jo said.

"You wouldn't be," Grace assured her. "You'd have your privacy and we'd have ours. The barn's close to the house, so if you needed anything it would be simple to reach me. There's a phone in the apartment, too, which I believe is still connected. If not, the line in the barn is hooked up."

The idea was gaining momentum in her mind. "Maybe I could...." Mary Jo said. As soon as she was settled, she'd call her brothers and explain that she'd decided to stay in Cedar Cove overnight. Besides, she was tired and depressed and didn't feel like celebrating. The idea of being by herself held more appeal by the minute.

Another plus was the fact that her brothers needed a break from her and her problems. For the last number of weeks, Mary Jo had been nothing but a burden to them, causing strife within the family. Thanks to her, the three of them were constantly bickering.

Ned was sympathetic to her situation and she loved him for it. But even he couldn't stand up to Linc, who took his responsibilities as head of the family much too seriously.

If her brothers were on their way to Cedar Cove, as she expected, she'd ask them firmly but politely to turn around. She'd tell them she was spending Christmas with David's family, which was, in fact, true. Sort of. By tomorrow evening, she would've met with Ben and Charlotte and maybe Olivia and the rest of David's Cedar Cove relatives. They'd resolve this situation *without* her brothers' so-called help.

"One thing," Grace said, her voice falling as she glanced over at Olivia.

"Yes?" Mary Jo asked.

"There's a slight complication."

Mary Jo should've known this was too good to be true.

"The barn's currently home to a...variety of animals," Grace went on to explain.

Mary Jo didn't understand why this should be a problem, nor did she understand Olivia's smug grin.

"There's an ox and several sheep, a donkey and—" she paused "—a camel."

"A *camel?*" Mary Jo repeated.

"A rather bad-tempered camel," Olivia put in.

Nodding, Grace pointed to her obviously bandaged arm. "You'd be well advised to keep your distance."

"That's, um, quite a menagerie you have in your barn."

"Oh, they don't belong to us," Grace said. "They're for the live Nativity scene, which ended last evening. We're housing them for the church."

"The animals won't bother me." Mary Jo smiled. "And I won't bother them."

Her smile grew wider as it occurred to her that she'd be spending Christmas Eve in a stable—something another Mary had done before her.

Chapter Six

Olivia reluctantly left the library by herself. Weak as she was these days, it made more sense for Mary Jo to go home with Grace. Nevertheless, Olivia felt a certain obligation toward this vulnerable young woman.

Olivia had never had positive feelings toward her stepbrother, and this situation definitely hadn't improved her impression of him. Ben's son could be deceptive and cruel. She knew very well that David had lied to Mary Jo Wyse. Sure, it took two to tango, as the old cliché had it—and two to get Mary Jo into her present state. But Olivia also knew that David would have misrepresented himself and, even worse, abdicated all responsibility for Mary Jo *and* his child. No wonder her family was in an uproar. Olivia didn't blame them; she would be, too.

The drive from the library to the Harbor Street Gallery took less than two minutes. Olivia hated driving such a short distance when at any other time in her life she would've walked those few blocks. The problem was that those blocks were a steep uphill climb and she didn't have the energy. The surgery and subsequent infection had sapped her of strength. Today, however, wasn't a day to dwell on the cancer that had struck her so unexpectedly, like a viper hiding in the garden. Today, Christmas Eve, was a day for gratitude and hope.

She parked outside the art gallery her brother had purchased and was renovating. Olivia had been the one to suggest he buy the gallery; he'd done so, and it seemed to be a good decision for him.

Will was waiting for her at the door. "Liv!" he said, bounding toward her in his larger-than-life way. He extended his arms for a hug. "Merry Christmas."

"Same to you," she said, smiling up at him. Her brother, although over sixty, remained a strikingly handsome man. Now divorced and retired, he'd come home to reinvent himself, leaving behind his former life in Atlanta. In the beginning Olivia had doubted his motives, but slowly he'd begun to prove himself, becoming an active member of the town—and his family—once again.

"I wanted to give you a tour of the gallery," Will told her as he led her inside.

The last time Olivia had visited the town's art gallery had been while Maryellen Bowman, Grace's daughter, was the manager. Maryellen had been forced to resign during a difficult pregnancy. The business had rapidly declined once she'd left, and eventually the gallery had gone up for sale.

Looking around, Olivia was astonished by the changes. "You did all *this* in less than a month?" The place barely resembled the old Harbor Street Gallery. Before Will had taken over, artwork had been arranged in a simple, straightforward manner—paintings and photographs on the walls, sculpture on tables.

Will had built distinctive multi-level glass cases and brought in other inventive means of displaying a variety of mediums, including a carefully designed lighting system. One entire wall was taken up with a huge quilt, unlike any she'd seen before. At first glance she had the impression of fire.

Close up, it looked abstract, with vivid clashing colors and surreal, swirling shapes. But, stepping back, Olivia identified an image that suddenly emerged—a dragon. It was fierce, angry, *red,* shooting out flames in gold, purple and orange satin against a background that incorporated trees, water and winding roads.

"That's by Shirley Bliss," Will said, following her gaze. "It took me weeks to convince her to let me put that up."

"It's magnificent." Olivia was in awe of the piece and couldn't tear her eyes from it.

"It isn't for sale, however."

"That's a shame."

Will nodded. "She calls it *Death.* She created it shortly after her husband was killed in a motorcycle accident." He slipped an arm through Olivia's. "Can't you just feel her anger and her grief?"

The quilt seemed to vibrate with emotions Olivia recognized from her own life—the time her thirteen-year-old son had drowned, more than twenty years ago. And the time, only weeks ago, that she'd been diagnosed with cancer. When she initially heard the physician say the word, she'd had a nearly irrepressible urge to argue with him. This *couldn't* be happening to her. There'd been some mistake.

That disbelief had been replaced by a hot anger at the unfairness of it. Then came numbness, then grief and finally resignation. With Jordan's death and with her own cancer, she'd experienced a tremendous loss that had brought with it fears of further loss.

Now, fighting her cancer—and that was how she thought of it, *her* cancer—she'd found a shaky serenity, even a sort of peace. That kind of acceptance was something she'd acquired with the love and assistance of her husband, Jack, her family and, as much as anyone, Grace, the woman who'd been her best friend all her life.

"My living quarters are livable now, too," Will was telling her. "I've moved in upstairs but I'm still sorting through boxes. Isn't it great how things worked out? Because of Mack," he added when Olivia looked at him quizzically.

"Getting the job here in town, you mean?"

"Yeah, since that meant he needed an apartment. At the same time, I needed out of the sublet, so it all came together perfectly."

After a quick turn around the gallery to admire the other pieces on display, Will steered her toward the door. "Where would you like to go for lunch?" he asked. "Anyplace in town. Your big brother's treating."

"Well, seeing you've got all that money burning a hole in your pocket, how about the Pancake Palace?"

Will arched his brows. "You're joking, aren't you?"

"No, I'm serious." The Pancake Palace had long been a

favorite of hers and in the past month or two, she'd missed it. For years, Grace and Olivia would head over to their favorite high school hangout after aerobics class on Wednesday night. The coconut cream pie and coffee was a reward for their exertions, and the Palace was where they always caught up with each other's news.

Goldie, their favorite waitress, had served them salty French fries and iced sodas back when neither of them worried about calories. These days their once-a-week splurge reminded them of their youth, and the nostalgic appeal of the place never faded.

Some of the most defining moments of their teenage years had occurred at the Pancake Palace. It was there that eighteen-year-old Grace admitted she was pregnant, shortly before graduation.

And years later, it'd been over coffee and tears that Olivia told her Stan had asked for a divorce after Jordan's death. And later, it was where they celebrated Olivia's appointment to the bench. The Pancake Palace was a place of memories for them, good and bad.

"The Pancake Palace? You're really serious?" Will said again. "I can afford a lot better, you know."

"You asked and that's my choice."

Will nodded. "Then off to the Palace we go."

Her brother insisted on driving and Olivia couldn't fault his manners. He was the consummate gentleman, opening the passenger door for her and helping her inside. The snow that had fallen earlier dusted the buildings and trees but had melted on the sidewalks and roads, leaving them slick. The slate-gray skies promised more snow, however.

Olivia had been out with her brother plenty of times and he'd never bothered with her car door. She was his sister and manners were reserved for others.

She wondered if Will's solicitude was linked to her illness. Although he might've been reluctant to admit it, Will had been frightened. His caring comforted her, particularly since they'd been at odds during the past few years.

He assisted her out of the car and opened the door to the Pancake Palace. They'd hardly entered the restaurant when Goldie appeared.

"Well, as I live and breathe, it's Olivia!" Goldie cried. Then she shocked Olivia by throwing both sinewy arms around her. "My goodness, you're a sight for sore eyes."

"Merry Christmas, Goldie," Olivia said.

The waitress had to be close to seventy and could only be described as "crusty." To Olivia's utter astonishment, Goldie pulled a hankie from her pink uniform pocket and dabbed at her eyes.

"I wasn't sure if I'd ever see you again," she said with a sniffle.

"Oh, Goldie…" Olivia had no idea what to say at this uncharacteristic display of affection.

"I just don't know what Grace and I would've done without you," Goldie said, sniffling even more. She wiped her nose and stuffed the hankie back in her pocket. Reaching for the coffeepot behind the counter, she motioned with her free hand. "Sit anyplace you want."

"Thank you, Goldie." Olivia was genuinely touched, since Goldie maintained strict control of who sat where.

Although Goldie had given her free rein, Olivia chose the booth where she'd sat with Grace every Wednesday night until recently. It felt good to slide across the cracked red vinyl cushion again. Olivia resisted the urge to close her eyes and breathe in the familiar scents. The coffee had always been strong and a hint of maple syrup lingered, although it was long past the breakfast hour.

Goldie automatically righted their coffee mugs and filled them. "We've got a turkey dinner with all the trimmings if you're interested," she announced.

Olivia still struggled with her appetite. "What's the soup of the day?"

Goldie frowned. "You aren't having just soup."

"But..."

"Look at you," the waitress chastised. "You're thin as a flagpole. If you don't want a big meal, then I suggest chicken pot pie."

"Sounds good to me," Will said.

Goldie ignored him. She whipped the pencil from behind her ear and yanked out the pad in her apron pocket. From sheer force of habit, or so Olivia suspected, she licked the lead. "Okay, what's it gonna be? And make up your mind, 'cause the lunch crowd's coming in a few minutes and we're gonna be real busy."

It was all Olivia could do to hide her amusement. "Okay, I'll take the chicken pot pie."

"Good choice." Goldie made a notation on her pad.

"I'm glad you approve."

"You're getting pie à la mode, too."

"Goldie!"

One hand on her hip, Goldie glared at her. "After all these years, you should know better than to argue with me." She turned to Will. "And that goes for you, too, young man."

Will raised his hands in acquiescence as Olivia sputtered. "I stand corrected," she said, grinning despite her efforts to keep a straight face.

Goldie left to place their order and Will grinned, too. "I guess *you* were told."

"I guess I was," she agreed. It was nice to know she'd been missed.

Grace would get a real kick out of hearing about this. Olivia would make a point of telling her when they met at the Christmas Eve service later that evening.

Looking out the window, Olivia studied the hand-painted snowman, surrounded by falling snow. The windowpane next to Will was adorned with a big-eyed reindeer. A small poinsettia sat on every table, and the sights and sounds of Christmas filled the room as "O, Little Town of Bethlehem" played softly in the background.

"Are you sure I can't convince you to join us for Christmas dinner?" Olivia asked her brother.

He shook his head. "I appreciate the offer, but you're not up for company yet."

"We're seeing Justine and her family tonight. It's just going to be Jack and me for Christmas Day."

"Exactly. The two of you don't need a third wheel."

"It wouldn't be like that," Olivia protested. "I hate the idea of you spending Christmas alone."

Will sat back. "What makes you think I'll be alone?"

Olivia raised her eyebrows. "You mean you won't?"

He gave a small noncommittal shrug.

"Will." She breathed his name slowly. She didn't want to bring up past history, but in her view, Will wasn't to be trusted with women. "You're seeing someone, aren't you?"

The fact that Will was being secretive didn't bode well. "Come on," she urged him. "Tell me."

He smiled. "It isn't what you think."

"She isn't married, is she?"

"No."

That, at least, was a relief.

"I'm starting over, Liv. My slate's clean now and I want to keep it that way."

Olivia certainly hoped so. "Tell me who it is," she said again.

Her brother relaxed and folded his hands on the table. "I've seen Shirley Bliss a few times."

Shirley Bliss. She was the artist who'd created the dragon, breathing fire and pain and anger.

"Shirley," she whispered. "The dragon quilt lady." Olivia hadn't even met the woman but sensed they could easily be friends.

"She's the one," Will said. "We're only getting to know each other but I'm impressed with her. She's someone I'd definitely like to know better."

"She invited you for Christmas?"

Will shifted his weight and looked out the window. "Well, not exactly."

Olivia frowned. "Either she did or she didn't."

"Let's put it like this. She hasn't invited me *yet*."

"Good grief, Will! It's Christmas Eve. If she was going to invite you, it would've been before now."

"Perhaps." He grinned boyishly. "Actually, I thought I'd stop by her place around dinnertime tomorrow with a small gift."

"Will!"

"Hey, you can't blame a man for trying."

"Will she be by herself?"

He shook his head. "She has two kids, a teenage daughter who's a talented artist, too, and a son who's in college. I haven't met him yet."

Before Will could say anything else, Goldie arrived at their booth, carrying two chicken pot pies. She set them down and came back with two huge pieces of coconut cream pie. "Make sure you save room for this," she told them.

"I'd like to remind you I didn't order any pie," Olivia said, pretending to disapprove.

"I know," Goldie returned gruffly. "It's on the house. Think of me as your very own elf. Merry Christmas."

"Merry Christmas to you, Goldie the Elf."

Will reached for his fork and smiled over at Olivia. "I have the feeling it's going to be a merry Christmas for us all."

Olivia had the very same feeling, despite—or maybe even because of—their unexpected visitor.

Chapter Seven

Linc gritted his teeth. It was after two, and the traffic through Tacoma was bumper to bumper. "You'd think it was a holiday or something," he muttered sarcastically.

Mel's eyebrows shot up and he turned to look at Ned in the backseat.

"What?" Linc barked.

"It *is* a holiday," Ned told him.

"Don't you think I *know* that? I'm joking!"

"Okay, okay."

"You're going to exit up here," Mel said, pointing to the exit ramp for Highway 16.

Linc sighed in relief. They were getting closer, and once they found Mary Jo he intended to give her a piece of his mind. She had no business taking off like this, not when her baby was due in two weeks. It just wasn't safe.

His jaw tightened as he realized it wasn't Mary Jo who annoyed him as much as David Rhodes. If Linc could just have five minutes alone with that jerk…

"I'll bet he's married," Linc said to himself. That would explain a lot. A married man having an affair would do anything he could to hide the fact that he had a wife. He'd strung Mary Jo along, fed her a bunch of lies and then left her to deal with the consequences all on her own. Well, that wasn't going to happen. No, sir. Not while Linc was alive. David Rhodes was going to acknowledge his responsibilities and live up to them.

"Who's married?" Mel asked, staring at him curiously.

"David Rhodes," he said. "Who else?"

The exit was fast approaching and, while they still had twenty miles to go, traffic would thin out once he got off the Interstate.

"He's not," Ned said blithely from the backseat.

"Isn't what?" Linc demanded.

"David Rhodes isn't married."

Linc glanced over his shoulder. "How do you know?"

"Mary Jo told me."

Ned and Mary Jo were close, and he was more apt to take a statement like that at face value.

"He probably lied about that along with everything else," Mel said, voicing Linc's own thoughts.

"He didn't," Ned insisted.

"How can you be so sure?"

"I checked him out on the internet," Ned continued with the same certainty. "It's a matter of public record. David Rhodes lives in California and he's been married and divorced twice. Both his marriages and divorces are listed with California's Department of Records."

Funny Ned had only mentioned this now. Maybe he had other information that would be helpful.

"You mean to say he's been married more than once?" Mel asked.

Ned nodded. "Yeah, according to what I read, he's been married twice. I doubt Mary Jo knows about the second time, though."

That was interesting and Linc wished he'd heard it earlier. "Did you find out anything else while you were doing this background search?" he asked. He eased onto the off ramp; as he'd expected, the highway was far less crowded.

"His first ex-wife, who now lives in Florida, has had problems collecting child support."

Linc shook his head. "Does that surprise anyone?"

"Nope," Mel said.

"How many children does he have?" Linc asked next.

"Just one. A girl."

"Does Mary Jo know this?" Mel asked. "About him being a deadbeat?"

"I didn't tell her," Ned admitted, adding, "I couldn't see any reason to upset her more than she already is."

"Good idea," Mel said. He leaned forward and looked up at the darkening sky. "Snow's starting again. The radio said there's going to be at least three inches."

"Snow," Linc groaned.

"Snow," Ned repeated excitedly. "That'll make a lot of little kids happy."

Mel agreed quickly. "Yeah, we'll have a white Christmas."

"Are either of *you* little kids?" Linc snapped. His nerves

were frayed and he'd appreciate it if his brothers took a more mature outlook.

"I guess I'm still a kid at heart," Ned said, exhaling a sigh.

Considering Linc's current frame of mind, it was a brave admission. With a slow breath, Linc made a concerted effort to relax. He was worried about Mary Jo; he couldn't help it. He'd wanted the best for her and felt that he'd failed both his sister and his parents.

To some extent he blamed himself for what had happened. Maybe he'd been too strict with her after she turned eighteen. But to his way of thinking, she was under his protection as long as she lived in the family home.

Not once had she introduced him to David Rhodes. Linc was convinced that if he'd met the other man, it would've taken him all of two seconds to peg David for a phony.

"What are you gonna say when we find her?" Ned asked.

Linc hadn't worked out the specifics. "Let's not worry about that now. Main thing is, we're going to put her in the truck and bring her home."

"What if she doesn't want to come with us?"

"Why wouldn't she? We're her family and it's Christmas Eve. Mary Jo belongs with us. Besides, that baby could show up anytime."

Mel seemed distinctly queasy at the prospect.

Thinking back, Linc knew he should have realized she was pregnant a lot earlier than he had. In fact, he hadn't recognized the signs at all; she'd *told* him and after that, of course, they were easy to see.

Not until the day Mary Jo rushed past him in the hallway and practically shoved him into the wall so she could get to the toilet in time to throw up did he have the slightest suspicion that anything was wrong. Even then he'd assumed she had a bad case of the flu.

Boy, had he been wrong. She had the flu, all right, only it was the nine-month variety.

It just hadn't occurred to him that she'd do something so dumb. An affair with the guy was bad enough, but to take that kind of chance…

Frowning, Linc glanced in his rearview mirror at his youngest brother. He was beginning to wonder about Ned. He'd never seemed as shocked as he or Mel had, and Mary Jo had always confided in him.

"How long have you known?" he asked casually.

Ned met Linc's gaze in the rearview mirror, his expression trapped. "Known what?"

"That Mary Jo was going to have a baby."

Ned looked away quickly and shrugged.

"She told you as soon as she found out, didn't she?"

Ned cleared his throat. "She might have."

"How early was that?" Linc asked, unwilling to let his brother sidestep the question.

"Early," Ned admitted. "I knew before David."

"You knew *that* early?" Mel shouted. "Why'd she tell you and not me?"

"Because you'd tell Linc," Ned told him. "She wanted to keep the baby a secret as long as she could."

Linc couldn't figure that one out. It wasn't like she'd be able to hide the pregnancy forever. And why hadn't she trusted him the way she did Ned? Although he prided himself on being stoic, that hurt.

Mel tapped his fingertips against the console. "Did she tell you how David Rhodes reacted to the news?"

Ned nodded. "She said he seemed pleased."

"Sure, why not?" Linc said, rolling his eyes. "The pregnancy wasn't going to inconvenience *him* any."

"I think that's why he could string Mary Jo along all this time," Ned suggested.

"You're probably right."

"I warned her, you know." Ned's look was thoughtful.

"When?"

"When she first started seeing him."

"You knew about David even before Mary Jo got pregnant?" Linc couldn't believe his ears. Apparently Mary Jo had shared all this information with Ned, who'd remained tight-lipped about most of it. If he wasn't so curious to uncover what his brother had learned, Linc might've been downright angry.

"So?" Mel said. "How'd she meet him?"

Ned leaned toward the front seat. "Rhodes works for the same insurance company. He's at corporate headquarters in San Francisco. Something to do with finances."

His sister worked in the accounting department, so that explained it, he supposed. "She should've come to work at our office the way I wanted," Linc said, and not for the first time. That was what he'd suggested when, against his wishes, Mary Jo had dropped out of college.

From her reaction, one would think he'd proposed slave labor. He never had understood her objections. He'd been willing to pay her top wages, as well as vacation and sick leave, and the work wasn't exactly strenuous.

She'd turned him down flat. Mary Jo wouldn't even consider working for Three Wyse Men Automotive. Linc regretted not being more forceful in light of what had happened. She might be almost twenty-four, but she needed his protection.

As they approached the Narrows Bridge, Linc's mood began to lighten somewhat. Yeah, Mary Jo needed him, and he assumed she'd be willing to admit that now. Not just him, either. She needed all three of her brothers.

Ned's idea that they bring gifts had been smart, a good way to placate her and prove how much she meant to them. Women, in his experience anyway, responded well to gifts.

Except that was probably the same technique David Rhodes had used.

"Did he buy her gifts?" Linc asked, frowning.

Ned understood his question, because he answered right away. "If you mean Rhodes, then yes, he got her a few."

"Such as?"

"Flowers a couple of times."

"Flowers!" Mel said.

"In the beginning, at any rate, and then after she was pregnant he bought her earrings."

Linc sat up straighter. "What kind?"

Ned snickered. "He said they were diamonds but one of them came loose so I dropped it off at Fred's for her. While he had it, I asked him to check it out."

Fred's was a local jewelry store the Wyse family had used for years. "Fake, right?"

"As phony as David Rhodes himself."

Mel twisted around and looked at Ned. "You didn't tell Mary Jo, did you?"

Ned shook his head. "I didn't want to add to her heart-ache."

"Maybe she already knows." His sister might be gullible but she wasn't stupid.

"I think she considered pawning it." Ned lowered his voice. "She didn't, so she might've guessed…."

The mere thought of his sister walking into a pawnshop with her pathetic bauble produced a stab of actual pain. "If she needed money, why didn't she come to me?" Linc demanded.

"You'll have to ask her that yourself."

"I plan to." Linc wasn't about to let this slide. "What does she need money for, anyway?"

"She wants her own place, you know."

No one needed to remind Linc of that. Mary Jo herself did a fine job of informing him at every opportunity. But it wasn't going to happen now. With a baby on the way, she wouldn't be leaving the family home anytime soon.

Linc liked that idea. He could keep an eye on her and on the baby, too. Even if he got married, which was by no means a sure thing, the house was big enough for all of them. His nephew would need a strong male influence, and he fully intended to provide that influence.

"How much farther?" Mel asked.

His brother was like a kid squirming in the front seat, asking "Are we there yet?" every five minutes.

"Hey, look," Ned said, pointing at the sky. "It's really coming down now."

"Did you think I hadn't noticed?" Linc didn't have much trouble driving in bad weather; it was all the *other* drivers who caused the problem. Snow in the Seattle area was infrequent and a lot of folks didn't know how to handle it.

"Hey," Mel said as they approached the first exit for Cedar Cove. "We're here."

"Right." Not having any more specific indication of where they should go, Linc took the exit.

"Where to now?" Mel asked.

Linc could've said, "Your guess is as good as mine." But he figured his guess was better. "We'll do what Mary Jo did," he said. "We'll chase down David's family. That's where she's going to be."

Mel nodded. "Whoever said the Wyse Men needed a star to guide them obviously never met the three of us."

Chapter Eight

Olivia couldn't wait to see her husband. For one thing, she wanted to tell him about her stepbrother, get his advice.

David Rhodes...that...that—she couldn't think of a word that adequately described how loathsome he was. She wanted him exposed. Humiliated, embarrassed, *punished*. Only the fact that Ben would be humiliated and embarrassed, too, gave her pause.

When Olivia pulled into her driveway on Lighthouse Road she was delighted to see that Jack was already home from the newspaper office. Impatiently, she grabbed the grocery bag of last-minute items and made her way into the house, using the entrance off the kitchen.

"Jack!" she called out as soon as she was inside.

"What's wrong?" Her husband met her in the kitchen and stopped short. "Someone's made *you* mad."

Olivia finished unwinding the muffler from around her

neck. "Why do you say that?" she asked, not realizing she'd been so obvious.

"Your eyes are shooting sparks. So, what'd I do this time?"

"It's not you, silly." She hung her coat on the hook along with the bright red scarf her mother had knit for her. She stuffed the matching hat and gloves in the pockets, then kissed Jack's cheek.

As she filled the electric teakettle and turned it on, Jack began to put the groceries away.

"Are you ready to talk about it?" he asked cautiously.

"It's David."

"Rhodes?"

"The very one. The man is lower than pond scum."

"That's not news."

Early in her mother's marriage to Ben, his son had tried to bilk Charlotte out of several thousand dollars. He'd used a ruse about needing some surgery his medical insurance wouldn't cover, and if not for Justine's intervention, Charlotte would have given him the money. David Rhodes was shameless, and he'd dishonored his father's name.

"Is he in town?" Jack asked. He took two mugs from the cupboard and set them on the counter; Olivia tossed a couple of Earl Grey teabags in the pot.

"No, or at least not as far as I'm aware. And frankly it's a good thing he isn't."

Jack chuckled. "I couldn't agree with you more, and I haven't got a clue what he's done to upset you now."

"He got a young girl pregnant."

Jack's eyebrows rose toward his hairline. "And you know this how?"

"I met her."

"Today?"

"Not more than two hours ago. She's young, probably twenty years younger than he is, and innocent. Or she was until David got hold of her. I swear that man should be shot!"

"Olivia!" He seemed shocked by her words. "That doesn't sound like you."

"Okay, that might be drastic. I'm just so furious I can hardly stand it."

Jack grinned.

Olivia glared at her husband. "You find this entertaining, do you?"

"Well, not about the young lady but I will admit it's a pleasant change to see color in your cheeks and your eyes sparkling, even if it's with outrage." He reached for her and brought her close enough to kiss her lips, allowing his own to linger. When he released her, he pressed his forehead to hers and whispered, "It's an even greater pleasure to know all this indignation isn't directed at me."

"I've never been anywhere near this upset with you, Jack Griffin."

"I beg to differ."

"When?"

"I remember one time," Jack said, "when I thought you were going to kick me out."

"I would *never* have done that." Her arms circled his waist.

They'd found ways to make their marriage work, ways to compromise between his nature—he was a slob, not to put too fine a point on it—and hers.

Olivia liked order. Their bathroom dilemma was a perfect example. She'd been driven to the brink of fury by the piles of damp towels, the spattered mirror, the uncapped toothpaste. The solution? They had their own bathrooms now. She'd kept the one off the master bedroom and he had the guest bath. Jack could be as sloppy as he wanted, as long as he closed the door and Olivia didn't have to see his mess.

"You're lucky I love you so much," Jack whispered.

"And why's that?" she asked, leaning back to look him in the eye.

"Because you'd be lost without me."

"Jack…"

The kettle started to boil, its piercing whistle enough to set the dogs in the next block howling. She tried to break free, but Jack held her fast. "Admit it," he insisted. "You're crazy about me."

"All right, all right, I'm crazy about you."

"And you'd be lost without me. Wouldn't you?"

"Jack!"

Chortling like a schoolboy, he let her go and she grabbed the kettle, relieved by the sudden cessation of that high-pitched shrieking.

Pouring the boiling water into the teapot, she covered it with a cozy and left the tea to steep. Then she opened the cookie jar and chose two of the decorated sugar cookies she'd baked a few days earlier with her grandson—a tree shape and a star. The afternoon had worn her out physically but she treasured every moment she'd spent in the kitchen with Leif.

Just as she was about to pour their tea, the phone rang.

"Want me to get that?" Jack called from the other room.

A glance at Caller ID told her it was Grace.

"I will," she told him. "Merry Christmas," she said into the receiver.

"Merry Christmas to you, too," her friend said in return. "I thought I'd check in and let you know how everything's going."

"So what's the update?"

"Everything's fine."

"Mary Jo's resting?"

"She was asleep the last time I looked, which was about five minutes ago. The girl must be exhausted. She told me she didn't get much sleep last night."

"She's in the apartment then, or at the house?"

"The apartment. Cliff's daughter and her family are already here, so…"

Olivia wasn't entirely comfortable with the idea of leaving Mary Jo alone, but it was probably for the best. This way she could relax undisturbed.

"There's something strange…."

"What?" Olivia asked.

"Well, for no reason I can understand, I decided to do a bit of housekeeping in the apartment yesterday. Cal's been gone a few weeks now, and I put clean sheets on the bed and fresh towels in the bathroom. It's as if…as if I was waiting for Mary Jo."

That was a little too mystical for Olivia. "I'm so glad this is working out," she said.

"She's an animal lover, too."

That didn't surprise Olivia. She sensed that Mary Jo had a gentleness about her, a soft heart, an interest in others.

"The minute I brought her into the barn, she wanted to see all the Nativity animals."

"You kept her away from that camel, didn't you?"

"I kept us both away," Grace was quick to tell her. "That beast is going to have to chew on someone else's arm."

"Yeah, David's would be ideal," Olivia said.

Grace laughed, but sobered almost immediately. "Listen, Mary Jo has a concern I'd like to talk to you about."

"Sure."

"She's got three older brothers who are most likely on their way into town, looking for her, as we speak."

"Does she *want* to be found?" Olivia asked.

"I think she does, only she wants to talk to Ben and Charlotte before her brothers do."

"She's not trying to protect David, is she?"

"I doubt it. What she's afraid of is that her brothers might try to insist that David marry her and she doesn't want to. At this point, she's accepted that she's better off without him."

"Smart decision."

"Yes, but it came at quite a price, didn't it?"

"True. A lesson with lifelong consequences."

"We all seem to learn our lessons the hard way," Grace said.

"I know I did." Her children, too, Olivia mused. Justine and James. As always, especially around the holidays, her mind wandered to Jordan, the son she'd lost that summer day all those years ago. Justine's twin.

"What time are Maryellen and Kelly coming by?" she asked Grace, changing the subject. Although Mary Jo would be staying in the barn, perhaps she should bring her over for dinner. Give her a chance to feel welcomed by Ben's second family. Cliff's daughter, Lisa, her husband and their little girl, April, were out doing some last-minute shopping, apparently, and not due back until late afternoon.

"My girls should be here around six."

"You're going straight to church after dinner?"

"That's the plan," Grace told her. "I was going to invite Mary Jo to join us."

"For dinner or Christmas Eve service?"

"Both, actually, but I'm having second thoughts."

"Why? And about what?"

"Oh, about inviting Mary Jo to dinner. I'm afraid it might be too much for her. We'll have five grandkids running around. You know how much racket children can make, and double that on Christmas Eve."

"Is there anything I can do for her?" Olivia asked. "Should I invite her to have dinner here?"

"I'm not sure. I'll talk to her when she wakes up and then I'll phone you."

"Thanks. And tell her not to worry about her brothers."

"I'll do that."

"See you tonight."

"Tonight," Olivia echoed.

After setting down the phone, Olivia poured the tea and placed both mugs on the table, followed by the plate of cookies, and called Jack into the kitchen again.

His eyes widened in overstated surprise. "Cookies? For me? You shouldn't have."

"I can still put them back."

"Oh, no, you don't." He grabbed the star-shaped cookie and bit off one point. "What's this in honor of?"

"I had pie with lunch. So I'm trying to be fair."

Knowing her disciplined eating habits, Jack did a double take. "You ate pie? At *lunch?*"

"Goldie made me do it."

"Goldie," he repeated. "You mean Will took you to the Pancake Palace?"

"It's where I wanted to go."

Jack sat down, scooped up the tree cookie and bit into that, too. "You're a cheap date."

"Not necessarily."

He ignored that remark. "Did you enjoy lunch with Will?" he asked, then sipped his tea. Jack was familiar with their sometimes tumultuous relationship.

"I did, although I'm a little worried." Olivia crossed her legs and held the mug in the palm of her hand. "He's interested in Shirley Bliss, a local artist."

"She's not married, is she?"

Olivia shook her head. "A widow."

Jack shrugged. "Then it's okay if he wants to see her."

"I agree. It's just that I don't know if I can trust my brother. It pains me to admit that, but still…" She left the rest unsaid. Jack knew her brother and his flaws as well as she did. "I want him to be successful here," she said earnestly. "He's starting over, and at this stage of his life that can't be easy."

"I don't imagine it will be," Jack agreed. "By the way, who was that on the phone?"

"Grace. She called to update me on Mary Jo."

"Problems?"

"Not really, but she said we need to keep an eye out for three irate brothers who might show up looking for her."

"A vigilante posse?"

"Not exactly." But now that Olivia thought about it, it might not be so bad if Mary Jo's brothers stumbled onto David Rhodes instead. "If her brothers find anyone, it should be David."

"There'd certainly be justice in that, but David's not going to let himself be found. And I think we should be focusing on the young woman, don't you?"

His tone was gentle, but Olivia felt chastened. "Yes—and her baby."

Chapter Nine

Mary Jo woke feeling confused. She sat up in bed and gazed around at the sparsely decorated room before she remembered where she was. Grace Harding had brought her home and was letting her spend the night in this apartment above the barn. It was such a kind thing to do. She was a stranger, after all, a stranger with problems who'd appeared out of nowhere on Christmas Eve.

Stretching her arms high above her head, Mary Jo yawned loudly. She was still tired, despite her nap. Her watch told her she'd been asleep for almost two hours. Two hours!

Other than in her first trimester, she hadn't required a lot of extra rest during her pregnancy, but that had changed in the past few weeks. Of course some of it could be attributed to David and his lies. Wondering what she should believe and whether he'd meant *any* of what he'd said had kept her awake many a night. Consequently she was tired during the day; while she was still working she'd nap during her lunch break.

Forcing her eyes shut, Mary Jo made an effort to cast David from her mind. She quickly gave up. Tossing aside the covers, she climbed out of bed, put on her shoes and left the apartment. The stairway led to the interior of the barn.

As soon as she stepped into the barn, several animals stuck their heads out of the stalls to study her curiously. The first she saw was a lovely horse. Grace had introduced her as Funny Face.

"Hello there, girl." Mary Jo walked slowly toward the stall door. "Remember me?" The mare nodded in what seemed to be an encouraging manner, and Mary Jo ran her hand down the horse's unusually marked face. The mare had a white ring around one eye and it was easy to see why the Hardings had named her Funny Face. Her dark, intelligent eyes made Mary Jo think of an old story she recalled from childhood—that animals can talk for a few hours after midnight on Christmas Eve—and she wondered what Funny Face would say. Probably something very wise.

The camel seemed curious, too, and thrust her long curved neck out of the stall, peering at Mary Jo through wide eyes, fringed with lush, curling lashes. Mary Jo had been warned to keep her distance. "Oh, no, you don't," she said, waving her index finger. "You're not going to lure me over there with those big brown eyes. Don't give me that innocent look, either. I've heard all about you."

After visiting a few placid sheep, another couple of horses and a donkey with a sweet disposition, Mary Jo walked out of the barn. She hurried toward the house through a light snowfall, wishing she'd remembered her coat. Even before she arrived, the front door opened and an attractive older gentleman held the screen.

"You must be Mary Jo," he said and thrust out his hand in greeting. "Cliff Harding."

"Hello, Mr. Harding," she said with a smile. She was about to thank him for his hospitality when he interrupted.

"Call me Cliff, okay? And come in, come in."

"All right, Cliff. Thank you."

Mary Jo entered the house and was greeted by the smell of roasting turkey and sage and apple pie.

"You're awake!" Grace declared as she came out of the kitchen. She wore an apron and had smudges of flour on her cheeks.

"I'm shocked I slept for so long."

"You obviously needed it," Grace commented, leading her into the kitchen. "I see you've met my husband."

"Yes." Mary Jo smiled again. Rubbing her palms nervously together, she looked from one to the other. "I really can't thank you enough for everything you've done for me."

"Oh, nonsense. It's the least we could do."

"I'm a stranger and you took me in without question and, well…I didn't think that kind of thing happened in this day and age."

That observation made Grace frown. "Really? It does here in Cedar Cove. I guess it's just how people act in small towns. We tend to be more trusting."

"I had a similar experience when I first moved here," Cliff said. "I wasn't accustomed to people going out of their way for someone they didn't know. I didn't believe it could be genuine.

Charlotte Jefferson—now Charlotte Rhodes—disabused me of *that* notion."

Despite everything, Mary Jo looked forward to meeting David's stepmother. The conversation would be difficult, but knowing that Charlotte was as kind as everyone else she'd met so far made all the difference.

"Really, Mary Jo," Grace continued. "All you needed was a friend and a helping hand. Anyone here would've done the same. Olivia wanted you to stay with her, too."

"Everyone's been so wonderful." Thinking about the willingness of these people to take her in brought a lump to her throat. She bent, with some effort, to stroke the smooth head of a golden retriever who lay on a rug near the stove.

"That's Buttercup," Grace said fondly as the dog thumped her tail but didn't stand up. "She's getting old, like the rest of us."

"Coffee?" Cliff walked over to the coffeemaker. "I'll make some decaf. Are you interested?" he asked, motioning in Mary Jo's direction with the pot.

"I'd love some. If it isn't any trouble."

"None whatsoever. I'm having a cup, too." Grace set out three mugs, then suddenly asked, "You didn't eat any lunch, did you?"

"No, but I'm not hungry."

"You might not be, but that baby of yours is," Grace said as if she had a direct line of communication to the unborn child. Without asking further, she walked to the refrigerator and poked her head inside. Adjusting various containers and bottles and packages, she took out a plastic-covered bowl.

"I don't want to cause you any extra work," Mary Jo protested.

"The work's already done. Cliff made the most delicious clam chowder," Grace said. "I'll heat you up some."

Now that Grace mentioned it, Mary Jo realized she really could use something to eat; she was feeling light-headed again. "Cliff cooks?" Her brothers were practically helpless around the kitchen and it always surprised her to find a man who enjoyed cooking.

"I am a man of many talents," Grace's husband answered with a smile. "I was a bachelor for years before I met Grace."

"If I didn't prepare meals, my brothers would survive on fast food and frozen entrées," she said, grinning. Thankfully her mother had taught her quite a bit before her death. The brothers had relied on Mary Jo for meals ever since.

The thought of Linc, Mel and Ned made her anxious. She'd meant to call, but then she'd fallen asleep and now… they could be anywhere. They'd be furious and frightened. She felt a blast of guilt; her brothers might be misguided but they loved her.

"If you'll excuse me a moment," she said urgently. "I need to make a phone call."

"Of course," Grace told her. "Would you like to use the house phone?"

She shook her head. "No, I have my cell up in the apartment. It'll only take a few minutes."

"You might have a problem with coverage. Try it and see. By the time you return, the coffee and soup will be ready."

Mary Jo went back to the barn and up the stairs to the

small apartment. She was breathless when she reached the top and paused to gulp in some air. Her pulse was racing. This had never happened before. Trying to stay calm, she walked into the bedroom where she'd left her purse.

Sitting on the bed, she got out her cell. She tried the family home first. But the call didn't connect, and when Mary Jo glanced at the screen, she saw there wasn't any coverage in this area. Well, that settled that.

She did feel bad but there was no help for it. She'd ask to make a long-distance call on the Hardings' phone, and she'd try Linc's cell, as well as the house. She collected her coat and gloves and hurried back to the house, careful not to slip in the snow.

A few minutes later, she was in the kitchen. As Grace had promised, the coffee and a bowl of soup were waiting for her on the table.

Mary Jo hesitated. She really hated to ask, hated to feel even more beholden. "If you don't mind, I'd appreciate using your phone."

"Of course."

"It's long distance, I'm afraid. I'd be happy to pay the charges. You could let me know—"

"Nonsense," Grace countered. "One phone call isn't going to make a bit of difference to our bill."

"Thank you." Still wearing her coat, Mary Jo went over to the wall phone, then remembered that Linc's number was programmed into her cell. Speed dial made it unnecessary to memorize numbers these days, she thought ruefully.

She'd have to go back to the apartment a second time.

Well, there was no help for that, either. "I'll need to get my cell phone," she said.

"I can have Cliff get it for you," Grace offered. "I'm not sure you should be climbing those stairs too often."

"Oh, no, I'm fine," Mary Jo assured her. She walked across the yard, grateful the snow had tapered off, and back up the steep flight of stairs, pausing as she had before to inhale deeply and calm her racing heart. Taking another breath, she went in search of her cell.

On the off chance the phone might work in a different location, Mary Jo stood on the Hardings' porch and tried again. And again she received the same message. No coverage.

Cell phone in hand, she returned to the kitchen.

"I'll make the call as quickly as I can," she told Grace, lifting the receiver.

"You talk as long as you need," Grace said. "And here, let me take your coat."

She found Linc's contact information in her cell phone directory and dialed his number. After a few seconds, the call connected and went straight to voice mail. Linc, it appeared, had decided to turn off his cell. Mary Jo wasn't sure what to make of that. Maybe he didn't *want* her to contact him, she thought with sudden panic. Maybe he was so angry he never wanted to hear from her again. When she tried to leave a message, she discovered that his voice mail was full. She sighed. It was just like Linc not to listen to his messages. He probably had no idea how many he'd accumulated.

"My brother has his cell off," Mary Jo said with a defeated shrug.

"He might be in a no-coverage zone," Grace explained. "We don't get good reception here at the ranch. Is it worth trying his house?"

Mary Jo doubted it, but she punched in the numbers. As she'd expected, no answer there, either. Her oldest brother's deep voice came on, reciting the phone number. Then, in his usual peremptory fashion, he said, "We're not here. Leave a message." Mary Jo closed her eyes.

"It's me," she began shakily, half afraid Linc would break in and start yelling at her. Grace had stepped out of the kitchen to give her privacy, a courtesy she appreciated.

"I'm in Cedar Cove," she said. "I'll be home sometime Christmas Day after I speak to David's parents. Probably later in the evening. Please don't try to find me. I'm with… friends. Don't worry about me. I know what I'm doing." With that she replaced the receiver.

She saw that Grace had moved into the dining room, setting the table. "Thank you," Mary Jo told her.

"You're very welcome. Is your soup still hot?"

Mary Jo had forgotten about that. "I'll check."

"If not, let me know and I'll reheat it in the microwave."

"I'm sure it'll be fine," she murmured. Even if it was stone-cold, she wouldn't have said so, not after everything Grace had done for her.

But as Mary Jo tried her first spoonful, she realized the temperature was perfect. She finished the entire bowl, then ate all the crackers and drank her decaf coffee after adding a splash of cream. As she brought her dishes to the sink, Grace returned to the kitchen. "My daughters will be here at six," she said, looking at the clock. "And my daughter-in-law and her family should be back soon. We're having dinner together and then we're leaving for the Christmas Eve service at our church."

"How nice." Mary Jo had missed attending church. She and her brothers just seemed to stop going after her parents' funeral. She still went occasionally but hadn't in quite a while, and her brothers didn't go at all.

"Would you like to join us?"

The invitation was so genuine that for a moment Mary Jo seriously considered it. "Thank you for the offer, but I don't think I should."

"Why not?" Grace pressed. "We'd love to have you."

"Thank you," Mary Jo said again, "but I should probably stay quiet and rest, like the EMT suggested."

Grace nodded. "Yes, you should take his advice, although we'd love it if you'd at least have dinner with us."

The invitation moved her so much that Mary Jo felt tears spring to her eyes. Not only had Grace and her husband taken her into their home, they wanted to include her in their holiday celebration.

"I can't believe you'd want me here with your family," she said.

"Why wouldn't we?" Grace asked. She seemed astonished by the comment. "You're our guest."

"But it's Christmas and you'll have your...your family here." She found it hard to speak.

"Yes, and they'll be delighted to meet you."

"But this isn't a time for strangers."

"Now, just a minute," Grace said. "Don't you remember the original Christmas story?"

"Of course I do." Mary Jo had heard it all her life.

"Mary and Joseph didn't have anywhere to stay, either, and strangers offered them a place," Grace reminded her. "A stable," she added with a smile.

"But I doubt those generous folks asked them to join the family for dinner," Mary Jo teased.

"That part we don't know because the Bible doesn't say, but I have to believe that anyone who'd lend their stable to those young travelers would see to their other needs, as well." Grace's warm smile wrapped its way around Mary Jo's heart. "Join us for part of the evening, okay? I'd love it if you met the girls, and I know they'd enjoy meeting you."

Mary Jo didn't immediately respond. Although she would've liked to meet Grace's family, she wasn't feeling quite right. "May I think about it?"

"Of course," Grace said. "You do whatever you need to do."

Leaning forward in the chair, Mary Jo supported her lower back with both hands, trying to ease the persistent ache. Sitting had become difficult in the last few weeks. It was as if the baby had latched his or her foot around one of her ribs and intended to hang on. Mary Jo was beginning to wonder if she'd ever find a comfortable position again.

"Can I help you with anything?" she asked.

Grace surveyed the kitchen. "No, I've got everything

under control. I thought I'd sit down with you for a few minutes."

Mary Jo nodded. "Yes, please. I'd like that."

"So would I," the other woman said. "Here, let me get us some fresh coffee. And what about some Christmas shortbread to go with it?"

Chapter Ten

At the fire station, Mack McAfee sat by himself in the kitchen, downing yet another cup of coffee. The only call so far that day had been for the young pregnant woman who'd had the dizzy spell at the library. For some reason, she'd stayed in his mind ever since.

Because he wasn't married, Mack had volunteered to work Christmas Eve and part of Christmas Day, allowing one of the other firefighters to spend the time with family. Unfortunately, his mother was none too happy that he'd agreed to work over the holidays.

Mack's parents lived in Cedar Cove and his sister had, too, until she'd left several months ago, her heart broken by that cowpoke who used to work for Cliff Harding. Linnette had taken off with no plan or destination and ended up in some Podunk town in North Dakota. She seemed to love her new home out there in the middle of nowhere. Mack didn't understand it, but then it wasn't his life.

He was happy for Linnette, knowing she'd found her niche.

She'd always said she wanted to live and work in a small rural town. As an experienced physician assistant, Linnette had a lot to offer a community like Buffalo Valley, North Dakota.

Gloria, Mack's oldest sister, had been given up for adoption as an infant; their relationship had only come to light in the past few years. Mack was just beginning to know her and so far he'd discovered that they had a surprising amount in common, despite their very different upbringings. She'd promised to stop by the house and spend part of Christmas with their parents, but she, too, was on the duty roster for tonight.

When Gloria had first moved into the area—with the goal of reconnecting with her birth family—she'd worked for the Bremerton police. Since then, however, she'd taken a job with the sheriff's department in Cedar Cove.

Mack's cell phone, attached to his waistband, chirped. He reached for it, not bothering to look at the screen. He already knew who was calling.

"Hi, Mom."

"Merry Christmas." Her cheerful greeting was strained and not entirely convincing.

"Thanks. Same to you and Dad."

"How's everything?"

His mother was at loose ends. Not having any of her children with her during the holidays was hard for her. "It's been pretty quiet here this afternoon," he said.

Corrie allowed an audible sigh to escape. "I wish you hadn't volunteered to work on Christmas."

This wasn't the first time his mother had brought it up. But as the firefighter most recently hired, he would've been assigned this shift anyway.

"It'll be lonely with just your father and me." Her voice fell and Mack sighed, wishing he could tell her what she wanted to hear.

"It'll be a wonderful Christmas," he said, sounding as positive as he could.

"I'm sure it'll be fine," she agreed in a listless voice. "I decided to cook a ham this year instead of turkey. It's far less work and we had a turkey at Thanksgiving. Of course, I'm going to bake your father's favorite potato casserole and that green bean dish everyone likes."

Mack didn't understand why his mother felt she had to review her dinner menu with him, but he let her chatter on, knowing it made her feel better.

"I was thinking," she said, abruptly changing the subject.

"Yes, Mom?"

"You should get married."

If Mack had been swallowing a drink at the time he would've choked. "I beg your pardon?"

"You're settling down here in Cedar Cove?"

He noticed that she'd made it a question. "Well, I wouldn't go that far."

"I would," she said. "You have a steady job." She didn't add that this was perhaps his tenth career change in the last six years. Mack was easily bored and tended to jump from job to job. He'd worked part-time for the post office, done construction, delivered for UPS and held half a dozen other short-term jobs since dropping out of college. He'd also renovated a run-down house and sold it for a tidy profit.

Mack's restlessness had contributed to the often acrimonious relationship he'd had with his father. Roy McAfee hadn't approved of Mack's need for change. He felt Mack was irresponsible and hadn't taken his life seriously enough. In some ways Mack supposed his father was right. Still, his new job with the fire department seemed to suit him perfectly, giving him the variety, the excitement and the camaraderie he craved. It also gave him a greater sense of purpose than anything else he'd done.

He and his dad got along better these days. Roy had actually apologized for his attitude toward Mack, which had come as a real shock. It had made a big difference in their relationship, though, and for that Mack was grateful.

"You think I should be *married*," he repeated, as though it was a foreign word whose meaning eluded him.

"You're twenty-eight."

"I know how old I am, Mom."

"It's time," she said simply.

"Really?" He found his mother's decree almost humorous.

"Have you met anyone special?" she asked.

"Mom!" he protested. Yet the picture of Mary Jo Wyse shot instantly into his mind. He knew from the conversation he'd overheard at the library that she was pregnant and single and that David Rhodes was her baby's father. He'd also heard a reference to Charlotte and Ben Rhodes. He was familiar with them, but completely in the dark about David.

"I'm not trying to pressure you," his mother said. "It's just that it would be nice to have grandchildren one day."

Mack chuckled. "If you want, I'll get to work on that first thing."

"Mack," she chastised, "you know what I mean."

He did but still enjoyed teasing her. While she was on the phone, he decided to take the opportunity to find out what he could about the father of Mary Jo's baby. "Can you tell me anything about David Rhodes?" he asked.

"David Rhodes," his mother said slowly. "Is he related to Ben Rhodes?"

"His son, I believe."

"Let me go ask your father."

"That's okay, Mom, don't bother. It's no big deal."

"Why'd you ask, then?"

"Oh, someone mentioned him, that's all." Mack was reluctant to bring up Mary Jo; for one thing, it'd been a chance encounter and he wasn't likely to see her again. Clearly she wasn't from here.

"Mack. Tell me."

"I treated a young woman at the library this morning."

"The pregnant girl?" Her voice rose excitedly.

Word sure spread fast in a small town, something Mack wasn't used to yet. "How do you know about Mary Jo?" he asked.

"Mary Jo," his mother said wistfully. "What a nice name."

She had a nice face to go with it, too, Mack mused and then caught himself. He had no business thinking about her. None whatsoever.

"I met Shirley Bliss in the grocery store earlier," his mother went on to say. "The last thing I wanted to do was make a dash to the store. You know how busy they get the day before a big holiday."

Actually, he didn't, not from experience, but it seemed logical enough.

"Anyway, I ran out of evaporated milk. I needed it for the green Jell-O salad I make every Christmas."

Mack remembered that salad well; it was one of his favorites. His mother had insisted on making it, he noted, even though Mack wouldn't be joining the family for dinner.

"I could've used regular milk, I suppose, but I was afraid it wouldn't taste the same. I don't like to use substitutes if it can be avoided."

"Shirley Bliss, Mom," he reminded her.

"Oh, yes. Shirley. I saw her at the store. She was with her daughter, Tanni."

"O-k-a-y." Mack dragged out the word, hoping she'd get to the point.

"That's a lovely name, isn't it?" his mother asked. "Her given name is Tannith."

"Tanni's the one who told you about Mary Jo?" he asked, bringing her back to the discussion.

"No, Shirley did." She hesitated. "Well, on second thought, it was Tanni's boyfriend, Shaw, who told her, so I guess in a manner of speaking it *was* her daughter."

"And how did Shaw hear?" he pressed, losing track of all these names.

"Apparently Mary Jo came into Mocha Mama's this morning and was asking him a lot of questions."

"Oh."

"And he suggested she ask Grace Harding about David Rhodes."

"I see." Well, he was beginning to, anyway.

"Shirley said Shaw told her that Mary Jo looked like she was about to deliver that baby any minute."

"She's due in two weeks."

"My goodness! Do you think David Rhodes is the baby's father?" his mother breathed, as if she'd suddenly made the connection. "It makes sense, doesn't it?"

He already knew as much but preferred not to contribute to the gossip obviously making the rounds. "Did Shirley happen to say where Mary Jo is right now?" Maybe someone should check up on her. Mack had recommended she rest for the remainder of the day but he didn't like the idea of her being alone.

"No," his mother said. "She'll be fine, won't she?"

"I assume so.…"

"Good."

"Where's Dad?" Mack asked.

His mother laughed softly. "Where do you think he is?"

It didn't take a private eye—which his father was—to know the answer to that. "Shopping," Mack said with a grin.

"Right. Your father's so efficient about everything else, yet he leaves gift-buying until the last possible minute."

"I remember that one year when the only store open was the pharmacy," he recalled. "He bought you a jigsaw puzzle of the Tower of London, two romance novels and some nail polish remover."

"And he was so proud of himself," Corrie said fondly.

"We all had a good time putting that puzzle together, didn't we?" It'd been one of their better Christmases, and the family still did jigsaw puzzles every holiday. A small family tradition had come about as a result of that particular Christmas and his father's last-minute gift.

"You'll call in the morning?" his mother asked.

"I will," Mack promised. "And I'll stop by the house as soon as I'm relieved. It'll be late tomorrow afternoon. Save me some leftovers, okay?"

"Of course," his mother said. "Gloria's schedule is the reverse of yours, so she's coming over in the morning." Corrie sounded slightly more cheerful as she said, "At least we'll see you both for a little while."

After a few words of farewell, Mack snapped his cell phone shut and clipped it back on his waistband.

He'd no sooner started getting everything ready for that night's dinner than Brandon Hutton sauntered into the kitchen. "You got company."

"Me?" Mack couldn't imagine who'd come looking for him. He was new in town and didn't know many people yet.

"Some guy and a woman," Brandon elaborated.

"Did they give you a name?" Mack asked.

"Sorry, no."

Mack walked toward the front of the building and as he neared he heard voices—one of them unmistakably his sister's.

"Linnette!" he said, bursting into the room.

"Mack." She threw herself into his arms for a fierce hug.

"What are you doing here?" he asked. The last he'd heard she was in Buffalo Valley and intended to stay there for the holidays.

She slipped one arm around his waist. "It's a surprise. Pete suggested it and offered to drive me, so here I am."

Mack turned to the other man. In a phone conversation the month before, Linnette had told him she'd met a farmer and that they were seeing each other. "Mack McAfee," he said, thrusting out his hand.

Pete's handshake was firm. "Pleased to meet you, Mack."

"Happy to meet you, too." He turned back to his sister. "Mom doesn't know?"

Linnette giggled. "She doesn't have a clue. Dad, either. It's going to be a total shock to both of them."

"When did you arrive?"

"About five minutes ago. We decided to come and see you first, then we're going to the house."

"Dad's out doing his Christmas shopping."

Linnette laughed and looked at Pete. "What did I tell you?"

"That he'd be shopping," Pete said laconically.

"Mom's busy cooking, I'll bet." This comment was directed at Mack.

"My favorite salad," he informed her. "Even though I won't be there, she's making it for me. I'm already looking forward to the leftovers. Oh, and she's doing a ham this year."

Linnette laughed again. "She discussed her Christmas menu with you?"

"In minute detail."

"Poor Mom," Linnette said.

"I wish I could see the expression on her face when you walk in the door."

"I love that we're going to surprise her." Linnette's wide grin was perhaps the best Christmas gift he could have received. His sister, happy again.

Mack hadn't seen her smile like this in…well, a year anyway.

"Call me later and let me know how long it takes Mom to stop crying."

"I will," Linnette said.

His sister and Pete left for the house, and Mack returned to the firehouse kitchen, where he was assigned cooking duty that evening. He resumed chopping onions for the vat of chili he planned to make—how was that for Christmas Eve dinner? He caught himself wishing he could be at his parents' place tonight, after all. Although he'd just met Pete, Mack sensed that he was a solid, hard-working, no-nonsense man. Exactly what Linnette needed, and someone Mack wanted to know better.

It seemed that Linnette had found the kind of person *she* needed, but had he? Mack shook his head.

And yet, he couldn't forget Mary Jo Wyse.

Which wasn't remotely logical, considering that their relationship consisted mostly of him taking her blood pressure.

And yet...

Chapter Eleven

Linc drove down Harbor Street, peering out at both sides of the street. Fortunately, the snow had let up—Ned was probably disappointed by that. He wasn't sure what he was searching for, other than some clue as to where he might locate his runaway sister. He'd give anything to see that long brown coat, that colorful striped scarf....

"Nice town," Ned commented, looking around.

Linc hadn't noticed. His mind was on Mary Jo.

"They seem to go all out with the Christmas decorations," Mel added.

Ned poked his head between the two of them and braced his arms against the back of their seats. "Lots of lights, too."

"There's only one that I can see," Linc said, concentrating on the road ahead. His brothers were so easily distracted, he thought irritably.

They exchanged knowing glances.

"What?" Linc barked. He recognized that look. In fact, he'd already seen it several times today.

"In case you weren't aware of it, there are lights on every lamppost all through town," Ned pointed out slowly, as if he was speaking to a child. "The street is decorated with Christmas lights. And that clock tower, too, with the Christmas tree in front of it."

"I was talking about traffic signals," Linc said.

"Oh, signals. Yeah, you're right about that." As Linc drove through the downtown area, there'd been just that one traffic light. Actually, he was going back to it. He made a sharp U-turn.

"Where are you going?" Mel asked, clutching the handle above the passenger window.

"Back to the light—the traffic light, I mean."

"Why?" Ned ventured with some hesitation.

Linc's mood had improved since they'd arrived in Cedar Cove. The traffic was almost nonexistent and his sister was here. Somewhere.

He tried to think like Mary Jo. Where could she be? It had started to get dark, although it was barely four in the afternoon. Twilight had already settled over the snowy landscape.

"Practically everything in town is closed for the day," Mel said, pressing his face against the passenger window like an anxious child.

"Stands to reason. It's Christmas Eve." Ned sounded as if he was stating something neither Linc nor Mel had discovered yet.

Linc waited for the light before making a sharp left-hand turn. The road ended at a small traffic circle that went around a totem pole. The building to the right with the large mural was the library, and there was a large, mostly vacant parking lot situated to his left. Directly in front of him was a marina and a large docked boat.

The sign read Passenger Ferry.

Linc immediately went through the traffic circle and pulled into the parking lot.

"Why are we stopping here?" Mel asked in surprise. "Not that I'm complaining. I could use a pit stop."

"Yeah, me, too," Ned chimed in. "Let's go, okay?"

"Come on," Mel said. "I wanna hit the men's room."

"How did Mary Jo get to Cedar Cove?" he asked them both, ignoring their entreaties. "The ferry, right? Isn't that what we figured?"

"Yeah, she must've taken it to Bremerton," Mel agreed. "And then she rode the foot ferry across from Bremerton to Cedar Cove." He pointed to the boat docked at the end of the pier.

Linc playfully ruffled his brother's hair. "Give the man a cigar."

Mel jerked his head aside. "Hey, don't do that." He combed his fingers through his hair to restore it to order.

Linc swung open the truck door and climbed out.

"Where you goin' now?" Mel asked, opening his own door.

"It's not for us to question why," Ned intoned and clambered out, too.

Linc sighed. "I'm going to ask if anyone saw a pregnant girl on the dock this morning."

"Good idea," Ned said enthusiastically. "Meanwhile, we'll visit that men's room over there."

"Fine," Linc grumbled, scanning the street as he waited for them. Unfortunately he hadn't found anyone to question in the vicinity of the dock. The only nearby place that seemed to be doing business was a pub—imaginatively called the Cedar Cove Tavern.

"I Saw Mommy Kissing Santa Claus" blasted out the door the instant Linc opened it. A pool table dominated one side of the establishment; a man was leaning over it, pool cue in hand, while another stood by watching. They looked over their shoulders when the three brothers came inside.

Linc walked up to the bar.

The bartender, who had a full head of white hair and was wearing a Santa hat, ambled over to him. "What can I get you boys?"

"Coke for me." Linc was driving, so he wasn't interested in anything alcoholic. Besides, he'd need a clear head once he tracked down his obstinate younger sister.

"I'll have a beer," Mel said. He propped his elbows on the bar as though settling in for a long winter's night.

"Coke," Ned ordered, sliding onto the stool on Linc's other side.

The bartender served them speedily.

Linc slapped a twenty-dollar bill on the scarred wooden bar. "You seen a pregnant woman around today?" he asked. "Someone from out of town?"

The man frowned. "Can't say I have."

"She's *real* pregnant." For emphasis Mel held both hands in front of his stomach.

"Then I definitely didn't," Santa informed them.

"She arrived by foot ferry," Ned told him. "Probably sometime midmorning."

"Sorry," Santa Claus said. "I didn't start my shift until three." He rested his bulk against the counter and called out, "Anyone here see a pregnant gal come off the foot ferry this morning?"

The two men playing pool shook their heads. The other patrons stopped their conversation, glanced at Linc and his brothers, then went back to whatever they were discussing.

"Doesn't look like anyone else did either," the bartender told them.

The brothers huddled over their drinks. "What we gotta do," Mel said, "is figure out what her agenda would be."

"She came to find David's parents," Ned reminded them. "*That's* her agenda."

"True." Okay, they both had a point. Turning back to the bartender, Linc caught his attention. "You know any people named Rhodes in the area?"

Santa nodded as he wiped a beer mug. "Several."

"This is an older couple. They have a son named David."

The bartender frowned. "Oh, I know David. He stiffed me on a sixty-dollar tab."

Yeah, they were talking about the same guy, all right. "What about his parents?"

"Ben and Charlotte," Santa folded his arms across his

chest. "Really decent folks. I don't have anything good to say about their son, though."

"Where do they live?"

"I'm not sure."

Looking around, Linc saw a pay phone near the restrooms. "I'll check if Ben Rhodes is in the phone book," he said, leaving his stool.

"Sounds like a plan," Santa muttered.

Linc removed the phone book from a small shelf. The entire directory was only half an inch thick. The Seattle phone book had a bigger section just of government agencies than the combined Cedar Cove White *and* Yellow Pages. He quickly found the listing for Ben and Charlotte Rhodes, then copied down the phone number and address.

"Got it," he announced triumphantly.

"Should we call?"

"Nope."

"Why not?" Mel asked. He walked back to the bar and downed the last of his beer.

"I don't want to give Mary Jo a heads-up that we're in town. I think the best thing to do is take her by surprise."

Ned nodded, although he seemed a bit uncertain.

Linc thanked the bartender, got some general directions and collected his change. He left a generous tip; it was Christmas Eve, after all. Then he marched toward the door, his brothers scrambling after him.

In the parking lot again, Linc climbed into the truck and started the engine. He'd noticed that Harbor Street angled up the hill. He guessed David's parents' street wasn't far from this main thoroughfare. Trusting his instincts, he returned to the traffic signal, took a left and followed the road until it intersected with Pelican Court.

Within five minutes of leaving the tavern, Linc was parked on Eagle Crest Avenue, outside Ben and Charlotte Rhodes's house.

The porch light was on, and there appeared to be a light on inside, too. The house was a solid two-story dwelling, about the same age as the one he shared with his brothers in Seattle. White Christmas lights were strung along the roofline and the bushes were lighted, too. There was a manger scene on the front lawn.

"This is a neat town," Mel said. "Did you see they have an art gallery? We passed it a couple of minutes ago."

"When did you get so interested in art?" Linc asked.

"I like art."

"Since when?"

"Since now. You want to make something of it?"

"No," Linc said, puzzled by Mel's defensiveness.

Linc walked up the steps leading to the front door while his brothers stood out on the lawn. Mel amused himself by rearranging the large plastic figures in the Nativity scene.

Linc felt smug. If Mary Jo thought she'd outsmarted him, she had a lesson to learn. He didn't want to be self-righteous, but he was going to teach his little sister that she wasn't nearly as clever as she seemed to think. He also wanted Mary Jo to understand that he had her best interests at heart—now and always.

He leaned hard against the doorbell, then waited several

minutes and when nothing happened, he pressed the bell a second time.

"Want me to scope out the backyard?" Ned called from the lawn.

"Sure."

His youngest brother took off and disappeared around the side of the house.

Mel trailed after Ned, while Linc stood guard on the porch. Since no one was bothering to answer—although there seemed to be people home—he stepped over to the picture window and glanced inside through the half-closed blinds.

A cat hissed at him from the windowsill on the other side. Or at least he assumed it was hissing, since its teeth were bared and its ears laid back. Startled, he took a deep breath and stepped away. Although there was a window between them, the cat glared at him maliciously, its intentions clear.

"Nice kitty, nice kitty," Linc remarked, although he knew the animal couldn't hear his attempt to be friendly. This cat was anything but. Linc didn't doubt for a moment that if he were to get inside the house, "nice kitty" would dig all his claws into him within seconds.

Linc hurried to the other side of the porch and leaned over the side, but that didn't provide him with any further information.

A minute or two later, his brothers were back. "The house is locked up. Door wouldn't budge."

This wasn't going the way Linc had planned. "Okay, so maybe they aren't home."

"Then where *are* they?" Mel demanded.

"How am I supposed to know?" Linc asked, growing irritated.

"You're the one with all the answers."

"Hey, hey," Ned said, coming to stand between his brothers. "Let's skip the sarcasm. We're looking for Mary Jo, remember?"

"Where is she?" Mel asked.

"I haven't got a clue," Ned returned calmly. "But someone must."

"Maybe we should ask a neighbor," Mel said.

"Be my guest." Linc motioned widely with his arm.

"Okay, I will. I'll try…that one." Mel marched down the steps, strode across the street and walked up to the front door. He pounded on it. Even from this distance Linc could hear his knock.

An older woman with pink rollers in her hair pulled aside the drape and peeked out.

"I just saw someone," Ned yelled. "There's someone inside."

Linc had seen her, too.

"Why isn't she answering the door?" Mel asked loudly, as if the two of them had some secret insight into this stranger.

"Would *you* answer if King Kong was trying to get in *your* front door?" Linc asked. Apparently Mel hadn't figured out that most people responded better to more sensitive treatment.

"Okay, fine," Mel shouted after several long minutes. "Be that way, lady."

"She just doesn't want to answer the door," Ned shouted back.

Mel ignored that and proceeded to the next house.

"Knock more quietly this time," Linc instructed.

Mel ignored that, too. Walking to the door, he pushed the buzzer, then turned and glanced over his shoulder. This house seemed friendlier, Linc thought. A large evergreen wreath hung on the door and lights sparkled from the porch columns.

Again no one answered.

Losing patience, Mel looked in the front window, framing his face with both hands. After peering inside for several seconds, he straightened and called out, "No one's home here."

"You want me to try?" Ned asked Linc. Mel wasn't exactly making friends in the neighborhood.

"Do you think it'll do any good?"

"Not really," Ned admitted.

A piercing blare of sirens sounded in the distance, disrupting the tranquility of the neighborhood.

Mel hurried back across the street. "Everyone seems to be gone. Except for the lady with those pink things in her hair."

Despite their efforts, they obviously weren't getting anywhere. "Now what?" Ned muttered.

"You got any ideas?" Linc asked his two brothers, yelling to be heard over the sirens.

"Nope," Mel said with a shrug.

"Me, neither," Linc said, not hiding his discouragement.

They sauntered back to the truck and climbed inside. Linc started the engine and was about to drive away from the curb when two sheriff's vehicles shot into the street and boxed him in.

The officers leaped out of their cars and pulled their weapons. "Get out of the truck with your hands up!"

Chapter Twelve

Mary Jo hadn't intended to spill her heart out to Grace, but the older woman was so warm, so sympathetic. Before long, she'd related the whole sorry tale of how she'd met and fallen in love with David Rhodes. By the time Mary Jo finished, there was a pile of used tissues on the table.

"You aren't the only one who's ever loved unwisely, my dear," Grace assured her.

"I just feel really stupid."

"Because you trusted a man unworthy of your love?" Grace asked, shaking her head. "The one who needs to be ashamed is David Rhodes."

"He isn't, though."

"No," Grace agreed. "But let me repeat a wise old saying that has served me well through the years."

"What's that?" Mary Jo asked. She dabbed tears from the corners of her eyes and blew her nose.

"Time wounds all heels," Grace said with a knowing smile. "It will with David, too."

Mary Jo laughed. "I guess the reverse is true, as well. I'll get over David and his lies…" Her voice trailed off. "Is everyone in Cedar Cove as nice as you and Cliff?" she asked a moment later.

The question seemed to surprise Grace. "I'd like to think so."

"Olivia—Ms. Griffin—certainly is." Mary Jo sighed and looked down at her hands. "That firefighter—what's his name again?"

"Mack McAfee. He's new to town."

What Mary Jo particularly remembered was that he had the gentlest touch and the most reassuring voice. She could still hear it if she closed her eyes. The way he'd knelt at her side and the protectiveness of his manner had calmed her, physically and emotionally.

"His parents live in town," Grace was explaining. "Roy McAfee is a retired Seattle detective turned private investigator, and his wife, Corrie, works in his office."

"Really." She recalled seeing Mr. McAfee's sign on Harbor Street. What a fascinating profession. She suspected Mack's father got some really interesting cases. Maybe not, though, especially in such a small town. Maybe she was just influenced by the mystery novels she loved and the shows she watched on television.

"I suppose I should change clothes before dinner," Grace said, rising from her chair with seeming reluctance. "I've enjoyed sitting here chatting with you."

"Me, too," Mary Jo told her. It'd been the most relaxing part of her day—except, of course, for her nap.

"I'll be back in a few minutes."

Mary Jo took that as her signal to leave. "I'll go to the apartment."

"Are you sure? I know Mack said you should rest but like I said, Cliff and I would be delighted if you joined our family for dinner."

"Where is Cliff?" she asked, glancing over one shoulder, assuming he must be somewhere within sight.

"He's out with his horses. They're his first love." Grace smiled as she said it.

Mary Jo had noticed the way Cliff regarded his wife. He plainly adored Grace and it was equally obvious that she felt the same about him. Mary Jo gathered they'd only been married a year or two. The wedding picture on the piano looked recent, and it was clear that their adult children were from earlier marriages.

Then, without letting herself consider the appropriateness of her question, Mary Jo said, "About what you said a few minutes ago... Have *you* ever loved unwisely?"

Grace sat down again. She didn't speak for a moment. "I did," she finally said. "I married young and then, after many years together, I was widowed. I'd just started dating again. It was a whole new world to me."

"Were you seeing Cliff?"

"Yes. He'd been divorced for years and dating was a new experience for him, too. I'd been married to Dan for over thirty years, and when another man—besides Cliff—paid attention to me, I was flattered. It was someone I'd had a crush on in high school."

"Did Cliff know about him?"

"Not at first. You see, this other man lived in another city and we emailed back and forth, and he became my obsession." Grace's mouth tightened. "I knew all along that he was married and yet I allowed our internet romance to continue. He said he was getting a divorce."

"It was a lie?"

"Oh, yes, but I believed him because I wanted to. And then I learned the truth."

"Did Cliff find out about this other man?"

Regret flashed in her eyes. "Yes—and as soon as he did, he broke off our relationship."

"Oh, no! You nearly lost him?"

"As I said, I'd learned the truth about Will by then and was crushed to lose Cliff over him. I was angry with myself for being so gullible and naive. I'd lost a wonderful man because of my foolishness. For a long time I could hardly look at my own face in the mirror."

"That's how I feel now," she whispered. *Will,* she thought. She'd heard that name before….

"It does get better, Mary Jo, I promise you that. Will, the man I was…involved with, did eventually lose his wife. She divorced him and, while I believe he had genuine feelings for me, it was too late. I wanted nothing more to do with him. So you see, he was really the one who lost out in all this."

"Cliff forgave you?"

"Yes, but it took time. I was determined never to give him cause to doubt me again. We were married soon after that and I can honestly say I've never been happier."

"It shows."

"Cliff is everything I could want in a husband."

The door off the kitchen opened just then, and Cliff came in, brushing snow from his jacket. He hung it on a peg by the door, then removed his boots. "When I left, you two were sitting right where you are now, talking away."

Grace smiled at him. "I was about to change my clothes," she said. "Keep Mary Jo entertained until I get back, will you?"

"Sure thing."

Grace hurried out, and Cliff claimed the chair next to Mary Jo. As he did, he eyed the crumpled tissues. "Looks like you two had a good heart-to-heart."

"We did," she said and then with a sigh told him, "I've been very foolish."

"I'm sure Grace told you we've all made mistakes in our lives. The challenge is to learn from those mistakes so we don't repeat them."

"I don't intend to get myself into this predicament ever again," Mary Jo said fervently. "It's just that…" She hesitated, uncertain how much to tell him about her brothers. "I feel like my family's smothering me. I have three older brothers and they all seem to think they know what's best for me and my baby."

"They love you," he said simply.

She nodded. "That's what makes it so difficult. With my parents gone, they feel *they* should be the ones directing my life."

"And naturally you take exception to that."

"Well, yes. But when I tried to live my life my *own* way and prove how adult I was, look what happened." She pressed both hands over her stomach, staring down at it. "I made a mistake, a lot of mistakes, but I discovered something… interesting after I found out I was pregnant."

"What's that?" Cliff asked. He stretched his long legs out in front of him and leaned back, holding his coffee mug. She noticed that his hand-knit socks had a whimsical pattern of Christmas bells, at odds with his no-nonsense jeans and shirt.

"Well, at first," she began, "as you can imagine, I was terribly upset. I was scared, didn't know what to do, but after a while I began to feel really excited. There was a new life inside me. A whole, separate human being with his or her own personality. This tiny person's going to be part David, part me—and all himself. Or herself," she added, refusing to accept her brothers' certainty that the baby was a boy.

Cliff smiled. "Pregnancy is amazing, isn't it? I can't pretend to know what a woman experiences, but as a man I can tell you that we feel utter astonishment and pride—and a kind of humbling, too."

"I think David might've felt like that in the beginning," Mary Jo whispered. He really had seemed happy. Very quickly, however, that happiness had been compromised. By fear, perhaps, or resentment. She wanted to believe he'd loved her as much as he was capable of loving anyone. She now realized that his capacity for feeling, for empathy, was limited. Severely limited. Barely a month after she learned she was pregnant with his baby, David had become emotionally distant. He continued to call and to see her when he was in town but those calls and visits came less and less frequently, and the instant she started asking questions about their future, he closed himself off.

"It's not all that different with my horses," Cliff was saying.

His words broke into her reverie. "I beg your pardon?" What did he mean? They hadn't been talking about horses, had they?

"I've bred a number of horses through the years and with every pregnancy I feel such a sense of hopefulness. Which is foolish, perhaps, since even the best breeding prospects don't always turn out the way you expect. Still…"

"I met Funny Face today."

Cliff's eyes brightened when she mentioned the mare. "She's my sweetheart," he said.

"She seems very special." Mary Jo remembered the moment of connection she'd felt with this horse.

"She is," Cliff said. "She's gentle and affectionate—a dream with the grandchildren. But as far as breeding prospects go, she was a disappointment."

"No." Mary Jo found that hard to believe.

"She's smaller than we thought she'd be and she doesn't have the heart of a show horse."

"But you kept her."

"I wouldn't dream of selling Funny Face. Even though she didn't turn out like Cal and I expected, we still considered her a gift."

Mary Jo released a long sigh. "That's how I feel about

my baby. I didn't plan to get pregnant and I know David certainly didn't want it, yet despite all the problems and the heartache, I've come to see this child as a gift."

"He definitely is."

"He?" She grinned. "Now you're beginning to sound like my brothers. They're convinced the baby's a boy."

"I was using *he* in a generic way," Cliff said. "Would you prefer a girl?"

"I…I don't know." She shrugged lightly. "There's nothing I can do about it, so I'll just leave it up to God." She was somewhat surprised by her own response. It wasn't something she would've said as little as six months ago.

During her pregnancy, she'd begun to reconsider her relationship with God. When she was involved with David, she'd avoided thinking about anything spiritual. In fact, she'd avoided thinking, period. The spiritual dimension of her life had shrunk, become almost nonexistent after her parents' death.

That had changed in the past few months. She thought often of the night she'd knelt by her bed, weeping and desperate, and poured out her despair, her fears and her hopes. It was nothing less than a conversation with God. That was probably as good a definition of prayer as any, she mused. Afterward, she'd experienced a feeling of peace. She liked to imagine her mother had been in the room that night, too.

"You've got everything you need?"

She realized Cliff had spoken. "I'm sorry, what did you say?" She hated to keep asking Cliff to repeat himself, but her mind refused to stay focused.

"I was asking if you have everything you need for the baby."

"Oh, yes… Thanks to my friends and my brothers." Mary Jo was grateful for her brothers' generosity to her and the baby. Their excitement at the idea of a nephew—or niece, as she kept telling them—had heartened her, even as their overzealous interference dismayed her.

Linc, who tended to be the practical one, had immediately gone up to the attic and brought down the crib that had once belonged to Mary Jo. He'd decided it wasn't good enough for her baby and purchased a new one.

Mary Jo had been overwhelmed by his thoughtfulness. She'd tried to thank him but Linc had brushed aside her gratitude as though it embarrassed him.

Mel was looking forward to having a young boy around—or a girl, as she'd reminded him, too—to coach in sports. She'd come home from work one day this month to find a tiny pair of running shoes and knew they'd come from Mel.

And Ned. Her wonderful brother Ned had insisted on getting her a car seat and high chair.

Mary Jo had knitted various blankets and booties, and her friends from the office had seen to her layette in what must have been one of the largest baby showers ever organized at the insurance company. Other than her best friend, Casey, no one had any inkling who the father was, and if they speculated, they certainly never asked. Regardless, their affection for Mary Jo was obvious and it made a difference in her life.

Just as Grace returned, Mary Jo heard the sound of a car

door closing. The front door opened a moment later and a girl of about five ran inside. "Grandma! Grandma!" she cried. "I'm an angel tonight! I'm an angel tonight!"

Grace knelt down, clasping the child's hands. "You're going to be an angel in the Christmas pageant?"

The little girl's head bobbed up and down. "In church tonight."

Grace hugged her granddaughter. "Oh, Katie, you'll be the best angel ever."

The girl beamed with pride. Noticing Mary Jo, she skipped over to her. "Hi, I'm Katie."

"Hi, Katie. I'm Mary Jo."

"You're going to have a baby, aren't you?"

"Yes, I am."

The door opened again and a young couple came in. The man carried a toddler, while the woman held a large quilted diaper bag.

"Merry Christmas, Mom," Grace's daughter said, kissing her mother's cheek. She turned to Mary Jo. "Hello, I'm Maryellen. And I'm so glad you're going to be joining us," she said, smiling broadly.

Mary Jo smiled back. She'd never expected this kind of welcome, this genuine acceptance. Tonight would be one of the most memorable Christmas Eves of her life.

If only her back would stop aching....

Chapter Thirteen

"Officer, let me explain," Linc said, trying his hardest to stay calm. His brothers stood on either side of him, arms raised high in the air. The deputy, whose badge identified him as Pierpont, appeared to have a nervous trigger finger.

The second officer was in his car, talking into the radio.

"Step away from the vehicle," Deputy Pierpont instructed, keeping his weapon trained on them.

The three brothers each moved forward one giant step.

"What were you doing on private property?" Pierpont bellowed as if he'd caught them red-handed inside the bank vault at Fort Knox.

"We're looking for our sister," Mel blurted out. "She ran away this morning. We've got to find her."

"She's about to have a baby," Linc said, feeling some clarification was required.

"Then why are you *here?*" the deputy asked, his tone none too friendly.

"Because," Linc said, fast losing patience, "this is where we *thought* she'd be."

The second officer approached them. His badge said he was Deputy Rogers. "We had two separate phone calls from neighbors who claimed three men were breaking into this house."

"We weren't breaking in!" Mel turned to his brothers to confirm the truth.

"I looked in the window," Linc confessed, shaking his head. "I didn't realize that was a crime."

Pierpont snickered. "So we got a Peeping Tom on our hands."

"There's no one at home!" Linc shouted. "There was nothing to peep at except a crazed cat."

"I tried to open the back door," Mel said in a low voice.

"Why'd you do that?" Rogers asked.

"Well, because…" Mel glanced at Linc.

As far as Linc was concerned, Mel was the one who'd opened his big mouth; he could talk his own way out of this.

"Go on," Rogers prodded. "I'd be interested to know why you tried to get into this house when your brother told us you were searching for your sister *and* that you knew there was no one here."

"Okay, okay," Mel said hurriedly. "I probably shouldn't have tried the door, but I suspected Mary Jo was inside and I wanted to see if that elderly couple was at home or just hiding from us."

"*I'd* hide if the three of you came pounding on my door." Again this was from Deputy Rogers.

"What did I tell you, Jim?" Pierpont said. Mel's comment seemed to verify everything the officers already believed. "Why don't we all go down to the sheriff's office so we can sort this out."

"Not without my attorney," Linc said in a firm voice. He wasn't going to let some deputy fresh out of the academy railroad him. "We didn't break any law. We came to the Rhodes residence in good faith. All we want...all we care about is locating our little sister, who's pregnant and alone and in a strange town."

At that point another car pulled up to the curb, and a middle-aged man stepped out, dressed in street clothes.

"Now you're really in for it," Pierpont said. "This is Sheriff Troy Davis."

As soon as Sheriff Davis walked toward them, Linc felt relieved. Troy Davis was obviously a seasoned officer and looked like a man he could reason with.

The sheriff frowned at the young deputies. "What's the problem here?"

They both started talking at once.

"We got a call from dispatch," Pierpont began.

"Two calls," Rogers amended.

"From neighbors, reporting suspicious behavior," Pierpont continued.

"The middle one here admits he was trying to open the back door."

Mel leaned forward. "Just checking to see if it was locked."

Linc groaned and turned to his brother. "Why don't you keep your trap shut before we end up spending Christmas in jail."

To his credit, Mel did seem chagrined. "Sorry, Linc. I wanted to help."

Linc appealed directly to the sheriff. "I understand we might have looked suspicious, peeking in windows, Sheriff Davis, but I assure you we were merely trying to figure out if the Rhodes family was at home."

"Are you family or friends of Ben and Charlotte's?" the man asked, studying them through narrowed eyes.

"Not exactly friends."

"Our sister knows Ben's son," Ned told them.

Mel nodded emphatically. "Knows him in the Biblical sense, if you catch my drift."

Linc wanted to kick Mel but, with all the law enforcement surrounding them, he didn't dare. They'd probably arrest him for assault. "Our sister's having David Rhodes's baby," he felt obliged to explain.

"Any day now," Mel threw in.

"And she disappeared," Ned added.

"If we're guilty of anything," Linc said, gesturing with his hands, "it's being anxious to locate our sister. Like I said, she's alone in a strange town and without family or friends."

"Did you check their identification?" the sheriff asked.

"We hadn't gotten around to that yet," Deputy Rogers replied.

"You'll see we're telling the truth," Linc asserted. "None of us have police records."

With the sheriff and his deputies watching carefully, Linc, Mel and Ned handed him their identification.

The sheriff glanced at all three pieces, then passed them to Pierpont. The young man swaggered over to his patrol car, apparently to check for any warrants or arrest records. He was back a couple of minutes later and returned their ID.

"They don't have records." He seemed almost disappointed, Linc thought.

The sheriff nodded. "What's your sister's name?"

"Mary Jo Wyse," Linc answered. "Can you tell us where we might find the Rhodes family? All we want to do is talk to them."

"Unfortunately Ben and Charlotte are out of the country," the sheriff said.

"You mean they aren't even in town?" Mel asked, sounding outraged. He turned to Linc. "What are we going to do *now?*"

"I don't know." Mary Jo must have discovered this information about the Rhodes family on her own. The only thing left for her to do was head back to Seattle. She wouldn't have any other options, which meant this entire venture through dismal traffic, falling snow and wretched conditions had been a complete waste of time.

"She's probably home by now and wondering where the three of us are," Linc muttered.

"Maybe." Ned shook his head. "But I doubt it."

"What do you mean, you doubt it?"

"Mary Jo can be stubborn, you know, and she was pretty upset last night."

"We should phone the house and see if she's there," Linc said, although he had a sneaking suspicion that Ned was right. Mary Jo wouldn't give up that easily.

"Sounds like a good idea to me," Sheriff Davis inserted.

Linc reached for his cell phone and called home. Five long rings later, voice mail kicked in. If his sister *had* gone back to Seattle, she apparently wasn't at the house.

"She's not there," Linc informed his brothers.

"What did I tell you?" Ned sighed. "I know Mary Jo, and she isn't going to turn tail after one setback."

This was more than a simple setback, in Linc's opinion. This was major.

"Have you tried her cell phone?" the sheriff suggested next.

"Yeah, we did. A few times. No answer," Linc said tersely.

"Try again."

"I'll do that now." Linc took out his phone again and realized he didn't know her number nor had he programmed it into his directory.

He cleared his throat. "Ah, Ned, could you give me the number for her cell?"

His youngest brother grabbed the phone from him and punched in Mary Jo's number, then handed it back.

Linc waited impatiently for the call to connect. After what seemed like minutes, the phone automatically went to voice mail. "She's not answering that, either."

"Maybe her cell battery's dead," the sheriff said. "It could be she's out of range, too."

Actually, Linc was curious as to why the sheriff himself had responded to dispatch. One would think the man had better things to do—like dealing with *real* criminals or spending the evening with his family. "Listen, Sheriff, is Cedar Cove so hard up for crime that the sheriff responds personally to a possible break-in?"

Troy Davis grinned. "I was on my way to my daughter's house for dinner when I heard the call."

"So you decided to come out here and see what's going on."

"Something like that."

Linc liked the sheriff. He seemed a levelheaded guy, whereas his deputies were overzealous newbies, hoping for a bit of excitement. He'd bet they were bored out of their minds in a quiet little town like Cedar Cove. The call about this supposed break-in had sent these two into a giddy state of importance.

"The only essential thing here is finding our sister," Linc reiterated to the sheriff.

"The problem is, we don't know *where* to find her," Ned put in.

The sheriff rubbed the side of his face. "Did you ask around town?"

No one at the pub had been able to help. "Not really. We asked the guys at some tavern, but they didn't seem aware of much except how full their glasses were."

The sheriff grinned and seemed to appreciate Linc's wry sense of humor.

"She's *very* pregnant," Ned felt obliged to remind everyone. "It isn't like someone wouldn't notice her."

"Yeah." Mel once more thrust his arms out in front of him and bloated his cheeks for emphasis.

Linc made an effort not to groan.

"Wait," Deputy Pierpont said thoughtfully. "Seems to me I heard something about a pregnant woman earlier."

That got Linc's attention. "Where?" he asked urgently. "When?"

"I got a friend who's a firefighter and he mentioned it."

"What did he say?"

Deputy Pierpont shrugged. "Don't remember. His name's Hutton. You could go to the fire station and ask."

"Will do." Linc stepped forward and shook hands with the sheriff and then, for good measure and goodwill, with each of the deputies. "Thanks for all your help."

Troy Davis nodded. "You tell your sister she shouldn't have worried you like this."

"Oh, I'll tell her," Linc promised. He had quite a few other things he planned to say to her, too.

After receiving directions to the fire station, they jumped back in the truck. Finally they were getting somewhere, Linc told himself with a feeling of satisfaction. It was just a matter of time before they caught up with her.

It didn't take them long to locate the fire station.

Rather than repeat their earlier mistakes—or what Linc

considered mistakes—he said, "Let me do the talking, understand?"

"Okay," Ned agreed.

"Mel?"

"Oh, all right."

They walked into the station house and asked to speak to the duty chief, who eyed them cautiously.

Linc got immediately to the point. "I understand that earlier today you responded to an incident involving a young pregnant woman. A firefighter named Hutton was mentioned in connection with this call. Is that correct?"

When the chief didn't reply, Linc added, "If so, we believe that's our sister."

The man raised his eyebrows, as if determined not to give out any information.

"She needs her family, chief."

There must've been some emotion in Linc's voice, some emotion he didn't even know he'd revealed, because the man hesitated, then excused himself. He returned a few minutes later, followed by a second man.

"This is Mack McAfee. He's one of the EMTs who took the call."

"You saw Mary Jo?" Linc asked. He extended his hand, and Mack shook it in a friendly fashion.

"I did."

Linc's relief was so great he nearly collapsed into a nearby chair. "That's great!"

"She's okay, isn't she?" Ned said anxiously. "She hasn't gone into labor or anything?"

"No, no, she had a dizzy spell."

"Dizzy?" Linc repeated and cast a startled look at his brothers.

"Does that mean what I think it means?" Mel asked.

Linc felt sick to his stomach. "I was twelve when Mary Jo was born and I remember it like it was yesterday. Mom got real dizzy that morning and by noon Mary Jo had arrived."

"That's not generally a sign of oncoming labor," Mack reassured him.

"It is in our family. Dad told me it was that way with each and every pregnancy. According to him, Mom had very quick deliveries and they all started with a dizzy spell. He barely made it to the hospital in time with Mary Jo. In fact—"

"She was born while Dad was parking the car," Mel said. "He dropped Mom off at the emergency door and then he went to look for a parking space."

That tale had been told around the kitchen table for years. Once their father had parked the car and made his way back to the hospital, he was met by the doctor, who congratulated him on the birth of his baby girl.

"Do you know where she is?" Linc asked with renewed urgency.

"You might talk to Grace Harding," Mack said.

"Who's Grace Harding?"

"The librarian." Mack paused for a moment. "Mary Jo was at the library when I treated her."

"The library?" That didn't make any sense to Linc. Why had Mary Jo gone to the library?

"What was she doing there?" Mel asked.

"That isn't as important as where she is now," Linc said. "Mack, do you have any idea where she might've gone after she left the library?" He remembered seeing it earlier. The building with the mural.

Mack shook his head. "She didn't say, although I told her to put her feet up and rest for a few hours."

"She must've gotten a hotel room." They should have realized that earlier. Of course! If Mr. and Mrs. Rhodes were out of town, that was exactly what Mary Jo would have done.

"I don't think so," Mack said. "I thought I'd check on her myself and discovered she isn't at any of the motels in town."

"Why not?"

"No rooms available."

"Where would she go?"

"My guess," Mack said slowly, "is to Grace Harding's house."

"Why her place?"

"Because it seems like the kind of thing Mrs. Harding would do. I have the Hardings' phone number. I could call if you'd like."

Linc couldn't believe their good fortune. "Please."

The firefighter was gone for what seemed like a long time. He returned wearing a grin. "You can talk to her yourself if you want."

Linc bolted to his feet, eager to hear the sound of his sister's voice. He'd been upset earlier—angry, worried, close to panic—but all he felt now was relief.

"She's at the Harding ranch in Olalla."

The three brothers exchanged smiling glances. "Is she all right?"

"She said she's feeling great, but she also said she's ready to go home if you're willing to come and get her."

"Wonderful." Linc couldn't have wished for anything more.

"I'll give you directions to the Harding place. She's on the phone now if you'd like to chat."

Linc grinned, following Mack to the office, his brothers on his heels.

This was finally working out. They'd get Mary Jo home where she belonged.

Chapter Fourteen

"No, please," Mary Jo said, looking at Grace and her family. "I want you to go to the Christmas Eve service, just like you planned."

"Are you positive?" Grace seemed uncertain about leaving her behind.

Mary Jo had bowed to their entreaties and been their guest for a truly wonderful dinner, but she had no intention of imposing on them any further that evening.

"I am." There was no reason for them to stay home because of her, either. This crazy adventure of hers was over; she'd admitted defeat. Her brothers were on their way and she'd be back in Seattle in a couple of hours.

"I'd like to meet those young men," Grace said. "But it sounds as if they'll get here while we're at church."

"You will meet them," Mary Jo promised. "Sometime after Christmas." In one short afternoon, she'd become strongly attached to both Grace Harding and Cliff. Her two daughters, her daughter-in-law, their husbands and the grandchildren had made Mary Jo feel like part of the family. They'd welcomed her without question, opened their hearts and their home to her, given her a place to sleep, a meal, the comfort of their company. In this day and age, Mary Jo knew that kind of unconditional friendship wasn't the norm. This was a special family and she planned to keep in touch with them.

While the fathers loaded up the kids and Cliff brought his car around, Grace lingered.

"You have our phone number?" she asked as they stood by the front door.

"Oh, yes. Cell numbers, too." Mary Jo patted her pants pocket. Grace had carefully written out all the numbers for her.

"You'll call us soon."

Mary Jo nodded. Grace was like the mother she'd lost—loving, protective, accepting. And now that she was becoming a mother herself, she valued her memory even more profoundly. It was Grace who'd reminded Mary Jo of everything her mother had been to her, of everything *she* wanted to be to her own child. Even though her baby wasn't born yet, she felt blessed. She was grateful for everything her pregnancy had brought her. A new maturity, the knowledge that she could rise to the occasion, that she had the strength to cope. This brand-new friendship. And, of course, the baby to come.

"If your brothers are hungry when they get here, there are plenty of leftovers," Grace was saying. "Tell them to help themselves."

"Thank you."

Cliff parked the car closer to the house and got out to open the passenger door. Still Grace lingered. "Don't hesitate to phone if you need *anything,* understand?"

"I won't—and thank you." Wearing her coat like a cloak, Mary Jo walked outside with her into the clear, beautiful night. Snow outlined the branches of trees, and the air was crisp.

"Wait in the house," Grace said.

"I'll be fine in the apartment. It's comfortable there."

The two women hugged and Grace slid into the car next to her husband. Maryellen, Kelly and Lisa, with their families, had already left for the church.

Grace lowered the window. "Thank you for being so patient with Tyler," she said, giving her an apologetic look.

Mary Jo smiled, completely enchanted with the six-year-old who'd received a drum for Christmas and had pounded away on it incessantly.

"He's a talented little boy." In fact, she loved all of Grace and Cliff's grandchildren.

"Now go inside before you get cold," Grace scolded.

But Mary Jo remained in the yard until the car lights faded from sight. Then, pulling her coat more snugly around her, she strolled toward the barn. Several of the participants in the live Nativity scene were inside a corral attached to the barn and she went there first.

"Hello, donkey," she said. "Merry Christmas to you."

As if he understood that she was talking to him, the donkey walked toward her until he was within petting range. Mary Jo stroked his velvety nose, then walked into the barn.

"Hello, everyone."

At the sound of her voice, Funny Face stuck her head over the stall door.

"Hi there," Mary Jo greeted the mare. "I hear you're very special to Cliff," she said. Funny Face nickered loudly in response.

Apparently curious about what was causing all the commotion, the camel poked her head out, too. "Sorry, camel," Mary Jo called, "but your reputation has preceded you and I'm not giving you a chance to bite *my* arm."

After several minutes of chatting with the other horses, Mary Jo washed her hands at a sink in the barn and headed up the stairs to the apartment. About halfway up, her back started to ache again. She pressed one hand against it and continued climbing, holding on to the railing with the other.

When she reached the apartment, she paused in the middle of removing her coat as she felt a powerful tightening across her stomach.

Was this labor?

She suspected it must be, but everything she'd heard and read stated that contractions began gradually. What she'd just experienced was intense and had lasted several long, painful seconds. Another contraction came almost right away.

Mary Jo checked her watch this time. Three minutes later there was a third contraction of equal severity.

Only three minutes.

At the class she'd attended, she'd learned that it wasn't uncommon for labor pains to start at fifteen-minute intervals. Perhaps hers had started earlier and she hadn't noticed.

That didn't seem possible, though. How could she be in labor and not know it? Except…there were all those family stories about her mother and how a dizzy spell always signaled the onset of labor. A dizzy spell like the one she'd had at the library…

The next pain caught her unawares and she grabbed her stomach and doubled over.

"*That* got my attention," she announced to the empty room.

Not sure what to do next, Mary Jo paced, deliberating on the best course of action. Her brothers were due any moment. If she told them she was in labor the second they arrived, they'd panic. One thing Mary Jo knew: she did *not* want her three brothers delivering this baby.

None of them had any experience or even the slightest idea of what to do. Linc would probably order the baby to wait until they could get to a hospital. Knowing Mel and his queasy stomach, he'd fall over in a dead faint, while Ned would walk around declaring that this was just perfect. He was going to be an uncle to a baby born on Christmas Eve—or Christmas Day, depending on how long this labor business was going to take.

Three minutes later, another pain struck and again Mary Jo bent double with the strength of it. She exhaled slowly and timed it, staring at her watch. This contraction lasted thirty seconds. Half a minute. It wasn't supposed to happen this fast! Labor was supposed to go on for hours and hours.

Mary Jo didn't know what to do or who to call. Her mind was spinning, her thoughts scrambling in a dozen different directions at once. She considered phoning Grace. If she was going to give birth here, at the ranch, she wanted a woman with her—and she couldn't think of anyone she'd rather have than Grace Harding. But Grace had left just a few minutes before and the only way to reach her was by cell phone. Unfortunately, as she'd learned earlier, coverage in this area was sporadic at best. And she hated to interfere with the Hardings' Christmas plans.

The second person she thought of was Mack McAfee. He'd been so kind, and he was a trained medical technician. He was calm and logical, which was exactly what she needed. He'd called—when was it? Half an hour ago—and urged her to go home with her brothers. There'd be plenty of time to talk to Ben and Charlotte Rhodes after the baby's birth. Her brothers wouldn't have the opportunity to confront David or his father now, anyway, and she'd manage, somehow or other, to prevent it in the future, too. While she was speaking with Linc, she'd realized how desperate her brothers had been to find her. Mary Jo hadn't meant to worry them like this.

If Linc or Mel or even Ned had reasoned with her like Mack had, she would've listened. Too late to worry about any of that now…

Mary Jo went back down the stairs to the barn. She didn't want to dial 9-1-1 and cause alarm the way she had with her dizzy spell at the library earlier, so she decided to call the fire station directly.

The barn phone was the same number as the house. Sure enough, when she picked up the receiver she saw that Caller

ID displayed the number of the last call received—the firehouse. Mary Jo pushed the redial button.

On the second ring, someone picked up. "Kitsap County Fire District."

Relief washed over her at the sound of Mack's voice. "Mack?"

There was a slight hesitation. "Mary Jo? Is that you?"

"Ye-es."

"What's wrong?"

"I... Grace and her family left for the Christmas Eve service about ten minutes ago. I didn't go because my brothers are on their way here."

"They haven't arrived yet?" He seemed surprised.

"Not yet."

Mack groaned. "I'll bet they're lost."

Mary Jo didn't doubt that for an instant.

"I'm sure they'll be there anytime," he said.

"I hate to bother you," she whispered and gasped at the severity of the next contraction.

"Mary Jo!"

Closing her eyes, she mentally counted until the pain subsided.

"What's wrong?" he asked urgently.

"I'm afraid I've gone into labor."

Mack didn't miss a beat. "Then I should get out there so I can transport you to the birthing center."

At the rate this was progressing, he'd better not lose any time. "Thank you," she said simply.

He must have sensed her fear, because he asked, "How far apart are the contractions?"

"Three minutes. I've been timing them."

"That's good."

"I didn't take all the birthing classes… I wish I had, but David said he'd take them with me and it never happened. I went once but that was just last week and—"

"You'll do fine. If you want, I'll stay with you."

"You?"

"I'm not a bad coach."

"You'd be a wonderful coach, but you have to remember I've only had the one class."

"Listen, instead of talking about it over the phone, why don't I hop in the aid car and drive over."

"Ri-ight." At the strength of the last contraction, Mary Jo was beginning to think this was an excellent idea.

"Where are you?"

"In the barn at the moment." She gave a small laugh.

"Why is that funny?"

"I'm with the animals from the live Nativity scene."

Mack laughed then, too. "That seems appropriate under the circumstances, but I want you to go to the house and wait for me there."

"I'd rather go back to the apartment if you don't mind." It was hard to explain but the place felt like home to her now, at least for this one night.

"Fine. Just don't lock the door. I'll be there soon, so hold on, okay?"

She didn't have any choice but to hold on. "Okay. But, Mack?"

"Yes?"

"Please hurry."

"You got it. I'm leaving now."

"No sirens, please," she begged, and Mack chuckled as if she'd made some mildly amusing joke.

Walking seemed to help, and instead of following Mack's instructions, she paced the length of the barn once, twice, three times.

She noticed that the camel was watching her every move. "Don't be such a know-it-all," she said. She'd swear the creature was laughing at her. "This isn't supposed to be happening yet."

A sheep walked up to the gate, bleating loudly, and Mary Jo wagged her index finger. "I don't want to hear from you, either."

All the horses in their stalls studied her with interest, but the only one who looked at her with anything that resembled compassion was Funny Face.

"Wish me well, Funny Face," Mary Jo whispered as she started back up the stairs. "I need all the good wishes I can get."

Absorbed in the cycle of pain and then relief, followed by pain again, Mary Jo lost track of time. Finally she heard a vehicle pull into the yard. A moment later, Mack entered the apartment, a second man behind him. They were both breathless; they must have run up the stairs.

Mary Jo was so grateful to see him she nearly burst into

tears. Clutching her belly, she walked over to Mack and said hoarsely, "I'm so glad you came."

"How's it going?"

"Not…good."

"Any sign of your brothers?"

She shook her head.

Mack glanced over his shoulder at the second EMT. "This is Brandon Hutton. Remember him from this morning?"

"Hi." Mary Jo raised her hand and wiggled her fingers.

"How far apart are the pains now?"

"Still three minutes, but they're lasting much longer."

Mack turned to the other man. "I think we'd better check her before we transport."

"I agree."

This was all so embarrassing, but Mary Jo would rather be dealing with Mack than any of her brothers. Mack would be impersonal about it, professional. And, most important of all, he knew what he was doing.

Taking her by the hand, Mack led her into the bedroom. He pulled back the sheets, then covered the bed with towels. Mary Jo lay down on the mattress and closed her eyes.

"Okay," Mack announced when he'd finished. "You're fully dilated. You're about to enter the second phase of labor."

"What does that mean?"

"Basically, it means we don't have time to take you to the hospital."

"Then who's going to deliver my baby?" she asked, fighting her tears.

"It looks like that'll be me," he said calmly.

Mary Jo held out her hand to him and Mack grabbed it in both of his.

"Everything's going to be fine," he said with such confidence she couldn't help believing him. "You can do this. And I'll be with you every step of the way."

Chapter Fifteen

"Admit it," Mel taunted, "we're lost."

"I said as much thirty minutes ago." Linc spoke through tightly clenched teeth. He didn't need his brother to tell him what he already knew.

"We should've gotten the Hardings' phone number," Ned commented from the backseat.

That was obvious. "You might've mentioned it at the time," Linc snapped. They'd been driving around for almost an hour and he had no idea where they were. Mack McAfee had drawn them a map but it hadn't helped; somehow they'd gone in the wrong direction and were now completely and utterly lost.

To further complicate matters, a fog had settled in over the area. It seemed they'd run the gamut of Pacific Northwest winter weather, and all within the last eight hours. There'd been sleet and snow, rain and cold. Currently they were driving through a fog so thick he could hardly see the road.

"Read me the directions again," he said.

Mel flipped on the interior light, which nearly blinded Linc. "Hey, turn that off!"

"I thought you wanted me to read these notes."

"You don't need the light," Ned told him. "I've got them memorized."

"So where are we?" Mel asked.

"You're asking *me?*" Linc muttered in frustration.

"Okay, okay." Mel sighed deeply. "Fighting isn't going to help us find Mary Jo."

"You're right." Linc pulled over to the side of the road and shifted to face his brothers. "Either of you have any other ideas?"

"We could go to the firehouse and start over," Mel said.

"Once we're there, we could get the Hardings' phone number," Ned added. "We could call and let Mary Jo know we're on our way."

Linc closed his eyes. "Fine. But have either of you geniuses figured out *how* to get back to the firehouse?"

"Ah…" Mel glanced at Ned, who shrugged his shoulders.

"I guess we can't do that, because we're lost."

"Exactly," Linc said. "Any *other* ideas?" He was feeling more helpless and frustrated by the second.

"We could always ask someone," Ned suggested next.

"Who are we supposed to ask?" Mel cried. "We haven't seen another car in over half an hour."

"There was a place down this road," Ned said in a tentative voice.

Linc stared at him. "Where?"

"You're sure about that?" Mel didn't seem to believe him, and Linc wasn't convinced, either.

"It's there, trust me." Ned's expression, however, did little to inspire Linc's confidence.

"I remember the name," his youngest brother said indignantly. "It was called King's."

"What kind of place was it?"

Ned apparently needed time to consider this.

"A tavern?" Linc asked.

Ned shook his head.

"A gas-and-go?" Mel offered.

"Could've been. There were a bunch of broken-down cars out front."

Linc didn't recall any such place. "How come I didn't see it?" he asked.

"'Cause you were driving."

That actually made sense. Concentrating on maneuvering down these back roads in the fog, it was all he could do to make sure his truck didn't end up in a ditch.

"I think I saw it, too," Mel said a moment later. "The building's set off the road, isn't it?"

Ned perked up. "Yes!"

"With tires edging the driveway?"

"That's the one!"

"Do we have a prayer of finding it again?" Linc asked his brothers.

Ned and Mel exchanged looks. "I think so," Ned told him.

"Good." Linc put the pickup back in gear. "Which way?"

"Turn around," Ned told him.

Linc started down the road, then thought to ask, "Are you sure this King's place is open?"

"Looked like it to me."

"Yeah," Mel concurred. "There were plenty of lights. Not Christmas lights, though. Regular lights."

Linc drove in silence for several minutes. Both his brothers were focused on finding this joint. Just when the entire trip seemed futile, Linc crested a hill and emerged out of the fog, which made a tremendous difference in visibility. Instantly he breathed easier.

"There!" Ned shouted, pointing down the roadway.

Linc squinted and, sure enough, he saw the place his brothers had been yapping about. Maybe there was some hope, after all.

Linc had no idea how his sister had ended up in the boondocks. He wished she'd stayed in town, but, oh, no, not Mary Jo.

As they neared the building, Linc noticed a sign that said King's. Linc could see what his brother meant; it was hard to tell exactly what type of business this was. The sign certainly didn't give any indication. True, there were beat-up old cars out front, so one might assume it was some sort of junk or salvage yard. The building itself was in ill repair; at the very least, it needed a coat of paint. There wasn't a single Christmas decoration in sight.

However, the Open sign in the window was lit.

Linc walked up to the door, peered in and saw a small restaurant, basically a counter with a few stools, and a convenience store. He went inside and strolled up to the counter, taking a seat. Mel and Ned joined him.

A large overweight man wearing a stained white T-shirt and a white apron waddled over to their end of the counter as if he'd been sitting there all day, waiting for them.

"Merry Christmas," Linc said, reaching for the menu.

"Yeah, whatever."

This guy was in a charming mood.

"Whaddaya want?" the cook asked.

"Coffee for me," Linc said.

"What's the special?" Mel asked, looking at a sign on the wall that said, *Ask About Our Daily Special.*

"Meat loaf, mashed potatoes, corn."

"If you want to order food, it's gotta be takeout," Linc told his brothers, although now that the subject had come up, Linc realized he was hungry, too. Famished, in fact.

"We do takeout," the cook said, filling Linc's mug with coffee that had obviously been in the pot far too long. It was black and thick and resembled liquid tar more than coffee.

"Is that fresh?" Linc risked asking.

"Sure is. Made it yesterday."

Linc pushed the mug away. "We'll take three meat loaf sandwiches to go," he said, making a snap decision.

"You want the mashed potatoes with that?"

"Can I have potato chips instead?" Ned inquired.

"I guess."

"Say," Linc said, leaning back on the stool. "Do you happen to know where the Harding ranch is?"

The cook scowled at him. "Who's askin'?"

Linc didn't want to get into long explanations. "A friend."

Cook nodded. "Cliff's a...neighbor."

"He is?" Maybe they were closer than Linc had thought.

"Raises the best horses around these parts." The cook sounded somewhat grudging as he said this.

Linc knew car engines inside out but didn't have a clue about horses, and he had no idea how to respond.

Fortunately he didn't have to. "You fellows interested in buying one of Cliff's horses?" the old curmudgeon asked.

"Not really." Linc hoped that wasn't disappointing news. "We're, uh, supposed to be meeting our sister, who's staying at the Harding place."

"We *had* directions," Mel explained.

"But we sort of got turned around."

"In other words, we're lost," Linc said.

"Lemme make you those sandwiches."

"What about giving us directions?"

King, or whatever his name was, sighed as if this was asking too much. "I could—for a price."

Linc slapped a ten-dollar bill on the counter.

The grouch eyed the money and shrugged. "That might get you there. Then again, it might not."

Linc threw in another ten. "This is all you're getting."

"Fine." He pocketed the money and slouched off toward the kitchen. "I'll be back with your order."

Ten minutes later, he returned with a large white bag packed with sandwiches, potato chips and canned sodas. Linc decided not to ask how old the meat loaf was. He paid the tab and didn't complain about the price, which seemed seriously inflated.

"About those directions?" Linc asked.

Ned took out the map the firefighter had drawn and spread it on the linoleum counter. The route from Cedar Cove to the Harding place looked pretty direct, and Linc didn't know how he'd managed to get so confused.

"The King's gonna set you straight," the grouch told them.

"Good, because we are *lost*," Mel said, dragging out the last word.

"Big-time lost," Ned added.

This was a point that did not need further emphasis. Linc would've preferred his brothers keep their mouths shut, but that wasn't likely to happen.

"Okay, you're here," King informed them, drawing a circle around their current location. He highlighted the street names at the closest intersection. "You're near the corner of Burley and Glenwood."

"Got it," Linc said.

"You need to head east."

"East," Linc repeated.

"Go down about two miles and you cross the highway via the overpass."

"Okay, got that."

The grouch turned the directions around and circled

the Harding ranch. "This is where Cliff and Grace Harding live."

"Okay."

"So, all you do after you cross the highway is go east. Keep going until you see the water, then turn left. The Harding place will be about three-quarters of a mile down the road on the left-hand side."

"Thanks," Linc said. Those directions seemed easy enough for anyone to follow. Even the three of them.

The grouch frowned at him, and Linc assumed he was hinting for more money, which he wasn't about to get. Grabbing their sandwiches, Linc handed the bag to his youngest brother and they piled out the door.

"Merry Christmas," Ned called over his shoulder. Apparently he hadn't grasped yet that this man wasn't doing any kind of celebrating.

The grouch's frown darkened. "Yeah, whatever."

Linc waited until they were back in the vehicle before he commented. "Miserable old guy."

"A regular Scrooge," Mel said.

Ned tore open the sack and passed one sandwich to Linc and another to Mel. Linc bit into his. The old grouch made a good meat loaf sandwich, surprisingly enough, and right now that compensated for a lot.

The three of them wolfed down the food and nearly missed the sign for the highway overpass.

"Hey, you two, I'm driving," Linc said, swallowing the last bite. "Pay attention, will you?"

"Sorry." Ned stared out at the road.

"He said to drive until we can see the water," Linc reminded them.

"It's dark," Mel protested. "How are we supposed to see water?"

"We'll know when we find it," Ned put in.

Linc rolled his eyes. "I hope you're right, that's all I can say."

Linc couldn't tell how far they'd driven, but the water never came into view. "Did we miss something?" he asked his brothers.

"Keep going," Mel insisted. "He didn't say *when* we'd see the water."

"He didn't," Linc agreed, but he had a bad feeling about this. The road wasn't straight ahead the way the grouch had drawn it on the map. It twisted and turned until Linc was, once again, so confused he no longer knew if he was going east or west.

"You don't think that King guy would've intentionally given us the wrong directions, do you?"

"Why would he do that?" Mel asked. "You paid him twenty bucks."

Linc remembered the look on the other man's face. He'd wanted more. "Maybe it wasn't enough."

"Maybe Mr. Scrooge back there needs three visitors tonight," Ned suggested. "If you know what I mean."

"He had three visitors—us."

"Yeah, and I think he was trying to con us," Linc muttered.

"I guess he succeeded," Mel said, just as Ned asked, "But why? What's the point?"

"The point is that he's trying to make us miserable," Linc said. "As miserable as he is, the old coot."

The three of them fell into a glum silence. It sure didn't feel like any Christmas Eve they'd ever had before.

Chapter Sixteen

By the time Grace and Cliff arrived at church for the Christmas Eve service, both her daughters and their husbands were already seated. So were Lisa, Rich and April. Maryellen held Drake, who slept peacefully in his mother's arms. Katie, as well as Tyler, were with the other local children getting ready for the big Christmas pageant.

Katie was excited about being an angel, although Tyler, who'd been assigned the role of a shepherd, didn't show much enthusiasm for his stage debut. If he displayed any emotion at all, it was disappointment that he couldn't bring his drum. Kelly had explained to him that the shepherds of the day played the flute, not drums, because drums would frighten the sheep. The explanation satisfied Tyler, who was of a logical disposition, but it didn't please him.

Grace and Cliff located a pew directly behind her daughters and Lisa. As they slipped in, Grace whispered that she'd prefer to sit closest to the aisle, craving the best possible view of her grandchildren's performances. Once they were seated, Cliff reached for her hand, entwining their fingers.

Maryellen turned around and whispered, "Is everything all right with Mary Jo?"

"I think so." Grace still didn't feel comfortable about leaving her alone. But Mary Jo had been adamant that Grace join her family, so she had. Now, however, she wished she'd stayed behind.

Cliff squeezed her hand as the white-robed choir sang Christmas hymns, accompanied by the organist. "O Come All Ye Faithful" had never sounded more beautiful.

Olivia and Jack, carrying his Santa hat, came down the aisle and slid into the pew across from Grace and Cliff. Justine and Seth accompanied them. From a conversation with Justine earlier in the week, Grace knew Leif had gotten the coveted role of one of the three Wise Men.

As soon as Olivia saw Grace, she edged out of her pew and went to see her friend. Olivia had wrapped a red silk scarf around her shoulders, over her black wool coat. Despite everything she'd endured, she remained the picture of dignity and elegance.

She leaned toward Grace. "How's Mary Jo?" she asked in a whisper.

Grace shrugged. "I left her at the house by herself, and now I wish I hadn't. Oh," she added, "apparently her brothers are in town...."

"Problems?"

Grace quickly shook her head. "Mary Jo actually seemed relieved to hear from them."

"Is she going home to Seattle with her family, then?" Olivia stepped sideways in the aisle to make room for a group of people trying to get past.

Grace nodded.

"How did they find out she was with you?" Olivia asked.

"They tracked her down through Mack McAfee. He phoned the house and talked to her. Then Mary Jo spoke with her oldest brother and decided it would be best to go back to Seattle." Grace had been with her at the time and was struck by the way Mary Jo's spirits had lifted. Whether that was because of her brothers or because of Mack… Grace tended to think it was the latter.

"Mack appeared to have a calming effect on her when I saw them at the library," Olivia said, echoing Grace's thoughts.

"I noticed it after she got off the phone, too. I gather he suggested she should go home with her brothers."

"I'm glad," Olivia said. "For her own sake and theirs. And for Mom and Ben's…" She paused. "As necessary as it is for them to know about this baby, I'd rather it didn't happen the second they got home."

"Her real fear was that her brothers were going to burst onto the scene and demand that David do the so-called honorable thing."

"David and the word *honor* don't belong in the same sentence," Olivia said wryly.

"Mary Jo's brothers were arriving any minute. I'd like to have met them. Or at least talked to them." Grace would've phoned the house, but by now Mary Jo should be well on her way to Seattle.

Olivia straightened. "We'll catch up after the service," she said and returned to the opposite pew, beside Jack.

No sooner had Olivia sat down than Pastor Flemming stepped up to the podium. He seemed to be...at peace. Relaxed, yet full of energy and optimism. The worry lines were gone from his face. Grace knew this had been a difficult year for the pastor and his wife, and she was glad their problems had been resolved.

"Merry Christmas," he said, his voice booming across the church.

"Merry Christmas," the congregation chanted.

"Before the children come out for the pageant, I'd like us all to look at the Christmas story again. For those of us who've grown up in the church, it's become a familiar part of our lives. This evening, however, I want you to forget that you're sitting on this side of history. Go back to the day the angel came to tell Mary she was about to conceive a child."

He opened his Bible and read the well-known passages from the Book of Luke. "I want us to fully appreciate Mary's faith," he said, looking up. "The angel came to her and said she'd conceive a child by the Holy Spirit and she was to name him Jesus, which in those days was a common name." He paused and gazed out at his congregation.

"Can you understand Mary's confusion? What the angel told her was the equivalent of saying to a young woman in our times that she's going to give birth to God's son and she should name him Bob."

The congregation smiled and a few people laughed outright.

"Remember, too," Pastor Flemming continued, "that although Mary was engaged to Joseph, she remained with her family. This meant she had to tell her parents she was with child. That couldn't have been easy.

"What do you think her mother and father thought? What if one of our daughters came to us and said she was pregnant? What if she claimed an angel had told her that the child had been conceived by the work of the Holy Spirit?" Again he paused, as if inviting everyone to join him in contemplating this scenario.

Pastor Flemming grinned. "Although I have two sons and no daughters, I know what *I'd* think. I'd assume that a teenage girl—or her boyfriend—would say anything to explain how this had happened."

Most people in the congregation smiled and agreed with nodding heads. Grace cringed a little, remembering as vividly as ever the day she'd told her parents she was pregnant. She remembered their disappointment, their anger and, ultimately, their support. Then she thought of Mary Jo and turned to exchange a quick glance with Olivia.

"And yet," the pastor went on, "this child, the very son of God, was growing inside her womb. Mary revealed remarkable faith, but then so did her family and Joseph, the young man to whom she was engaged."

Something briefly distracted the pastor and he looked to his left. "I can see the children are ready and eager to begin their performance, so I won't take up any more time. I do want to say this one thing, however. As a boy, taking part in a Christmas pageant just like this, I was given the role of a shepherd standing guard over his sheep when the angel came to announce the birth of the Christ Child. When I grew up, I chose, in a sense, the very same job—that of a shepherd. Every one of you is a member of my flock and I care for you deeply. Merry Christmas."

"Merry Christmas," the congregation echoed.

As he stepped down from the podium, the children took their positions on the makeshift stage. Grace moved to the end of her pew to get a better view of the proceedings. Katie stood proudly in place, her gold wings jutting out from her small shoulders and her halo sitting crookedly atop her head. She couldn't have looked more angelic if she'd tried.

Tyler had borrowed one of Cliff's walking sticks to use as a staff. He was obviously still annoyed to be without his precious drum, glaring at the congregation as if to inform them that he was doing this under protest. Grace had to smother a laugh.

Oh, how Dan would've loved seeing his grandchildren tonight. Their grandson was like his grandfather in so many ways. A momentary sadness came over her and not wanting anyone to sense her thoughts, Grace looked away. She didn't often think about Dan anymore. She'd loved her first husband, had two daughters with him, and through the years they'd achieved a comfortable life together.

But Dan had never been the same after Vietnam. For a lot of years, Grace had blamed herself and her own failings for his unhappiness. Dan knew that and had done his best to make things right in the letter he wrote her before his death.

Christmas Eve, however, wasn't a night for troubled memories. The grandchildren Dan would never know were onstage, giving the performances of their young lives.

Out of the corner of her eye, Grace noticed Angel, the church secretary, rushing down the side aisle and toward the front. She went to the first pew, where Pastor Flemming sat with his wife, Emily.

Angel whispered something in his ear and the pastor nodded. He left with her. Apparently there was some sort of emergency.

"Look, there's a star in the East," Leif Gunderson, Olivia's grandson, shouted. As one of the three Wise Men, he pointed at the church ceiling.

"Let us follow the star," the second of the Wise Men called out.

It wasn't until Cliff tapped her arm that she realized Angel was trying to get her attention. She stood in the side aisle and motioned with her finger for Grace to come out.

"What's that about?" Cliff asked as she picked up her purse.

"I don't know. I'll tell you as soon as I find out."

He nodded.

Grace hurried down the center aisle to the foyer, reaching it just as Angel did. "What's going on?" she asked.

"It's a miracle I was even in the office," Angel said.

This confused Grace. "What do you mean?"

"For the phone call," she explained. "I went to get a pair of scissors. Mrs. Murphy, the first-grade Sunday School teacher, needed scissors and I thought there was a pair in my desk."

"The phone call," Grace reminded her.

"Oh, yes, sorry. It was from some young firefighter."

"Mack McAfee?" Grace blurted out.

"No, no, Brandon Hutton. At any rate, he wanted to speak to the pastor."

"Has there been an accident?"

"No… I don't know. I think it would be best if you talked to Pastor Flemming yourself. He asked me to get you."

Dave Flemming was on the phone, a worried expression on his face. When he saw Grace, he held out the receiver. "You'd better take this."

Grace dismissed her first fear, that there'd been an accident. Everyone she loved, everyone who was important to her here in Cedar Cove, was inside the church.

"This is Grace Harding," she said into the receiver, her voice quavering slightly.

"Ms. Harding, this is EMT Hutton from the Kitsap County Fire District. We received a distress call from a young woman who's currently at your home."

Grace gasped. "Mary Jo? She's still at the house? Is she all right?"

"I believe so, ma'am. However, she's in labor and asking for you."

"Won't you be transporting her to the hospital? Shouldn't I meet you there?" Grace would notify Cliff and they could go together.

From the moment she'd left the house, some instinct

had told her she should've stayed with Mary Jo. Some inner knowledge that said Mary Jo would be having her baby not in two weeks but *now*. Tonight.

"We won't be transporting her, Ms. Harding."

"Good heavens, why not?" Grace demanded, wondering if it was a jurisdictional matter. If so, she'd get Olivia involved.

"It appears Ms. Wyse is going to give birth imminently. We don't have time to transport her."

"She's not alone, is she?"

"No, ma'am. EMT McAfee is with her."

Mack. Thank goodness. "What about her brothers?" she asked. Surely they'd arrived by now.

"There's no one else here, ma'am."

Grace's heart started to pound. "I'll get there as soon as possible."

"One last thing," Officer Hutton added. "Do you normally keep camels in your barn?"

"No. But be warned. She bites."

"She's already attempted to take a piece out of me. I managed to avoid it, though."

"Good."

She set down the receiver and turned to Pastor Flemming. "A young woman who's staying with us has gone into labor."

"So I understand."

"I'll collect my husband and get going." Grace hated to miss the pageant but there was nothing she could do about it.

Returning to the pew, she explained to Cliff what was

happening. Maryellen twisted around and Grace told her, too.

"She doesn't have anything for the baby, does she?" Maryellen asked.

Grace hadn't even thought of that. She had blankets and a few other supplies for her grandchildren, but the disposable diapers would be far too big.

"Jon and I will stop by the house and get some things for Mary Jo and the baby and drop them off. I'm sure I still have a package of newborn-size diapers, too."

Grace touched her daughter's shoulder, grateful for Maryellen's quick thinking.

"We'll bring Lisa, Rich and April back to the house," Kelly whispered. "I wouldn't miss this for the world."

"Me, neither," Lisa said. "There couldn't be a more ideal way to celebrate Christmas!"

Chapter Seventeen

"You're doing great," Mack assured Mary Jo.

"No, I'm not," she cried, exhaling a harsh breath. Giving birth was hard, harder than she'd ever envisioned and the pain...the pain was indescribable.

The second EMT came back into the bedroom. "I talked to your friend and she's on her way."

"Thank God." It was difficult for Mary Jo to speak in the middle of a contraction. The pain was so intense and she panted, imitating Mack who'd shown her a breathing exercise to help deal with it.

Mack held her hand and she squeezed as tight as she could, so tight she was afraid she might be hurting him. If that was the case, he didn't let on.

"Get a cool damp washcloth," Mack instructed the other man.

"Got it." As though thankful for something to do, Brandon Hutton shot out of the room and down the hallway to the bathroom.

"I'm going to check you again," Mack told her.

"No!" She clung to his hand, gripping it even tighter. "I need you here. Beside me."

"Mary Jo, I have to see what position the baby's in."

"Okay, okay." She closed her eyes. Sweat poured off her forehead. Now she knew why giving birth was called *labor*. This was the hardest thing she'd ever done. Unfortunately there wasn't time to go to any more classes, or to finish reading the books she'd started…. She'd thought she had two more weeks. If only she hadn't waited for David, or believed him when he said he wanted to attend the classes with her. *This* was what she got for trusting him.

Suddenly liquid gushed from between her legs. "What was that?" she cried.

"Your water just broke."

"Oh." She'd forgotten about that. She had a vague recollection of other women's stories about their water breaking.

"That's good, isn't it?" she asked. What she hoped was that it meant her baby was almost ready to be born and this agony would come to an end.

"It's good," he told her.

"It'll be better now, right?"

Mack hesitated.

"What's wrong?" she demanded. "Tell me."

"Your labor may intensify."

This had to be a cruel joke. "Intensify." She couldn't imagine how the pains could get any stronger than they were now. "What do you mean…intensify?"

"The contractions will probably last longer…."

"Oh, no," she moaned.

Although she'd discovered this was Mack's first birth, he knew so much more than she did. He'd at least studied it and obviously paid attention during class. Mack had joked that he was getting on-the-job training—and so was she, but that part didn't seem so amusing anymore.

"The baby's fully in the birth canal. It won't be long now, Mary Jo. Just a few more pains and you'll have your baby."

"Thank God." Mary Jo didn't know how much more of this she could take.

"Rest between contractions," Mack advised.

Brandon Hutton returned with a damp washcloth. Mack took it from him and wiped her face. The cool cloth against her heated skin felt wonderfully refreshing.

At the approach of another pain, she screamed, "Mack! Mack!"

Instantly he was at her side, his hand holding hers. Her fingers tightened around his.

"Count," she begged.

"One, two, three…"

The numbers droned on and she concentrated on listening to the even cadence of Mack's voice, knowing that by the time he reached fifty, the contraction would ease.

Halfway through, she started to pant. And then felt the instinctive urge to bear down. Arching her back, Mary Jo pushed with every ounce of her strength.

When the pain passed, she was too exhausted to speak.

Mack wiped her forehead again and brushed the damp hair from her face.

"Water," she mumbled.

"Got it!" Brandon Hutton tore out of the room, like a man on a quest.

Recovering from the pain, she breathed deeply, her chest heaving. She opened her eyes and looked up at Mack. His gaze was tender.

"How much longer?" she asked, her voice barely a whisper.

"Soon."

"I can't stand much more of this…I just can't." Tears welled in her eyes and rolled down the sides of her face.

Mack dabbed at her cheeks. As their eyes met, he gave her an encouraging smile. "You can do it," he said. "You're almost there."

"I'm glad you're with me."

"I wouldn't want to be anywhere else," he told her. They continued to hold hands.

Brandon came back with the water. "Here," he said.

Mack took the glass and held it for Mary Jo, supporting her head. "Just a sip or two," he cautioned.

She nodded and savored each tiny sip.

The sound of a car door slamming echoed in the distance.

"Grace," Mary Jo said, grateful the other woman had finally come home.

"I'll bring her up." Brandon disappeared from the room.

Another pain approached. "No…no…" she whimpered, gathering her resolve to get through this next contraction.

She closed her eyes and clung to Mack, thanking God once more that she wasn't alone. That Mack was with her…

Mack automatically began to count. Again she felt the urge to push. Gritting her teeth, she bore down, grunting loudly for the first time, straining her entire body.

"Mary Jo." Grace's serene voice broke through the haze of pain. "I came as soon as I heard."

The contraction eased and Mary Jo collapsed onto the mattress, sweat blinding her eyes.

"The baby's in the birth canal," Mack told her friend.

"What would you like me to do?" Grace asked.

"Hold on to her hand and count off the seconds when the contractions come."

"No…don't leave me." Mary Jo couldn't do this without Mack at her side.

"I need to deliver the baby," he explained, his words so gentle they felt like a warm caress. "Grace will help you."

"I'm here," Grace said.

"Okay." Reluctantly Mary Jo freed Mack's hand.

Grace slipped into his spot. "I don't want to hurt you," Mary Jo said.

"How would you do that?" Grace asked, clasping her hand.

Somehow she found the strength to smile. "I squeeze hard."

"You aren't going to hurt me," Grace said reassuringly. "You squeeze as hard as you need to and don't worry about me." She reached for the damp cloth and wiped Mary Jo's flushed and heated face.

"I…don't have anything for the baby," she whispered. That thought suddenly struck Mary Jo and nearly devastated her. Her baby wasn't even born yet, and already she was a terrible mother. Already she'd failed her child.

"That's all been taken care of."

"But…I don't even have a blanket."

"Maryellen and Jon are stopping at their house for diapers and baby blankets and clothes for a newborn."

"But…"

"Maryellen still has all of Drake's clothes, so that should be the least of your worries, okay?"

"Okay." A weight lifted from her heart.

Another pain approached. Mary Jo could feel herself pushing the infant from her womb. She gritted her teeth, bearing down with all her strength.

Grace, her voice strong and confident, counted off the seconds. Again, when the pain was over, Mary Jo collapsed on the bed.

In the silence that followed, Mary Jo could hear the sound of her own harsh breathing. Then in the distance she heard the laughter of children.

"The kids…"

"The grandchildren are outside with Cliff," Grace said.

"Laughing?"

"Do you want me to tell Cliff to keep them quiet?"

"No…no. It's…joyful." This was the way it should be on Christmas Eve. Hearing their happiness gave her hope. Her baby, no matter what the future held, would be born surrounded by people who were generous and kind.

Giving birth in a barn, the stalls below filled with beasts, children running and laughing outside, celebrating the season, hadn't been part of Mary Jo's plan. And yet—it was perfect.

So perfect.

This was a thousand times better than being alone with strangers in a hospital. None of her brothers would've been comfortable staying with her through labor. Maybe Ned, but even her youngest brother, as much as he loved her, wouldn't have done well seeing her in all this pain.

Mack had been with her from the first, and now Grace.

"Thank you," she whispered to them both.

"No, Mary Jo, thank *you*," Grace whispered back. "We're so honored to be helping you."

"I'm glad you're with me." She smiled tremulously at Grace, then Mack. How she wished she'd fallen in love with him instead of David. Mack was everything a man should be.…

Another pain came, and she locked her eyes with his for as long as she could until the contraction became too strong. She surrendered to it, whimpering softly.

"The head's almost there," Mack said when the pain finally released her. "Your baby has lots of brown hair."

"Oh…"

"Another pain or two and this will be over," Grace promised.

"Thank God, thank God," Mary Jo said fervently.

"You're going to be a good mother," Grace told her.

Mary Jo wanted to believe that. Needed to believe it. All

night, she'd been tortured with doubts and, worse, with guilt about arriving at this moment totally unprepared.

"I *want* to be a good mother."

"You already are," Mack said.

"I love my baby."

"I know." Grace whisked the damp hair from her brow.

Mary Jo was drenched in sweat, her face streaked with tears. "I'm never going through this again," she gasped, looking at Grace. "I can't believe my mother gave birth four times."

"All women think that," Grace said. "I know I did. While I was in labor with Maryellen, I told Dan that if this baby wasn't the son he wanted, he was out of luck because I wasn't having another one."

"You did, though."

"As soon as you hold your baby in your arms, nothing else matters. You forget the pain."

Footsteps clattered up the stairs. "Mom?"

It was Maryellen, Grace's daughter.

"In here," Grace called out.

Maryellen hurried into the room, then paused when she saw Mary Jo and smiled tearfully. Her arms were heaped with baby clothes.

A pain overtook Mary Jo. Again it was Mack she looked to, Mack who held her gaze, lending her his strength.

She was grateful that Grace was at her side, but most of the time it had been Mack who'd guided and encouraged her. He had a way of comforting her that no one else seemed to have, not even Grace.

"You're doing so well," Mack said to her. "We have a shoulder...."

Mary Jo sobbed quietly. It was almost over. The baby was leaving her body. She could feel it now, feel the child slipping free and then the loud, fierce cry that resounded in the room.

Her relief was instantaneous.

She'd done it! Despite everything, she'd done it.

With her last reserves of strength, Mary Jo rose up on one elbow.

Mack held the child in his arms and Brandon had a towel ready. Mack turned to her and she saw, to her astonishment, that there were tears in his eyes.

"You have a daughter, Mary Jo."

"A daughter," she whispered.

"A beautiful baby girl."

Her own tears came then, streaming from her eyes with an intensity of emotion that surprised her. She hadn't given much thought to the sex of this child, hadn't really cared. Her brothers were the ones who'd insisted she'd have a son.

They'd been wrong.

"A daughter," she whispered again. "I have a daughter."

Chapter Eighteen

"The natives are getting restless," Jon Bowman reported to Grace when she came down from the apartment. After watching the birth of Mary Jo's baby, Grace felt ecstatic. She couldn't describe all the emotions tumbling through her. Joy. Excitement. Awe. Each one held fast to her heart.

Katie, April and Tyler raced around the yard, screaming at the top of their lungs, chasing one another, gleeful and happy. Jon went to quiet them, but Grace stopped him.

"Let them play," she told her son-in-law. "They aren't hurting anything out here."

"Kelly and Lisa are inside making hot cocoa," Cliff said, joining Grace. "And Paul's looking after Emma." He slid his arm around her waist. "Everything all right up there?" He nodded toward the barn.

"Everything's wonderful. Mary Jo had a baby girl."

"That's marvelous!" Cliff kissed her cheek. "I bet you never guessed you'd be delivering a baby on Christmas Eve."

Grace had to agree; it was the last thing she'd expected.

She was thankful Mary Jo hadn't been stuck in some hotel room alone. These might not have been the best of circumstances, but she'd ended up with people who genuinely cared for her and her baby.

Grace didn't know Roy and Corrie McAfee's son well, but Mack had proved himself ten times over. He was a capable, compassionate young man, and he'd been an immeasurable help to Mary Jo. In fact, Grace doubted *anyone* could have done more.

After he'd delivered that baby girl, Mack had cradled the infant in his arms and gazed down on her with tears shining in his eyes. An onlooker might have thought he was the child's father.

The other EMT actually had to ask him to let go of the baby so he could wash her. After that, Grace had wrapped the crying baby in a swaddling blanket and handed her to Mary Jo.

The two EMTs were finishing up with Mary Jo and would be transporting her and the baby to the closest birthing center. Maryellen had stayed to discuss breastfeeding and to encourage and, if need be, assist the new mother.

Grace had felt it was time to check on the rest of her family.

"It's certainly been a full and busy night," Cliff said.

"Fuller than either of us could've imagined," Grace murmured.

A car pulled into the yard. "Isn't that Jack's?" Cliff asked, squinting into the lights.

"Yes—it's Olivia and Jack." Grace should've known Olivia

wouldn't just go home after Christmas Eve services. She'd briefly told Olivia what was happening before she'd hurried out of the church, fearing she'd caused enough of a distraction as it was.

Jack parked next to Cliff's vehicle. Before he'd even turned off the engine, Olivia had opened her door. "How's everything?" she asked anxiously as she stepped out of the car.

"We have a baby girl."

Olivia brought her hands together and pressed them to her heart. "I'm so *pleased*. And Mary Jo?"

"Was incredible."

"You delivered the baby?"

"Not exactly. But I was there."

Being with Mary Jo had brought back so many memories of her own children's births. Memories that were clear and vivid. The wonder of seeing that beautiful, perfectly formed child. The elation. The feeling of womanly power. She remembered it all.

"If not you, then who?" Olivia asked.

"Mack McAfee. The other EMT, Brandon, was there, too, but it was Mack who stayed with Mary Jo, who helped her through the worst of it. By the time I arrived, the baby was ready to be born."

"I'm sure she was happy to see you."

Mary Jo had been, but she hadn't really needed Grace; she and Mack had worked together with a sense of ease and mutual trust.

Grace almost felt as if she'd intruded on something very private. The communication between Mack and Mary Jo had been—she hesitated to use this word—*spiritual*. It was focused entirely on the birth, on what each needed to do to get that baby born. Grace felt moved to tears, even now, as she thought about it.

"Grandma, listen!" Tyler shouted. He pounded on his drum, making an excruciating racket.

Grace covered her ears. "Gently, Tyler, gently."

Tyler frowned as he looked up at her. "I was playing my best for you."

"Remember the song about the little drummer boy?" Olivia asked him.

Tyler nodded eagerly. "It's my favorite."

"It says in the song that he went pa-rum-pum-pum-pum, right?"

Tyler nodded again.

"It doesn't say he beat the drum like crazy until Baby Jesus's mother put her hands over her ears and asked him to go next door and play."

Tyler laughed. "No."

"Okay, try it more slowly now," Grace said.

Tyler did, tapping on the drum in a soft rhythm that was pleasing to the ear.

"Lovely," Grace told her grandson.

"Can I play for the ox and the lamb?" he asked.

"In the song they kept time, remember?"

Grinning, Tyler raced away to show his cousins what he'd learned and to serenade the animals.

"Come in for a cup of coffee," Cliff suggested to Olivia and Jack.

"We should head home," Jack said. His arm rested protectively on Olivia's shoulders.

"I just wanted to make sure everything turned out well," Olivia explained. "Do you think I could see Mary Jo and the baby for a few minutes?"

"I don't see why not," Grace said with a smile.

The two women left the men outside while Grace led the way up to the small apartment. Brandon Hutton sat on the top step with his medical equipment, filling out paperwork. He shifted aside and they skirted around him.

"Mary Jo?" Grace asked, standing in the doorway to the bedroom. "Would it be okay if Olivia came in to see the baby?"

"Of course. That would be fine," Mary Jo said.

When they walked into the bedroom, they found Mary Jo sitting up, holding her baby in her arms.

"Oh, my," Olivia whispered as she reached the bed. "She's so tiny."

"She didn't feel so tiny a little while ago." Mary Jo looked up with a comical expression. "I felt like I was giving birth to an elephant."

"It was worth it, though," Olivia said and ran her finger over the baby's head. "She's just gorgeous."

"I never would've believed how much you can love such a tiny baby." Mary Jo's voice was full of wonder. "I thought my heart would burst with love when Mack put her in my arms."

"Do you have a name for her?" Grace asked.

"Not yet. I had one picked out, but now I'm not sure."

"She's a special baby born on a special night."

"I was thinking the same thing," Mary Jo said, kissing the newborn's forehead. Her gaze fell lovingly on the child. "When I was first pregnant...I was so embarrassed and afraid, I prayed God would just let me die. And now...now I see her as an incredible gift."

Grace had felt that way when she discovered she was pregnant with Maryellen all those years ago. It was shortly before her high school graduation; she'd been dating Dan Sherman and their relationship had always been on-again, off-again. She'd dreaded telling him she was pregnant, even more than she'd dreaded telling her parents.

For weeks she'd kept her secret, embarrassed and ashamed. But like Mary Jo, she'd learned to see the pregnancy as an unexpected gift, and the moment Maryellen was placed in her arms, Grace had experienced an overwhelming surge of love. The birth hadn't been easy, they never really were, but as soon as she saw her daughter, Grace had recognized that every minute of that pain had been worth the outcome.

"If you need anything," Olivia was saying to Mary Jo, "make sure you give me a call."

"Thank you. That's so kind."

Olivia turned to Mack, who hovered in the background. "Are you taking her to the birthing center in Silverdale?"

He nodded. "We'll be leaving in about ten minutes."

"Then I won't keep you," Olivia said. "I'll stop by some-time tomorrow afternoon," she promised Mary Jo.

"Oh, please don't," Mary Jo said quickly. "It's Christ-mas—spend that time with your family. I'll get in touch soon. Anyway, I'll be with my own family." She looked up, her eyes widening.

"Mary Jo?" Grace asked in alarm. "What's wrong?"

"Oh, my goodness!"

"What is it?" Mack's voice was equally worried.

"My brothers," Mary Jo said. "They never showed up."

"That's true." The entire matter had slipped Grace's mind. "Mary Jo's brothers were due here—" she checked her watch "—three hours ago."

"Where could they be?" Mary Jo wailed.

Grace tried to reassure her. "They're probably lost. It's easy enough with all these back roads. They've never been in this area before, have they?"

Mary Jo shook her head.

"Don't worry. When they arrive, I'll tell them what happened and where to find you."

Mary Jo smiled down at the infant cradled in her arms. "They'll hardly believe I had the baby—but then it's hard for me to believe, too."

"I'll call you tomorrow," Olivia said.

"Thank you, but please…"

"Yes?"

"Don't tell your parents about the baby yet. Give them a chance to settle back into their routine before you let them know about David and me…and the baby."

"I won't say a word until you and I agree the time is right."

Mary Jo nodded.

Grace was impressed that Mary Jo wanted to spare Ben

and Charlotte the unsavory news of David's betrayal until they were more prepared to accept it.

"I'll leave you now," Olivia told her. "But like I said, if you need *anything,* anytime, please call. You're practically family, you know."

Mary Jo thanked her softly. "You all feel like family to me.... Everyone's been so wonderful."

Grace walked down the stairs with Olivia. She was surprised to see Jack and Cliff still outside, huddled with the children.

"What's Cliff up to now?" Grace wondered aloud.

Jack glanced over. "You gotta see this!" he said, waving at Olivia. He sounded like a giddy child.

As soon as Grace saw the huge carton of fireworks Cliff had dragged out, she groaned. "Cliff!"

"I was saving them for New Year's Eve, but I can't think of a better night for celebrating, can you?"

"What about the horses?"

"They're all safe in their stalls. Don't worry about them."

"And Buttercup? She hates that kind of noise."

"She's locked in the house."

"Can we, Grandpa, can we?"

The children were jumping up and down, clapping their hands with enthusiasm.

"Why right now?" Grace asked.

Cliff sent her a look of pure innocence. "I was just casting about for a way to keep the grandkids entertained."

"Oh, all right." She sighed loudly, holding back a grin.

"Okay if we stay and watch?" Jack said.

Grace and Olivia glanced at each other. As they'd often had occasion to observe, most men were little boys at heart.

"If you must," Olivia murmured.

The front door opened and Kelly stepped out with her husband, Paul, who still held the baby. Grace's daughter balanced a large tray filled with mugs and Lisa followed with a tin of Christmas cookies.

"Anyone for hot chocolate?" Kelly asked.

"I'd love a cup," Olivia said.

"Me, too," Grace put in.

Paul gestured at the kids. "What's going on?"

"Fireworks in a few minutes," Grace told him.

"Wow! Great idea."

"Men," Olivia whispered under her breath, and then both Olivia and Grace broke into giggles, just like they had when they were schoolgirls.

Chapter Nineteen

"How did we get so lost—twice?" Linc groaned. The only thing left to do was return to Cedar Cove and start over. That *sounded* easy enough, except that he no longer knew how to find the town.

"That King did us wrong," Mel said.

"You think?" Linc asked sarcastically. He was past frustration, past impatience and past losing his cool. All he wanted was to track down his pregnant sister and bring her home. That shouldn't be such an impossible task, and yet…

"I'm never going back to King's," Ned said in disgust.

"Me, neither," Mel spat. "If I ever go back to Cedar Cove, which is unlikely."

Frankly, Linc was of the same mind, at least as far as King went. The man had blackmailed him into paying for directions and then completely misled him. True, the sandwiches weren't bad, but he'd overcharged for them. The old coot had an evil streak a mile wide. If he thought it was fun to misdirect them, then he had a perverse sense of humor, too. Perverse? Downright twisted!

"Let's find a phone that works," Ned suggested, not for the first time. His brother had harped on that for the last half hour. Their cell phones were useless out here. But it wasn't as if there was a phone booth sitting on the side of the road just waiting for them to appear.

"Okay, you find one, Ned, and I'll be more than happy to pay for the call."

Ned didn't respond, which was definitely for the best.

"What we need is a sign," Mel said.

Linc bit off another sarcastic comment. They needed a sign, all right, and it had better be one from heaven. He could only imagine what Mary Jo must be thinking. By now his sister probably figured they'd abandoned her, yet nothing could be further from the truth.

"What's that?" Ned shouted, pointing into the distance.

"What's what?" Linc demanded.

"There," Mel said, leaning forward and gazing toward the sky.

Linc saw a flash of light. He pulled over to the side of the road and climbed out of the truck. He needed to stretch his legs, anyway, and the cold air would revive him. Sure enough, someone was setting off fireworks. The sky burst with a spectacular display of lights.

"Wow, that was a big one," Mel said, like a kid at a Fourth of July display.

His brothers didn't seem to appreciate the gravity of

their situation. "Okay, it's nice, but how's that going to help us?"

"You said I should find a phone," Ned pointed out. "Whoever's setting off those fireworks must have a phone, don't you think?"

"Yeah, I guess," Linc agreed. He leaped back into the truck, his brothers with him. "Guide me," he said and jerked the transmission into Drive.

"Turn right," Ned ordered.

"I can't!"

"Why not?"

"I'd be driving across someone's pasture, that's why." Obviously Linc was the only one with his eye on the road.

"Then turn as soon as you reach an intersection," Mel told him.

Linc had never liked taking instructions from his younger brothers. He gritted his teeth. As the oldest, he'd always shouldered responsibility for the others. He had no choice now, however—not that things had worked out all that well with *him* in charge.

At the first opportunity, Linc made a sharp right-hand turn, going around the corner so fast the truck teetered on two wheels. It came down with a bounce that made all three of them hit their heads on the ceiling. "Now what?"

"Pull over for a minute."

"Okay." Linc eased to a stop by the side of the road.

"There!" Mel had apparently seen another display in the heavens. "That star!"

"Which way?" Linc asked with a sigh.

"Go straight."

Linc shook his head. The road in front of him was anything but straight. It twisted and curved this way and that.

"Linc," Mel said, glaring at him. "Go!"

"I'm doing the best I can." He came to a straight patch in the road and floored the accelerator. If anyone had told him he'd be chasing around a series of dark roads, desperately seeking guidance from a fireworks display, he would've laughed scornfully. Him, Mr. Great Sense of Direction? Lost? He sighed again.

"We're getting close," Mel said.

"Okay, stop!" Ned yelled.

Linc slammed on the brakes. The three of them jerked forward and just as abruptly were hurled back. If not for the seat belts, they would've been thrown headfirst into the windshield.

"Hey!" Mel roared.

"Maybe don't stop *quite* so suddenly," Ned added in a voice that was considerably less hostile.

"Sorry."

"Wait, wait, wait." Mel cocked his head toward the sky. "Okay, continue down this road." Mercifully it was flat and straight.

"Here," Ned said a minute later.

Once more Linc slammed on the brakes, only this time his brothers were prepared and had braced themselves.

"Look!" Ned shouted. "This is it. We're here!"

Linc didn't know what he was talking about. "We're where?"

"The Harding ranch," Mel answered.

Then Linc saw. There, painted on the rural route box, was the name Cliff Harding. To his left was a pasture and a large barn.

"I think I see a camel," Linc said. He'd heard about people raising llamas before but not camels.

"Are you sure?" Ned mumbled. "Maybe it's just an ugly horse."

"A camel? No way," Mel insisted.

"I say it's a camel." Linc wondered if his brother's argumentative nature had something to do with being a middle child. Ned, as the youngest, was usually the reasonable one, the conciliator. Whereas he—

"A *camel?*" Mel repeated in an aggressive tone. "What would a camel be doing here?"

"Does it matter?" Ned broke in. "This is where Mary Jo's waiting for us."

"Right." Linc turned into the long driveway that led to the house and barn. The fireworks had stopped, but some kind of party seemed to be taking place, because the yard was filled with people. There was a bunch of little kids running around and the atmosphere was festive and excited.

"There's an aid car here." Ned gestured urgently in its direction.

"Do you think someone's hurt?" Mel asked.

"No," Linc said slowly, thoughtfully. This was what he'd feared from the first. The minute he'd heard about Mary Jo's dizzy spell he'd suspected she was about to give birth. "I think Mary Jo might have had her baby."

"But she isn't due for another two weeks," Mel said.

Ned opened the truck door. "Instead of discussing it, let's go find out."

A middle-aged woman approached as Linc got out of the truck. "You must be Mary Jo's brothers," she said. "I'm Grace Harding. Merry Christmas!"

The woman looked friendly, and Linc appreciated the pleasant greeting. "Merry Christmas to you, too. Sorry for the delay."

"We got lost."

How helpful of Mel to point out the obvious.

"Some guy named King gave us the wrong directions."

"King's Gas and Grocery?" A man came up to them, extending his hand. "Cliff Harding."

"That's the one," Ned answered.

Cliff pinched his lips together, but didn't speak.

Linc shook hands with Grace's husband. "Linc Wyse," he said, introducing himself. "My brothers, Ned and Mel."

Hands were shaken and greetings exchanged all around.

"We were wondering if you were ever going to find the place," Cliff told them.

"If it hadn't been for the fireworks, we probably wouldn't have," Mel admitted.

Linc ignored him and glanced at the aid car. "Mary Jo?" He couldn't bring himself to finish the question.

Grace nodded. "She had the baby."

"A boy," Mel said confidently. "Right?" His eyes lit up with expectation.

"A girl."

"A girl?" Linc was shocked. "Mary Jo had a girl?"

"You sound disappointed," Grace said, studying him closely.

"Not…disappointed. Surprised."

Ned felt obliged to explain. "For some reason, we were all sure she was having a boy."

"Well, she didn't. You have a niece."

"We have a niece," Linc said to his brothers. Mel gave him a congratulatory slap on the back that nearly sent him reeling. He suddenly realized what this all meant. He was an *uncle*. He hadn't thought of himself in those terms until that very moment.

"The EMTs are bringing Mary Jo and the baby down now," Grace was saying.

"Can we see the baby?" Linc asked.

"And talk to Mary Jo?" Mel added.

Grace warmed them with a smile. "I'm sure you can."

A little boy raced up to her. "Grandma, Grandma, can I play my drum for the baby and Mary Jo?"

Grace crouched down so she was eye level with her grandson. "Of course, Tyler, but remember you have to play quietly so you won't disturb the baby."

"Okay!"

Two EMTs rolled Mary Jo toward the aid car on a gurney.

As soon as she saw her brothers, Mary Jo—holding the sleeping newborn in one arm—stretched out the other. "Linc, Mel, Ned…oh, my goodness, you're here!"

They hurried to her side.

"You had a girl," Mel said, staring down at the bundle in her arms.

"She looks just like you," Ned commented.

"No, she doesn't," Linc chimed in. "She looks like the Wyse family—like all of us."

"And like herself," Mary Jo said.

"I'm sorry we were so late," Ned apologized.

"Yeah, we got lost."

If Mel announced that to one more person, Linc might be tempted to slug him.

"Where are they taking you?" he asked.

"To the birthing center in Silverdale," one of the EMTs answered.

"You won't have any trouble finding it," Cliff assured them. "I'll draw you a map."

"No, thanks." Mel shuddered noticeably.

"We'd better follow the aid car," Linc said.

"Mary Jo, we brought you gifts."

"Thank you, Ned." Her face softened as she looked at the three of them. "That's so sweet."

"We're sorry about the things we said." Again this came from Ned, who was more willing to acknowledge that he was wrong than either Mel or Linc.

"Yeah," Mel agreed.

Linc muttered something under his breath, hoping it would pass for an apology. He did feel bad about the way everything had gone and the pressure they'd put on Mary Jo. They hadn't meant to. Their intentions had been good, although he could see now that they'd gone too far. Still, he wasn't letting David Rhodes off the hook. The man had responsibilities and Linc was as determined as ever to see that he lived up to them.

"Linc, Mel, Ned, I want you to meet Mack McAfee," his sister said, her arm out to the EMT. "Oh, I forgot. You guys met earlier."

Linc nodded at the other man. So did Mel and Ned.

"Great to see you again," Mack said. "And congratulations on your brand-new niece. Oh, and this is my partner, Brandon Hutton."

Once more the brothers nodded.

"I couldn't have managed without them," Mary Jo said fervently.

Linc thanked them both. "Our family's much obliged to you for everything you've done."

"Just part of the job," Brandon said.

"It was an honor," Mack told them. "I have to tell you this was the best Christmas Eve of my life."

"And mine," Mary Jo said. She looked at Mack, and the two of them seemed to maintain eye contact for an extra-long moment.

"Now, Grandma?" Tyler stepped up to Grace, a small drum strapped over his shoulders.

"Now, Tyler."

The youngster set his sticks in motion. Pa-rum-pum-pum-pum, pa-rum-pum-pum-pum.

Linc glanced over at the barn and saw the ox and the

lamb in the paddock. They seemed to be keeping time to the drum, bowing their heads with each slow beat.

Mary Jo was right. This was the best Christmas Eve of his life. Of *all* their lives.

Chapter Twenty

Mary Jo woke to find Mack McAfee standing in the doorway of her private hospital room. "Mack," she whispered. Her heart reacted to the sight of him, pounding extraordinarily hard. She hadn't been certain she'd ever see him again.

"How are you feeling?" he asked, walking into the room.

"Fine." Actually, she was sore and tired and eager to get home, to be with her family.

"I brought you something."

"You did?" She sat up in bed and self-consciously brushed her fingers through her hair.

Mack produced a bouquet of roses, which he'd been hiding behind his back. "For you, Mary Jo." He bowed ever so slightly.

"My goodness, where'd you get these on Christmas Day?"

He raised his eyebrows. "I have my ways."

"Mack."

ot them in the hospital gift shop."

someone I knew who had a key and she

Mary Jo brought the fragrant flowers to her nose and breathed in their fresh scent. The vase was lovely, too. "You shouldn't have, but I'm thrilled you did."

"I wasn't sure your brothers would remember to send flowers."

Her brothers. Just thinking about the three of them, all bumbling and excited, made her want to laugh. They'd practically shoved each other out of the way last night, fussing over her and the baby. They'd been full of tales about their misadventures in Cedar Cove and the people they'd met and their near-arrest. Mel had a few comments about a meat loaf sandwich, too—and then they'd all decided they were hungry again. Their gifts of the gold coin, the perfume and the incense lay on the bedside table.

When they'd arrived at the hospital, her brothers wouldn't let her out of their sight—until the physician came into the room to examine her and then they couldn't leave fast enough.

They'd returned for a few minutes an hour later—apparently well-fed—to wish her a final good-night, promising to come back Christmas Day. Then they'd all trooped out again.

"I stopped at the nursery to see..." Mack paused. "Do you have a name for her yet?"

Mary Jo nodded. "Noelle Grace."

"Noelle for the season and Grace after Grace Harding."

Mary Jo smiled, nodding again.

"I like it," Mack said. "The name's just right. Elegant and appropriate."

His approval pleased her. She didn't want to think too closely about how much his opinion meant to her—or why. She understood that they'd shared something very special, something intimate, while she was in labor. But that didn't mean the bond they'd experienced would last, no matter how much she wanted it to. Mack had come into her life for a brief period of time. Soon she'd go back to Seattle with her family, and he'd go on living here, in Cedar Cove. It was unlikely that she'd see him again; there was no real reason to. The thought was a painful one.

"Noelle Grace was a joy to behold," Mack said with a grin.

"Was she asleep?"

"Nope, she was screaming her head off."

Mary Jo instantly felt guilty. "Oh, the staff should've woken me. It's probably her feeding time."

Mack pulled up a chair and sat down beside the bed. "Nope, she just needed her diaper changed and to be held a little."

"Did someone hold her?" The nursery was crowded with newborns and there were only a couple of nurses on duty.

"I did," Mack admitted, somewhat embarrassed.

"You?"

"I hope you don't mind."

"Of course I don't! I—I'm just surprised they'd let you."

"Yes, well…" Mack looked away and cleared his throat. "I might've led the nurse to believe that Noelle and I are… related."

Mary Jo burst out laughing. "Mack, you didn't!"

"I did. And I have to say that the minute I settled her in my arms, Noelle calmed down, stopped crying and looked straight up at me."

"You brought her into the world, after all." She probably didn't need to remind Mack of that; nevertheless, she wanted him to know she hadn't forgotten what he'd done for her.

The night before, she'd told her brothers that she would never have managed if not for Mack, and that was true. He'd been her salvation. She wanted to tell him all this, but the right words escaped her. Besides, she wasn't sure she could say what was in her heart without getting teary-eyed and emotional.

"I'm so glad you stopped by… I was going to write you and Brandon and thank you for everything."

"It's our job." Those had been Brandon's words, too, and in his case, she assumed they were true. But Mack… Dismissing her appreciation like that—it hurt. Not wanting him to see how his offhand comment had upset her, she stared down at the sheet, twisting it nervously.

Mack stood and reached for her hand, entwining their fingers.

"Let me explain," he said. "It *is* part of what we agreed to do when we took the job with the fire department." He paused for a moment. "But the call from you wasn't an ordinary one."

"How so?" she asked and looked up, meeting his eyes.

"I've never delivered a baby before."

"I know. Me, neither," she said and they smiled at each other.

"It was one of the highlights of my life, being there with you and Noelle."

"Mine, too—I mean, you being there."

"Thank you." His words were low and charged with intent. He leaned forward and braced his forehead against hers. "If it's okay with you…"

"What?" she asked breathlessly.

"I'd like to see Noelle sometime."

"See her?"

"See both of you."

"Both of us," she repeated, afraid she was beginning to sound like an echo.

"As long as it's okay with you," he said again.

She nodded, trying not to act too excited. "If you want."

"I want to very much."

"I'll be back in Seattle," she said.

"I don't mind the drive."

"Or you could take the ferry."

"Yes." Mack seemed just as eager to visit as she was to have him come by. "When?"

She wanted him there as soon as possible. "The doctor said he'd release Noelle and me this afternoon. My brothers are picking us up at three."

"Is tomorrow too soon?" he asked.

Mary Jo was convinced the happiness that flowed through

her must have shone from her eyes. She didn't think she could hide it if she tried. "That would be good," she said shyly.

"Merry Christmas, Mary Jo."

"Merry Christmas, Mack."

Just then the nurse came in carrying Noelle. "It's lunchtime," she said cheerfully.

Mary Jo held out her arms for her baby, born on Christmas Eve in Cedar Cove, the town that had taken her in. A town whose people had sheltered her and accepted her. The town that, one day, she'd love to call home.

Home for her and Noelle.

* * * * *

Call Me Mrs Miracle

To
Dan and Sally Wigutow
and
Caroline Moore
in appreciation for bringing
Mrs Miracle
to life

Chapter One

Need a new life?
God takes trade-ins.
—Mrs. Miracle

Jake Finley waited impatiently to be ushered into his father's executive office—the office that would one day be his. The thought of eventually stepping into J. R. Finley's shoes excited him. Even though he'd slowly been working his way through the ranks, he'd be the first to admit he still had a lot to learn. However, he was willing to do whatever it took to prove himself.

Finley's was the last of the family-owned department stores in New York City. His great-grandfather had begun the small mercantile on East 34th Street more than seventy years earlier. In the decades since, succeeding Finleys had opened branches in the other boroughs and then in nearby towns. Eventually the chain had spread up and down the East Coast.

"Your father will see you now," Mrs. Coffey said. Dora Coffey had served as J.R.'s executive assistant for at least twenty-five years and knew as much about the company as Jake did—maybe more. He hoped that when the time came she'd stay on, although she had to be close to retirement age.

"Thank you." He walked into the large office with its panoramic view of the Manhattan skyline. He'd lived in the city all his life, but this view never failed to stir him, never failed to lift his heart. No place on earth was more enchanting than New York in December. He could see a light snow drifting down, and the city appeared even more magical through that delicate veil.

Jacob R. Finley, however, wasn't looking at the view. His gaze remained focused on the computer screen. And his frown told Jake everything he needed to know.

He cleared his throat, intending to catch J.R.'s attention, although he suspected that his father was well aware of his presence. "You asked to see me?" he said. Now that he was here, he had a fairly good idea what had initiated this summons. Jake had hoped it wouldn't happen quite so soon, but he should've guessed Mike Scott would go running to his father at the first opportunity. Unfortunately, Jake hadn't had enough time to prove that he was right—and Mike was wrong.

"How many of those SuperRobot toys did you order?" J.R. demanded, getting straight to the point. His father had never been one to lead gently into a subject. "Intellytron," he added scornfully.

"Also known as Telly," Jake said in a mild voice.

"How many?"

"Five hundred." As if J.R. didn't know.

"What?"

Jake struggled not to flinch at his father's angry tone, which was something he rarely heard. They had a good relationship, but until now, Jake hadn't defied one of his father's experienced buyers.

"For how many stores?"

"Just here."

J.R.'s brow relaxed, but only slightly. "Do you realize those things retail for two hundred and fifty dollars apiece?"

J.R. knew the answer to that as well as Jake did. "Yes."

His father stood and walked over to the window, pacing back and forth with long, vigorous strides. Although in his early sixties, J.R. was in excellent shape. Tall and lean, like Jake himself, he had dark hair streaked with gray and his features were well-defined. No one could doubt that they were father and son. J.R. whirled around, hands linked behind him. "Did you clear the order with…anyone?"

Jake was as straightforward as his father. "No."

"Any particular reason you went over Scott's head?"

Jake had a very good reason. "We discussed it. He didn't agree, but I felt this was the right thing to do." Mike Scott had wanted to bring a maximum of fifty robots into the Manhattan location. Jake had tried to persuade him, but Mike wasn't interested in listening to speculation or taking what he saw as a risk—one that had the potential of leaving them with a huge overstock. He relied on cold, hard figures and years of purchasing experience. When their discussion was over, Mike still refused to go against what he considered his own better judgment. Jake continued to argue, presenting internet research and what his gut was telling him about this toy. When he'd finished, Mike Scott had countered with a list of reasons why fifty units per store would be adequate. *More* than adequate, in his opinion. While Jake couldn't disagree with the other man's logic, he had a strong hunch that the much larger order was worth the risk.

"You *felt* it was right?" his father repeated in a scathing voice. "Mike Scott told me we'd be fortunate to sell fifty in each store, yet you, with your vast experience of two months in the toy department, decided the Manhattan store needed ten times that number."

Jake didn't have anything to add.

"I don't suppose you happened to notice that there's been a downturn in the economy? Parents don't *have* two hundred and fifty bucks for a toy. Not when a lot of families are pinching pennies."

"You made me manager of the toy department." Jake wasn't stupid or reckless. "I'm convinced we'll sell those robots before Christmas." As manager, it was his responsibility—and his right—to order as he deemed fit. And if that meant overriding a buyer's decision—well, he could live with that.

"You think you can sell *all* five hundred of those robots?" Skepticism weighted each word. "In two weeks?"

"Yes." Jake had to work hard to maintain his air of confidence. Still he held firm.

His father took a moment to consider Jake's answer, walking a full circle around his desk as he did. "As of this morning, how many units have you sold?"

That was an uncomfortable question and Jake glanced down at the floor. "Three."

"Three." J.R. shook his head and stalked to the far side of the room, then back again as if debating how to address the situation. "So what you're saying is that our storeroom has four hundred and ninety-seven expensive SuperRobots clogging it up?"

"They're going to sell, Dad."

"It hasn't happened yet, though, has it?"

"No, but I believe the robot's going to be the hottest toy of the season. I've done the research—this is the toy kids are talking about."

"Maybe, but let me remind you, *kids* aren't our customers. Their parents are. Which is why no one else in the industry shares your opinion."

"I know it's a risk, Dad, but it's a calculated one. Have faith."

His father snorted harshly at the word *faith*. "My faith died along with your mother and sister," he snapped.

Involuntarily Jake's eyes sought out the photograph of his mother and sister. Both had been killed in a freak car accident on Christmas Eve twenty-one years ago. Neither Jake nor his father had celebrated Christmas since that tragic night. Ironically, the holiday season was what kept Finley's in the black financially. Without the three-month Christmas shopping craze, the department-store chain would be out of business.

Because of the accident, Jake and his father ignored anything to do with Christmas in their personal lives. Every December twenty-fourth, soon after the store closed, the two of them got on a plane and flew to Saint John in the Virgin Islands. From the time Jake was twelve, there hadn't been a Christmas tree or presents or anything else that would remind him of the holiday. Except, of course, at the store....

"Trust me in this, Dad," Jake pleaded. "Telly the SuperRobot will be the biggest seller of the season, and pretty soon Finley's will be the only store in Manhattan where people can find them."

His father reached for a pen and rolled it between his fingers as he mulled over Jake's words. "I put you in charge of the toy department because I thought it would be a valuable experience for you. One day you'll sit in this chair. The fate of the company will rest in your hands."

His father wasn't telling him anything Jake didn't already know.

"If the toy department doesn't show a profit because you went over Mike Scott's head, then you'll have a lot to answer for." He locked eyes with Jake. "Do I make myself clear?"

Jake nodded. If the toy department reported a loss as a result of his judgment, his father would question Jake's readiness to take over the company.

"Got it," Jake assured his father.

"Good. I want a report on the sale of that robot every week until Christmas."

"You'll have it," Jake promised. He turned to leave.

"I hope you're right about this toy, son," J.R. said as Jake opened the office door. "You've taken a big risk. I hope it pays off."

He wasn't the only one. Still, Jake believed. He'd counted on having proof that the robots were selling by the time his father learned what he'd done. Black Friday, the day after Thanksgiving, which was generally the biggest shopping day of the year, had been a major disappointment. He'd fantasized watching the robots fly off the shelves.

It hadn't happened.

Although they'd been prominently displayed, just one of the expensive toys had sold. He supposed his father had a point; in a faltering economy, people were evaluating their Christmas budgets, so toys, especially expensive ones, had taken a hit. Children might want the robots but it was their parents who did the buying.

Jake's head throbbed as he made his way to the toy department. In his rush to get to the store that morning, he'd skipped his usual stop at a nearby Starbucks. He needed his caffeine fix.

"Welcome to Finley's. May I be of assistance?" an older woman asked him. The store badge pinned prominently on her neat gray cardigan told him her name was Mrs. Emily Miracle. Her smile was cheerful and engaging. She must be the new sales assistant Human Resources had been promising him—but she simply wouldn't do. Good grief, what were they thinking up in HR? Sales in the toy department could be brisk, demanding hours of standing, not to mention dealing with cranky kids and short-tempered parents. He needed someone young. Energetic.

"What can I show you?" the woman asked.

Jake blinked, taken aback by her question. "I beg your pardon?"

"Are you shopping for one of your children?"

"Well, no. I—"

She didn't allow him to finish and steered him toward the center aisle. "We have an excellent selection of toys for any age group. If you're looking for suggestions, I'd be more than happy to help."

She seemed completely oblivious to the fact that he was the department manager—and therefore her boss. "Excuse me, Mrs….." He glanced at her name tag a second time. "Mrs. Miracle."

"Actually, it's Merkle."

"The badge says Miracle."

"Right," she said, looking a bit chagrined. "HR made a mistake, but I don't mind. You can call me Mrs. Miracle."

Speaking of miracles… If ever Jake needed one, it was now. Those robots *had* to sell. His entire future with the company could depend on this toy.

"I'd be more than happy to assist you," Mrs. Miracle said again, breaking into his thoughts.

"I'm Jake Finley."

"Pleased to meet you. Do you have a son or a daughter?" she asked.

"This is *Finley's* Department Store," he said pointedly.

Apparently this new employee had yet to make the connection, which left Jake wondering exactly where HR found their seasonal help. There had to be someone more capable than this woman.

"Finley," Mrs. Miracle repeated slowly. "Jacob Robert is your father, then?"

"Yes," he said, frowning. Only family and close friends knew his father's middle name.

Her eyes brightened, and a smile slid into place. "Ahh," she said knowingly.

"You're acquainted with my father?" That could explain why she'd been hired. Maybe she had some connection to his family he knew nothing about.

"No, no, not directly, but I *have* heard a great deal about him."

So had half the population on the East Coast. "I'm the manager here in the toy department," he told her. He clipped on his badge as he spoke, realizing he'd stuck it in his pocket. The badge said simply "Manager," without including his name, since his policy was to be as anonymous as possible, to be known by his role, not his relationship to the owner.

"The manager. Yes," she said, nodding happily. "This works out beautifully."

"What does?" Her comments struck him as odd.

"Oh, nothing," she returned with the same smile.

She certainly looked pleased with herself, although Jake couldn't imagine why. He doubted she'd last a week. He'd see about getting her transferred to a more suitable department for someone her age. Oh, he'd be subtle about it. He had no desire to risk a discrimination suit.

Jake examined the robot display, hoping that while he'd been gone another one might have sold. But if that was the case, he didn't see any evidence of it.

"Have you had your morning coffee?" Mrs. Miracle asked.

"No," he muttered. His head throbbed, reminding him of his craving for caffeine.

"It seems quiet here at the moment. Why don't you take your break?" she suggested. "The other sales associate and I can handle anything that comes along."

Jake hesitated.

"Go on," she urged. "Everyone needs their morning coffee."

"You go," he said. He was, after all, the department manager, so he should be the last to leave.

"Oh, heavens, no. I just finished a cup." Looking around, she gestured toward the empty aisles. "It's slow right now but it's sure to pick up later, don't you think?"

She was right. In another half hour or so, he might not get a chance. His gaze rested on the robots and he pointed in their direction. "Do what you can to interest shoppers in those."

"Telly the SuperRobot?" she said. Not waiting for his reply, she added, "You won't have any worries there. They're going to be the hottest item this Christmas."

Jake felt a surge of excitement. "You heard that?"

"No…" she answered thoughtfully.

"Then you must've seen a news report." Jake had been waiting for exactly this kind of confirmation. He'd played a hunch, taken a chance, and in his heart of hearts felt it had been a good decision. But he had four hundred and ninety-seven of these robots on his hands. If his projections didn't pan out, it would take a long time—like maybe forever—to live it down.

"Coffee," Mrs. Miracle said, without explaining why she was so sure of the robot's success.

Jake checked his watch, then nodded. "I'll be back soon."

"Take whatever time you need."

Jake thanked her and hurriedly left, stopping by HR on his way out. The head of the department, Gloria Palmer, glanced up when Jake entered the office. "I've got a new woman on the floor this morning. Emily Miracle," he said.

Gloria frowned. "Miracle?" She tapped some keys on her computer and looked back at Jake. "I don't show anyone with that name working in your department."

Jake remembered that Emily Miracle had said there'd been an error on her name tag. He rubbed his hand across his forehead, momentarily closing his eyes as he tried to remember the name she'd mentioned. "It starts with an *M*—McKinsey, Merk, something like that."

Gloria's phone rang and she reached for it, holding it between her shoulder and ear as her fingers flew across the keyboard. She tried to divide her attention between Jake and the person on the line. Catching Jake's eye, she motioned toward the computer screen, shrugged and shook her head.

Jake raised his hand and mouthed, "I'll catch you later."

Gloria nodded and returned her attention to the caller. Clearly she had more pressing issues to attend to just then. Jake would seek her out later that afternoon and suggest Mrs. Miracle be switched to another department. A less demanding one.

As he rushed out the door onto Thirty-fourth and headed into the still-falling snow, he decided it would be only fair to give the older woman a chance. If she managed to sell one of the robots while he collected his morning cup of java, he'd consider keeping her. And if she managed to sell *two*, she'd be living up to her name!

Chapter Two

If God is your copilot, trade places.
—Mrs. Miracle

Friday morning, and Holly Larson was right on schedule—even a few minutes ahead. This was a vast improvement over the past two months, ever since her eight-year-old nephew, Gabe, had come to live with her. It'd taken effort on both their parts to make this arrangement work. Mickey, Holly's brother, had been called up by the National Guard and sent to Afghanistan for the next fifteen months. He was a widower, and with her parents doing volunteer medical work in Haiti, the only option for Gabe was to move in with Holly, who lived in a small Brooklyn apartment. Fortunately, she'd been able to turn her minuscule home office into a bedroom for Gabe.

They were doing okay, but it hadn't been easy. Never having spent much time with children Gabe's age, the biggest adjustment had been Holly's—in her opinion, anyway.

Gabe might not agree, however. He didn't think sun-dried tomatoes with fresh mozzarella cheese was a special dinner. He turned up his nose and refused even one bite. So she was learning. Boxed macaroni and cheese suited him just fine, although she couldn't tolerate the stuff. At least it was cheap. Adding food for a growing boy to her already strained budget had been a challenge. Mickey, who was the manager of a large grocery store in his civilian life, sent what he could but he had his own financial difficulties; she knew he was still paying off his wife's medical bills and funeral expenses. And he had a mortgage to maintain on his Trenton, New Jersey, home. Poor Gabe. The little boy had lost his mother when he was an infant. Now his father was gone, too. Holly considered herself a poor replacement for either parent, let alone both, although she was giving it her best shot.

Since she had a few minutes to spare before she was due at the office, she hurried into Starbucks to reward herself with her favorite latte. It'd been two weeks since she'd had one. A hot, freshly brewed latte was an extravagance these days, so she only bought them occasionally.

Getting Gabe to school and then hurrying to the office was as difficult as collecting him from the after-school facility at the end of the day. Lindy Lee, her boss, hadn't taken kindly to Holly's rushing out the instant the clock struck five. But the child-care center at Gabe's school charged by the minute when she was late. *By the minute.*

Stepping out of the cold into the warmth of the coffee shop, Holly breathed in the pungent scent of fresh coffee. A cheery evergreen swag was draped across the display case. She dared not look because she had a weakness for cranberry scones. She missed her morning ritual of a latte and a scone almost as much as she did her independence. But giving it up was a small sacrifice if it meant she could help her brother and Gabe. Not only that, she'd come to adore her young nephew and, despite everything, knew she'd miss him when her brother returned.

The line moved quickly, and she placed her order for a skinny latte with vanilla flavoring. The man behind her ordered a large coffee. He smiled at her and Holly smiled back. She'd seen him in this Starbucks before, although they'd never spoken.

"Merry Christmas," she said.

"Same to you."

The girl at the cash register told Holly her total and she opened her purse to pay. That was when she remembered— she'd given the last of her cash to Gabe for lunch money. It seemed ridiculous to use a credit card for such a small amount, but she didn't have any choice. She took out her card and handed it to the barista. The young woman slid it through the machine, then leaned forward and whispered, "It's been declined."

Hot embarrassment reddened her face. She'd maxed out her card the month before but thought her payment would've been credited by now. Scrambling, she searched for coins in the bottom of her purse. It didn't take her long to realize she didn't have nearly enough change to cover the latte. "I have a debit card in here someplace," she muttered, grabbing her card case again.

"Excuse me." The good-looking man behind her pulled his wallet from his hip pocket.

"I'm...I'm sorry," she whispered, unable to meet his eyes. This was embarrassing, humiliating, downright mortifying.

"Allow me to pay for your latte," he said.

Holly sent him a shocked look. "You don't need to do that."

The woman standing behind him frowned impatiently at Holly. "If I'm going to get to work on time, he does."

"Oh, sorry."

Not waiting for her to agree, the stranger stepped forward and paid for both her latte and his coffee.

"Thank you," she said in a low, strangled voice.

"I'll consider it my good deed for the day."

"I'll pay for your coffee the next time I see you."

He grinned. "You've got a deal." He moved down to the end of the counter where she went to wait for her latte. "I'm Jake Finley."

"Holly Larson." She extended her hand.

"Holly," he repeated.

"People assume I was born around Christmas but I wasn't. Actually, I was born in June and named after my mother's favorite aunt," she said. She didn't know why she'd blurted out such ridiculous information. Perhaps because she still felt embarrassed and was trying to disguise her chagrin with conversation. "I do love Christmas, though, don't you?"

"Not particularly." Frowning, he glanced at his watch. "I've got to get back to work."

"Oh, sure. Thank you again." He'd been thoughtful and generous.

"See you soon," Jake said as he turned toward the door.

"I owe you," she said. "I won't forget."

He smiled at her. "I hope I'll run into you again."

"That would be great." She meant it, and next time she'd make sure she had enough cash to treat him. She felt a glow of pleasure as Jake left Starbucks.

Holly stopped to calculate—it'd been more than three months since her last date. That was pitiful! Three months. Nuns had a more active social life than she did.

Her last relationship had been with Bill Carter. For a while it had seemed promising. As a divorced father, Bill was protective and caring toward his young son. Holly had only met Billy once. Unfortunately, the trip to the Central Park Zoo hadn't gone well. Billy had been whiny and overtired, and Bill had seemed to want *her* to deal with the boy. She'd tried but Billy didn't know her and she didn't know him, and the entire outing had been strained and uncomfortable. Holly had tried—unsuccessfully—to make the trip as much fun as possible. Shortly thereafter, Bill called to tell her their relationship wasn't "working" for him. He'd made a point of letting her know he was interested in finding someone more "suitable" for his son because he didn't feel she'd make a good mother. His words had stung.

Holly hadn't argued. Really, how could she? Her one experience with Billy had been a disaster. Then, just a month after

Bill's heartless comment, Gabe had entered her life. These days she was more inclined to agree with Bill's assessment of her parenting skills. She didn't seem to have what it took to raise a child, which deeply concerned her.

Things were getting easier with Gabe, but progress had been slow, and it didn't help that her nephew seemed to sense her unease. She had a lot to learn about being an effective and nurturing parent.

Dating Bill had been enjoyable enough, but there'd never been much chemistry between them, so not seeing him wasn't a huge loss. She categorized it as more of a disappointment. A letdown. His parting words, however, had left her with doubts and regrets.

Carrying her latte, Holly walked the three blocks to the office. She actually arrived a minute early. Working as an assistant to a fashion designer sounded glamorous but it wasn't. She didn't get to take home designer purses for a fraction of their retail price—except for the knockoff versions she could buy on the street—or acquire fashion-model hand-me-downs.

She was paid a pittance and had become the go-to person for practically everyone on staff, and that added up to at least forty people. Her boss, Lindy Lee, was often unreasonable. Unfortunately, most of the time it was Holly's job to make sure that whatever Lindy wanted actually happened. Lindy wasn't much older than Holly, but she was well connected in the fashion world and had quickly risen to the top. Because her work as a designer of upscale women's sportswear was in high demand, Lindy Lee frequently worked under impossible deadlines. One thing was certain; she had no tolerance for the fact that Holly now had to stick to her official nine-to-five schedule, which meant her job as Lindy Lee's assistant might be in jeopardy. She'd explained the situation with Gabe, but her boss didn't care about Holly's problems at home.

Rushing to her desk, Holly set the latte down, shrugged off her coat and readied herself for the day. She was responsible for decorating the office for Christmas, and so far, there just hadn't been time. On Saturday she'd bring Gabe into the office and the two of them would get it done. That meant her own apartment would have to wait, but…oh, well.

Despite her boss's complaints about one thing or another, Holly's smile stayed in place all morning. A kind deed by a virtual stranger buffered her from four hours of commands, criticism and complaints.

Jack…no, Jake. He'd said his name was Jake, and he was cute, too. Maybe *handsome* was a more accurate description. Classically handsome, like those 1940s movie stars in the old films she loved. Tall, nicely trimmed dark hair, broad shoulders, expressive eyes and…probably married. She'd been too shocked by his generosity to see whether he had a wedding band. Yeah, he was probably taken. Par for the course, she thought a little glumly. Holly was thirty, but being single at that age wasn't uncommon among her friends. Her parents seemed more worried about it than she was.

Most of her girlfriends didn't even *think* about settling down until after they turned thirty. Holly knew she wanted a husband and eventually a family. What she hadn't expected was becoming a sole parent to Gabe. This time with her nephew was like a dress rehearsal for being a mother, her friends told her. Unfortunately, there weren't any lines to memorize and the script changed almost every day.

At lunch she heated her Cup-a-Soup in the microwave and logged on to the internet to check for messages from Mickey. Her brother kept in touch with Gabe every day and sent her a quick note whenever he could. Sure enough, there was an email waiting for her.

From: "Lieutenant Mickey Larson" <larsonmichael@ goarmy.com>
To: "Holly Larson"<hollylarson@msm.com>
Sent: December 10
Subject: Gabe's email

Hi, sis,
Gabe's last note to me was hilarious. What's this about you making him put down the toilet seat? He thinks girls should do it themselves. This is what happens when men live together. The seat's perpetually up.
Has he told you what he wants for Christmas yet? He generally mentions a toy before now, but he's been suspiciously quiet about it this year. Let me know when he drops his hints.
I wish I could be with you both, but that's out of the question. Next year for sure.
I know it's been rough on you having to fit Gabe into your apartment and your life, but I have no idea what I would've done without you.

By the way, I heard from Mom and Dad. The dental clinic Dad set up is going well. Who'd have guessed our parents would be doing volunteer work after retirement? They send their love...but now that I think about it, you got the same email as me, didn't you? They both sound happy but really busy. Mom was concerned about you taking Gabe, but she seems reassured now.

Well, I better get some shut-eye. Not to worry—I reminded Gabe that when he's staying at a house with a woman living in it, the correct thing to do is put down the toilet seat.

Check in with you later.

Thank you again for everything.

Love,

Mickey

Holly read the message twice, then sent him a note. She'd always been close to her brother and admired him for picking up the pieces of his life after Sally died of a rare blood disease. Gabe hadn't even been a year old. Holly had a lot more respect for the demands of parenthood—and especially single parenthood—now that Gabe lived with her.

At five o'clock, she was out the door. Lindy Lee threw her an evil look, which Holly pretended not to see. She caught the subway and had to stand, holding tight to one of the poles, for the whole rush-hour ride into Brooklyn.

As she was lurched and jolted on the train, her mind wandered back to Mickey's email. Gabe hadn't said anything about Christmas to her, either. And yet he had to know that the holidays were almost upon them; all the decorations in the neighborhood and the ads on TV made it hard to miss. For the first time in his life, Gabe wouldn't be spending Christmas with his father and grandparents. This year, there'd be just the two of them. Maybe he'd rather not celebrate until his father came home, she thought. That didn't seem right, though. Holly was determined to make this the best Christmas possible.

Not once had Gabe told her what he wanted. She wondered whether she should ask him, maybe encourage him to write Santa a letter—did he still believe in Santa?—or try to guess what he might like. Her other question was what she could buy on a limited income. A toy? She knew next to nothing about toys, especially the kind that would intrigue an eight-year-old boy. She felt besieged by even more insecurities.

She stepped off the subway, climbed the stairs to the street and hurried to Gabe's school, which housed the after-hours activity program set up for working parents. At least it wasn't snowing anymore. Which was a good thing, since she'd forgotten to make Gabe wear his boots that morning.

What happened the first day she'd gone to collect Gabe still made her cringe. She'd been thirty-two minutes late. The financial penalty was steep and cut into her carefully planned budget, but that didn't bother her nearly as much as the look on Gabe's face.

He must have assumed she'd abandoned him. His haunted expression brought her to the edge of tears every time she thought about it. That was the same night she'd prepared her favorite dinner for him—another disaster. Now she knew better and kept an unending supply of hot dogs—God help them both—plus boxes of macaroni and cheese. He'd deign to eat carrot sticks and bananas, but those were his only concessions, no matter how much she talked about balanced nutrition. He found it hilarious to claim that the relish he slathered on his hot dogs was a "vegetable."

She waited by the row of hooks, each marked with a child's name. Gabe ran over the instant he saw her, his face bright with excitement. "I made a new friend!"

"That's great." Thankfully Gabe appeared to have adjusted well to his new school and teacher.

"Billy!" he called. "Come and meet my aunt Holly."

Holly's smile froze. This wasn't just any Billy. It was Bill Carter, Junior, son of the man who'd broken up with her three months earlier.

"Hello, Billy," she said, wondering if he'd recognize her.

The boy gazed up at her quizzically. Apparently he didn't. Or maybe he did remember her but wasn't sure when they'd met. Either way, Holly was relieved.

"Can I go over to Billy's house?" Gabe asked. The two boys linked arms like long-lost brothers.

"Ah, when?" she hedged. Seeing Bill again would be difficult. Holly wasn't eager to talk to the man who'd dumped her—especially considering why. It would be uncomfortable for both of them.

"I want him to come tonight," Billy said. "My dad's making sloppy joes. And we've got marshmallow ice cream for dessert."

"Well…" Her meals could hardly compete with that—not

if you were an eight-year-old boy. Personally, Holly couldn't think of a less appetizing combination.

Before she could come up with a response, Gabe tugged at her sleeve. "Billy doesn't have a mom, either," he told her.

"I have a mom," Billy countered, "only she doesn't live with us anymore."

"My mother's in heaven with the angels," Gabe said. "I live with my dad, too, 'cept he's in Afghanistan now."

"So that's why you're staying with your aunt Holly." Billy nodded.

"Yeah." Gabe reached for his jacket and backpack.

"I'm sorry, Billy," she finally managed to say, "but Gabe and I already have plans for tonight."

Gabe whirled around. "We do?"

"We're going shopping," she said, thinking on her feet.

Gabe scowled and crossed his arms. "I hate shopping."

"You won't this time," she promised and helped him put on his winter jacket, along with his hat and mitts.

"Yes, I will," Gabe insisted, his head lowered.

"You and Billy can have a playdate later," she said, forcing herself to speak cheerfully.

"When?" Billy asked, unwilling to let the matter drop.

"How about next week?" She'd call or email Bill so it wouldn't come as a big shock when she showed up on his doorstep.

"Okay," Billy agreed.

"That suit you?" Holly asked Gabe. She wanted to leave *now*, just in case Bill was picking up his son today. She recalled that their housekeeper usually did this—but why take chances? Bill was the very last person she wanted to see.

Gabe shrugged, unhappy with the compromise. He let her take his hand as they left the school, but as soon as they were outdoors, he promptly snatched it away.

"Where are we going shopping?" he asked, still pouting as they headed in the opposite direction of her apartment building. The streetlights glowed and she saw Christmas decorations in apartment windows—wreaths, small potted trees and strings of colored lights. So far Holly hadn't done anything. Perhaps this weekend she'd find time to put up their tree—after she'd finished decorating the office, of course.

"I thought we'd go see Santa this evening," Holly announced.

"Santa?" He raised his head and eyed her speculatively.

"Would you like that?"

Gabe seemed to need a moment to consider the question. "I guess."

Holly assumed he was past the age of believing in Santa but wasn't quite ready to admit it, for fear of losing out on extra gifts. Still, she didn't feel she could ask him. "I want you to hold my hand while we're on the subway, okay?"

"Okay," he said in a grumpy voice.

They'd go to Finley's, she decided. She knew for sure that the store had a Santa. Besides, she wanted to look at the windows with their festive scenes and moving parts. Even in his current mood, Gabe would enjoy them, Holly thought. And so would she.

Chapter Three

Exercise daily—walk with the Lord.
—Mrs. Miracle

It was the second Friday in December and the streets were crowded with shoppers and tourists. As they left the subway, Holly kept a close watch on Gabe, terrified of becoming separated. She heaved a sigh of relief when they reached Finley's Department Store. The big display windows in the front of the fourteen-story structure were cleverly decorated. One showed a Santa's workshop scene, including animated elves wielding hammers and saws. Another was a mirrored pond that had teddy bears skating around and around. Still another, the window closest to the doors, featured a huge Christmas tree, circled by a toy train running on its own miniature track. The boxcars were filled with gaily wrapped gifts.

With the crowds pressing against them, Gabe and Holly

moved from window to window, stopping at the final one. "Isn't that a great train set?" she asked.

Gabe nodded.

"Would you like one of those for Christmas?" she murmured. "You could ask Santa."

Gabe glanced up at her. "There's something else I want more."

"Okay, you can tell Santa that," she said.

They headed into the store, and had difficulty getting through the revolving doors, crushed in with other shoppers. "Can we go home and have dinner when we're done seeing Santa?" Gabe asked.

"Of course. What would you like?"

If he said hot dogs or macaroni and cheese Holly promised herself she wouldn't scream.

"Mashed potatoes with gravy and meat loaf with lots of ketchup."

That would take a certain amount of effort but was definitely something she could do. "You got it."

Gabe cast her one of his rare smiles, and Holly placed her hand on his shoulder. This was progress.

The ground floor of Finley's was crammed. The men's department was to the right and the cosmetics and perfume counters directly ahead. Holly inched her way forward, Gabe close by her side.

"We need to get to the escalator," she told him, steering the boy in that direction. She hoped that once they got up to the third floor, the crowds would have thinned out, at least a little.

"Okay." He voluntarily slipped his hand in hers.

More progress. Visiting Santa had clearly been a stroke of genius on her part.

Her guess about the crowds was accurate. When they reached the third floor Holly felt she could breathe again. If it wasn't for Gabe, she wouldn't come within ten miles of Thirty-fourth on a Friday night in December.

"Santa's over there," Gabe said, pointing.

The kid obviously had Santa Claus radar. Several spry elves in green tights and pointy hats surrounded the jolly old man in the red suit. This guy was good, too. His full white beard was real. He must've just gotten off break because he wore a huge smile.

The visit to Santa was free but for an extra twenty dollars, she could buy a picture. They'd stopped at an ATM on their way to the subway and she'd gotten cash. Although she couldn't help feeling a twinge at spending the money, a photo of Gabe with Santa would be the perfect Christmas gift for Mickey.

The line moved quickly. Gabe seemed excited and happy, chattering away about this and that, and his mood infected Holly. She hadn't felt much like Christmas until now. Classic carols rang through the store and soon Holly was humming along.

When it was Gabe's turn, he hopped onto Santa's knee as if the two of them were old friends.

"Hello there, young man," Santa said, adding a "Ho, ho, ho."

"Hello." Gabe looked him square in the eyes.

"And what would you like Santa to bring you?" the jolly old fellow inquired.

Her nephew didn't hesitate. "All I want for Christmas is Telly the SuperRobot."

What in heaven's name was that? A robot? Even without checking, Holly knew this wasn't going to be a cheap toy. A train set—a small one—she could manage, but an electronic toy was probably out of her price range.

"Very well, young man, Santa will see what he can do. Anything else you're interested in?"

"A train set," Gabe said, his eyes serious. "But I *really* want Intellytron."

"Intellytron," Holly muttered to herself.

Santa gestured at the camera. "Now smile big for me, and your mom can collect the photograph in five minutes."

"Okay." Gabe gave Santa a huge smile, then slid off his knee so the next child in line could have a turn. It took Holly a moment to realize that Gabe hadn't corrected Santa about who she was.

Holly went around to the counter behind Santa's chair to wait for the photograph, accompanied by Gabe.

"I don't know where Santa will find one of those robots," she said, trying to get as much information as she could.

"All the stores have them," Gabe assured her. "Billy wants an Intellytron, too."

So she could blame Billy for this sudden desire. But since this was the only toy Gabe wanted, she'd do her best to make sure that Intellytron the SuperRobot would be wrapped and under the tree Christmas morning.

"Maybe I should see what this robot friend of yours looks like," she suggested. A huge sign pointing to the toy department was strategically placed near Santa's residence. This, Holly felt certain, was no coincidence.

"Toys are this way," Gabe said, leading her by the hand.

Holly dutifully followed. "What if they don't have the robot?" she asked.

"They will," he said with sublime confidence.

"But what if they don't?"

Gabe frowned and then tilted his chin at a thoughtful angle. "Can Santa bring my dad home?"

Holly's heart sank. "Not this year, sweetheart."

"Then all I really want is my robot."

She'd been afraid of that.

They entered the toy department and were met by a grandmotherly woman with a name badge that identified her as Mrs. Emily Miracle.

"Why, hello there," the woman greeted Gabe with a smile.

Gabe immediately smiled back at her. "Hello."

"I see you've been to visit Santa." She nodded at the photo Holly was holding.

"Yup," Gabe said happily. "He was nice."

"Did you tell Santa what you want for Christmas?"

"Intellytron the SuperRobot," he replied.

"Telly is a wonderful toy. Let me show you one."

"Please," Holly said, hoping against hope that the robot was reasonably priced. If fate was truly with her, it would also be on sale.

Mrs. Miracle took them to a display on the other side of the department, directly across from the elevator. The robots would be the first toys seen by those stepping off. She wondered why they weren't by the escalator, but then it dawned on her. Mothers with young children usually came up via elevator. The manager of this department was no dummy.

"Look!" Gabe said, his eyes huge. "It's Telly! He's here. I told you he would be. Isn't he the best *ever?*"

"Would you like to see how he works?" the grandmotherly saleswoman asked.

"Yes, please."

Holly was impressed by Gabe's politeness, which she'd never seen to quite this degree. Well, it was December, and this was the one toy he wanted more than any other. The saleswoman took down the display model and started to demonstrate it when a male voice caught Holly's attention.

"Hello again."

She turned to face Jake, the man she'd met in Starbucks that morning. For a moment she couldn't speak. Eventually she croaked out a subdued hello.

He looked curiously at Gabe. "Your son?"

"My nephew," she said, recovering her voice. "Gabe's living with me for the next year while his father's in Afghanistan."

"Nephew," he repeated, and his eyes sparked with renewed interest.

"I brought Gabe here to visit Santa and he said that what he wants for Christmas is Intellytron the SuperRobot."

"An excellent choice. Would you like me to wrap one for you now?"

"Ah…" Holly paused. "I need to know how much they are first." Just looking at the toy told her she wasn't getting off cheap.

"Two hundred and fifty dollars."

Holly's hand flew to her heart. "*How* much?"

"Two hundred and fifty dollars."

"Oh." She swallowed. "Will there be a sale on these later? A big sale?"

Jake shook his head. "I doubt it."

"Oh," she said again.

Jake seemed disappointed, too.

Holly bit her lip. This was the only gift Gabe had requested. He'd indicated mild interest in a train set, but that was more at her instigation. Watching his eyes light up as the robot maneuvered itself down the aisle filled her with a sense of delight. He loved this toy and it would mean so much to him. "I get my Christmas bonus at the end of next week. Will you still have the robot then?" Never mind that Lindy Lee might be less than generous this year.…

"We should have plenty," Jake told her.

"Thank goodness," Holly said gratefully.

"We've sold a number today, but I brought in a large supply so you shouldn't have anything to worry about."

"Wonderful." She could hardly wait for Gabe to unwrap this special gift Christmas morning. Tonight, the spirit of Christmas had finally begun to take root in her own heart. Seeing the joy of the season in Gabe's eyes helped her accept that this year would be different but could still be good. Although she and Gabe were separated from their family, she intended to make it a Christmas the two of them would always remember.

"I want to thank you again for buying my latte this morning," she said to Jake. She was about to suggest she pay him back, because she had the cash now, but hesitated, hoping for the opportunity to return the favor and spend more time with him.

"Like I said, it was my good deed for the day."

"Do you often purchase a complete stranger a cup of coffee?"

"You're the first."

She laughed. "Then I'm doubly honored."

"Aunt Holly, did you see? Did you see Telly move?" Gabe asked, dashing to her side. "He can talk, too!"

She'd been so involved in chatting with Jake that she'd missed most of the demonstration. Other children had come over to the aisle, drawn by the robot's activities; in fact, a small crowd had formed to watch. Several boys Gabe's age were tugging at their parents' arms.

"We'll have to see what Santa brings," Holly told him.

"He'll bring me Telly, won't he?"

Holly shrugged, pretending nonchalance. "We'll have to wait and see."

"How many days until Christmas?" Gabe asked eagerly.

"Today's the tenth, so...fifteen days."

"That long?" He dragged out the words as if he could barely hang on all those weeks.

"The time will fly by, Gabe. I promise."

"Excuse me," Jake said as he turned to answer a customer's question. Her query was about the price of the robot, and the woman had nearly the same reaction as Holly. Two hundred and fifty dollars! A lot of money for a toy. Still, in Gabe's case it would be worth it.

Mrs. Miracle brought out the display robot to demonstrate again, and Gabe and a second youngster watched with rapt attention. The older woman was a marvel, a natural with children.

"So, you're the manager here," Holly said once Jake was free.

He nodded. "How'd you guess?" he asked with a grin.

"Your badge, among other things." She smiled back at him. "I was just thinking how smart you were to place Santa next to the toy section."

"That wasn't my idea," Jake said. "Santa's been in that location for years."

"What about the Intellytron display across from the elevator?"

"Now, that *was* my idea."

"I thought as much."

Jake seemed pleased that she'd noticed. "I'm hoping it really takes off."

"Well, if Gabe's interest is any indication, I'm sure it will."

He seemed to appreciate her vote of confidence.

"Look!" Gabe said, grabbing Holly's hand. He pointed to a couple who were removing a boxed unit of Intellytron from the display. "My robot will still be here by Christmas, won't he?"

"Absolutely," she assured him.

Jake winked at her as Mrs. Miracle led the young couple toward the cash register.

"Hiring Mrs. Miracle was a smart move, too," she said.

"Oh, I can't really take credit for that," Jake responded.

"Well, you're lucky, then. She's exactly right for the toy department. It's like having someone's grandmother here. She's helping parents fulfill all their children's Christmas wishes."

Jack glanced at the older woman, then slowly nodded. "I guess so," he said, sounding a bit uncertain.

"Haven't you seen the way kids immediately take to her?" Holly asked.

"Not only can't I take credit for her being here, it's actually a mistake."

"A mistake," Holly echoed. "You're joking! She's *perfect*. It wouldn't surprise me if you sold out the whole toy department with her working here."

"Really?" He said this as if Holly had given him something to think about.

"I love her name, too. Mrs. Miracle—it has such a nice Christmas sound."

"That's a mistake, as well. Her name's not really Miracle. HR spelled it wrong on her badge, and I asked that it be corrected."

"Oh, let her keep the badge," Holly urged. "Mrs. Miracle. It couldn't be more appropriate."

Jake nodded again. "Perhaps you're right."

Mrs. Miracle finished the sale and joined them. "Very nice meeting you, Gabe and Holly," she said warmly.

Holly didn't remember giving the older woman her name. Gabe must have mentioned it.

"You, too, Emily," she said.

"Oh, please," she said with a charming smile. "Just call me Mrs. Miracle."

"Okay," Gabe piped up. "We will."

Chapter Four

Lead me not into temptation.
I can find the way myself.
—J. R. Finley

"I thought we'd bake cookies today," Holly said on Saturday morning as Gabe sat at the kitchen counter eating his breakfast cereal. When he didn't think she was looking, he picked up the bowl and slurped what was left of his milk.

"Cookies?" Gabe said, frowning. "Can't we just buy them?"

"We could," Holly answered, "but I figured it would be fun to bake them ourselves."

Gabe didn't seem convinced. "Dad and I always got ours at the store. We never had to *work* to get them."

"But it's fun," Holly insisted, unwilling to give up quite so easily. "You can roll out the dough. I even have special cookie cutters. After the cookies are baked and they've cooled down, we can frost and decorate them." She'd hoped this Christmas tradition would appeal to Gabe.

He slid down from his chair and carried his bowl to the dishwasher. "Can I go on the computer?"

"Sure." Holly made an effort to hide her disappointment. She'd really hoped the two of them would bond while they were baking Christmas cookies. Later, she intended to go into the office and put up decorations—with Gabe's help. She wanted that to be fun for him, too.

Gabe moved to the alcove between the kitchen and small living room with its sofa and television. Holly was astonished at how adept the eight-year-old was on the computer. While he logged on, she brought out the eggs and flour and the rest of the ingredients for sugar cookies and set them on the kitchen counter.

Gabe obviously didn't realize she could see the computer screen from her position. She was pleased that he was writing his father a note.

From: "Gabe Larson"<gabelarson@msm.com>
To: "Lieutenant Mickey Larson" <larsonmichael@ goarmy.com>
Sent: December 11
Subject: Cookies

Hi, Dad,
Guess what? Aunt Holly wants me to bake cookies. Doesn't she know I'm a BOY? Boys don't bake cookies. It's bad enough that I have to put the toilet seat down for her. I

hope you get home soon because I'm afraid she's going to turn me into a girl!
Gabe

Holly tried to conceal her smile. "Would you like to go into the city this afternoon?" she asked as she added the butter she'd cubed to the sugar in the mixing bowl.

Gabe turned around to look at her. "You aren't going to make me go shopping, are you?"

"No. I'll take you to my office. Wouldn't you like that?"

"Yes," he said halfheartedly.

"I have to put up a few decorations. You can help me."

"Okay." Again he showed a decided lack of enthusiasm.

"The Rockefeller Center Christmas tree is up," she told him next.

Now, that caught his interest. "Can we go ice-skating?"

"Ah…" Holly had never gone skating. "Maybe another time, okay?"

Gabe shrugged. "Okay. I bet Billy and his dad will take me."

The kid had no idea how much that comment irritated her. However, Holly knew she had to be an adult about it. She hadn't phoned Bill to discuss the fact that his son and her nephew were friends. She would, though, in order to arrange a playdate for the two boys.

"I thought we'd leave after lunch," she said, resuming their original conversation.

"Okay." Gabe returned to the computer and was soon involved

in a game featuring beasts in some alien kingdom. Whatever it was held his attention for the next ten minutes.

Using the electric mixer, Holly blended the sugar, butter and eggs and was about to add the dry ingredients when Gabe climbed up on the stool beside her.

"I've never seen anyone make cookies before," he said.

"You can watch if you want." She made an effort to sound matter-of-fact, not revealing how pleased she was at his interest.

"When we go into the city, would it be all right if we went to Finley's?" he asked.

Holly looked up. "I suppose so. Any particular reason?"

He stared at her as if it should be obvious. "I want to see Telly. He can do all kinds of tricks and stuff, and maybe Mrs. Miracle will be there."

"Oh."

"Mrs. Miracle said I could stop by anytime I want and she'd let me work the controls. She said they don't normally let kids play with the toys but she'd make an exception." He drew in a deep breath. "What's an 'exception'?"

"It means she'll allow you to do it even though other people can't."

"That's what I thought." He leaned forward and braced his elbows on the counter, nodding solemnly at this evidence of his elevated status—at least in Mrs. Miracle's view.

As soon as the dough was mixed, Holly covered it with plastic wrap and put it inside the refrigerator to chill. When she'd finished, she cleaned off the kitchen counter. "You want to lick the beaters?" she asked.

Gabe straightened and looked skeptically at the mixer. "You can do that?"

"Sure. That's one of the best parts of baking cookies."

"Okay."

She handed him one beater and took the second herself.

Gabe's eyes widened after his first lick. "Hey, this tastes *good*."

"Told you," she said with a smug smile.

"Why can't we just eat the dough? Why ruin cookies by baking 'em?"

"Well, they're not cookies unless you bake them."

"Oh."

Her response seemed to satisfy him.

"I'm going to roll the dough out in a few minutes. Would you help me decide which cookie cutters to use?"

"I guess." Gabe didn't display a lot of enthusiasm at the request.

Holly stood on tiptoe to take down the plastic bag she kept on the upper kitchen shelf. "Your grandma Larson gave these to me last year. When your dad and I were your age, we used to make sugar cookies."

Gabe sat up straighter. "You mean my dad baked cookies?"

"Every Christmas. After we decorated them, we chose special people to give them to."

Gabe was always interested in learning facts about Mickey. Every night he asked Holly to tell him a story about his father as a boy. She'd run out of stories, but it didn't matter; Gabe liked hearing them again and again.

"You gave the cookies to special people? Like who?"

"Well…" Holly had to think about that. "Once I brought a plate of cookies to my Sunday school teacher and one year—" she paused and smiled "—I was twelve and had a crush on a boy in my class, so I brought the cookies to school for him."

"Who'd my dad give the cookies to?"

"I don't remember. You'll have to ask him."

"I will." Gabe propped his chin on one hand. "Can I take a plate of cookies to Mrs. Miracle?"

Holly was about to tell him that would be a wonderful idea, then hesitated. "The problem is, if I baked the cookies and decorated them, they'd be from me and not from you."

Gabe frowned. "I could help with cutting them out and stuff. You won't tell anyone, will you?"

"Not if you don't want me to."

"I don't want any of my friends to think I'm a sissy."

She crossed her heart. "I promise not to say a word."

"Okay, then, I'll do it." Gabe dug into the bag of cookie cutters and made his selections, removing the Christmas tree, the star and several others. Then, as if a thought had suddenly struck him, he pointed at her apron. "I don't have to put on one of those, do I?"

"You don't like my apron?"

"They're okay for girls, but not boys."

"You don't have to wear one if you'd rather not."

He shook his head adamantly.

"But you might get flour on your clothes, and your friends

would guess you were baking." This was a clever argument, if she did say so herself.

Gabe nibbled on his lower lip, apparently undecided. "Then I'll change clothes. I'm not wearing any girlie apron."

"That's fine," Holly said, grinning.

The rest of the morning was spent baking and decorating cookies. Once he got started, Gabe appeared to enjoy himself. He frosted the Christmas tree with green icing and sprinkled red sugar over it.

Then, with a sideways glance at Holly, he promptly ate the cookie. She let him assume she hadn't noticed.

"Who are you giving your cookies to?" Gabe asked.

Actually, Holly hadn't thought about it. "I'm not sure." A heartbeat later, the decision was made. "Jake."

"The man in the toy department at Finley's?"

Holly nodded. "He did something kind for me on Friday. He bought my coffee."

Gabe cocked his head. "Is he your boyfriend?"

"Oh, no. But he's very nice and I want to repay him." She got two plastic plates and, together, they arranged the cookies. Holly bundled each plate in green-tinted cellophane wrap and added silver bows for a festive look.

"You ready to head into town?" she asked.

Gabe raced into his bedroom for his coat, hat and mittens. "I'm ready."

"Me, too." The truth was, Holly felt excited about seeing Jake again. Of course, there was always the possibility that he wouldn't be working today—but she had to admit she hoped he was. Her reaction surprised her; since Bill had broken off their relationship she'd been reluctant to even consider dating someone new.

Meeting Jake had been an unexpected bonus. He'd been so— She stopped abruptly. Here she was, doing it again. Jake had paid for her coffee. He was obviously a generous man... or he might've been in a rush to get back to the store. Either way, he'd been kind to her. But that didn't mean he was *attracted* to her. In reality it meant nada. Zilch. Zip. Gazing down at the plate of cookies, Holly felt she might be pushing this too far.

"Aunt Holly?"

She looked at her nephew, who was staring quizzically at her. "Is something wrong?" he asked.

"Oh, sorry... No, nothing's wrong. I was just thinking maybe I should give these cookies to someone else."

"How come?"

"I...I don't know."

"Give them to Jake," Gabe said without a second's doubt. "Didn't you say he bought your coffee?"

"He did." Gabe was right. The cookies were simply a way of thanking him. That was all. She was returning a kindness. With her quandary settled, they walked over to the subway station.

When they arrived at Finley's, the streets and the store were even more crowded than they'd been the night before. Again Holly kept a close eye on her nephew. She'd made a contingency plan—if they did happen to get separated, they were to meet in the toy department by the robots.

They rode up on the escalator, after braving the cosmetics

aisles, with staff handing out perfume samples. Gabe held his nose, but Holly was delighted to accept several tiny vials of perfume. When they finally reached the toy department, it was far busier than it had been the previous evening. Both Gabe and Holly studied the display of robots. There did seem to be fewer of the large boxes, but Jake had assured her there'd be plenty left by the time she received her Christmas bonus. She sincerely hoped that was true.

The moment Gabe saw Mrs. Miracle, he rushed to her side. "We made you sugar cookies," he said, giving her the plate.

"Oh, my, these are lovely." The grandmotherly woman smiled. "They look good enough to eat."

"You *are* supposed to eat them," Gabe said with a giggle.

"And I will." She bent down and hugged the boy. "Thank you so much."

Gabe whispered, "Don't tell anyone, but I helped Aunt Holly make them."

Holly was standing close enough to hear him and exchanged a smile with Mrs. Miracle.

"You should be proud of that," Mrs. Miracle said as she led him toward the Intellytron display, holding the plate of cookies aloft. "Lots of men cook. You should have your aunt Holly turn on the Food Network so you see for yourself."

"Men bake cookies?"

"Oh, my, yes," she told him. "Now that you're here, why don't we go and show these other children how to work this special robot. You can be my assistant."

"Can I?" Wide-eyed, Gabe looked at Holly for permission.

She nodded, and Mrs. Miracle and Gabe went to the other side of the toy department. Holly noticed that Jake was busy with customers, so she wandered down a randomly chosen aisle, examining the Barbie dolls and all their accoutrements. She felt a bit foolish carrying a plate of decorated cookies.

As soon as he was free, Jake made a beeline toward her. "Hi," he said. "I didn't expect to see you again so soon."

"Hi." Looking away, she tried to explain the reason for her visit. "Gabe wanted to check out his robot again. After that, we're going to my office and then Rockefeller Center to see the Christmas tree…but we decided to come here first." The words tumbled out so quickly she wondered if he'd understood a thing she'd said.

He glanced at the cookies.

"These are for you," she said, shoving the plate in his direction. "Sugar cookies. In appreciation for my latte."

"Homemade sugar cookies," he murmured as if he'd never seen anything like them before.

He continued to stare at the plate for an awkward moment. Holly was afraid she'd committed a social faux pas.

"My mother used to bake sugar cookies every Christmas," Jake finally said. His eyes narrowed, and the memory seemed to bring him pain.

Holly had the absurd notion that she should apologize.

"I remember the star and the bell." He spoke in a low voice, as though transported through the years. "Oh, and look, that one's a reindeer, and of course the Christmas tree with the little cinnamon candies as ornaments."

"Gabe actually decorated that one," she said.

He looked up and his smile banished all doubt. "Thank you, Holly."

"You're welcome, Jake."

"Excuse me." A woman spoke from behind Holly. "Is there someone here who could show me the electronic games?"

Jake seemed reluctant to leave her, and Holly was loath to see him go. "I'll be happy to help you," he said. He set the cookies behind the counter and escorted the woman to another section of the department.

Holly moved to the area where Gabe and Mrs. Miracle were demonstrating Intellytron. A small crowd had gathered, and Gabe's face shone with happiness as he put the robot through its paces. In all the weeks her nephew had lived with her, she'd never seen him so excited, so fully engaged. She knew Gabe wanted this toy for Christmas; what Holly hadn't understood until this very second was just how much it meant to him.

Regardless of the cost, Holly intended to get her nephew that robot.

Holiday Sugar Cookies
(from *Debbie Macomber's Cedar Cove Cookbook*)

This foolproof sugar cookie recipe makes a sturdy, sweet treat that's a perfect gift or a great addition to a holiday cookie platter.

- 2 cups (4 sticks) unsalted butter, at room temperature
- 2 cups brown sugar
- 2 large eggs
- 2 teaspoons vanilla extract or grated lemon peel
- 6 cups all-purpose flour, plus extra for rolling
- 2 teaspoons baking powder
- 1 teaspoon salt

1. In a large bowl with electric mixer on medium speed, cream butter and sugar until light and fluffy. Add eggs and vanilla; beat until combined.

2. In a separate bowl, combine flour, baking powder and salt. Reduce mixer speed to low; beat in flour mixture just until combined. Shape dough into two disks; wrap and refrigerate at least 2 hours or up to overnight.

3. Preheat oven to 350°F. Line baking sheets with parchment paper. Remove 1 dough disk from the refrigerator. Cut disk in half; cover remaining half. On a lightly floured surface with floured rolling

pin, roll dough ¼-inch thick. Using cookie cutters, cut dough into as many cookies as possible; reserve trimmings for rerolling.

4. Place cookies on prepared sheets about 1 inch apart. Bake 10 to 12 minutes (depending on the size of cookies) until pale gold. Transfer to wire rack to cool. Repeat with remaining dough and rerolled scraps.

TIP: Decorate baked cookies with prepared frosting or sprinkle unbaked cookies with colored sugars before putting them in the oven.

Makes about 48 cookies.

Chapter Five

*People are like tea bags—you have to drop them
in hot water before you know how strong they are.*
—Mrs. Miracle

"Sugar cookies," Jake said to himself. A rush of memories swarmed him. Memories of his mother and sister at Christmas. Spicy scents in the air—cinnamon and ginger and cloves. Those sensory memories had been so deeply buried, he'd all but forgotten them.

"We sold three of the SuperRobots this afternoon," Mrs. Miracle said, breaking into his thoughts.

Just three? Jake felt a sense of dread. He'd need to sell a lot more than three a day to unload the five hundred robots he'd ordered. He checked the computer, which instantly gave him the total number sold since Black Friday. When he saw the screen, his heart sank down to his shoes. This wasn't good. Not good at all. Jake had made a bold decision, hoping to prove himself to his father, and he was about to fall flat on his face.

"I'll be leaving for the night," Mrs. Miracle announced. "Karen—" the other sales associate "—is already gone."

He glanced at his watch. Five after nine. "By all means. You've put in a full day."

"So have you."

As the owner's son, Jake was expected to stay late. He wouldn't ask anything of his staff that he wasn't willing to do himself. That had been drilled into him by his father, who lived by the same rules.

"It's a lovely night for a walk in the park, don't you think?" the older woman said wistfully.

Jake lived directly across from Central Park. He often jogged through the grounds during the summer months, but winter was a different story.

Mrs. Miracle patted him on the back. "I appreciate that you let me stay here in the toy department," she said.

Jake turned to look at her. He hadn't said anything to the older woman about getting her transferred. He couldn't imagine HR had, either. He wondered how she'd found out about his sudden decision to keep her with him. Actually, it'd been Holly's comment about having a grandmotherly figure around that had influenced him. That, and Emily's obvious rapport with children.

"Good night, Mrs. Miracle," he said.

"Good night, Mr. Finley. Oh, and I don't think you need to worry about that robot," she said. "It's going to do very well. Mark my words."

Now it appeared the woman was a mind reader, too.

"I hope you're right," he murmured.

"I am," she said, reaching for her purse. "And remember, this is a lovely evening for a stroll through the park. It's an excellent way to clear your head of worries."

Again, she'd caught him unawares. Jake had no idea he could be so easily read. Good thing he didn't play high-stakes poker. That thought amused him as he finished up for the day and left the store.

He was grateful not to run into his father because J.R. would certainly question him about those robots. No doubt his father already knew the dismal truth; the click of a computer key would show him everything.

When Jake reached his apartment, he was hungry and restless. He unwrapped the plate of cookies and quickly ate two. If this wasn't his mother's recipe, then it was a very similar one. They tasted the same as the cookies he recalled from his childhood.

Standing by the picture window that overlooked the park, he remembered the Christmas his mother and sister had been killed. The shock and pain of it seemed as fresh now as it'd been all those years ago. No wonder his father still refused to celebrate the holiday. Jake couldn't, either.

When he looked out, he noticed how brightly lit the park was. Horse-drawn carriages clattered past, and although he couldn't hear the clopping of the horses' hooves, it sounded in his mind as clearly as if he'd been out on the street. He suddenly saw himself with his parents and his sister, all huddled under a blanket in a carriage. The horse had been named Silver, he remembered, and the snow had drifted softly down. That was almost twenty-one years ago, the winter they'd died, and he hadn't taken a carriage ride since.

Mrs. Miracle had suggested he go for a walk that evening. An odd idea, he thought, especially after a long day spent dealing with harried shoppers. The last thing he'd normally want to do was spend even more time on his feet. And yet he felt irresistibly attracted to the park. The cheerful lights, the elegant carriages, the man on the corner selling roasted chestnuts, drew him like a kid to a Christmas tree.

None of this made any sense. He was exhausted, doubting himself and his judgment, entangled in memories he'd rather ignore. Perhaps a swift walk would chase away the demons that hounded him.

Putting on his coat, he wrapped the cashmere scarf around his neck. George, the building doorman, opened the front door and, hunching his shoulders against the wind, Jake hurried across the street.

"Aunt Holly, can we buy hot chestnuts?"

The young boy's voice immediately caught Jake's attention. He turned abruptly and came face-to-face with Holly Larson. The fourth time in less than twenty-four hours.

"Jake!"

"Holly."

They stared at each other, both apparently too shocked to speak.

She found her voice first. "What are you doing here?"

He pointed to the apartment building on the other side

of the street. "I live over there. What are you doing here this late?"

"How late *is* it?"

He checked his watch. "Twenty to ten."

"Ten!" she cried. "You've got to be kidding. I had no idea it was so late. Hurry up, Gabe, it's time we got to the subway."

"Can we buy some chestnuts first?" he asked, gazing longingly at the vendor's cart.

"Not now. Come on, we have to go."

"I've never had roasted chestnuts before," the boy complained.

"Neither have I," Jake said, although that wasn't strictly true, and stepped up to the vendor. "Three, please."

"Jake, you shouldn't."

"Oh, come on, it'll be fun." He paid for the chestnuts, then handed bags to Holly and Gabe.

"I'm not sure how we got this far north," Holly said, walking close to his side as the three of them strolled down the street, eating chestnuts. "Gabe wanted to see the carriages in the park."

"Lindy told me about them." Gabe spoke with his mouth full. "Lindy Lee."

"Lindy Lee's my boss," Holly explained. "The designer."

Jake knew who she was, impressed that Holly worked for such a respected industry name.

"We went into Holly's office to decorate for Christmas, and Lindy was there and she let me put up stuff around her desk. That's when she told me about the horses in the park," Gabe said.

"Did you go for a ride?" Jake asked.

Gabe shook his head sadly. "Aunt Holly said it costs a lot of money."

"It is expensive," Jake agreed. "But sometimes you can make a deal with the driver. Do you want me to try?"

"Yeah!" Gabe said excitedly. "I've never been in a carriage before—not even once."

"Jake, no," Holly whispered, and laid a restraining hand on his arm. "I should get him home and in bed."

"Aunt Holly, *please!*" The eight-year-old's plaintive cry rang out. "It's Saturday."

"You're turning down a carriage ride?" Jake asked. He saw the dreamy look that came over Holly as a carriage rolled past—a white carriage drawn by a midnight-black horse. "Have you ever been on one?"

"No…"

"Then that settles it. The three of us are going." Several carriages had lined up along the street. Jake walked over to the first one and asked his price, which he willingly paid. All that talk about negotiating had been just that—talk. This was the perfect end to a magical day. Magical because of a plate of silly sugar cookies. Magical because of Holly and Gabe. Magical because of Christmas, reluctant though he was to admit it.

He helped Holly up into the carriage. When she was seated, he lifted Gabe so the boy could climb aboard, too.

Finally he hoisted himself onto the bench across from Holly and Gabe. They shared a thick fuzzy blanket.

"This is great," Gabe exclaimed. "I can hardly wait to tell my dad."

Holly smiled delightedly. "I'm surprised he's still awake," she said. "We've been on the go for hours."

"There's nothing like seeing Christmas through the eyes of a child, is there?"

"Nothing."

"Reminds me of when I was a kid…"

The carriage moved into Central Park and, even at this hour, the place was alive with activity.

"Oh, look, Gabe," Holly said, pointing at the carousel. She wrapped her arm around the boy, who snuggled closer. "We'll go on the carousel this spring."

He nodded sleepily. The ride lasted about thirty minutes, and by the time they returned to the park entrance, Gabe's eyes had drifted shut.

"I was afraid this would happen," Holly whispered.

"We'll go to my apartment, and I'll contact a car service to get you home."

Holly shook her head. "I…appreciate that, but we'll take the subway."

"Nonsense," Jake said.

"Jake, I can't afford a car service."

"It's on me."

"No." She shook her head again. "I can't let you do that."

"You can and you will. If I hadn't insisted on the carriage ride, you'd have been home by now."

She looked as if she wanted to argue more but changed her mind. "Then I'll graciously accept and say thank-you. It's been a magical evening."

Magical. The same word he'd used himself. He leaped down, helped her and Gabe out, then carried Gabe across the street. The doorman held the door for them.

"Evening, Mr. Finley."

"Evening, George."

Holly followed him onto the elevator. When they reached the tenth floor and the doors glided open, he led the way down the hall to his apartment. He had to shift the boy in his arms to get his key in the lock.

Once inside Holly looked around her, eyes wide. By New York standards, his apartment was huge. His father had lived in it for fifteen years before moving to a different place. This apartment had suited Jake, so he'd taken it over.

"I see you're like me. I haven't had time to decorate for Christmas, either," she finally said. "I was so late getting the office done that I had to come in on a Saturday to do it."

"I don't decorate for the holidays," he said without explaining the reasons. He knew he probably sounded a little brusque; he hadn't meant to.

"I suppose you get enough of that working for the store."

He nodded, again avoiding an explanation. He laid a sleeping Gabe on the sofa.

"I'll see how long we'll have to wait for a car," he said. The number was on speed dial; he used it often, since he didn't own a car himself. In midtown Manhattan car ownership could be more of a liability than a benefit. He watched Holly walk over to the picture window and gaze outside. Apparently she found the scene as mesmerizing as he had earlier. Although he made every effort to ignore Christmas, it stared back at him from the street, the city, the park. New York was always intensely alive but never more so than in December.

The call connected with the dispatcher. "How may I help you?"

Jake identified himself and gave his account number and address, and was assured a car would be there in fifteen minutes.

"I'll ride with you," Jake told her when he'd hung up the phone.

His offer appeared to surprise her. "You don't need to do that."

"True, but I'd like to," he said with a smile.

She smiled shyly back. "I'd like it, too." Walking away from the window, she sighed. "I don't understand why, but I feel like I've known you for ages."

"I feel the same way."

"Was it only yesterday morning that you paid for my latte?"

"You were a damsel in distress."

"And you were my knight in shining armor," she said warmly. "You're still in character this evening."

He sensed that she wanted to change the subject because she turned away from him, resting her gaze on something across the room. "You know, you have the ideal spot for a Christmas tree in that corner," she said.

"I haven't celebrated Christmas in more than twenty years," Jake blurted out, shocking himself even more than Holly.

"I beg your pardon?"

Jake went back into the kitchen and found that his throat had gone dry and his hands sweaty. He never talked about his mother and sister. Not with anyone. Including his father.

"You don't believe in Christmas?" she asked, trailing after him. "What about Hanukkah?"

"Neither." He'd dug himself into a hole and the only way out was to explain. "My mother and sister were killed on Christmas Eve twenty-one years ago. A freak car accident that happened in the middle of a snowstorm, when two taxis collided."

"Oh, Jake. I'm so sorry."

"Dad and I agreed to forget about Christmas from that point forward."

Holly moved to his side. She didn't say a word and he was grateful. When people learned of the tragedy—almost always from someone other than him—they rarely knew what to say or how to react. It was an uncomfortable situation and still painful; he usually mumbled some remark about how long ago the accident had been and then tried to put it out of his mind. But he *couldn't,* any more than his father could.

Holly slid her arms around him and simply laid her head against his chest. For a moment, Jake stood unmoving as she held him. Then he placed his own arms around her. It felt as though she was an anchor, securing him in an unsteady sea. He needed her. *Wanted* her. Before he fully realized what he was doing, he lifted her head and lowered his mouth to hers.

The kiss was filled with urgency and need. She slipped her arms around his neck, and her touch had a powerful effect on him.

He tangled his fingers in her dark shoulder-length hair and brought his mouth to hers a second time. Soon they were so involved in each other that it took him far longer than it should to hear the ringing of his phone.

He broke away in order to answer; as he suspected, the car was downstairs, waiting. When he told Holly, she immediately put on her coat. Gabe continued to sleep as Jake scooped him up, holding the boy carefully in both arms.

George opened the lobby door for them. Holly slid into the vehicle first, and then as Jake started to hand her the boy, he noticed a movement on the other side of the street.

"Jake?" Holly called from the car. "Please, there's no need for you to come. You've been so kind already."

"I want to see you safely home," he said as he stared across the street. For just an instant—it must have been his imagination—he was sure he'd seen Emily Merkle, better known as Mrs. Miracle.

Chapter Six

Forbidden fruit creates many jams.
—Mrs. Miracle

The phone rang just as Holly and Gabe walked into the apartment after church the next morning. For one wild second Holly thought it might be Jake.

Or rather, *hoped* it was Jake.

Although she'd been dead on her feet by the time they got to Brooklyn, she couldn't sleep. She'd lain awake for hours, thinking about the kisses they'd shared, replaying every minute of their time together. All of this was so unexpected and yet so welcome. Jake was—

"Hello," she said, sounding breathless with anticipation.

"What's this I hear about you turning my son into a girl?"

"Mickey!" Her brother's voice was as clear as if he were in the next room. He tried to phone on a regular basis, but it wasn't easy. The most reliable form of communication had proved to be email.

"So you're baking cookies with my son, are you?" he teased.

"We had a blast." Gabe was leaping up and down, eager to speak to his father. "Here, I'll let Gabe tell you about it himself." She passed the phone to her nephew, who immediately grabbed it.

"Dad! Dad, guess what? I went to Aunt Holly's office to help her decorate and then she took me to see the big tree at Rockefeller Center and we watched the skaters and had hot chocolate and then we walked to Central Park and had hot dogs for dinner, and, oh, we went to see Mrs. Miracle. I helped Aunt Holly roll out cookies and…" He paused for breath.

Evidently Mickey took the opportunity to ask a few questions, because Gabe nodded a couple of times.

"Mrs. Miracle is the lady in the toy department at Finley's," he said.

He was silent for a few seconds.

"She's really nice," Gabe continued. "She reminds me of Grandma Larson. I gave her a plate of cookies, and Aunt Holly gave cookies to Jake." Silence again, followed by "He's Aunt Holly's new boyfriend and he's really, really nice."

"Maybe I should talk to your father now," Holly inserted, wishing Gabe hadn't been so quick to mention Jake's name.

Gabe clutched the receiver in both hands and turned his back, unwilling to relinquish the phone.

"Jake took us on a carriage ride in Central Park and then…" Gabe stopped talking for a few seconds. "I don't know what happened after that 'cause I fell asleep."

Mickey was asking something else, and although Holly strained to hear what it was, she couldn't.

Whatever his question, Gabe responded by glancing at Holly, grinning widely and saying, "Oh, yeah."

"Are you two talking about me?" she demanded, half laughing and half annoyed.

She was ignored. Apparently Gabe felt there was a lot to tell his father, because he cupped his hand around the mouthpiece and whispered loudly, "I think they *kissed*."

"Gabe!" she protested. If she wanted her brother to know this, she'd tell him herself.

"Okay," Gabe said, nodding. He held out the phone to her. "Dad wants to talk to you."

Holly took it from him and glared down at her nephew.

"So I hear you've found a new love interest," Mickey said in the same tone he'd used to tease her when they were teenagers.

"Oh, stop. Jake and I hardly know each other."

"How'd you meet?"

"At Starbucks. Mickey, please, it's nothing. I only met him on Friday." It felt longer than two days, but this was far too soon to even suggest they were in a relationship.

"Gabe doesn't seem to feel that's a problem."

"Okay, so I took Jake a plate of cookies like Gabe said—it

was just a thank-you for buying me a coffee—and…and we happened to run into him last evening in Central Park. It's no big deal. He's a nice person and, well…like I said, we've just met."

"But it looks promising," her brother added.

Holly hated to acknowledge how true that was. Joy and anticipation had surged through her from the moment she and Jake kissed. Still, she was afraid to admit this to her brother—and, for that matter, afraid to admit it to herself. "It's too soon to say that yet."

"Ah, so you're still hung up on Bill?"

Was she? Holly didn't think so. If Bill had ended the relationship by telling her the chemistry just wasn't there, she could've accepted that. Instead, he'd left her with serious doubts regarding her parenting abilities.

"Is that it?" Mickey pressed.

"No," she said. "Not at all. Bill and I weren't really meant to be together. I think we both realized that early on, only neither of us was ready to be honest about it."

"Mmm." Mickey made a sound of agreement. "Things are going better with Gabe, aren't they?"

"Much better."

"Good."

"He's adjusting and so am I." This past week seemed to have been a turning point. They were more at ease with each other. Gabe had made new friends and was getting used to life without his father—and with her. She knew she insisted on rules Mickey didn't bother with—like making their beds every morning, drinking milk with breakfast and, of course, putting the toilet seat down. But Gabe hardly complained at all anymore.

"What was it he told Santa he wanted for Christmas?" Mickey asked.

"So he emailed you about the visit with Santa, did he?"

"Yup, he sent the email right after he got home. He seemed quite excited."

"It's Intellytron the SuperRobot."

At her reference to the toy, Gabe's eyes lit up and he nodded vigorously.

"We found them in Finley's Department Store. Mrs. Miracle, the woman Gabe mentioned, works there...and Jake does, too."

"Didn't Gabe tell me Jake's name is Finley?" Mickey asked. "He said he heard Mrs. Miracle call him that—Mr. Finley. Is he related to the guy who owns the store?"

"Y-e-s." How dense could she be? Holly felt like slapping her forehead. She'd known his name was Finley from the beginning and it hadn't meant a thing to her. But now...now she realized Jake was probably related to the Finley family— was possibly even the owner's son. No wonder he could afford to live where he did. He hadn't given the price of the carriage ride or the car service a second thought, either.

She had the sudden, awful feeling that she was swimming in treacherous waters and there wasn't a life preserver in sight.

"Holly?"

"I...I think he must be." She'd been so caught up in her

juvenile fantasies, based on the coincidence of their meetings, that she hadn't paid attention to anything else.

"You sound like this is shocking news."

"I hadn't put two and two together," she confessed.

"And now you're scared."

"I guess I am."

"Don't be. He puts his pants on one leg at a time like everyone else, if you'll pardon the cliché. He's just a guy."

"Right."

"You don't seem too sure of that."

Holly wasn't. A chill had overtaken her and she hugged herself with one arm. "I need to think about this."

"While you're thinking, tell me more about this robot that's got my son so excited."

"It's expensive."

"How…expensive?"

Holly heard the hesitation in her brother's voice. He had his own financial problems. "Don't worry—I've got it. This is on me."

"You're sure about that?"

"Positive." The Christmas bonus checks were due the following Friday. If all went well, hers should cover the price of the toy with enough left over for a really special Christmas dinner.

Christmas.

When she woke that morning, still warm under the covers, Holly's first thought had been of Jake. She'd had the craziest idea that…well, it was out of the question now.

What Jake had confided about his mother and sister had

nearly broken her heart. The tragedy had not only robbed him of his mother and sibling, it had destroyed his pleasure in Christmas. Holly had hoped to change that, but the mere notion seemed ridiculous now. She'd actually planned to invite Jake to spend Christmas Day with her and Gabe. She knew now that he'd never accept. He was a Finley, after all, a man whose background was vastly different from her own.

Half-asleep, she'd pictured the three of them sitting around her table, a lovely golden-brown turkey with sage stuffing resting in the center. She'd imagined Christmas music playing and the tree lights blinking merrily, enhancing the celebratory mood. She couldn't believe she'd even considered such a thing, knowing what she did now.

"I have a Christmas surprise coming your way," Mickey said. "I'm just hoping it arrives in time for the holidays."

"It doesn't matter," she assured her brother, dragging her thoughts away from Jake. She focused on her brother and nephew—which was exactly what she intended to do from this point forward. She needed to forget this romantic fantasy she'd invented within a day of meeting Jake Finley.

"I can guarantee Gabe will like it and so will you," Mickey was saying.

Holly couldn't begin to guess what Mickey might have purchased in Afghanistan for Christmas, but then her brother had always been full of surprises. He'd probably ordered something over the internet, she decided.

"Mom and Dad mailed us a package, as well," she told him. "The box got here this week."

"From Haiti? What would they be sending?"

"I don't have a clue," she said. Once the tree was up she'd arrange the gifts underneath it.

"You're going to wait until Christmas morning, aren't you?" he asked. "Don't open anything before that."

"Of course we'll wait." Even as kids, they'd managed not to peek at their gifts.

Mickey laughed, then grew serious. "This won't be an ordinary Christmas, will it?"

Holly hadn't dwelled on not being with her parents. Her father, a retired dentist, and her mother, a retired nurse, had offered their services in a health clinic for twelve months after the devastating earthquake. They'd been happy about the idea of giving back, and Holly had been happy for them. This Christmas was supposed to be Mickey, Gabe and her for the holidays—and then Mickey's National Guard unit had been called up and he'd left to serve his country.

"It could be worse," she said, and her thoughts involuntarily went to Jake and his father, who refused to celebrate Christmas at all.

"Next year everything will be different," Mickey told her.

"Yes, it will," she agreed.

Her brother spoke to Gabe for a few more minutes and then said goodbye. Gabe was pensive after the conversation with his father and so was Holly, but for different reasons.

"How about toasted cheese sandwiches and tomato soup for lunch?" she suggested, hoping to lighten the mood. "That was your dad's and my favorite Sunday lunch when we were growing up."

Gabe looked at her suspiciously. "What kind of cheese?"

Holly shrugged. "Regular cheese?" By that she meant the plastic-wrapped slices, Gabe's idea of cheese.

"You won't use any of that buffalo stuff, will you?"

She grinned. "Buffalo mozzarella. Nope, this is plain old sliced regular cheese in a package."

"Okay, as long as the soup comes from a can. That's the way Dad made it and that's how I like it."

"You got it," she said, and moved into the kitchen.

Gabe sat on a stool and watched her work, leaning his elbows on the kitchen counter. Holly wasn't fooled by his intent expression. He wasn't interested in spending time with her; he was keeping a close eye on their lunch in case she tried to slip in a foreign ingredient. After a moment he released a deep sigh.

"What's that about?" she asked.

"I miss my dad."

"I know you do, sweetheart. I miss him, too."

"And Grandma and Grandpa."

"And they miss us."

Gabe nodded. "It's not so bad living with you. I thought it was at first, but you're okay."

"Thanks." She hid a smile and set a piece of buttered bread on the heated griddle, then carefully placed a slice of processed cheese on top before adding the second piece of bread. She planned to have a plain cheese sandwich herself—one with *real* cheese.

Obviously satisfied that she was preparing his lunch according to his specifications, Gabe clambered off the stool. "Can we go to the movies this afternoon?"

"Maybe." She had to be careful with her entertainment budget, especially since there were additional expenses coming up this month. "It might be better if we got a video."

"Can I invite a friend over?"

She hesitated a moment, afraid he might want to ask his new friend, Billy.

"Sure," she said. "How about Jonathan Krantz?" Jonathan was another eight-year-old who lived in the building, and Caroline, his mother, sometimes babysat for her.

That was acceptable to Gabe.

After lunch they walked down to the neighborhood video store, found a movie they could both agree on and then asked Jonathan to join them.

Holly did her best to pay attention to the movie; however, her mind had a will of its own. No matter how hard she tried, all she could think about was Jake. He didn't phone and that was just as well. She wasn't sure what she would've said if he had.

Then again, he hadn't asked for her phone number. Still, he could get it easily enough if he wanted….

Late Sunday night, after Gabe was asleep, Holly went on the computer and did a bit of research. Sure enough, Jake was related to the owner. Not only that, he was the son and heir.

Monday morning, Holly dropped Gabe off at school and took the subway into Manhattan. As she walked past

Starbucks, she felt a twinge of longing—for more than just the coffee they served. This was where she'd met Jake. Jake Finley.

As she walked briskly past Starbucks, the door flew open and Jake Finley dashed out, calling her name.

Holly pretended not to hear.

"Holly!" he shouted, running after her. "Wait up!"

Chapter Seven

Coincidence is when God chooses
to remain anonymous.
—*Mrs. Miracle*

"Wait up!" Jake called. Holly acted as if she hadn't heard him. Jake knew better. She was clearly upset about something, although he couldn't figure out what. His mind raced with possibilities, but he couldn't come up with a single one that made sense.

Finally she turned around.

Jake relaxed. Just seeing her again brought him a feeling of happiness he couldn't define. He barely knew Holly Larson, yet he hadn't been able to forget her. She was constantly in his thoughts, constantly with him, and perhaps the most puzzling of all was the *rightness* he felt in her presence. He couldn't think of any other way to describe it.

Jake had resisted the urge to contact her on Sunday,

afraid of coming on too strong. They'd seen quite a bit of each other in the past few days, seemingly thrown together by fate. Coincidence? He supposed so, and yet... It was as though a providential hand was behind all this. Admittedly that sounded fanciful, even melodramatic. Nevertheless, four chance meetings in quick succession was hard to explain.

With someone else, a different kind of woman, Jake might have suspected these meetings had been contrived, and certainly this morning's was pure manipulation on his part. He'd hoped to run into her casually. But he hadn't expected to see Holly walk directly past the coffee shop. He couldn't allow this opportunity to pass.

She looked up at him expectantly; she didn't say anything.

"Good morning," he said, unsure of her mood.

"Hi." She just missed making eye contact.

He felt her reluctance and frowned, unable to fathom what he might have done to upset her. "What's wrong?" he asked.

"Nothing."

"Then why won't you look at me?"

The question forced her to raise her eyes and meet his. She held his gaze for only a fraction of a second before glancing away.

The traffic light changed and, side by side, they crossed the street.

"I'd like to take you to dinner," he said. He'd decided that if he invited her out on a real date they could straighten out the problem, whatever it was.

"When?"

At least she hadn't turned him down flat. That was encouraging. "Whenever you say." He'd rearrange his schedule if necessary. "Tonight? Tomorrow? I'm free every evening. Or I can be." He wanted it understood that he wasn't involved with anyone else. In fact, he hadn't been in a serious relationship in years.

His primary goal for the past decade had been to learn the retail business from the ground up, and as a result his social life had suffered. He worked long hours and that had taken a toll on his relationships. After his last breakup, which was in… Jake had to stop and think. June, he remembered. Had it really been that long? At any rate, Judith had told him it was over before they'd really begun.

At the time he'd felt bad, but agreed it was probably for the best. Funny how easily he could let go of a woman with hardly a pause after just four weeks. Judith had been attractive, successful, intelligent, but there'd been no real connection between them. The thought of letting Holly walk out of his life was a completely different scenario, one that filled him with dread.

All he could think about on Sunday was when he'd see her again. His pride had influenced his decision not to call her; he didn't want her to know how important she'd become to him in such a short time. Despite that, he'd gone to Starbucks first thing this morning.

"Tonight?" she repeated, referring to his dinner invitation. "You mean this evening?"

"Sure," he said with a shrug. "I'm available Tuesday night if that's better for you."

She hesitated, as if considering his offer. "Thanks, but I don't have anyone to look after Gabe."

"I could bring us dinner." He wasn't willing to give up that quickly.

Her eyes narrowed. "Why are you trying so hard?"

"Why are you inventing excuses not to see me?"

He didn't understand her reluctance. Saturday, when he'd dropped her off at her Brooklyn apartment and kissed her good-night, she'd practically melted in his arms. Now she couldn't get away from him fast enough.

Holly stared down at the sidewalk. People hurried past them and around them. They stood like boulders in the middle of a fast-moving stream, neither of them moving, neither talking.

"I...I didn't know who you were," she eventually admitted. "Not until later."

"I told you my name's Jake Finley." He didn't pretend not to understand what she meant. This wasn't the first time his family name had intimidated someone. He just hadn't expected that sort of reaction from Holly. He'd assumed she knew, and that was part of her charm because it hadn't mattered to her.

"I know you did," she countered swiftly. "And I feel stupid for not connecting the dots."

He stiffened. "And my name bothers you?"

"Not really," she said, and her gaze locked with his before

she slowly lowered her lashes. "I guess it does, but not for the reasons you're assuming."

"What exactly am I assuming?" he asked.

"That I'd use you."

"For what?" he demanded.

"Well, for one thing, that robot toy. We both know how badly Gabe wants it for Christmas and it's expensive and you might think I…"

"*What* would I think?" he asked forcefully when she didn't complete her sentence.

"That I'd want you to get me the toy."

"Would you ask me to do that?" If she did, he'd gladly purchase it—retail price—on her behalf.

"No. Never." Her eyes flared with the intensity of her response. She started to leave and Jake followed.

"Then it's a moot point." He began to walk, carefully matching his longer stride to her shorter one. "Under no circumstances will I purchase that toy for you. Agreed?"

"Agreed," she said.

"Anything else?"

Holly looked at him and then away. "I don't come from a powerful family or know famous people or—"

"Do you think I care?"

"No, but if you did, you'd be plain out of luck."

He smiled. "That's fine with me."

"Okay," she said, stopping abruptly. "Can you explain why you want to see me?"

Jake wished he had a logical response. He felt drawn to her in ways he hadn't with other women. "I can't say for sure, but deep down I feel that if we were to walk away from each other right now, I'd regret it."

"You do?" she asked softly, and pressed her hand to her heart. "Jake, I feel the same way. What's happening to us?"

He didn't have an answer. "I don't know." But he definitely felt it, and that feeling intensified with each meeting.

They started walking again. "So, can I see you tonight?" he asked. That was important, necessary.

Her face fell. "I wasn't making it up, about not having anyone to take care of Gabe. If you were serious about bringing us dinner…"

"I was."

Her face brightened. "Then that would work out perfectly."

"Do you like take-out Chinese?" he asked, thinking Gabe would enjoy it, as well.

"Love it."

"Me, too, but you'll have to use chopsticks."

"Okay, I'll give it a try."

"Great." Jake breathed easier. Everything was falling into place, just the way he'd hoped it would. He glanced at his watch and grimaced. He was late for work. He hoped Karen or Mrs. Miracle had covered for him.

Retreating now, taking two steps backward, he called out to Holly, "Six-thirty? At your place?"

She nodded eagerly. "Yes. And thank you, Jake, thank you so much."

He raised his hand. "See you tonight."

"Tonight," she echoed, and they both turned and hurried off to their respective jobs.

Jake's step was noticeably lighter as he rushed toward the department store. By the time he arrived, ten minutes later than usual, he was breathless. He'd just clocked in and headed for the elevator when his father stopped him, wearing a frown that told him J.R. wasn't happy.

"Are you keeping bankers' hours these days?"

"No," Jake told him. "I had an appointment." A slight stretch of the truth.

"I was looking for you."

"Any particular reason?" Jake asked. He'd bet his lunch break this sudden interest in the toy department had to do with those robots.

His father surprised him, however, with a completely different question. "I heard from HR that you requested a transfer for one of the seasonal staff...."

"Mrs. Miracle."

"Who? No, that wasn't the name."

"No, it's Merkle or Michaels or something like that. The name badge mistakenly says Miracle, and she insisted that's what we call her."

His father seemed confused, which was fine with Jake. He felt he was being rather clever to keep J.R.'s attention away from the robots.

J.R. ignored the comment. "You asked for this Mrs. Miracle or whoever she is to be transferred and then you changed your mind. Do I understand correctly?"

"Yes. After I made the initial request, I realized she was a good fit for the department—a grandmotherly figure who relates well to kids *and* parents. She adds exactly the right touch."

"I see," his father murmured. "Okay, whatever you decide is fine."

That was generous, seeing that *he* was the department head, Jake mused with more affection than sarcasm.

"While I have you, tell me, how are sales of that expensive robot going?"

Jake wasn't fooled. His father already knew the answer to that. "Sales are picking up. We sold a total of twenty-five over the weekend."

"Twenty-five," his father said slowly. "There're still a lot of robots left in the storeroom, though, aren't there?"

"Yes," Jake admitted.

"That's what I thought."

He made some additional remark Jake couldn't quite grasp, but it didn't sound like something he wanted to hear, anyway, so he didn't ask J.R. to repeat it.

As he entered the toy department, clipping on his "Manager" badge, Jake was glad to see Mrs. Miracle on duty.

"Good morning, Mr. Finley," she said, looking pleased with herself.

"Good morning. I apologize for being late—"

"No problem. I sold two Intellytrons this morning."

"Already?" This was encouraging news and improved his workday almost before it had started. "That's wonderful!"

"They seem to be catching on."

The phone rang just then, and Jake stepped behind the

counter to answer. The woman at the other end of the line was looking for Intellytron and sighed with audible relief when Jake assured her he had plenty in stock. She asked that he hold one for her.

"I'll be happy to," Jake said. He found Mrs. Miracle watching him, smiling, when he ended the conversation. "I think you might be right," he said. "That was a woman calling about Intellytron. She sounded excited when I told her we've got them."

Mrs. Miracle rubbed her palms together. "I knew it." The morning lull was about to end; in another half hour, the store would explode with customers. Since toys were on the third floor, it took time for shoppers to drift up the escalators and elevators, so they still had a few minutes of relative peace. Jake decided to take advantage of it by questioning his rather unusual employee.

"I thought I saw you on Saturday night," he commented in a nonchalant voice, watching her closely.

"Me?" she asked.

Jake noted that she looked a bit sheepish. "Did you happen to take a walk around Central Park around ten or ten-thirty?"

"My heavens, no! After spending all day on my feet, the last thing I'd do is wander aimlessly around Central Park. At that time of night, no less." Her expression turned serious. "What makes you ask?"

"I could've sworn that was you I saw across from the park."

She laughed as though the question was ludicrous. "You're joking, aren't you?"

"No." Jake grew even more suspicious. Her nervous reaction seemed to imply that she wasn't being completely truthful. "Don't you remember? You suggested I take a stroll through the park."

"I said that?"

"You did," he insisted. He wasn't about to be dismissed quite this easily. "You said it would help clear my head."

"After a long day at work? My goodness, what was I thinking?"

Jake figured the question was rhetorical, so he didn't respond. "I met Holly Larson and her nephew there," he told her.

"My, that was a nice coincidence, wasn't it?"

"Very nice," he agreed.

"Are you seeing her again?" the older woman asked.

"Yes, as a matter of fact, I am." He didn't share any details. The less she knew about his personal life, the better. Mrs. Miracle might appear to be an innocent senior citizen, but he had his doubts. Not that he suspected anything underhanded or nefarious. She seemed... Jake couldn't come up with the right word. He liked Mrs. Miracle and she was an excellent employee, a natural saleswoman. And yet... He didn't really know much about her.

And what he did know didn't seem to add up.

Chapter Eight

Aspire to inspire before you expire.
—Mrs. Miracle

Holly felt as if she was walking on air the rest of the way into the office. It didn't matter how rotten her day turned out to be; no one was going to ruin it after her conversation with Jake.

She'd spent a miserable Sunday and had worked herself into a state after she'd discovered Jake's position with the department store. Son and heir. Now, having talked to him, she realized her concerns were irrelevant. Okay, so his family was rich and influential; that didn't define him or say anything about the person he really was.

The question that, inevitably, kept going around and around in her mind was why someone like Jake Finley would be interested in *her*. The reality was that he could have his pick of women. To further complicate the situation, she was taking care of Gabe. Lots of men would see her nephew as an encumbrance. Apparently not Jake.

Holly was happy they'd gotten this settled. She felt reassured about his interest—and about the fact that he'd promised not to purchase the robot for her. Mickey had offered, too, but she knew he was financially strapped. Besides, getting Gabe this toy for Christmas—as *her* gift to him—was important to Holly.

She couldn't entirely explain why. Maybe because of Bill's implication that she wasn't good with kids. She had something to prove—if not to Bill or Mickey or even Jake, she had to prove it to herself. Nothing was going to keep her from making this the best possible Christmas for Gabe.

Holly entered her cubicle outside Lindy Lee's office and hung up her coat. She'd been surprised to find her boss in the office on Saturday afternoon and had tried to keep Gabe occupied so he wouldn't pester her. Unfortunately, Holly's efforts hadn't worked. She'd caught Gabe with Lindy Lee twice. One look made her suspect Lindy didn't really appreciate the intrusion. As soon as they'd finished putting up the decorations, Holly had dragged Gabe out with her. But this morning, as she looked around the office, she was pleased with her work. The bright red bulbs that hung outside her cubicle created an air of festivity. She couldn't help it—she started singing "Jingle Bells."

"Where is that file?" Lindy Lee shouted. She was obviously in her usual Monday-morning bad mood. Her employer was sorting through her in-basket, cursing impatiently under her breath.

Of course, Lindy Lee didn't mention *which* file she needed. But deciphering vague demands was all part and parcel of Holly's job. And fortunately she had a pretty good idea which one her boss required.

Walking into Lindy Lee's office, Holly reached across the top of the desk, picked up a file and handed it to her.

Lindy Lee growled something back, opened the file and then smiled. "Thank you."

"You're welcome," Holly said cheerfully.

The designer eyed her suspiciously. "What are *you* so happy about?" she asked.

"Nothing...I met up with a friend this morning, that's all."

"I take it this *friend* is a man."

Holly nodded. "A very special man."

"Honey, don't believe it." She laughed as though to say Holly had a lot to learn about the opposite sex. "Men will break your heart before breakfast and flush it down the toilet just for fun."

Holly didn't bother to explain about Jake. Lindy Lee's experience with men might be far more extensive than her own, but it was obviously different. Jake would never do anything to hurt her; she was sure of it. Besides, Lindy Lee socialized in different circles—Jake's circles, she realized with a start. Still, Holly couldn't make herself believe Jake was the kind of man who'd mislead her. Even though they'd known each other so briefly, every instinct she had told her she could trust him, and she did.

No irrational demand or bad temper was going to spoil her day, Holly decided. Because that evening she was seeing Jake.

Holly guessed wrong. Her day was ruined.

Early that afternoon she slipped back into her cubicle after delivering Lindy Lee's latest sketches to the tech department, where they'd be translated into patterns, which would then be sewn up as samples. Lindy was talking to the bookkeeper and apparently neither one noticed that she'd returned.

Holly hadn't intended to listen in on the conversation, but it would've been impossible not to with Lindy Lee's office door wide open. In Holly's opinion, if Lindy wanted to keep the conversation private, then it was up to her to close the door.

"Christmas bonuses are due this Friday," Marsha, the bookkeeper, reminded their boss.

"Due." Lindy Lee pounced on the word. "Since when is a bonus *due?* It's my understanding that a bonus is exactly that—a bonus—an extra that's distributed at my discretion."

"Well, yes, but you've given us one every year since you went out on your own."

"That's because I could afford to."

"You've had a decent year," Marsha said calmly.

Holly wanted to stand and cheer. Marsha was right; profits were steady despite the economy. The staff had worked hard, although their employer took them for granted. Lindy Lee didn't appear to notice or value the team who backed her both personally and professionally. More times than she cared to count, Holly had dropped off and picked up Lindy's dry cleaning or run errands for her. She often went above and beyond anything listed in her job description.

Not once had she complained. The way Holly figured it, her main task was to give Lindy Lee the freedom to be creative and do what she did best and that was design clothes.

"A *decent* year, perhaps," Lindy Lee repeated. "But not a stellar one."

"True," Marsha agreed. "But you're holding your own in a terrible economy."

"All right, I'll reconsider." Lindy Lee walked over to the window, her back to Holly. Not wanting to be caught listening, Holly quietly stood. There was plenty to do away from her desk—like filing. Clutching a sheaf of documents, she held her breath as she waited for Lindy's decision.

"Everyone gets the same bonus as last year," Lindy Lee said with a beleaguered sigh.

Holly released her breath.

"Everyone except Holly Larson."

Her heart seemed to stop.

"Why not Holly?" Marsha asked.

"She doesn't deserve it," Lindy Lee said flippantly. "She's out of the office at the stroke of five and she's been late for work a number of mornings, as well."

The bookkeeper was quick to defend Holly. "Yes, but she's looking after her nephew while her brother's in Afghanistan. This hasn't been easy for her, you know."

Lindy Lee whirled around and Holly moved from her line

of vision in the nick of time. She flattened herself against the wall and continued to listen.

"Yes, yes, I met the boy this weekend. She brought him on Saturday when she came in to decorate."

"On her own time," Marsha said pointedly.

"True, but if she managed her time better, Holly could've done it earlier. As it is, the decorations are up much later than in previous years. If I was giving out bleeding-heart awards this Christmas, I'd make sure Holly got one. No, I won't change my mind," she snapped as Marsha began to protest. "A bonus is a bonus, and as far as I'm concerned Holly doesn't deserve one. It's about merit, you know, and going the extra mile, and she hasn't done that."

Holly gasped.

"But—"

"I've made my decision."

Marsha didn't argue further.

Holly didn't blame her. The bookkeeper had tried. Holly felt tears well up but blinked them away. She was a good employee; she worked hard. While Lindy Lee was correct—these days she *did* leave the office on time—there'd been many a night earlier in the year when she'd stayed late without being asked. She'd often gone that extra mile for her employer. Yet all Lindy seemed to remember was the past three months.

She felt sick to her stomach. So there'd be no bonus for her. Although the amount of money wasn't substantial—maybe five hundred dollars—it would've made all the difference. But somehow, she promised herself, she'd find a way to buy Gabe his special Christmas toy.

* * *

Even though she was distracted by her financial worries, Holly managed to enjoy dinner with Jake and Gabe that evening. Jake brought chopsticks along with their take-out Chinese—an order large enough to feed a family of eight. Several of the dishes were new to Holly. He'd chosen moo shu pork and shrimp in lobster sauce, plus barbecue pork, egg rolls, fried rice and almond fried chicken.

Gabe loved every minute of their time with Jake. As he so eloquently said, "It's nice being around a guy."

"I don't know," Jake commented as he slipped his arm around Holly's waist. "Women aren't so bad."

Gabe considered his comment carefully. "Aunt Holly's okay, I guess."

"You *guess*," she sputtered. Using her chopsticks she removed the last bit of almond fried chicken from her nephew's plate.

"Hey, that was mine," Gabe cried.

"That's what you get for criticizing women," Holly told him, and then, to prove her point, she reached for his fried dumpling, too. In retaliation, Gabe reached across for her egg roll, dropping it on the table.

Jake immediately retrieved it and stuck one end in his mouth. "Five-second rule," he said just before he bit down.

When they'd finished, they cleared the table and settled down in front of the television.

As Jake flipped through the channels, Gabe asked, "When are we gonna put up the Christmas tree?"

"This week," Holly told him. She'd need to budget carefully

now that she wasn't going to get her bonus. The tree—she'd hoped to buy a real one—was an added expense she'd planned to cover with the extra money. This year she'd have to resort to the small artificial tree she'd stuck in the back of her coat closet.

The news that she wouldn't be receiving the bonus was devastating. Holly's first instinct had been to strike back. If everyone else was getting a bonus, it didn't seem fair that she wasn't. Still, Lindy Lee had a point. Holly hadn't been as dedicated to her job since Gabe came into her life. She had other responsibilities now.

That afternoon she'd toyed with the idea of looking for a new job. She could walk out—that would show Lindy Lee. Reason quickly asserted itself. She couldn't leave her job and survive financially. It could take her months to find a new one. And although this was an entry-level position, the chance to advance in the fashion world was an inducement she simply couldn't reject that easily. She'd made friends at the office, too. Friends like Marsha, who'd willingly defended her to their employer.

Besides, if she left her job, there'd be dozens who'd leap at the opportunity to take her place. No, Holly would swallow her disappointment and ride this out until Mickey returned. Next Christmas would be different.

"Can Jake help decorate the Christmas tree?" Gabe asked.

Jake was sitting next to her and Holly felt him tense. His face was pale, his expression shocked.

"Jake." Holly said his name softly and laid her hand on his forearm. "Are you okay?"

"Sure. Sorry, no decorating trees for me this year," he said in an offhand way.

"Why not?" Gabe pressed. "It's really fun. Aunt Holly said she'd make popcorn and we'd have cider. She has some ornaments from when she and my dad were kids. She won't let me see them until we put up the tree. It'll be lots of fun." His young face pleaded with Jake to reconsider.

Holly gently placed her hand on her nephew's shoulder. "Jake said another time," she reminded him. Jake hadn't participated in any of the usual Christmas traditions or activities in more than twenty years, ever since he'd lost his mother and sister.

"But there won't be another time," her nephew sulked. "I'll be with my dad next year."

"Jake's busy," Holly said, offering yet another excuse.

"Sorry to let you down, buddy," Jake told Gabe. "We'll do something else, all right?"

Gabe shrugged, his head hanging. "Okay."

"How about if I take you ice-skating at Rockefeller Center? Would you like that?"

"Wow!" In his excitement, Gabe propelled himself off the sofa and landed with a thud on the living room carpet. "I wanted to go skating last Saturday but Aunt Holly doesn't know how."

"She's a girl," Jake said in a stage whisper. Then he looked at her and grinned boyishly. "Frankly, I'm glad of it."

"As you should be," she returned under her breath.

"When can we go?" Gabe wasn't letting this opportunity slip through his fingers. He wanted to nail down the date as soon as possible. "I took skating lessons last winter," he said proudly.

Jake hesitated. "I'll need to get back to you once I see how everything goes at the store. It's the Christmas season, you know, so we might have to wait until the first week of the new year. How about Sunday the second?"

"That *long?*"

"Yes, but then I'll have more time to show you some classic moves. Deal?"

Gabe considered this compromise and finally nodded. "Deal." They clenched their fists and bumped them together to seal the bargain.

The three of them sat side by side and watched a rerun of *Everybody Loves Raymond* for the next half hour. Jake was beside her, his arm around her shoulders. Gabe sat to her left with his feet tucked beneath him.

When the program ended, Gabe turned to Jake. "Do you want me to leave the room so you can kiss my aunt Holly?"

"Gabe!" Holly's cheeks were warm with embarrassment.

"What makes you suggest that?" Jake asked the boy.

Gabe stood in the center of the room. "My dad emailed and said if you came to the apartment, I should dis-discreetly leave for a few minutes, only I don't know what that word means. I think it means you want to kiss Aunt Holly without me watching. Right?"

Jake nodded solemnly. "Something like that."

"I thought so. Okay, I'm going to go and get ready for bed." He enunciated each word as if reading a line of dialogue from an unfamiliar play.

Jake winked at Holly. "Pucker up, sweetheart," he said, doing a recognizable imitation of Humphrey Bogart.

Holly rolled her eyes and clasped her hands prayerfully. "Ah, sweet romance."

As soon as the bedroom door closed, Jake pulled her into his arms. The kiss was everything she'd remembered and more. They kissed repeatedly until Gabe came back and stood in front of them. He cleared his throat.

"Should I go away again?" he asked.

"No, that's fine," Holly said. She had trouble speaking.

"Your timing is perfect," Jake assured the boy.

Jake left shortly after that, and once she'd let him out of the apartment, Holly leaned against the door, still a little breathless. Being with Jake was very nice, indeed, but she had something else on her mind at the moment—Intellytron the SuperRobot and how she was going to afford one before Christmas.

Chapter Nine

It's hard to stumble when you're down on your knees.
—Shirley, Goodness and Mercy,
friends of Mrs. Miracle

Holly gave the situation regarding Gabe and the robot careful thought during the sleepless night that followed their dinner. She'd asked Jake about it when Gabe was out of earshot.

"There are still plenty left," he'd told her.

"But they're selling, aren't they?"

"Yes, sales are picking up."

That was good for him but unsettling for her. If she couldn't afford to pay for the robot until closer to Christmas, then she'd need to make a small deposit and put one on layaway now. She didn't know if Finley's offered that option; not many stores did anymore. She'd have to check with Jake.

She dared not take a chance that Intellytron would sell out before she had the cash.

While she was dead set against letting Jake purchase the robot for her, she hoped he'd be willing to put one aside, even if layaway wasn't a current practice at higher-end department stores. If she made their lunches, cut back on groceries and bought only what was absolutely necessary, she should be able to pay cash for the robot just before Christmas.

Tuesday morning she packed a hard-boiled egg and an apple for lunch. For Gabe she prepared a peanut butter and jelly sandwich, adding an apple for him, too, plus the last of the sugar cookies. Gabe hadn't been happy to take a packed lunch. He much preferred to buy his meal with his friends. But it was so much cheaper for him to bring it—and, at this point, necessary, although of course she couldn't tell him why. The leftover Chinese food figured into her money-saving calculations, too. It would make a great dinner.

On her lunch hour, after she'd eaten her apple and boiled egg, Holly hurried to Finley's to talk to Jake. She'd been uneasy from the moment she'd learned she wasn't getting a Christmas bonus. She wouldn't relax until she knew the SuperRobot would still be available the following week.

Unfortunately, Jake wasn't in the toy department.

"He's not here?" Holly asked Mrs. Miracle, unable to hide her disappointment.

"He's with his father just now," the older woman told her, and then frowned. "I do hope the meeting goes smoothly. It can be difficult to read the senior Mr. Finley sometimes.

But I have faith that all will end well." Her eyes twinkled as she spoke.

Holly hoped she'd explain, and Mrs. Miracle obliged.

"In case you didn't hear, Jake went over the department buyer's head when he ordered those extra robots," she confided, "and that's caused some difficulty with his father. J. R. Finley has a real stubborn streak."

Mrs. Miracle seemed very well informed about the relationship between Jake and his father. "The robots are selling, though. Isn't that right?" she asked, again torn between pleasure at Jake's success and worry about laying her hands on one of the toys. The display appeared to be much smaller than last week.

"Thankfully, yes," Mrs. Miracle told her. "Jake took quite a risk, you know?"

Holly shook her head.

"Jake tried to talk Mike Scott into ordering more of the robots, but Mike refused to listen, so Jake did what he felt was best." Her expression sobered. "His father was not pleased, to put it mildly."

"But you said they're selling."

"Oh, yes. We sold another twenty-five over the weekend and double that on Monday." She nodded sagely. "I can only assume J.R. is feeling somewhat reassured."

"That's great." Holly meant it, but a shiver of dread went through her.

"Several of our competitors have already sold out," Mrs. Miracle said with a gleeful smile.

"That's terrific news." And it was—for Finley's. Parents

searching for the toy would now flock to one of the few department stores in town with enough inventory to meet demand.

"How's Gabe?" Mrs. Miracle asked, changing the subject.

"He's doing fine." Holly chewed her lip, her thoughts still on the robot. "Seeing how well the robot's selling, would it be possible for me to set one aside on a layaway plan?"

The older woman's smile faded. "Oh, dear, the store doesn't have a layaway option. They haven't in years. Is that going to be a problem for you?"

Holly wasn't surprised that layaway was no longer offered, but she figured it was worth asking. Holly clutched her purse. "I...I don't know." Her mind spinning, she looked hopefully at the older woman. "Do you think you could hold one of the robots for me?" She hated to make that kind of request, but with her credit card temporarily out of commission and no layaway plan, she didn't have any other choice. The payment she'd made on her card would've been processed by now, but she didn't dare risk a purchase as big as this.

"Oh, dear, I'm really not sure."

"Could you ask Jake for me?" Holly inquired. She'd do it herself if he was there.

"Of course. I just don't think I could go against store policy, being seasonal staff and all."

"I wouldn't want you to do that, Mrs. Miracle."

"However, I'm positive Jake would be happy to help if he can." She leaned closer and lowered her voice. "He's rather sweet on you."

Sweet? That was a nice, old-fashioned word. "He's been wonderful to me and Gabe."

"So I understand. Didn't he bring you dinner last night?"

Holly wondered how Mrs. Miracle knew about that, unless Jake had mentioned it. No reason not to, she supposed. "Yes, and it was a lovely evening," she said. The only disappointment had come when Gabe asked him to help decorate the tree and Jake refused. The mere suggestion had distressed him. She hadn't realized that the trauma of those family deaths was as intense and painful as if the accident had just happened. If it was this traumatic for Jake, Holly could only imagine what it was like for his father.

"Did you know Jake and his father leave New York every Christmas Eve?" Mrs. Miracle whispered.

It was as if the older woman had been reading her mind. "I beg your pardon?"

"Jake and his father leave New York every Christmas Eve," she repeated.

Holly hadn't known this and wasn't sure what to say.

"Isn't that a shame?"

Holly shrugged. "Everyone deals with grief differently," she murmured. Her brother handled the loss of his wife with composure and resolve. That was his personality. Practical. Responsible. As he'd said himself, he couldn't fall apart; he had a boy to raise.

Sally had been sick for a long while, giving Mickey time to prepare for the inevitable—at least to the extent anyone can. He'd loved Sally and missed her terribly, especially in the beginning. Yet he'd gone on with his life, determined to be a good father.

Perhaps the difference was that for the Finleys, the deaths had come suddenly, without warning. The family had awakened the morning of Christmas Eve, excited about the holiday. There'd been no indication that by the end of the day tragedy would befall them. The shock, the grief, the complete unexpectedness of the accident, had remained an unhealed wound all these years.

"He needs you," Mrs. Miracle said.

"Me?" Holly responded with a short laugh. "We barely know each other."

"Really?"

"We met last week, remember?"

"Last week," she echoed, with that same twinkle in her eye. "But you like him, don't you?"

"Yes, I guess I do," Holly admitted.

"You should invite him for a home-cooked dinner."

Funny, Holly had been thinking exactly that. She'd wait, not wanting to appear too eager—although heaven knew that was how she felt. And of course there was the problem of her finances....

"I'd like to have Jake over," she began. "He—"

"Did I hear someone mention my name?" Jake said from behind her.

"Jake!" She turned to face him as his assistant moved away to help a young couple who'd approached the department. From the corner of her eye, Holly saw that the husband and wife Mrs. Miracle had greeted were pointing at the SuperRobot.

Mrs. Miracle picked up a box and walked over to the cash register to ring up the sale.

"Holly?" Jake asked.

"I need to put Intellytron on layaway but Mrs. Miracle told me you don't do that," she said in a rush.

"Sorry, no. I thought you were going to use your Christmas bonus to purchase the robot this week."

"I'm not getting one," she blurted out. She was close to tears, which embarrassed her.

"Listen, I'll buy the robot for Gabe and—"

"No," she broke in. "We already talked about that, remember? I won't let you."

"Why not?"

"Because...I just won't. Let's leave it at that."

He frowned but reluctantly agreed. "Okay, if that's the way you want it."

"That's the way it has to be."

"At least let me hold one for you," Jake said before she could compose herself enough to ask.

"You can do that?"

Jake nodded. "Sure. I'll set one aside right away and put your name on it. I'll tell everyone on staff that it isn't to be sold. How does that sound?"

She closed her eyes as relief washed over her. "Thank you. That would be perfect."

"Are you all right now?" He placed his hand on her shoulder in a comforting gesture.

"I'm fine. I apologize if I seem unreasonable."

"I understand."

"You do?" Holly wasn't convinced she could explain it herself. She just knew she had to do this. For Gabe, for Mickey…and for herself. The robot had become more than a toy. It was a symbol of her commitment to her nephew and her desire to give him the Christmas he deserved.

She saw that the department was busy and she was keeping Jake from his customers. "I have to get back to the office," she said.

He grinned. "Next time maybe you could stay longer."

Holly smiled back. "Next time I will."

"I'll call you. You're in the phone directory?"

She nodded, hoping she'd hear from him soon. "See you, Jake."

"See you, Holly."

As she walked toward the elevator, Mrs. Miracle joined her. "Mr. Finley suggested I take my lunch hour now," she said as they stepped into the empty car together. "What I feel like having is fried chicken."

"Fried chicken," Holly echoed. "My mother, who was born and raised in the South, has a special family recipe but she hasn't made it in years. I can't even remember the last time we ate fried chicken." In this age of heart-healthy diets, her mother had focused on lean, low-carb meals.

"A special recipe?" Mrs. Miracle murmured. "I'll bet it was good."

"The best." Now that she thought about it, Holly figured she might have a copy in her kitchen. "Mom put together a book of family recipes for me when I left home. I wonder if she included that one." Fried chicken was the ultimate comfort food and would make a wonderful dinner when she invited Jake over—sometime in the new year.

"She probably did. That sounds just like her."

"You know my mother?" Holly asked, surprised.

"No…no, but having met you, I know she must be a very considerate woman, someone who cares about family and traditions."

What a lovely compliment. The kind words helped take the sting out of her employer's refusal to give Holly a Christmas bonus. Lindy Lee was a modern-day Scrooge as far as Holly was concerned.

That evening, as dinner heated in the microwave, Holly searched through her kitchen drawers for the notebook where her mother had written various recipes passed down through her family.

"What would you think of homemade fried chicken for Christmas?" Holly asked Gabe. It wasn't the traditional dinner but roast turkey with all the fixings was out of her budget now. If Gabe considered her fried chicken a success, she'd serve it again when Jake came over.

"I've had take-out chicken. Is that the same?"

"The same?" she repeated incredulously. "Not even close!"

"Then I've never had it." He shrugged. "If it's not frozen or out of a can Dad doesn't know how to make it," Gabe said. "Except for macaroni and cheese in the box." He sat down at the computer and logged on to the internet, preparing to send an email to his father, as he did every night. He hadn't typed more than a few words when he turned and looked at Holly. "What's for dinner tonight?"

"Leftover Chinese. You okay with that?"

"Sure." Gabe returned to the computer screen.

Ten minutes later, he asked, "Can you invite Jake for Christmas dinner?"

"He won't be able to come."

"Why not?"

"He's going away for Christmas."

Gabe was off the internet and playing one of his games, jerking the game stick left and right as he battled aliens. "Why?"

"You'll have to ask him."

"I will." Apparently he'd won the battle because he let go of the stick and faced her. "You're going to see him again, right? You want to, don't you?"

Even an eight-year-old boy could easily see through her.

"I hope so."

"Me, too," Gabe said, then added, "Billy wants me to come over after school on Friday. I can go, can't I?" He regarded her hopefully.

The boys had obviously remained friends. "I'll clear it with his dad first." Holly had been meaning to talk to Bill before this. She'd make a point of doing it soon, although she wasn't looking forward to contacting him.

The good news was that she'd found the recipe in her mother's book.

Fried Chicken

(from *Debbie Macomber's Cedar Cove Cookbook*)

The key to crisp fried chicken is cooking at a high temperature. Stick a candy or deep-frying thermometer in the chicken as you fry to make sure the oil temperature remains between 250° and 300°F.

  1 whole chicken (about 3½ pounds),
      cut into 10 pieces
  1 quart buttermilk
  2 tablespoons Tabasco or other hot sauce
  2 cups all-purpose flour
Salt and pepper, to taste
  2 large eggs
  1 teaspoon baking powder
  ½ teaspoon baking soda
Vegetable oil or shortening

1. Rinse chicken. In a large bowl or resealable plastic bag, combine buttermilk and Tabasco. Add chicken pieces, turn to coat. Refrigerate, covered, for at least 8 hours and up to 16, turning the pieces occasionally. Remove chicken from buttermilk; shake off excess. Arrange in a single layer on large wire rack set over rimmed baking sheet. Refrigerate, uncovered, for 2 hours.

2. Measure flour into large shallow dish; whisk in some salt and pepper. In a medium bowl, beat eggs,

baking powder and baking soda. Working in batches of 3, drop chicken pieces in flour and shake dish to coat. Shake excess flour from each piece. Using tongs, dip chicken pieces into egg mixture, turning to coat well and allowing excess to drip off. Return chicken pieces to flour; coat again, shake off excess and set on wire rack.

3. Preheat oven to 200°F. Set oven rack to middle position. Set another wire rack over a rimmed baking sheet, and place in oven. Line a large plate with paper towels. Pour oil about ½ inch up the side of a large, heavy skillet. Place skillet over high heat; let pan warm until oil shimmers.

4. Place half of chicken, skin-side down, in hot oil. Reduce heat to medium and fry 8 minutes, until deep golden brown. Turn chicken pieces; cook an additional eight minutes, turning to fry evenly on all sides. Using tongs, transfer chicken to paper towel –lined plate. After draining, transfer chicken to wire rack in oven. Fry remaining chicken, transferring pieces to paper towel–lined plate to drain, then to wire rack in oven to keep warm.

Serves 4 to 6.

Chapter Ten

May you live all the days of your life.
—Mrs. Miracle

Emily Merkle smiled to herself. This latest assignment was going well. She enjoyed the ones that took place during the Christmas season most of all. She hadn't expected the romance between Jake and Holly to develop quite this quickly, so that was a bonus. Those two were very good together—and good for each other.

She attached her name badge to her sweater and hung her purse in the employee locker, then headed up to the toy department. She'd grown fond of Jake Finley. He was a kindhearted young man, a bit reserved, to be sure, but willing to take a risk he believed in. The robots were one example of that, his pursuit of Holly another.

Walking toward the elevator, she saw J. R. Finley, who'd just come into the hallway. He stopped, and his eyes automatically went to her badge.

"Mrs. Miracle," he said thoughtfully. He seemed to be mulling over where he'd heard it before.

"Mr. Finley," she said in the same thoughtful tone.

"To the best of my recollection, we don't have an employee here at Finley's named Miracle."

Emily was about to identify herself, but before she could, J.R. continued.

"I pride myself on knowing the name of every employee at the Thirty-fourth Street Finley's. Including seasonal staff." He narrowed his eyes. "Just a minute. I remember my son mentioning you earlier."

"The name is Merkle," Emily told him. "Emily Merkle."

Finley shook his head. "Can't say I'm familiar with that name, either."

"If you check with HR, I'm sure—"

"You're working with my son in the toy department, aren't you?" he said abruptly.

Emily frowned. "Are you always this rude, or are you making an exception in my case?"

He blinked twice.

He was used to everyone kowtowing to him. Well, *she* wouldn't do it.

"I beg your pardon?"

Emily met his look boldly. "I was saying something, young man."

J.R.'s head reared back and he released a howl of laughter. "*Young* man? My dear woman, it's been a long time since anyone referred to me as young."

Compared to her, he was practically in diapers. "That's beside the point."

He seemed confused.

"As I was saying," Emily continued politely, "if you care to check with HR, you'll find that I was hired last week as seasonal help."

"Only last week?" J.R. smiled at her. "That explains it, then."

"It does, indeed." She started down the hallway and was surprised when J.R. kept pace with her.

"You *are* working with my son, correct?"

"Yes. The toy department is extremely busy this time of year, as you well know." She glanced pointedly at her watch, wanting him to realize she should be on the floor that very moment.

"My son made a huge error in judgment by ordering five hundred of those expensive robots."

She was puzzled by his willingness to discuss business—and family—matters with a short-term employee. But she couldn't let his comment go unchallenged. "You think so, do you?" she asked mildly.

He gave her a startled look, as if no one had dared question his opinion before. "I know so," he insisted.

Emily was curious as to why he felt Jake was wrong and he was right. "Please tell me why you're so convinced your son's about to fail."

"Good grief, woman—"

"Call me Mrs. Miracle."

"Fine, Mrs. Miracle. Do you realize exactly how many of these…Intellytromps he needs to sell by Christmas? That's less than two weeks from now. It'll never happen."

"They're Intelly*trons*."

"Tromps, trons, whatever. They won't sell. Mark my words. It would take a miracle." He grinned broadly, obviously thinking himself very clever.

"You called?" she said, and laughed.

J.R. apparently didn't like the fact that she'd responded to his joke with one of her own. Instead of laughing, he scowled.

"Never mind," she said with a sigh. "I just wish you had more faith in your son."

He quickly took offense. "My son is my concern."

"He *is* your concern," she agreed. "And your future. So, it's time you trusted his judgment."

She'd really ruffled his feathers now. He grew red in the face and puffed up like an angry rooster, his chest expanding. "Now listen here. I won't have an employee talking to me as if I'm some messenger boy."

Emily stood her ground. "Someone needs to tell you the truth and it might as well be me."

"Is that so?"

He sounded like a third-grader exchanging insults on the playground.

"You need to give your son a bit of leeway to make his own mistakes instead of second-guessing all his decisions."

He opened and closed his mouth as if he couldn't speak fast enough to say what was on his mind. He thrust out one hand. "Your badge."

So he intended to fire her. "You don't want to do that," she told him calmly.

"I will not have an insubordinate employee working in my store!"

"I'm temporary help," she reminded him. "I'll be gone soon enough."

"I expect you gone *today.*"

"Sorry, I'm afraid that would be impossible. You'll need to reconsider."

Once again he couldn't seem to speak. "Are…are you refusing to leave the premises?" he finally managed to sputter.

"Jacob Robert, settle down. You've always had a problem with your temper, haven't you? Now, take a deep breath and listen to me. You do not want to fire me this close to Christmas."

"Are you threatening me?" he growled. "And how do you know my middle name?"

"Not in the least," she said, answering his first question and ignoring his second.

"I'm calling Security and having you escorted from the building. Your check will be mailed to you."

"Security?" The image of two beefy security guards lifting her by the arms and marching her outside was so comical it made Emily laugh.

That seemed to infuriate him even more. "Do you find this humorous?"

"Frankly, yes." She wouldn't lie; the man was insufferable. Oh, heavens, she did have her work cut out for her. "Now, if you'll excuse me, your son needs my help."

His jaw sagged as she scurried past him and walked quickly to the elevator.

As she suspected, the toy department was in chaos. Poor Jake was run ragged—thanks, in part, to his father, who'd taken too much pleasure in making her late for her shift. That man was about to meet his match. Emily Merkle was not going to let one overstuffed, pigheaded man stand in the way of her mission.

She'd been on the floor for thirty minutes or so when J.R. unexpectedly showed up. When he saw how busy the department was, he did a double take.

"Don't stand there gawking," Emily said as she marched past him, leading a customer to the cash register. Brenda and Karen, also on duty, were bustling around, answering questions, ringing up sales, demonstrating toys.

He stared at her blankly.

"Help," she told him. "We could use an extra pair of hands, in case you hadn't noticed."

"Ah…" He froze, as if he didn't know where to start.

"That couple over there," Emily said, pointing in the direction of the board games. "They have a three-year-old and a six-year-old and they're looking for suggestions. Give them a few."

"Ah…"

"Don't just stand there with your mouth hanging open," she ordered. "Get to work!"

To his credit, J.R. rolled up his sleeves and dug in. J. R. Finley might know the name of every employee in his store—with minor exceptions, of course—but he was in way over his head when it came to recommending board games. To *her* credit, Emily kept her mouth shut.

At four o'clock there was a slight lull. "Dad," Jake greeted his father. "What brings you down here?"

J.R. squinted at Emily but didn't answer.

"Whatever it was, I'm grateful." He turned to Emily. "How many Intellytrons did we sell this afternoon?"

"Sixteen."

"Fabulous!" Jake couldn't conceal his excitement.

His father, however, looked as though he needed to sit down, put up his feet and have a cup of hot tea. In Emily's view, it would do the man good to work the floor once in a while. He might actually learn something that way.

"I came to talk to you about this woman." J.R. stabbed a menacing finger at Emily.

"Ah, you mean Mrs. Miracle," Jake said fondly. "She's a wonder, isn't she?"

"She's a nuisance," J.R. snapped. "I want her fired."

Jake laughed, which was clearly the opposite reaction of what his father expected.

"This is not a joke."

"Yes, it is," Jake insisted. "Didn't you see what a madhouse this place was? It's like that every day now. I can't afford to lose Mrs. Miracle."

Emily sauntered over to J.R.'s side and whispered saucily, "Told you so."

He shook his finger. "I don't care if I have to work this department on my own," he yelled, "I will not tolerate insubordination."

"Excuse me, Dad, I've got another customer."

"I do, too," Emily said. "But you can keep standing there for a while. You make a nice fixture."

A kid of about five stepped in front of J.R. and stared up at him. "Is that a trick, mister?"

J.R. lowered his arms. "What, son?"

The boy was completely enthralled. "The way you get your cheeks to puff out like that."

Difficult though it was, Emily managed not to laugh. The boy was quite observant. J.R. had the puffing of cheeks down to an art form.

Jake finished with his customer and hurried back to his father. "Dad, I am *not* firing Mrs. Miracle."

"No, you're not. I am," J.R. said. "It will give me great pleasure to make sure she never works in this store again."

"What did she do that was so terrible?" Jake demanded.

"She insulted me and meddled in my personal affairs," his father burst out.

"How?" Jake asked, calm and collected. He was the perfect contrast to his father, who waved both arms wildly and spoke loudly enough to attract attention from every corner of the third floor.

When J.R. didn't answer, Jake shrugged and said, "Sorry, Dad, I need her."

Emily smiled ever so sweetly.

"She's out of here," J.R. roared, making a chopping motion

with his arm. She thought he resembled an umpire signaling a strikeout.

Jake shook his head. "She's our best sales associate by a mile, so if she goes, we might as well close down the entire department. You wouldn't want that, would you, Dad?"

J.R. hesitated.

"And if we close the department, you won't have a chance to prove how wrong I was by ordering five hundred Intellytrons," he said, as if that should be sufficient inducement to keep her on staff.

Emily suspected J.R. wanted Jake to fall flat on his face over this robot. He'd pay a high price for being right—and, as a matter of fact, he was dead wrong. She'd seen for herself how popular the toy was. She'd hoped it would be and had done her best to sell it. However, after the past twenty-four hours, she didn't need to try very hard; the toy sold itself. Apparently, its sudden popularity had begun like so many trends, on the West Coast. Now, the moment someone heard that Finley's still had robots in stock, they dashed over. Then they couldn't whip out their credit cards fast enough.

"I'd better stay," Emily murmured to Jake. "As much as I'd like to walk away right now, I wouldn't give your father the satisfaction."

J.R. stomped his foot.

"Are you having a temper tantrum?" she asked sweetly.

Jake only laughed. "Dad, I think it might be best if you went back to your office now. Or you could go home."

"This is *my* store and I'll stay anywhere I darn well please."

Jake leaned closer to his father and whispered, "You're scaring off my customers."

"Oh, sorry."

"We want customers, don't we, Dad? Isn't that the whole idea?"

"Don't get smart with me," J.R. muttered.

"Yes, Dad." Jake winked at Emily, who winked back.

J.R. must have caught sight of what they were doing. "What's that about?"

"What?" Emily asked, again the picture of politeness.

"What?" Jake echoed.

Seeing that he'd forfeited even the pretense of control, J.R. sighed. "Forget it."

"I can stay on, then?" Emily asked the store owner.

"Why ask me? I seem to have lost complete control of this company to a man I no longer recognize—my son." With that he marched toward the elevator that would deliver him to his private office on the fourteenth floor.

Chapter Eleven

People are funny. They want the front of the bus,
the middle of the road and the back of the church.
  —Mrs. Miracle

Holly knew she couldn't postpone calling Bill Carter, since the boys wanted to get together two days from now. It would be petty to allow her awkward relationship with Bill to stand in the way of her nephew being friends with his son.

The problem was how to approach him. She waited until Gabe was in bed on Wednesday night. Then she drew in a deep breath and looked up Bill's home number, which she'd made a point of erasing from her mind—and her phone. She hated feeling nervous about this. It was a courtesy call and nothing more.

Bill picked up on the fourth ring, when she was about to hang up, almost relieved he hadn't answered. Then all of a sudden, she heard, "Hello."

"Bill, it's Holly."

"Do you realize what time it is?"

"Uh, yes… It's nine-thirty. Am I calling too late?"

He didn't respond immediately. "I know why you're calling and I—"

"You do?" So all this angst had been for nothing. She should've noticed earlier how silly she was being, how badly she'd overreacted.

"It's about Tiffany, isn't it?"

"No…who's Tiffany?"

"You mean you *don't* know?"

Obviously she didn't. "Sorry, I think we're talking at cross-purposes here. I don't know any Tiffany—well, other than the one I met through work. I'm calling about Billy."

"My son?"

He sounded both relieved and worried, which confused Holly. "Listen, can we start over?" she asked.

"It's too late for that."

Just how obtuse *was* the man? "I don't mean our relationship, Bill. I was referring to our conversation."

"Just tell me why you called," he said, with more than a hint of impatience.

"I'm trying to, but you keep interrupting me. This isn't an easy phone call for me and your attitude's not helping." If Bill was a decent human being, he should understand this was difficult and appreciate the courage it had taken her to contact him. The fact that he didn't angered her. "No wonder the two of us aren't dating anymore," she muttered.

"Okay, fine. But what's that got to do with my son?"

She sighed loudly. "Since you haven't worked it out for yourself, I'll tell you. Billy and Gabe have become friends."

"Yeah? So what?"

"Well, I—" Before she could answer his rudely phrased question, he broke in.

"Wait a minute," he said suspiciously. "How do you know my son's friends with this kid?"

The way he said it practically implied that Holly had been stalking his son. "That's the most ridiculous question I've ever heard! I know because Gabe's my nephew."

"So?"

"So Billy wants Gabe to come home with him after school on Friday."

"Fine. And this concerns you how?"

"I thought I should tell you we're related."

"That still doesn't explain why you're calling. Shouldn't Gabe's parents clear this with me? Not you."

Holly gritted her teeth at his offensive tone. What she'd ever seen in this man was completely lost on her now. At the moment, she was grateful he'd broken it off.

"I have custody of Gabe," she said calmly. She didn't feel like describing how that had come about; it was none of his business—and besides, she wanted to keep the conversation as short as possible.

"*You* have custody?"

The question grated on her nerves. "Yes, *me,* and it's working out very nicely, I might add."

"Ah…" Bill apparently hadn't figured out yet how to react.

Holly had no intention of allowing him to make any more derogatory comments about her mothering skills. She launched right into her question, not giving him a chance to say much of anything. "Is it still okay if Gabe comes to your house after school?"

"Uh, sure."

"Do you have the same housekeeper looking after Billy as before?"

The suspicious voice was back. "Why do you ask?"

"Because I don't want Gabe visiting Billy if there isn't any adult supervision." The after-school program only went until five-thirty, and Bill was often home much later than that, which meant the part-time housekeeper picked the boy up and then stayed at the apartment to supervise him.

"Oh, yeah, Mrs. Henry still looks after Billy from five-thirty to seven, except for the nights I have social engagements. Then she stays until I get home."

He seemed to delight in letting her know—in what he probably thought was a subtle fashion—that he'd started dating again. Well, she had social engagements, too, even if they mostly involved going out with friends, but was mature enough not to mention it. Let him think what he liked.

Holly waited a moment, hoping he'd realize how juvenile his reaction had been. "Talking civilly isn't so hard, is it?" she asked.

"No," he agreed.

"Great. Now that's settled, what time would you like me to pick Gabe up?"

"You'll pick him up?"

"Would you rather bring him back to my apartment?" That certainly made it easier for her. Maybe he didn't want Holly showing up at his house, but if so, she didn't care enough to be offended.

"I can do that," he said.

"Fine."

"Fine," he echoed.

"What time should I expect you?"

"Seven-thirty, I guess."

"I'll be here."

She was about to disconnect when Bill's soft chuckle caught her off guard. "So Gabe's your nephew, huh?"

"I already told you that."

"You did. His last name's Larson?"

"Yes, Gabe Larson." She didn't see the humor in this. "I apologize for calling so late, but I thought it would be best if you and I talked when Gabe was in bed."

"Did you think I'd refuse to let the two boys be friends?"

"I wasn't sure. Our last conversation wasn't very pleasant and, well, it seemed better to ask."

"I'm glad you did."

She was glad to hear that because he sure hadn't acted like it.

Holly met Jake for lunch on Thursday. He'd called her at the office that morning and suggested a nearby restaurant; thankfully he'd insisted on buying. She might've sounded a bit too eager to accept, because she was sick of making do with leftovers. By cutting back, packing lunches and not spending a penny more than necessary Holly had managed to save seventy-five dollars toward the robot. According to her calculations, she'd have the funds to make the purchase but it would be close. Every cent counted.

Jake had arrived at the restaurant before her and secured a booth. "Hi," he said with a smile when she slid in across from him.

"Hi. This is nice. Thanks so much." She reached for the menu and quickly scanned the day's specials. She was so hungry, Jake would be fortunate if she could limit her selection to one entrée. As it was, she ordered a cup of wild-mushroom soup, half a turkey sandwich with salad and a slice of apple pie à la mode for dessert.

Jake didn't seem to mind.

"That was delicious," she said as she sat back half an hour later and pressed her hands over her stomach. "I probably ate twice as much as any other woman you've ever gone out with."

"It's a relief to be with someone who isn't constantly worried about her weight."

"I do watch my calories but I've been doing without breakfast, and lunches have been pretty skimpy and—"

"No breakfast?"

"That's not entirely accurate. I have breakfast, sort of. Just not much."

"And the reason is?"

Holly wished she'd kept her mouth shut. She pretended

not to hear his question and glanced at her watch instead. "Oh, it's almost one. I should get back to work."

"Holly." Jake wasn't easily distracted. "Answer the question."

Her shoulders sagged. "I really do need to go."

"You're going without breakfast to save money for the robot, aren't you?"

"Sorry, I have to run." She slid out of the booth and grabbed her coat and purse. "Oh, before I forget. Gabe wanted me to invite you to come and watch us decorate our Christmas tree tomorrow night, if you can. He'll be at a friend's place and won't get home until seven-thirty."

He hesitated, and Holly knew why. "I won't be able to leave the store until at least nine," he said.

"I let Gabe stay up until ten on Friday and Saturday nights."

He hesitated again. Holly hadn't forgotten his reaction when Gabe had first mentioned decorating for Christmas. She knew that, like his father, he ignored the holiday—apart from being surrounded by all that bright and shiny yuletide evidence at the store. Perhaps it was selfish of her, but she wanted to show him the joy of Christmas, prove that not all his Christmas memories were bad. She was convinced there must be happy remembrances, too, and she hoped to revive those so he could let go of the past. Holly held her breath as she waited for his response.

Jake stared into the distance for what seemed like a long time before he said, "Okay, I'll come."

Her breath whooshed out in relief and she gave him her

brightest, happiest smile. "Thank you, Jake." She finished putting on her coat, hoping he understood how much she appreciated his decision.

"Can we do this again?" he asked. "It's been crazy in the toy department. Mrs. Miracle insisted I take my lunch break early—and she said I should invite you. I need to get back to work, but I wanted to see you."

"I wanted to see you, too."

They left the restaurant together and went their separate ways. Holly's spirits were high. She'd cleared the air with Bill as much as possible, and Gabe had been excited to learn he'd be able to go to his friend's house on Friday.

When she returned to work, she found her boss on the phone, talking in her usual emphatic manner. Despite the fact that Holly wouldn't be receiving a Christmas bonus, she'd tried not to let that influence her job performance.

As soon as Lindy Lee saw her, she waved one arm to get her attention.

Holly stepped into her employer's office. "You're back late from lunch," Lindy said as she slammed down the phone.

"I have an hour lunch," Holly reminded her. She rarely took that long and often ate at her desk. Taking the full time allotted her was the exception rather than the rule.

"It's one-fifteen," Lindy Lee said pointedly, tapping her index finger against her wristwatch.

"And I left the office at twelve-thirty. Technically I still have fifteen minutes." Holly could see that she might have said more than necessary and decided it would be best to stop while she was ahead. "Is there something you need me to do?" she asked.

Frowning, Lindy handed her a thick file folder. "I need you to get these sketches over to Design."

"Right away." She took the folder and hurried out of the office, catching the elevator to the sixth floor. As she entered the design department she caught sight of one of the models regularly hired by the company. Tiffani White was tall, slim and elegant and she possessed about as perfect a body as one could hope to have. She was a favorite of Lindy Lee's and no wonder. The model showed Lindy's creations to their peak potential.

Tiffani saw Holly and blinked, as if she had trouble placing her, which was odd. They'd spent a fair amount of time together, since Holly had been backstage at several runway events with her.

"Lindy Lee asked me to deliver these sketches," she said to the head of the technical department. She turned to Tiffani.

"Hi, Tiff," she said casually.

"Hi." The model smiled—a smile that didn't quite reach her eyes.

Holly smiled back, but there was something strange going on. Tiffani had always been friendly. They'd even had coffee together now and then. Once, nearly a year ago when she'd been dating Bill, they'd run into Tiffani and—

Just a minute!

Thoughts and memories collided inside Holly's head. The conversation with Bill the night before played back in her mind. He'd made an unusual comment when they'd first spoken, mentioning the name Tiffany—or rather, Tiffani, with an *i*. The pieces were falling into place….

"Tiffani," Holly said. "I talked to Bill the other night."

"You did?"

"Yes, and your name came up."

The model brought one beautifully manicured hand to her mouth. "It did? Then you know?"

"Well, not everything."

"I wanted him to tell you before now, but Bill said it wasn't really any of your business. I told him that sometimes we see each other at work and it would make things better for me if you knew."

"So the two of you are…dating?"

"Actually we're…talking about marriage."

Marriage. Bill was planning to *marry* Tiffani? This didn't make sense. The model was about the least motherly woman Holly had ever met; she'd even told Holly she didn't like children. And she'd demonstrated it, too. They'd had a shoot earlier in the year with a couple of child models and Tiffani had been difficult and cranky all day. She'd made it clear that she didn't enjoy being around kids.

Holly wondered if Bill had any idea of the other woman's feelings. Probably not, she thought uncharitably. All he saw was Tiffani's perfect body and how good she looked on his arm.

In some ways, she had to concede, Bill and Tiffani were a good match. Bill had his own graphic design business and often hosted clients. Tiffani would do well entertaining, but

Holly suspected she didn't have a lot to offer as a stepmother to Billy.

Yet that'd been the excuse Bill had used when he'd broken off *their* relationship.

That was exactly what it'd been. An excuse, and a convenient one. He'd wanted Holly out of his life and he didn't care how badly he hurt her to make that happen. Granted, the relationship would've ended anyway, but in the process of hastening its demise, he'd damaged her confidence—in herself and in her maternal instincts.

Bill Carter was a jerk, no question about it. Tiffani was welcome to him.

Chapter Twelve

*Be ye fishers of men. You catch 'em
and God'll clean 'em.*
—Mrs. Miracle

"Can I go see Telly the robot after school?" Gabe asked as Holly walked him to school Monday morning.

"Not today," she said, stepping up her speed so she'd make it to work on time. The last thing she needed was to show up late. As it was, Gabe would get out of school at eleven-thirty this morning for winter break, and there was no after-school care today. Thankfully her neighbor, Caroline Krantz, had children of her own, including a son, Jonathan, who was Gabe's age, and Gabe enjoyed going there. Today, however, he obviously had a different agenda.

"But it's been so *long* since I saw him and I want—"

"I know. I'm sorry, Gabe. But Christmas will be here soon," she said, cutting him off.

"Do you think Santa's going to bring me my robot?"

"We won't find out until Christmas, will we?" she said, ushering him along. At the school, she bent down and kissed his cheek. "Remember, you're going to Mrs. Krantz's house with Jonathan after school."

"Yeah," he said, kicking at the sidewalk with the toe of his boot.

"Call me at the office when you get there, okay?"

"Okay."

Holly watched him walk into the building and then half ran to the subway station.

She was jostled by the crowd and once again had to stand, clutching the pole as she rode into the city. Her weekend had been everything she'd hoped for. Jake had stopped by on Friday night, arriving later than expected. She'd assembled the small artificial tree, which she'd bought years before; she would've preferred a real one but didn't want to spend the money this year. Then she'd draped it with lights, and she and Gabe had carefully arranged the ornaments. They were almost done by the time Jake came over, and Gabe insisted that he place the angel on top of the tree. Holly wasn't sure how he'd react to that request. At first he'd hesitated until she explained it was an honor and that it meant a lot to Gabe. Then he reluctantly set the angel on the tree.

Maybe it wasn't up to her to change—or try to change— his feelings about Christmas, but she hoped to coax him by creating new memories and by reminding him of happy ones from his own childhood.

On Friday, after school and his playdate with Billy, Gabe

had been exhausted by ten o'clock. Holly tucked him in, and then she and Jake had cuddled and kissed in front of the television. She couldn't remember what TV program they'd started to watch because they were soon more focused on each other than on the TV.

Thinking about Friday night with Jake made her tingle with excitement and anticipation. Bill could have his Tiffani. Holly would rather be with Jake. Their relationship held such promise….

Unfortunately, Jake was so busy at the store on Saturday that a couple of quick phone calls had to suffice. On Sunday evening he came to the apartment, bringing a take-out pizza and a bottle of lovely, smooth merlot—the best wine she'd had in ages. Jake had been full of tales about the store, and especially how well Intellytron was now selling. Rumor had it that Finley's was the only place in Manhattan that had the robot available, and customers had flooded the store, many of them going straight from Santa's throne to the toy department. No one else had guessed that Intellytron would be one of the hottest retail trends of the season.

While Holly was thrilled for Jake, she was still concerned that there wouldn't be any left once she could afford to make the purchase. Jake had again assured her she didn't need to worry; he'd put one aside for Gabe. It was safely hidden away in the back of the storeroom, with a note that said it wasn't to be sold.

Holly dashed into the office just in time. She saw Lindy Lee glance at her watch but Holly knew she had three minutes to spare. While Lindy Lee might not appreciate her new work habits, she was well within the bounds of what was required. Before Gabe's advent into her life, she'd often arrived early and stayed late. That wasn't possible now, and she was paying the price for her earlier generosity, which Lindy Lee had quickly taken for granted. Still, she enjoyed her job and believed she was a credit to her employer, even if Lindy didn't agree.

"Good morning," she said to her boss, sounding more cheerful than she felt. Holly was determined not to allow Lindy Lee's attitude to affect her day.

At noon, Holly began to check her watch every few minutes. She kept her cell phone on her desk, ready to receive Gabe's call. He should be phoning any time now; school was out, and he'd be going home with Jonathan. At twelve-thirty Holly started to worry. Gabe should be at the Krantzes'. Why hadn't he called? She felt too anxious to eat the crackers and cheese she'd brought, too anxious to do anything productive. She'd give him until one-fifteen and then she'd call.

At one-thirteen, her cell phone chirped, and she recognized the Krantzes' number. Holly heaved a grateful sigh. "Hello," she said.

"Holly?" It was Caroline.

"Oh, hi. Did everything go as scheduled? Did Gabe and Jonathan walk home from school together?"

"Well, that's the reason I'm phoning. Gabe didn't come home with Jonathan."

A chill raced down her spine. "What do you mean?"

"He told Jonathan there was something he needed to do

first, so Jonathan came home by himself. I…I feel really bad about this."

"Where is he?" Holly asked, struggling not to panic.

"That's just it. I don't know."

There was a huge knot in Holly's chest, and she found it difficult to breathe. How could she tell her brother that Gabe had gone missing?

Panicked thoughts surged through her mind. He'd been abducted, kidnapped, held for ransom. Or even worse, simply taken, never to be seen or heard from again.

"I'll call you if I hear anything," Caroline told her. "I'd go look myself but I can't leave the children. If he's not here in an hour, we'll reassess, call the police. In the meantime, I'll phone some of the other kids' parents."

"Yes… Thank you." Holly disconnected the line, her cell phone clenched in her fist.

"Holly?" Lindy Lee asked, staring at her. "What's wrong?"

Holly didn't realize she'd bolted to her feet. She felt herself swaying and wondered if she was going to faint. "My—my nephew's missing."

"Missing," Lindy Lee repeated. "What do you mean, missing?"

"He didn't show up at the sitter's house after school."

Lindy Lee looked at her watch. "It's a bit early for him to be out of school, isn't it?"

"No, not today," she said, panic making her sound curt. She was torn by indecision. Her first inclination was to contact the police immediately, not to wait another hour as

Caroline had suggested. They should start a neighborhood search. Ask questions.

She wondered crazily if she should get his picture to the authorities so they could place it on milk cartons all across America.

Her cell phone chirped again and she nearly dropped it in her rush to answer.

"Yes?" she blurted out.

"Holly, it's Jake."

"I don't have time to talk now. Gabe's missing and we've got to contact the police and get a search organized and—"

"Gabe's with me," Jake interrupted.

She sank into her chair, weak with relief. "He's with you?"

"Yes. He came into the city."

"On his own?" This was unbelievable!

"Yup."

"You mean to say he walked from school to the subway station, took the train and then walked to Finley's by *himself?*" It seemed almost impossible to comprehend. She held her head in one hand and leaned back in her chair, eyes closed. She remembered what he'd said that morning, about wanting to see the robot, but she'd had no idea he'd actually try to do it.

"Would you like to talk to him?" Jake was asking.

"Please."

"Aunt Holly?" Gabe's voice was small and meek.

"So," she said, releasing a long sigh. Although the urge to lambaste him was nearly overwhelming, she resisted.

"You didn't walk home with Jonathan the way you were supposed to?"

"No."

"Can you tell me why?"

"Because…"

"Because *what?*"

"I wanted to see Intellytron again and you said we couldn't and I thought, well, I know you have to work and everything, but I could come by myself, so I did. I remembered to take the green line and then I walked from the subway station." Despite the fact that he was obviously in trouble, there was a hint of pride in his voice.

Gabe had traveled into the city on his own just to see his favorite toy. The possibility hadn't even occurred to her. Holly suppressed the urge to break into sobs.

"I'm coming to get you right this minute," she declared. "Stay with Jake and Mrs. Miracle, and I'll be there as soon as I can. Now put Jake back on the phone."

His voice, strong and clear, came through a moment later. "Holly, it's Jake."

"I'm on my way."

"He'll be fine until you get here," he said.

"Thank you, thank you so much." This time, the urge to weep nearly overcame her.

"Everything's fine. Relax."

"I'm trying." She closed her cell, then looked up to see her boss standing in front of her desk.

"I take it you've located the little scoundrel?"

Holly nodded. "He came into the city on his own. Would

it be okay if I brought him to the office for the rest of the day?" Taking him back to Brooklyn would be time-consuming and Lindy Lee would no doubt dock her pay. Holly needed every penny of her next paycheck. "I promise he won't make a sound."

Lindy Lee considered the request, then slowly nodded. "I enjoyed meeting Gabe that Saturday.... I wouldn't mind seeing him again."

Lindy Lee wanted to see Gabe again? *This* was an interesting development, as well as an unexpected one. Her employer wasn't the motherly type—to put it mildly. Lindy Lee was all about Lindy Lee.

Grabbing her coat and purse, Holly rushed over to Finley's, calling Caroline Krantz en route. The store was crowded, and by the time she reached the third floor Holly felt as though she'd run a marathon. She saw Mrs. Miracle first, and the woman's eyes brightened the instant she noticed Holly.

"You don't have a thing to worry about, my dear. Gabe is perfectly safe with Jake."

"Aunt Holly!" Gabe raced to her side and Jake followed.

"You're in a lot of trouble, young man," she said sternly, hands on her hips.

Gabe hung his head. "I'm sorry," he whispered, his voice so low she could hardly hear it.

Customers thronged the toy department, several of them carrying the boxes that held the SuperRobot. A line had already formed at the customer service desk, and she noted that a couple of extra sales associates were out on the floor today. Everyone was busy.

"You'll have to come back to the office with me," Holly told Gabe. "I'm warning you it won't be nearly as much fun as it would've been with Jonathan and his mother."

"I know," he muttered. "Am I grounded?"

"We'll discuss that once we're home."

"Okay, but nothing happened…."

"You mean nothing other than the fact that you nearly gave me a heart attack."

Jake murmured a quick goodbye and started to leave to help a customer but Mrs. Miracle stopped him. "I'll take care of them," she said. "Besides, I believe there was something you wanted to ask Holly?"

"There was?" He looked surprised, wrinkling his brow as if he couldn't recall any such question.

"The Christmas party," Mrs. Miracle said under her breath. "You mentioned asking Holly to go with you."

Jake's mouth sagged open. "I'd thought about it, but I didn't realize I'd said it out loud." Now, instead of looking surprised, he seemed confused. "My father and I usually just make a token appearance."

"This year is different," the older woman insisted. "You need to be there for your staff. After all, the toy department's the busiest of the whole store at Christmastime. And," she continued sagely, "I predict record sales this year. Your staff needs to know you appreciate them."

"But…"

"I can't go," Holly said, resolving the issue. "There's no one to watch Gabe."

"Oh, but there is, my dear," Mrs. Miracle told her.

Holly frowned. Finding someone to stay with Gabe had always been a problem. She didn't want to impose on Caroline any more than she already did, especially since her neighbor wouldn't take any payment. With Jake they'd managed to work around it, which was easy enough, since Jake had mostly come to her apartment.

"I'll be more than happy to stay with Gabe while the two of you attend the party," Mrs. Miracle said.

It was generous of her to offer, but Holly couldn't accept. She shook her head. "You should be at the party yourself, Mrs. Miracle."

"Oh, heavens, no. After a full day on my feet I'll look forward to sitting in that comfy blue chair of yours. The one your parents gave you."

Before she could question how Mrs. Miracle knew about her chair, Jake asked, "Would you like to go to the party with me?" His eyes met hers, and she found herself nodding.

"Yes," she whispered. "When is it?"

"Wednesday night, after the store closes."

"Wednesday," she repeated.

"I'll pick you up at nine-thirty. I know that's late but—"

"I'll be ready."

"I'll come over a bit earlier," Mrs. Miracle added. "The two of you will have a *lovely* evening." She spoke with the utmost confidence, as if no other outcome was possible.

Holly and Gabe left a few minutes later, and Jake walked them to the elevator. "I'll see you Wednesday," he said as he pressed the button.

"Listen, Jake, you don't need to do this. I mean, it's fairly obvious you didn't intend to ask me and—"

"I'd really like it if you'd come to the party with me," he said, and she couldn't doubt his sincerity.

"Then I will," she murmured. "I'll look forward to it."

In the elevator, Holly remembered Mrs. Miracle's comment. The woman had never been to her apartment and yet somehow she knew about the chair her parents had given her. Furthermore, she seemed to know her address, too.

Oh, well. Gabe had probably told her. He obviously felt comfortable with the older woman and for that Holly could only be grateful.

Chapter Thirteen

Cars are not the only thing recalled by their maker.
—Mrs. Miracle

On Wednesday at nine-fifteen, Emily stood at Holly's door, her large purse draped over one arm and her knitting bag in the other hand. Holly answered, smiling in welcome. She absolutely sparkled. In her fancy black dress and high heels, her hair gathered up and held in place with a jeweled comb, she looked stunning.

"Mrs. Miracle, I can't thank you enough." Holly stepped aside so Emily could enter the apartment. "Tonight wouldn't be possible if not for you."

"The pleasure's all mine," she said. She put down her bags, then unwrapped the knitted scarf from around her neck and removed her heavy wool coat. Holly hung them in the hallway closet as Emily arranged her bags by the chair, prepared to settle down for the evening. The toy department had kept her busy all day and she was eager to get off her feet.

Holly followed her into the small living room. "I feel bad that you won't be attending the party."

"Oh, no, my dear." Emily dismissed her concern. "I'm not a party girl anymore." She chuckled at her own humor. "Besides, I intend to have a good visit here with my young friend Gabe."

"He's been pretty subdued since the episode on Monday. He's promised to be on his best behavior."

"Don't you worry. We'll have a grand time together." And they would.

"Hi, Mrs. Miracle."

She was surprised to see Jake standing on the other side of the room. He'd arrived early, she thought approvingly, and he looked quite debonair in his dark suit and red tie. She'd seen an improvement in his attitude toward Christmas, mostly due to Holly and Gabe. And she had it on excellent authority that it would improve even more before the actual holiday.

"Gabe's on the computer," Holly said, pointing at the alcove between the living room and kitchen. "He's had his dinner and he can stay up until ten tonight."

Gabe twisted around and waved.

Emily waved back. "I'll make sure he's in bed by ten."

Jake held Holly's coat and the young woman slipped her arms into the sleeves. "I appreciate your volunteering to watch Gabe," he said with a smile for Emily.

"As I told Holly, I'm delighted to do it." She walked over to where Gabe sat at the small desk and put her hand on his shoulder. "Now, you two go. Have fun."

Holly kissed the top of Gabe's head. "Be good."

"I will," the boy said without taking his eyes from the screen.

Holly and Jake left, and Emily had to grin as she glanced over Gabe's shoulder at the message he was emailing his father.

From: "Gabe Larson"<gabelarson@msm.com>
To: "Lieutenant Mickey Larson" <larsonmichael@goarmy.com>
Sent: December 22
Subject: Me and Aunt Holly

Hi, Dad,
I made Aunt Holly cry. Instead of going to Jonathan's house like I was supposed to, I went to see the robot. I was afraid the store would run out before Santa got my Intellytron. Aunt Holly came and picked me up and when we were outside she started to cry. When I asked her why she was crying she said it was because she was happy I was safe.
Are you mad at me? I wish Aunt Holly had gotten mad instead of crying. I felt awful inside and got a tummy ache. She took me back to her office and made me sit quiet all afternoon. But that was okay because I knew I didn't do the right thing. Her boss is real pretty. I don't think she's

around kids much because she talked to me like I was in kindergarten or something. I think she's nice, though. You said you had a gift coming for me for Christmas. It isn't here yet. I know I was bad, so you don't have to send it if you don't want. I'm sorry I made Aunt Holly cry.

Love,

Gabe

Emily sank down in the big comfortable chair, rested her feet on the matching ottoman and took out her knitting. She turned on the television and had just finished the first row when Gabe joined her. He didn't say anything for a long time, but Emily could see his mind working.

After a while he said, "My dad's going to be mad at me."

"It was brave of you to tell him you did something you weren't supposed to," she murmured.

Gabe looked away. "I told him he doesn't need to send me anything for Christmas. He said there was a special gift on the way but it hasn't come. He probably won't send it now."

"Don't be so sure." She pulled on the skein of yarn as she continued knitting.

"What if Santa finds out what I did?" His face crumpled in a frown. "Do you think maybe he won't bring me the robot 'cause I went to Finley's by myself and I didn't tell anyone where I was going?"

"Well, now, that remains to be seen, doesn't it?"

Gabe climbed onto the sofa and rested his head against

the arm. "I didn't think Aunt Holly would be so worried when I didn't go to Jonathan's house after school. She got all weird."

"Weird?"

"Yeah. When we were still at her office, all of a sudden she put her arms around my neck and hugged me really hard. Isn't that weird?"

Emily shrugged but didn't answer. "Are you ready for Christmas?" she asked instead.

Gabe nodded. "I made Aunt Holly an origami purse. A Japanese lady came to my school and showed us how to fold them. She said they were purses, but it looks more like a wallet to me, all flat and skinny." He sighed dejectedly. "I wrapped it up but you can't really see where the wrapping stops and the gift starts."

"I bet Holly will really like the purse because you made it yourself," Emily said with an encouraging smile.

"I made my dad a gift, too. But Aunt Holly and I mailed off his Christmas present a long time ago. They take days and days to get to Afghanistan so we had to go shopping before Thanksgiving and wrap up stuff for my dad. Oh, we mailed him the picture of me and Santa, too. And I made him a key ring. And I sent him nuts. My dad likes cashews. I've never seen a cashew in the shell, have you?"

"Why, yes, as a matter of fact I have," she said conversationally.

Gabe sat up. "What do they look like?"

"Well, a cashew is a rather unusual nut. My goodness, God

was so creative with that one. Did you know the cashew is both a fruit *and* a nut?"

"It is?"

"The fruit part looks like a small apple and it has a big stem."

The boy's eyes were wide with curiosity.

"The stem part is the nut, the cashew," she explained.

"Wow."

"And they're delicious," she said. "Good for you, too," she couldn't resist adding.

"What are you doing for Christmas?" Gabe asked.

"I've been invited to a party, a big one with lots of celebrating. I'll be with my friends Shirley, Goodness—"

"Goodness? That's a funny name."

"Yes, you're right. Anyway, the party preparations have already begun. It won't be long now."

"Oh." Gabe looked disappointed.

"Why the sad face?"

"I was going to ask you to come here for Christmas."

Emily was touched by his invitation. "I know you'll have a wonderful Christmas with Holly," she said.

"I invited Aunt Holly's boss, too."

She had to make an effort to hide her smile. This was all working out very nicely. Very nicely, indeed.

"Lindy didn't say she'd come for sure but she might." He paused. "She said to call her Lindy, not Ms. Lee like Aunt Holly said I should."

"Well, I hope she comes."

"Me, too. I think she's lonely."

"So do I," Emily agreed. The boy was very perceptive for his age, she thought.

"I asked her what she wants for Christmas and she said she didn't know. Can you *believe* that?"

In Emily's experience, many people walked through life completely unaware of what they wanted—or needed. "I brought along a book," she said, changing the subject. "Would you like to read it to me?" She'd put the children's book with its worn cover on the arm of her chair.

Gabe considered this. "I'm not in school now. Can you read it to me?"

"The way your dad used to when you were little?" she asked.

Gabe nodded eagerly. "I used to sit on his lap and he'd read me stories until I fell asleep." His face grew sad. "I miss my dad a lot."

"I know you do." Emily set aside her knitting. "Would you like to sit in my lap?"

"I'm too big for that," he insisted.

Emily could see that despite his words he was mulling it over. "You're not too big," she assured him.

Indecision showed on his face. Gabe wanted to snuggle with her, yet he hesitated because he was eight now and eight was too old for such things.

"What book did you bring?" he asked.

"It's a special one your grandma Larson once read to your dad and your aunt Holly."

"Really? How'd you know that?"

"Oh, I just do. It's the Christmas story."

"I like when the angels came to announce the birth of Baby Jesus to the shepherds."

She closed her eyes for a moment. "It was the most glorious night," she said. "The sky was bright and clear and—"

"And the angels sang," Gabe finished enthusiastically. "Angels have beautiful voices, don't they?"

"Yes, they do," Emily confirmed. "They make music we know nothing about here on earth…I'm sure," she added quickly. "Glorious, heavenly music."

"They do?" He cocked his head to one side.

"You'll hear it yourself one day, many years from now."

"What about you? When will you hear it?"

"Soon," she told him. He climbed into her lap and she held him close. He really was a sweet boy and would become a fine young man like his father. He'd be a wonderful brother to his half brother and half sister, as well—but she was getting ahead of herself.

"Tell me more about the angels," Gabe implored. "Is my mom an angel now?"

"No, sweetheart. Humans don't become angels. They're completely separate beings, although both were created by God."

"How come you know so much about angels?"

"I read my Bible," she said, and he seemed to accept her explanation.

"I never knew my mom," he said somberly. "Dad has pictures of her at the house, I look at her face and she smiles at me but I don't remember her."

"But you do understand that she loved you very much, right?"

"Dad said she did, and before she died she made him promise that he'd tell me every night how much she loved me."

"I know," she whispered.

"Do you think there are lots of angels in heaven?" Gabe asked.

"Oh, yes, and there are different kinds of angels, too."

"What kinds are there?"

"Well, they have a variety of different tasks. For instance, Gabriel came to Mary as a messenger. Other angels are warriors."

"When I get to heaven, I want to meet the warrior angels."

"And you shall."

"Do you think I was named after the angel Gabriel?" he asked.

Emily pressed her cheek against the top of his head, inhaling the clean, little-boy scent of his hair. "Now, that's something you'll need to ask your father when you see him."

"Okay, I will."

"Gabriel had one of the most important tasks ever assigned," Emily said. "He's the angel God sent to tell Mary about Baby Jesus."

He yawned. "Can people see angels?"

Emily's mouth quivered with a smile she couldn't quite suppress. "Oh, yes, but most people don't recognize them."

Gabe lifted his head. "How come?"

"Not all angels show their wings," she said.

"They don't?"

"No, some angels look like ordinary people."

"How come?"

"Well, sometimes God sends angels to earth. But if people saw their wings, they'd get all excited and they'd miss the lesson God wanted to teach them. That's why angels are often disguised."

"Are they always disguised?"

"No, some are invisible. Other times they look like ordinary people."

"Do angels only come to teach people a lesson?"

"No, they come to help, too."

Gabe yawned again. "How do angels help?"

"Oh, in too many ways to count."

He thought about that for a while, his eyelids beginning to droop.

"Are you ready for me to read you the story?" Emily asked.

"Sure." He rested his head against her shoulder as she opened the book. She read for a few minutes before she noticed that Gabe had fallen asleep. And she hadn't even gotten to the good part.

Chapter Fourteen

When you flee temptation,
don't leave a forwarding address.
—Shirley, Goodness and Mercy,
friends of Mrs. Miracle

The Christmas party was well under way by the time Holly and Jake arrived. When they entered the gala event, the entire room seemed to go still. Holly kept her arm in Jake's, self-conscious about being the center of attention.

"Why's everyone looking at us?" she whispered.

Jake patted her hand reassuringly. "My father and I usually show up toward the end of the party, say a few words and then leave. No one expected me this early."

He'd mentioned that before. Still, she hadn't realized his arrival would cause such a stir. Jake immediately began to walk through the room, shaking hands and introducing Holly. At first she tried to keep track of the names, but soon gave up. She was deeply impressed by Jake's familiarity with the staff.

"How do you remember all their names?" she asked when she had a chance.

"I've worked with them in each department," he explained. "My father felt I needed to know the retail business from the mail room up."

"You started in the mail room?"

"I did, but don't for a minute consider the mail room unimportant. I made that mistake and quickly learned how vital it is."

"Your father is a wise man."

"He is," Jake said. "And a generous one, too. But he'd describe himself as *fair*. He's always recognized the value of hiring good people and keeping them happy. I believe it's why we've managed to hold on to the company despite several attempts to buy us out."

It went without saying that Jake intended to follow his father's tradition of treating employees with respect and compensating them generously.

Ninety minutes later Holly's head buzzed with names and faces. They sipped champagne and got supper from the buffet; the food was delicious. Numerous people commented happily on seeing Jake at the party.

His father appeared at about midnight and immediately sought out his son and Holly.

"So this is the young lady you've talked about," J. R. Finley said, slapping Jake jovially on the back.

"Dad, meet Holly Larson."

J.R. shook her hand. "I'm pleased to meet you, young lady. You've made a big impression on my son."

Holly glanced at Jake and smiled. "He's made a big impression on me."

J. R. Finley turned to his son. "When did you get here?"

"Before ten," Jake said.

His father frowned, then moved toward the microphone. As was apparently his practice, he gave a short talk, handed out dozens of awards and bonuses and promptly left.

The party wound down after J.R.'s speech. People started to leave, but almost every employee, singly and in groups, approached Jake to thank him for attending the party. Holly couldn't tell how their gratitude affected Jake, but it had a strong impact on her.

"They love you," she said when they went to collect their coats.

"They're family," Jake said simply.

She noticed that he didn't say Finley's employees were *like* family but that they *were* family. The difference was subtle but significant. J.R. had lost his wife and daughter and had turned to his friends and employees to fill the huge hole left by the loss of his loved ones. Jake had, too.

As they stepped outside, Holly was thrilled by the falling snow. "Jake, look!" She held out her hand to catch the soft flakes that floated down from the night sky. "It's just so beautiful!"

Jake wrapped his scarf more securely around his neck. "I can't believe you're so excited about a little snow."

"I love it…. It's so Christmassy."

He grinned and clasped her hand. "Do you want to go for a short walk?"

"I'd love to." It was cold, but even without boots or gloves or a hat, Holly felt warm, and more than that, *happy*.

"Where would you like to go?" Jake asked.

"Wherever you'd like to take me." Late though it was, she didn't want the night to end. Lindy Lee had never thrown a Christmas party for her staff. Maybe she'd talk to Lindy about planning one for next December; she could discuss the benefits—employee satisfaction and loyalty, which would lead to higher productivity. Those were the terms Lindy would respond to. Not appreciation or enjoyment or fun. Having worked with Lindy as long as she had, Holly suspected her employer wasn't a happy person. And she wasn't someone who cared about the pleasure of others.

"I thought this would be a miserable Christmas," Holly confessed, leaning close to Jake as they moved down the busy sidewalk. They weren't the only couple reveling in the falling snow.

"Why?" Jake asked. "Because of your brother?"

"Well, yes. It's also the first Christmas without my parents, and then Mickey got called up for Afghanistan so there's just Gabe and me."

"What changed?"

"A number of things, actually," she said. "Meeting you, of course."

"Thank you." He bent down and touched his lips to hers in the briefest of kisses.

"My attitude," she said. "I was worried that Gabe would resent living with me. For months we didn't really bond."

"You have now, though, haven't you?"

"Oh, yes. I didn't realize how much I loved him until he went missing the other day. I…I don't normally panic, but I did then."

Holly was still surprised by how accommodating her employer had been during and after that crisis. First Lindy Lee had allowed Gabe to come to the office and then she'd actually chatted with him. Holly didn't know what the two of them had talked about, but her employer had seemed almost pleasant afterward.

"Remember the other night when you and Gabe decorated your Christmas tree?" Jake asked.

"Of course."

"Gabe asked me about mine."

"Right." It'd been an awkward moment. Gabe had been full of questions. He couldn't understand why some people chose not to make Christmas part of their lives. No tree. No presents. No family dinner. The closest Jake and his father got to celebrating the holidays was their yearly sojourn to the Virgin Islands.

Holly knew this was his father's way of ignoring the holiday. Jake and J.R. left on Christmas Eve and didn't return until after New Year's.

She was sure they'd depart sooner if they could. The only reason they stayed in New York as long as they did was because of the business. The holiday season made their year financially. Without the last-quarter sales, many retailers would struggle to survive. Finley's Department Store was no different.

"You told Gabe you didn't put up a tree," Holly reminded him.

"I might've misled him."

"You have a tree?" After everything he'd said, that shocked her.

"You'll see." His stride was purposeful as they continued walking. She soon figured out where they were headed.

"I can't wait," she said with a laugh.

When they reached Rockefeller Center, they stood gazing up at the huge Christmas tree, bright with thousands of lights and gleaming decorations. Jake gestured toward it. "*That's* my Christmas tree," he said.

"Gabe's going to be jealous that I got to see it again—with you."

Music swirled all around them as Jake slipped his arm about her waist. "When I was young, I found it hard to give up the kind of Christmas I'd known when my mother and sister were alive. Dad refused to have anything to do with the holidays but I still wanted the tree and the gifts."

Holly hadn't fully grasped how difficult those years must've been for him.

"Dad said if I wanted a Christmas tree, I could pick one in the store and make it my own. Better yet, I could claim the one in Rockefeller Center and that's what I did."

Instinctively she knew Jake had never shared this information with anyone else.

"Well, you've got the biggest, most beautiful Christmas tree in the city," she said, leaning her head against his shoulder.

"I do," he murmured.

"Jake," she said carefully. "Would you consider having Christmas dinner with Gabe and me?"

He didn't answer, and she wondered if she'd crossed some invisible line by issuing the invitation. Nevertheless she had to ask.

"I know that would mean not joining your father when he leaves for the Caribbean, but you could fly out the next day, couldn't you?" Holly felt she needed to press the issue. If he was ever going to agree, it would be tonight, after he'd witnessed how much it meant to Finley's employees that he'd attended their party.

"I could fly out later," he said. "But then I'd be leaving my father alone on the saddest day of his life."

"I'd like to invite him, too."

Jake's smile was somber and poignant. "He'll never come, Holly. He hates anything to do with Christmas—outside of the business, anyway."

"Maybe so, but I'd still like to ask him." She wasn't sure why she couldn't simply drop this. It took audacity to invite two wealthy men to her small apartment, when their alternative was an elaborate meal in an exotic location.

She was embarrassed now. "I apologize, Jake. I don't know what made me think you'd want to give up the sunshine and warmth of a Caribbean island for dinner with me and Gabe."

"Don't say that! I want to be with you both."

"But you don't feel you can leave your father."

"That's true, but maybe it's time I started creating traditions of my own. I'd be honored to spend Christmas Day with the two of you," he said formally.

Holly felt tears spring to her eyes. "Thank you," she whispered.

She turned to face him. He smiled as she slid her hands up his chest and around his neck. Standing on the tips of her toes with a light snow falling down on them, she pressed her mouth to his.

Jake held her tight. Holly sensed that they'd crossed a barrier in their relationship and established a real commitment to each other.

"When I come, I'll bring the robot for Gabe and hide it under the tree so it'll be a real surprise."

"I'll give you the money on Friday—Christmas Eve."

Christmas Eve.

"Okay." She knew he'd rather not take it, but there was no question—she had every intention of paying.

Jake called his car service, and a limousine met them at Rockefeller Center fifteen minutes later. When he dropped her off at the apartment Mrs. Miracle was sound asleep, still in the blue chair. Jake helped her out to the car, then had the driver take her home. Holly was touched by his thoughtfulness.

Even after Jake had left, Holly had trouble falling asleep. Her mind whirled as she relived scenes and moments of what had been one of the most memorable evenings of her life. When the alarm woke her early Thursday morning, she couldn't get up and just dozed off again. She finally roused herself, horrified to discover that she was almost half an hour behind schedule.

She managed to drag herself out of bed, gulp down a cup of coffee and get Gabe up and dressed and over to the Krantzes'.

Filled with dread, Holly rushed to work. As she yanked off her coat, she heard her name being called. Breathless, she flew into Lindy Lee's office; as usual, Lindy looked pointedly at her watch.

Holly tried to apologize. "I'm sorry I'm late. I'll make up the twenty-five minutes, I promise."

Lindy Lee raised one eyebrow. "Make sure you do."

Holly stood waiting for the lecture that inevitably followed. To her astonishment, this time it didn't. "Thank you for understanding."

"See to it that this doesn't happen again," her employer said, dismissing Holly with a wave of her hand.

"It won't…I just couldn't seem to get moving this morning." Thinking she'd probably said too much already, she started to leave, then remembered her resolve to discuss a Christmas party with Lindy Lee.

Aware that Holly was lingering, Lindy Lee raised her head and frowned. "Was there something else?"

"Well, yes. Do you mind if I speak freely?"

"That depends on what you have to say." Lindy Lee held her pen poised over a sheet of paper.

"I was at the employees' party for Finley's Department Store last evening," she said, choosing her words carefully.

"It was a wonderful event. The employees work together as a team and…and they feel such loyalty to the company. You could just tell. They feel valued, and I doubt there's anything they wouldn't do to help the company succeed."

"And your point is?" Lindy Lee said impatiently.

"My point is we all need to work as a team here, too, and it seemed to me that maybe we should have a Christmas party."

Lindy Lee leaned back in her chair and crossed her arms. "In a faltering economy, with flat sales and an uncertain future, you want me to throw a *Christmas party?*"

"It's…it's just an idea for next year," Holly said, and regretted making the suggestion. Still, she couldn't seem to stop. "The future is always uncertain, isn't it? And there'll always be ups and downs in the economy. But the one constant is the fact that as long as you're in business you'll have a staff, right? And you need them to be committed and—"

"I get it," Lindy Lee said dryly.

Holly waited.

And waited.

"Let me think about it," Lindy Lee finally mumbled.

She'd actually agreed to think about it. Now, this was progress—more progress than Holly had dared to expect.

Chapter Fifteen

The best vitamin for a Christian is B1.
—Mrs. Miracle

Jake Finley was in love. Logically, he knew, it was too soon to be so sure of his feelings, and yet he couldn't deny his heart. Love wasn't about logic. He'd been attracted to Holly from the moment he met her, but this was more than attraction. He felt…connected to Holly, absorbed in her. He thought about her constantly. Over the years he'd been in other relationships, but no woman had made him feel the way Holly did.

When he arrived at work Thursday morning, he went directly to his father's office. Dora Coffey seemed surprised to see him.

"Is my father in yet?" Jake asked her.

"Yes, he's been here for a couple of hours. You know your father—this store is his life."

"Does he have time to see me?" Jake asked next. "No meetings or conference calls?"

"He's free for a few minutes." She left her desk and announced Jake, who trailed behind her.

When Jake entered the office, his father stood. "Good morning, son. What can I do for you?" He gestured for Jake to take a seat, which he did, and settled back in his own chair.

Jake leaned forward, unsure where to start. He should've worked out what he was going to say before coming up here.

"I suppose you want to gloat." J.R. chuckled. "You were right about that robot. Hardly anyone else forecast this trend. I turned on the TV this morning and there was a story on Telly the SuperRobot. Hottest toy of the season, they said. Who would've guessed it? Not me, that's for sure."

"Not Mike Scott, either," Jake added, although he didn't fault the buyer.

"True enough. And yet Mike was the first to admit he didn't see this coming."

So Scott had mentioned it to J.R. but not to him. Still, it must've taken real humility to acknowledge that he'd been wrong.

"I'm proud of you, son," J.R. continued. "You went with your gut and you were right to do it."

Jake wondered what would've happened if Finley's had been stuck with four hundred leftover robots. Fortunately, however, he wouldn't have to find out.

"I checked inventory this morning, and we have less than twenty of the robots in stock."

Jake didn't need to point out the benefits of being the only store in the tristate area with *any* robots in stock. Having a supply—even a rapidly dwindling supply—of the season's most popular toy brought more shoppers into the store and created customer loyalty.

"They're selling fast. The entire quantity will be gone before Christmas."

"Good. Good," his father said. He grinned as he tilted back in his high leather chair. "Oh, I enjoyed meeting your lady friend last night."

"Holly enjoyed meeting you."

"She's special, isn't she?"

Jake was astonished that his father had immediately discerned his feelings for Holly. "Yes, but… What makes you say that?" He had to ask why it had been so obvious to his father.

J.R. didn't respond for a moment. Finally he said, "I recognized it from the way you looked at her. The way you looked at each other."

Jake nodded but didn't speak.

"I remember when I met your mother." There was a faraway expression in his eyes. "I think I fell in love with Helene as soon as I saw her. She was the daughter of one of my competitors and so beautiful I had trouble getting out a complete sentence. It's a wonder she ever agreed to that first date." He smiled at the memory.

So rarely did his father discuss his mother and sister that

Jake kept quiet, afraid that any questions would distract J.R. He craved details, but knew he had to be cautious.

"I loved your mother more than life itself. I still do."

"I know," Jake said softly.

"She wasn't just beautiful," he murmured, and the same faraway look stole over him. "She had a heart unlike anyone I've ever known. Everyone came to her when they needed something, whether it was a kind word, a job, some advice. She never turned anyone away." His face, so often tense, relaxed as he sighed. "I felt that my world ended the day your mother and Kaitlyn died. Since then you've been my only reason for going on."

"Well, I hope your grandchildren will be another good reason," Jake teased, hoping to lighten the moment.

J.R. gave a hearty laugh. "They certainly will. So…I was right about you and Holly."

"It's too early to say for sure," Jake hedged. Confident though he was about his own feelings, he didn't want to speak for Holly. Not yet…

"But you *know*."

"It looks…promising."

Slapping the top of his desk, J.R. laughed again. "I thought so. I'm happy for you, Jake."

"Thanks, Dad." But he doubted J.R. would be as happy when he found out what that meant, at least as far as Christmas was concerned.

"Oh, before I forget," J.R. said with exquisite timing. "Dora's ordered the plane tickets for Christmas Eve. We leave JFK at seven and land in Saint John around—"

"Dad, I'll need to change my ticket," Jake said, interrupting his father.

That brought J.R. up short. "Change your ticket? Why?"

"I'll join you on the twenty-sixth," Jake explained. "Holly invited me to spend Christmas Day with her and her nephew."

J.R.'s frown was back as he mulled over that statement. "You're going to do it?"

"Yes. I told her I would."

J.R. stood and walked to the window, turning his back to Jake. "I don't know what to say."

"Holly invited you, too."

"You told her it was out of the question, didn't you?"

More or less. "You'd be welcome if you chose to come."

Slowly J.R. turned around. "Well," he said with a sigh, "I suppose it was unrealistic of me not to realize times are changing." He paused. "I look forward to our vacation every year."

Jake had never thought of their trip to the Caribbean as a getaway. His father always brought work with him and they spent their week discussing trends, reading reports and forecasting budgets. It was business, not relaxation.

"You call it a *vacation?*" Jake asked, amused.

"Well, yes. What would you call it?" J.R. frowned in confusion.

Jake hesitated, then decided to tell the truth, even if his father wasn't ready to hear it. "I call it an escape from reality—but not from work. A vacation is supposed to be fun, a break, a chance to do nothing or else do something completely out of the ordinary. Not sit in a hotel room and do exactly the same thing you'd be doing here."

J.R.'s frown deepened.

"Admit it, Dad," Jake said. "You don't go to the islands to lounge on the beach or snorkel or take sightseeing trips. Far from it. You escape New York because you can't bear to be here over Christmas."

J.R. shook his head.

Jake wasn't willing to let it go. "From the time Mom and Kaitlyn died, you've done everything possible to pretend there's no Christmas.

"As a businessman you need the holidays to survive financially but if it wasn't for that, you'd ban anything to do with Christmas from your life—and mine."

J.R. glared at Jake. "I believe you've said enough."

"You need to accept that Christmas had nothing to do with the accident. It happened, and it changed both our lives forever, but it was a fluke, a twist of fate. I wish with everything in me that Mom and Kaitlyn had stayed home that afternoon, but the fact is, they didn't. They went out, and because their cab collided with another one, they were killed."

"Enough!" J.R. shouted.

Jake stood. "I didn't mean to upset you, Dad."

"If that's the case, then you've failed. I *am* upset."

Jake regretted that; nevertheless, he felt this had to be said. "I'm tired of running away on Christmas Eve. You can do it if you want, but I'm through."

"Fine. Spend the day with Holly if you prefer. It's not going to bother me."

"I wish you'd reconsider and join us."

J.R. tightened his lips. "No, thanks. You might think I'm hiding my head in the sand, but the truth is, I enjoy the islands."

Jake might have believed him if J.R. had walked along the beach even once or taken any pleasure in their surroundings. Instead, he worked from early morning to late evening, burying himself in his work in a desperate effort to ignore the time of year—the anniversary of his loss.

"Yes, Dad," Jake said rather than allow their discussion to escalate into a full-scale argument.

"You'll come the next day, then?"

Jake nodded. He'd make his own flight arrangements. They always stayed at the same four-star hotel, the same suite of rooms.

"Good."

Jake left the office and hurried down to the toy department. He was surprised to see Mrs. Miracle on the floor. According to the schedule she wasn't even supposed to be in. That was his decision; since she'd volunteered to watch Gabe, he'd given her the day off.

"I didn't expect to see you this morning," he said.

"Oh, I thought I'd come in and do a bit of shopping myself."

"I didn't realize you had grandchildren," he said. In fact, he knew next to nothing about Mrs. Miracle's personal life, including her address. He'd offered to have the driver take her home and she'd agreed, but only on the condition that he be dropped off first. For some reason, he had the impression that she lived close to the store....

"So how'd the meeting with your father go?" she asked, disregarding his remark about grandchildren.

"How did you know that's where I was?" Jake asked, peering at her suspiciously.

"I didn't, but you looked so concerned, I guessed it had to do with J.R."

"It went fine," he said, unwilling to reveal the details of his conversation with an employee, even if she'd become a special friend. He didn't plan to mention it to Holly, either. All he'd say was that he'd extended the dinner invitation to his father and J.R. had thanked her but sent his regrets.

"I'm worried about J.R.," Mrs. Miracle said, again surprising him.

"Why? He's in good health."

"Physically, yes, he's doing well for a man of his age."

"Then why are you worried?" Jake pressed.

Instead of answering, the older woman patted his back. "I'm leaving in a few minutes. Would you like me to wrap Gabe's robot before I go?"

"Ah, sure," he said.

"You *are* taking it with you when you go to Holly's for Christmas, aren't you?"

"Yes."

"Then I'll wrap it for you. I'll get some ribbon and nice paper from the gift-wrapping kiosk."

"Thank you," Jake said, still wondering what she'd meant about J.R.

The older woman disappeared, leaving Jake standing in the toy department scratching his head. He valued Mrs. Miracle as an employee and as a new friend, and yet every now and then she'd say something that totally confused him. How did she know so much about him and his father? Perhaps she'd met his parents years ago. Or...

Well, he couldn't waste time trying to figure it out now.

Jake was walking to the customer service counter when his cell phone rang. Holly. He answered immediately.

"Can you talk?" she asked. "I know it's probably insane at the store, but I had to tell you something."

"What is it? Everything okay?"

"It's my boss, Lindy Lee. Oh, Jake, I think I'm going to cry."

"What's wrong?" he asked, alarmed.

"Nothing. This is *good*. Lindy just called me into her office. I spoke with her this morning about a Christmas party. I saw what a great time your employees had. I thought it would help morale, so I mentioned it to Lindy Lee."

"She's going to have a party?"

"No, even better than that. I can have a real Christmas dinner now with a turkey and stuffing and all the extras like I originally planned. I...I'd decided to make fried chicken because I couldn't really afford anything else, and now I can prepare a traditional meal."

"You got your bonus?"

"Yes! And it's bigger than last year's, so I can pay for the robot now."

"That's fabulous news!"

"It is, Jake, it really is." She took a deep breath. "If you don't mind, I'd like to call your father and invite him personally."

Jake's smile faded. "I should tell you I already talked to Dad about joining us on Christmas Day."

"I hope he will."

"Don't count on it." Jake felt bad about discouraging her. "I think he'd like to, but he can't let go of his grief. He feels he'd dishonor the memory of my mother and sister if he celebrated Christmas. For him, their deaths and Christmas are all tied together."

"Oh, Jake, that's so sad."

"Yes…" He didn't say what he knew was obvious—that, until now, the same thing had been true of him.

"I'm looking forward to spending the day with you," Jake said, and he meant every word. "Can you meet me for lunch this afternoon?" he asked, not sure he could wait until Christmas to see her again.

When she agreed, he smiled, a smile so wide that several customers looked at him curiously…and smiled back.

Chapter Sixteen

Happiest are the people who give
the most happiness to others.
—Mrs. Miracle

That same morning Lindy Lee called Holly into her office again. Saving the document she was working on, Holly grabbed a pad and pen and rushed inside. Gesturing toward the chair, Lindy invited her to sit. This was unusual in itself; Lindy Lee never went out of her way to make Holly comfortable. In fact, it was generally the opposite.

"I've given your suggestion some thought," she said crisply.

"You mean about the Christmas party for next year?"

Lindy Lee's eyes narrowed. "Of course I mean the Christmas party. I want you to organize one for tomorrow."

"*Tomorrow?* But—"

"No excuses. *You're* the one who asked for this."

"I'll need a budget," Holly said desperately. It was a little late to be organizing a party. Every caterer in New York would've been booked months ago. Finding a restaurant with an opening the day before Christmas would be hopeless. What was she thinking when she'd suggested the idea to Lindy Lee? Hadn't she emphasized that she was talking about the *following* year? Not this one? Holly hardly knew where to start.

Lindy Lee glared at her. "I'm aware that you'll require a budget. Please wait until I'm finished. You can ask your questions then."

"Okay, sorry." Holly wasn't sure how she was supposed to manage this on such short notice.

Lindy explained that she'd close the office at two, that she wanted festive decorations and Christmas music, and that attendance was mandatory. "You can bring your nephew if you like," she added, after setting a more than generous budget.

"In other words, the family of staff is included?"

"Good grief, no."

"But Gabe's family."

"He's adorable. He even—" Lindy Lee stopped abruptly.

Holly was in complete agreement about Gabe's cuteness, but it wouldn't go over well if Gabe was invited and no one else's children were. "The others might get upset," Holly said, broaching the subject cautiously. "I mean, if I bring Gabe and no other children are allowed, it might look bad."

Lindy Lee sat back and crossed her arms, frowning. "If we invite family, then the place will be overrun with the little darlings," she muttered sarcastically. She sighed. "*Should* we include them?"

Holly shook her head. "There are too many practical considerations. People with kids would have to go home and pick them up and… Well, I think it's too much trouble, so let's not."

"Okay," Lindy said with evident relief.

"I'll get right on this."

"You might invite Gabe to the office again," Lindy Lee shocked her by saying. "Maybe in the new year."

Holly wondered if she'd misunderstood. "You want me to bring Gabe into the office?"

"A half day perhaps," her boss said, amending her original thought.

"Okay." So Gabe had succeeded in charming Lindy Lee, something Holly had once considered impossible.

Lindy Lee turned back to her computer, effectively dismissing Holly. Head whirling with the difficulty of her assignment, Holly returned to her own desk. She immediately got a list of nearby restaurants and began making calls, all of which netted quick rejections. In fact, the people she spoke with nearly laughed her off the phone. By noon she was growing desperate and worried.

"How's it going?" Lindy Lee asked as she stepped out of her office to meet someone for lunch. "Don't answer. I can tell by the look on your face."

"If only we'd scheduled the party a bit sooner…"

"You shouldn't have waited until the last minute to spring it on me," she said, laying the blame squarely on Holly.

That seemed unfair and a little harsh, even for Lindy Lee.

"We could have our event here in the building," Lindy Lee suggested, apparently relenting. "The sixth floor has a big open space. Check with them and see if that's available."

"I'll do it right away."

"Good," Lindy said, and turned to leave.

"I'll make this party happen," Holly promised through gritted teeth.

"I'll hold you to that," Lindy Lee tossed over her shoulder on her way out the door.

As soon as she'd left, Holly called the sixth floor. As luck would have it, the only time available was the afternoon of Christmas Eve—exactly what she needed. That solved one problem, but there was still an equally large hurdle to jump. Finding a caterer.

Despite the urgency of this task, Holly kept her lunch date with Jake. These last days before Christmas made getting away for more than a few minutes difficult for him. Yet he managed with the help of his staff who, according to Jake, were determined to smooth the course of romance. Mrs. Miracle, God bless her, had spearheaded the effort.

Holly picked up a pastrami on rye at the deli and two coffees, and walked to Finley's; that was all they really had time for. Now that she'd been assured of her Christmas bonus, Holly had resumed the luxury of buying lunch. When she arrived at the store, white bag in hand, Jake was busy with a customer.

Mrs. Miracle saw her and came over to greet Holly. "My dear, what's wrong?"

Once again Holly was surprised at how readable she must be. "I'm on an impossible mission," she said.

"And what's that?" the older woman asked.

Holly explained. As soon as she'd finished, Mrs. Miracle smiled. "I believe I can help you."

"You can?" she asked excitedly.

"Yes, a friend of mine just opened a small restaurant in the Village. She's still getting herself established, but she'd certainly be capable of handling this party. What are you planning to serve? Sandwiches? Appetizers? Cookies? That sort of thing?"

"The party will be in the early afternoon, so small sandwiches and cookies would be perfect. It doesn't have to be elaborate." At this point she'd accept almost anything.

"I'll get you my friend's number."

"Yes, please, and, Mrs. Miracle, thank you so much."

"No problem, my dear. None whatsoever." The older woman beamed her a smile. "By the way, I've set up a table in the back of the storeroom for you and Jake to have your lunch."

"How thoughtful."

"You go on back and Jake'll be along any minute. Meanwhile, I'll get you that phone number."

"Thanks," she said again. "Could you tell me your friend's name?"

"It's Wendy," she said. "Now don't you worry about a thing, you hear?"

Feeling deeply relieved, Holly went to the storeroom. Sure enough, Mrs. Miracle had set up a card table, complete with a white tablecloth and a small poinsettia in the middle. Holly put down the sandwich, plus a couple of pickles and the two cups of coffee.

Jake came in a few minutes later, looking harassed. He kissed her, then took his place. "It's crazy out there," he said, slumping in his chair.

"I can tell." She noticed that the rest of the staff was diligently avoiding the storeroom, no doubt under orders from Mrs. Miracle.

He reached for his half of the massive sandwich. "I sold the last of the robots this morning."

"That's wonderful!"

"It is and it isn't," he said between bites. "I wish I'd ordered another hundred. We could've sold those, as well. Now we have to turn people away. I hate disappointing anyone."

"Is there any other store in town with inventory?"

"Nope, and believe me, I've checked. Another shipment is due in a week after Christmas but by then it'll be too late."

Holly hated to bring up the subject of Gabe's Intellytron, but she needed Jake's reassurance that the one he'd set aside hadn't been sold in the robot-buying frenzy. "You still have Gabe's, don't you?"

Still chewing on his sandwich, Jake nodded. "Mrs. Miracle wrapped it herself. It's sitting right over there." He pointed to a counter across from her. The large, brightly decorated package rested in one corner.

"I'm so grateful you did this for me," she told him. Meeting

Jake had been one of the greatest blessings of the year—in so many ways.

"Thank Mrs. Miracle, too," he said. "She wasn't even supposed to be in today, but she ended up staying to help us out."

The few minutes they'd grabbed flew by much too quickly. Jake stood, kissed her again, and they left the storeroom together. As they stepped onto the floor, Mrs. Miracle handed her a slip of paper. "The name of the restaurant is Heavenly Delights and here's the number."

"Heavenly Delights," Holly repeated. "I'll give your friend a call as soon as I'm back at my desk."

"You do that."

Holly tucked the paper in her coat pocket and nearly danced all the way to the office. With a little help from Mrs. Miracle, she'd be able to pull off a miracle of her own—she'd organize this Christmas party, regardless of the difficulties and challenges.

Once at her desk, Holly reached for the phone and called the number Mrs. Miracle had written down for her.

"Hello." A woman answered on the third ring.

"Hello," Holly returned brightly. "Is this Wendy?"

"Yes. And you are?"

"I'm Holly Larson, and I'm phoning on behalf of Lindy Lee."

"Lindy Lee, the designer?" Wendy sounded impressed.

"Yes," Holly answered. "I know I'm probably calling at the worst time, but I felt I should contact you as soon as possible." She assumed the restaurant would be busy with the lunch crowd.

"No, no, this is fine."

"I was given your phone number by Emily Miracle."

"Who?"

"Oh, sorry. Her badge says Miracle, but that's a mistake. Rather than cause a fuss, she asked that we call her Mrs. Miracle, although that's not actually her name. I apologize, but I can't remember what it is. I'm so accustomed to calling her Mrs. Miracle." Holly hoped she wasn't rambling.

"Go on," Wendy urged without commenting on all the confusion about names.

"Long story short, she suggested I call you about catering Lindy Lee's Christmas party for her employees."

"She did?"

"Yes… She highly recommended you and the restaurant."

"What restaurant?"

"Heavenly Delights," Holly said. Wendy must own more than one. "The location in the Village."

"Heavenly Delights," Wendy gasped, then started to laugh. "Heavenly Delights?"

"Yes." Holly's spirits took a sharp dive; nevertheless, she forged ahead. "I'm wondering if you could work us into your schedule."

"Oh, dear."

Holly's spirits sank even further. "You can't do it?"

"I didn't say that."

Her emotions went from hopeful to disheartened and back again. "Then you could?"

"I…I don't know what to say." The woman seemed completely overwhelmed.

Yes, I can do it would certainly make Holly's day, but the words weren't immediately forthcoming.

"Unfortunately, the party's scheduled for tomorrow afternoon—Christmas Eve." Holly suspected that, by then, practically everyone in the restaurant business would be closing down and heading home to their families. As an incentive, she mentioned the amount she could offer. The catering would take up most of the budget, with a little left over for decorations.

"That sounds fair," Wendy said.

"Would you be able to accommodate us?" she asked hopefully. "We're talking about forty people, give or take."

"I…"

Holly closed her eyes, fearing the worst.

"I think I could. However, there's something you should know."

"What's that?"

"First, I can't imagine who this Mrs. Miracle is."

"As I said, that isn't her real name. But I can find out for you, if you like."

"No, it doesn't matter. What I wanted to tell you is that I don't have a restaurant."

"No restaurant?" Holly's mouth went dry.

"The thing is, I've been talking with my daughter about opening one. She's attending culinary school. I've been praying about it, too. However, a lot of problems stand in the way—one of which is money."

"Oh."

"When I applied for a loan, the bank officer asked me what we intended to call the restaurant. Lucie and I have gone over dozens of names and nothing felt right. Our specialty would be desserts…. I like the name Heavenly Delights. If you don't mind, I'll borrow it."

"I… That's the name Mrs. Miracle gave me."

"Well, if *she* doesn't mind, we'll definitely use it." She paused. "Maybe I know her, but right now I can't figure out who she is."

"Um, so if you don't have a restaurant yet, you can't cater the event?"

"I can't," Wendy agreed. "But perhaps Lucie and her friends from culinary school could."

"Really?" Holly asked excitedly.

"Give me your number and I'll call her to see if we can make this happen."

"Great!"

Holly fidgeted until Wendy called back five minutes later. "We'll do it," Wendy told her. "Lucie talked to several of her colleagues and they're all interested. I can promise you'll *love* their menu. Lucie's already working on it."

"Fabulous. Thank you! Oh, thank you so much." Her relief was so great that she felt like weeping.

She disconnected just as Lindy returned from lunch

"The party's all set," Holly said happily.

"Really?" She'd impressed Lindy Lee, which was no small feat.

"Christmas Eve from two to four."

Her employer nodded. "Good job, Holly."

Holly closed her eyes and basked in the glow of Lindy Lee's approval.

Chapter Seventeen

We don't change God's message.
His message changes us.
—Mrs. Miracle

Jake glanced at his watch and felt a surge of relief. Five-thirty on Christmas Eve; in half an hour, the store would close its doors for the season.

Finley's would open again on the twenty-sixth for the year-end frenzy. He felt good that toy sales for this quarter were twenty percent higher than the previous year. He attributed the boost in revenue to Intellytron the SuperRobot. Jake felt vindicated that his hunch had been proven right. He'd be proud to take these latest figures to his father. While the robot alone didn't explain the increase, the fact that it was available at Finley's had brought new customers into the store.

Holly was occupied with her boss and the Christmas party,

which she'd arranged for Lindy Lee at the last moment. The poor girl had worked herself into a nervous state to pull off the event, and Jake was confident that the afternoon had gone well. He knew Holly had obsessed over each and every detail.

No doubt exhausted, she'd go home to her Brooklyn apartment as soon as she was finished with the cleanup. Jake would come by later that evening to spend time with her and Gabe. The three of them would enjoy a quiet dinner and then attend Christmas Eve services at her church.

It felt strangely luxurious not to be rushing away from the city with his father, although Jake was saddened that he hadn't been able to convince J.R. to join them on Christmas Day.

His cell chirped, and even before he looked, Jake knew it was Holly.

"Hi," he said. "How'd the party go?"

"Great! Wonderful. Even Lindy Lee was pleased. The caterers did a fabulous job, above and beyond my expectations. Wendy told me that Heavenly Delights plans to specialize in desserts and they should. Everything was spectacular."

"I'm glad."

"Don't forget to bring over Gabe's gift tonight," she said in a tired voice. As he'd expected, Holly was worn out.

"Sure thing."

"We'll hide it in my bedroom until he goes to sleep, and then we can put it under the tree. That way it'll be the first thing he sees Christmas morning."

"Sounds like a plan."

"I'll distract him when you arrive so you can shove it in my closet."

"Okay."

She hesitated. "Are you sure you can't talk your father into coming for Christmas dinner?"

"I don't think so, Holly. He isn't ready to give up his... vacation." He nearly choked on the word.

"Ask him again, would you?" she said softly.

"I will," he agreed with some reluctance, knowing it wouldn't have any effect.

"And thank Mrs. Miracle for me. She saved the day with this recommendation."

"Of course. Although I believe she's already left."

"She'll be back, won't she?"

"As seasonal help, she'll stay on until the end of January when we finish inventory." The older woman had been a real success in the department. She'd reassured parents and entertained their kids. If she was interested, Jake would like to offer her full-time employment.

He ended his conversation with Holly and went into the storeroom to pick up Gabe's robot.

He stopped short. The package that had lain on the counter, the package so beautifully wrapped by Mrs. Miracle, was missing.

Gone.

"Karen," Jake said, walking directly past a customer to confront one of the other sales associates. If this was a practical joke, he was not amused. "Where's the robot that was on the counter in the storeroom?" he demanded, ignoring the last-minute shopper she was assisting.

Karen blinked as though he was speaking in a foreign language. "I beg your pardon?"

"The wrapped gift in the storage room?" he repeated.

"I...I don't have a clue."

"You know what I'm talking about, don't you?"

Her face became flushed. "I'm not sure."

"It was wrapped and ready for delivery and now it's missing." Jake couldn't believe anyone would steal the robot. He knew his employees, and there wasn't a single one who was capable of such a deed. He'd stake his career on it.

"Did you ask John?"

"No." Jake quickly sought out the youngest sales associate. John had just finished with a customer and looked expectantly at Jake.

"The robot's missing," he said without preamble.

John stared back at him. "The one in the storeroom?"

"Are there any others in this department?" he snapped. If there were, he'd grab one and be done with it. However, no one knew better than Jake that there wasn't an Intellytron to be had.

"I saw it," Gail said, joining them.

Relief washed over Jake. Someone had moved it without telling him; that was obviously what had happened. The prospect of facing Holly and telling her he didn't have the robot didn't bear thinking about.

That morning, the moment she'd received her Christmas bonus, Holly had rushed over to Finley's to pay for the toy.

Her face had been alight with happiness as she described how excited Gabe would be when he found his gift under the Christmas tree. That robot meant so much to the boy. If Jake didn't bring it as promised, Holly might not forgive him. He hoped that wouldn't happen, but the thought sent a chill through him nonetheless.

Frances, another sales associate, came over, too. "Mrs. Miracle had it," she said.

"When?"

"This morning," Frances explained. "She didn't mention it to you?"

"No." Jake shook his head. "What did she do with it?"

Frances stared down at the floor. "She sold it."

"*Sold* it?" Jake exploded. This had to be some kind of joke—didn't it? "How could she do that? It was already paid for by someone else." That robot belonged to Gabe Larson. She knew that as well as anyone.

"Why would she sell it?" he burst out again, completely bewildered.

"I…I don't know. You'll have to ask her," Frances said. "I'm so sorry, Mr. Finley. I'm sure there's a logical explanation."

There'd better be. Not that it would help now.

Sick at heart, Jake left the department and went up to his father's office. Dora had already gone home; the whole administrative floor was deserted. He didn't know what he'd tell Holly. He should've taken the robot to his apartment and kept it there. Then he could've been guaranteed that nothing like this would happen. Still, berating himself now wouldn't serve any useful purpose.

Preparing for his flight, J. R. Finley was busy stuffing paperwork in his computer case when Jake entered the office. J.R. looked up at him. "What's the matter with you? Did you decide to come with me, after all?"

"No. Have you decided to stay in New York?" Jake countered.

"You're kidding, right?"

Jake slumped into a chair and ran his fingers through his hair. "Gabe's robot is missing," he said quietly. "Emily Miracle, or whatever her name is, sold it."

"Mrs. Miracle?" J.R.'s face tightened and he waved his index finger at Jake. "I told you that woman was up to no good, butting into other people's business. She's a troublemaker. Didn't I tell you that?"

"Dad, stop it. She's a sweet grandmotherly woman."

"She's ruined a little boy's Christmas and you call that *sweet?*" He made a scoffing sound and resumed his task of collecting papers and shoving them into his case.

"Do you have any connections—someone who can locate a spare Intellytron at the last minute?" This was Jake's only hope.

Frowning, his father checked his watch. "I'll make some phone calls, but I can't promise anything."

Jake was grateful for whatever his father could do. "What about your flight?"

J.R. looked at his watch again and shrugged. "I'll catch a later one."

Jake started to remind his father that changing flights at

this point might be difficult, but stopped himself. If J.R. was going to offer his assistance, Jake would be a fool to refuse.

"I'll shut down the department and meet you back here in twenty minutes," Jake said.

His father had picked up his phone and was punching out numbers. One thing Jake could be assured of—if there was a single Intellytron left in the tristate area, J.R. would locate it and have it delivered to Gabe.

He hurried back to the toy department and saw that the last-minute customers were being ushered out, bags in hand, and the day's sales tallied. The store was officially closed. His staff was waiting to exchange Christmas greetings with Jake so they could go home to their families.

"Is there anything we can do before we leave?" John asked, speaking for the others.

"No, thanks. You guys have been great. Merry Christmas, everyone!"

As soon as they'd left, he got Mrs. Miracle's contact information and called the phone number she'd given HR. To his shock, a recorded voice message informed him that the number was no longer in service. That wasn't the only shock, either—she'd handed in her notice that afternoon.

He groaned. Mrs. Miracle was unreachable and had absconded with precious information regarding the robot—like why she'd sold it and to whom.

Jake returned to his father's office to find him pacing the floor with the receiver pressed to his ear. J.R. glanced in Jake's direction, then quickly looked away. That tight-lipped expression told Jake everything he needed to know—his father hadn't been successful.

He waited until J.R. hung up the phone.

"No luck," Jake said, not bothering to phrase it in the form of a question.

J.R. shook his head. "Everyone I talked to said as far as they knew we're the only store in five states to have the robot."

"*Had*. We sold out."

"Apparently there isn't another one to be found anywhere till after Christmas."

Jake had expected that. A sick feeling attacked the pit of his stomach as he sank into a chair and sighed loudly. "I appreciate your help, Dad. Thanks for trying."

"I'm sorry I couldn't do more." J.R. nodded and placed a consoling hand on Jake's shoulder. "I know how you feel."

Jake doubted that but he wasn't in the mood to argue.

"Holly's special," J.R. said. "I've known that since the first time you mentioned her."

"She is." Jake was in full agreement there.

"If it'd been your mother who needed that thing, I would've moved heaven and earth to make sure she got it."

He reconsidered. Maybe his father *did* know what he was feeling. He'd done his utmost to keep Holly and Gabe from being disappointed. Unfortunately, nothing he or J.R. did now would make any difference. It was simply too late.

"Every Intellytron in New York State and beyond is wrapped and under some youngster's tree," J.R. said.

Jake rubbed his face. "I'll come up with something to tell Holly and Gabe," he said, thinking out loud.

"Is there anything else the boy might like?" his father asked.

The only toy Gabe had referred to, at least in Jake's hearing, was the robot. He'd even risked Holly's wrath and traveled into the city on his own just to see it again and watch it in action.

"What about a train set?" his father suggested. "Every little boy wants a train set."

Jake had. He'd longed for one the Christmas his mother and sister had died. But there'd been no presents the next morning or any Christmas morning since the accident.

"He might," Jake said. "But—"

"Well, we have one of those."

Jake wondered what his father was talking about. As head of the toy department Jake was well aware of the inventory left in stock and there were no train sets. This season had been record-breaking in more ways than one; not only the robot but a number of other toys had sold out. The trains, a popular new doll, a couple of computer games… "Exactly where is there a train set?" he asked. "Unless you mean the one in the window…"

"Not the display train. A brand-new one. Except that it's twenty-one years old." J.R. swallowed visibly. "I have it," he said. "It's still wrapped in the original paper. Your mother bought it for you just before…" He didn't need to finish the sentence.

"Mom bought me the train set I wanted?" Jake asked, his voice hoarse with emotion.

J.R. grinned. "You were spoiled, young man. Your mother loved you deeply. And your little sister adored you."

A sense of loss hit him hard and for a moment that was all Jake could think about. "You kept the train set all these years?" he finally asked.

J.R. nodded solemnly. "I always meant to give it to you but I could never part with it. In a way, holding on to it was like…having your mother still with me. I could pretend it was Christmas Eve twenty-one years ago and she hadn't died. Don't worry, I didn't *actually* believe that, but I could indulge the fantasy of what Christmas should've been. That train set made the memory so real…."

"And you're willing to give it up for Gabe?"

"No" was his father's blunt reply. "I'm willing to give it up for *you*."

Jake smiled and whispered, "Thanks, Dad."

"You're welcome. Now we've got a bit of digging to do. I don't remember where I put that train set but I know it's somewhere in the condo. Or maybe the storage locker. Or…"

"Do we have time? Did you change your flight?"

"Flight?" J.R. repeated, then seemed to remember he was scheduled to fly out that evening. Shaking his head, he muttered, "It's fine. I'll catch one tomorrow if I have to."

Jake didn't want to pressure his father, but he'd promised Holly he'd invite J.R. to dinner at her apartment. Although he'd already tried once, he'd ask again. If he was going to disappoint her on one front, then the least he could do was surprise her on another.

"Since you're apparently staying over..." he began.

"Yes?"

"Have Christmas dinner with Holly and Gabe and me tomorrow afternoon. Will you do that, Dad?"

His father took a long moment to consider the invitation. Then, as if the words were difficult to say, he slowly whispered, "I believe I will. Something tells me your mother would want me to."

Chapter Eighteen

God isn't politically correct.
He's just correct.
—Mrs. Miracle

Holly set the phone down and forced herself to keep the smile on her face. Gabe's robot was missing. Because Gabe was in earshot, she couldn't ask Jake the questions that clamored in her mind. He'd said something about Mrs. Miracle, but Holly had been too disheartened to remember what followed.

Adding to her distress, Jake had said there was something he needed to do with his father, which meant he'd have to renege on dinner that night. In addition to the bad news about the missing robot, Jake had passed on some good news, too. Evidently his father had changed his plans and would be joining them on Christmas Day, after all, which delighted Holly and greatly encouraged her. She recognized that this was no small concession on J.R.'s part.

"Isn't Jake coming for dinner?" Gabe asked, looking up from his handheld video game. He lay on the sofa as he expertly manipulated the keys.

"I... No. Unfortunately, Jake has something else he has to do," Holly explained, doing her best to maintain an even voice. "Something really important," she emphasized.

Gabe frowned and sat up. "What's more important than Christmas Eve?"

Again Holly made an effort to pretend nothing was wrong. "We'll have to ask when we see him tomorrow," she said airily.

Her nephew slouched back onto the sofa. His downcast look prompted Holly to sit beside him. She felt as depressed as Gabe did, but was trying hard not to show it. In the larger scheme of life, these disappointments were minor. Nevertheless, she'd hoped to give Gabe a very special gift this year. And she'd hoped—so had Gabe—to spend Christmas Eve with Jake.

"Did Jake promise to come tomorrow?"

"He'll be here."

"But he said he'd come for dinner tonight, too—and he didn't."

"We'll have a wonderful time this evening, just the two of us." She slipped her arm around his small frame and squeezed gently.

Gabe didn't seem too sure of that. "Can I email my dad?"

"Of course." Holly would come up with ways to keep them both occupied until it was time to walk to church for the Christmas Eve service. They could watch a Christmas movie; Gabe might enjoy *The Bishop's Wife,* Holly's favorite, or *A Christmas Carol* with Alastair Sim as the ultimate Scrooge. Still cheering herself up, she headed into her kitchen to start frying the chicken, which had been marinating in buttermilk since six that morning. They'd have turkey tomorrow, but tonight she'd make the meal she associated with her mother... with comfort.

Gabe leaped up from the sofa and hurried into the kitchen. "Can we invite Mrs. Miracle for dinner?" he asked excitedly.

"Oh, Gabe, I wish we'd thought of that sooner."

"I like Mrs. Miracle."

"I like her, too." The older woman had never mentioned whether she had family in the area, which made Holly wonder if she was spending this evening by herself.

Gabe returned to writing his email. "Dad's surprise didn't come, did it?" he said in a pensive voice.

Holly suddenly realized it hadn't. This complicated everything. Not only wouldn't she be able to give her nephew the only toy he'd requested for Christmas, but the gift his father had mailed hadn't arrived, either.

"He might be mad at me for going into the city by myself," Gabe murmured.

"Oh, sweetie, I'm positive that's not it."

Before she could finish her reassurances, the doorbell chimed. Hoping, despite everything, that it was Jake, Holly answered the door, still wearing her apron. To her astonishment, Emily Miracle was standing in the hall.

"I hope you don't mind me dropping in unexpectedly like this."

"Mrs. Miracle! Mrs. Miracle!" Gabe rushed to the door. "We were just talking about you." He grabbed her free hand and tugged her into the apartment. "Can you stay for dinner? Aunt Holly's making fried chicken and there's corn and mashed potatoes and cake, too. You can stay, can't you? Jake said he was coming and now he can't."

"Oh, dear," Emily said, laughing softly. "I suppose I could. I came by to bring you my Christmas salad. It's a family favorite and I wanted to share it with you."

"That's so nice of you, Emily," Holly said, adding a place setting to the table. Her mood instantly lightened.

"Jake *said* he'd come," Gabe pouted.

"He's doing something important," Holly reminded her nephew.

"I'm sure he is," Emily said, giving Holly a covered ceramic bowl and removing her coat. "It isn't like Jake to cancel at the last moment without a good reason. He's a very responsible young man—in his personal life and in business, too. He'll do his father proud." She held out her hands for the bowl.

"You mean *does* his father proud," Holly corrected, passing it back. She had every confidence that Jake would one day step up to the helm at Finley's, but that was sometime in the future. Jake seemed to think it might take as long as five years, and he said that suited him fine.

"Yes, that's what I mean. I've enjoyed working with him

this Christmas season." Emily made her way into the kitchen and put her salad in the refrigerator.

"Can you come to church with us?" Gabe asked, following her. "It's Christmas Eve, and there's a special program and singing, too."

"I'd like that very much, but unfortunately I already have other plans."

"We're grateful you could have dinner with us," Holly said. She waited until Gabe had left the room before she asked Emily about the robot.

"Do you have any idea what happened to the you-know-what Jake put aside?" She spoke guardedly because the apartment was small and she wanted to ensure that Gabe didn't hear anything that would upset him.

Mrs. Miracle was about to answer when he dashed into the kitchen again.

Grasping the situation, she immediately distracted him. "Do you want to help me fill the water glasses?" she asked.

"Okay," Gabe agreed.

Emily poured water into the pitcher, which she handed to Gabe. Holding it carefully, he walked over to the dining area, which was actually part of the living room. The older woman turned to Holly. "I think there was a misunderstanding between Jake and me," she said in a low voice. "I'll clear everything up as soon as I can."

"Please do," Holly whispered. She tried to recall her conversation with Jake. He seemed to imply that Emily had sold the robot to someone else. That didn't seem possible. She'd never do anything to hurt a little boy; Holly was convinced of it.

The fried chicken couldn't have been better; in fact, it was as good as when her mother had prepared this dish. Holly had wanted tonight's meal to be memorable for Gabe, and because Mrs. Miracle was with them, it was.

During dinner, Emily entertained them with story after story of various jobs she'd taken through the years. She'd certainly had her share of interesting experiences, working as a waitress, a nanny, a nurse and now a salesperson.

All too soon, it was time to get ready for church. Holly reluctantly stood up from the table.

"Everything was lovely," Mrs. Miracle told her with a smile of appreciation. "I've never had chicken that was more delicious." She carried her empty dessert plate to the kitchen sink. "And that coconut cake…"

"I liked the sauce best," Gabe chimed in, putting his plate in the sink, too.

"I loved the salad," Holly said, and was sincere. "I hope you'll give me the recipe."

"Of course. I'll be happy to write it out for you now if you'll get me some paper and a pen."

Holly tore a page from a notebook and grabbed Gabe's Santa pen; minutes later, Mrs. Miracle handed her the recipe with a flourish. "Here you go." Then she frowned at her watch. "Oh, my. I hate to run, but I'm afraid I must."

"No, no, don't worry," Holly assured her. "We have to leave for church, anyway. I'm just glad you could be with us this evening. It meant a lot to Gabe and me."

The older woman bent down and kissed the boy's cheek. "This is going to be a very special Christmas for you, young man. Just you wait. It's one you'll remember your whole life. Someday you'll tell your grandchildren about the best Christmas of your life."

"Do you really think so?" Gabe asked, eyes alight with happiness.

She reached for her coat and put it on before she hugged Holly goodbye. "It's going to be a special Christmas for you, as well, my dear."

Holly smiled politely. Maybe Mrs. Miracle was right, but it definitely hadn't started out that way.

Gabe woke at six o'clock Christmas morning. He knocked on Holly's bedroom door and shouted, "It's Christmas!" Apparently he suspected she might have forgotten.

Holly opened one eye. Still half-asleep, she sat up and stretched her arms above her head.

"Can we open our presents?" Gabe asked, leaping onto her bed.

"What about breakfast?" she said.

"I'm not hungry. You aren't, either, are you?" The question had a hopeful lilt, as though any thought of food would be equally irrelevant to her.

"I could eat," she said.

Gabe's face fell.

"I could eat…later," she amended.

His jubilant smile reappeared.

"Shall we see what Santa brought you?" she asked, tossing

aside her covers. She threw on her housecoat and accompanied him into the living room, where the gifts beneath the small tree awaited their inspection.

Gabe fell to his knees and began rooting through the packages she'd set out the night before, after he'd gone to sleep. He must've known from the size of the wrapped boxes that the robot wasn't among them. He sat back on his heels. "Santa didn't get me Intellytron, did he?"

"I don't know, sweetie. I hear Santa sometimes makes late deliveries."

"He does?" Hope shone in his face. "When?"

"That I can't say." Rather than discuss the subject further, Holly hurried into the kitchen.

While she put on a pot of coffee, Gabe arranged the gifts in two small piles. Most of them had been mailed by Holly's parents, and Gabe's didn't take long to unwrap. He was wonderful, sweetly expressing gratitude and happiness with his few gifts. A number of times Holly had to wipe tears from her eyes.

"I hope you're not too disappointed," she said when she could speak. "I know how badly you wanted the robot—and I'm sure Santa has one for you but it might be a little late."

Gabe looked up from the new video game she'd purchased on her way home from work. "I bet I'll still get Intellytron. Mrs. Miracle said this was going to be my best Christmas ever, remember? And it wouldn't be without my robot." He jumped up and slid his arms around Holly's neck and gave her a tight hug.

She opened her gifts after that—a book from her parents,

plus a calendar and a peasant-style blouse. And the origami purse from Gabe, which brought fresh tears to her eyes.

They had a leisurely breakfast of French toast and then, while Gabe played with his new video game, Holly got the turkey in the oven. The doorbell rang around eleven o'clock.

Jake and his father came in, carrying a large wrapped box between them. Holly's heartbeat accelerated. It must be Intellytron, although the box actually seemed too big.

"Merry Christmas," Jake said, and held her close. "Don't get excited—this isn't what you think it is," he whispered in her ear just before he kissed her.

"Merry Christmas, young man," J.R. said, and shook Gabe's hand.

"What's that?" Gabe asked, eyeing the box Jake had set on the carpet.

"Why don't you open it and see?" J.R. suggested.

Jake stood at Holly's side with his arm around her waist. "I'm sorry I had to cancel last night," he said in a low voice.

"It's fine, don't worry."

"Mrs. Miracle came over," Gabe said as he sat on the floor beside the box.

"Emily Miracle?" Jake frowned. "Did she happen to deliver something?" he asked, his eyes narrowing.

"She brought a Christmas salad for dinner," Gabe told him, tearing away the ribbon. He looked up. "We didn't eat it all. Do you want to taste it?" He wrinkled his nose. "For green stuff, it was pretty good."

"I wouldn't want to ruin my dinner," J.R. said, smiling down at him. "Go ahead, young man, and let 'er rip."

Gabe didn't need any encouragement. He tore away the wrapping paper. "It's a train set," he said. "That was the second thing on my Christmas list, after Intellytron. Can we set it up now?"

"I don't see why not," Jake told him and got down on his knees with Gabe. "I wanted one when I was around your age, too."

"Did you get one?" Gabe asked.

Jake looked at his father, who sat on the sofa, and nodded. "I certainly did, and it was the best train set money could buy."

Gabe took the engine out of the box. "Wow, this is heavy."

"Let's lay out the track first, shall we?"

Holly sat on the sofa next to Jake's father. "I'm so glad you could have dinner with us."

"I am, too." A pained look came over him and he gave a slight shake of his head. "I was sure I'd never want to celebrate Christmas again, but I've decided it's time I released the past and started to prepare for the future."

"The future?" she repeated uncertainly.

"Grandchildren," J.R. said with a sheepish grin. "I have the distinct feeling that my son has met the woman he's going to love as much as I loved his mother."

Embarrassed, Holly looked away. With all her heart she hoped she was that woman.

"Jake would be furious with me if he knew I'd said anything. It's too soon—I realize that. He probably isn't aware of how strongly he feels, but I know. I've seen my son with other women. He's in love with you, the same way I was in love with Helene."

Holly was about to make some excuse about dinner and return to the kitchen when the doorbell chimed again. Everyone looked at her as if she knew who it would be.

"I…I wonder who that is," she murmured, walking to the door.

"It could be Mrs. Miracle," Gabe said hopefully.

Only it wasn't.

Holly opened the apartment door to find her brother standing there in his army fatigues, wearing a smile of pure happiness. In his arms he held a large wrapped box.

"Mickey!" she screamed. He put down the box and hugged her fiercely.

"Dad!" Gabe flew off the floor as though jet-propelled and launched himself into his father's arms.

Eyes closed, Mickey held the boy for a long, long time.

Merry Christmas, Holly thought, tears slipping down her face. Just as Emily Miracle had predicted, this was destined to be the best Christmas of Gabe's life.

DEBBIE MACOMBER

Baby Arugula Salad with Goat Cheese, Pecans and Pomegranate Seeds
(from *Debbie Macomber's Cedar Cove Cookbook*)

This salad is a lively blend of sharp arugula, tangy goat cheese, mellow pecans and tart pomegranates. If you can't find arugula, substitute any delicate salad green.

- 1 small shallot, minced
- 3 tablespoons balsamic vinegar
- 1 teaspoon Dijon mustard
- Salt and pepper, to taste
- ½ cup extra-virgin olive oil
- 10 to 12 cups baby arugula (about 10 ounces)
- 1 cup pomegranate seeds (from one pomegranate)
- ½ cup toasted pecans, chopped
- 1 cup crumbled goat cheese

1. In a measuring cup, whisk shallot, vinegar, mustard, salt and pepper until combined. Slowly pour oil in a stream until blended.

2. In a large serving bowl, combine arugula, pomegranate seeds and pecans. Add dressing; toss to coat. Top salad with cheese; toss once.

TIP: Extra-virgin olive oil, which comes from the first cold pressing of the olives, has a stronger, purer flavor than virgin olive oil. Since it is more expensive, most cooks prefer to use it only for salad and other uncooked dishes. Virgin olive oil is better for sautéing.

Serves 8.

Chapter Nineteen

Searching for a new look? Have your faith lifted!
—Mrs. Miracle

Mickey stepped into the apartment, still holding Gabe, and extended his hand to Jake. "You must be Jake Finley."

"And you must be Holly's brother, Mickey."

"I am."

"What's in there?" Gabe asked, looking over his father's shoulder at the large box resting on the other side of the open door.

"That's a little something Santa asked me to deliver," Mickey told his son. Gabe squirmed out of his arms and raced back into the hallway. He stared at Holly and his grin seemed to take up his whole face. "I think I know what it is," he declared before pushing the box inside. "Aunt Holly told me Santa sometimes makes deliveries late."

No one needed to encourage him to unwrap the gift this time. He tore into the wrapping paper, which flew in all directions. As soon as he saw the picture of Intellytron on the outside of the box, Gabe gave a shout of exhilaration.

"It's my robot! It's my robot!"

"Wherever did you find one?" J.R. asked Mickey. The older man stepped forward and extended his hand. "J. R. Finley," he said.

"He bought it at Finley's," Jake answered in a confused tone.

"Our department store?" J.R. sounded incredulous. "When?"

"My guess is that it was late on Christmas Eve." Again, Jake supplied the answer.

"And how do you know all this?" Holly had a few questions of her own.

"Because that's the gift wrap Mrs. Miracle used."

"But...who sold it to him?" J.R. appeared completely befuddled by this latest development.

"Mrs. Miracle," Jake and Holly murmured simultaneously.

"He's right," Mickey said as he sat on the couch next to his son, who remained on the floor. "I remember her name badge. Mrs. Miracle. We talked for a few minutes."

Thankfully, Gabe was too involved with his robot to listen.

"I had a chance to go into the city yesterday," Mickey told them.

"Wait." Holly held up her hand. "You've got some splainin'

to do, Lieutenant Larson. Why are you in New York in the first place?"

Mickey laughed. "Don't tell me you don't want me here?"

"No, no, of course I do! But you might've said something."

"I couldn't."

"Security reasons?" Holly asked.

"No, just that I wasn't sure I'd get the leave I was hoping for. I've been sent back for specialized training—I'll be at Fort Dix for the next six weeks. I didn't want to say anything to Gabe yet, in case it fell through. I could tell from his emails that he was starting to adjust to life here with you. It would've been cruel to raise his hopes, only to have Uncle Sam dash them. Turns out I was on duty until nine this morning...so here I am. I thought I'd bring Gabe his Christmas surprise."

"You might've mentioned it to *me*," Holly said with more than a little consternation.

"True, but I had to take your poor track record with keeping secrets into consideration."

"I can keep a secret," she insisted.

"Oh, yeah? What about the time you told Candi Johnson I had a crush on her?"

"I was twelve years old!"

Jake chuckled and she sent him a stern look. If Mickey had asked her not to say anything about his possible visit, she wouldn't have uttered a word. Then it occurred to her that he'd hinted at it when he referred to the surprise he was sending Gabe. Fantastic, stupendous, *exhilarating* though this was, a Christmas visit was the last thing she'd expected.

"But why buy the robot?" Holly asked. "I told you I'd get it for Gabe."

"Yes, but you were going without lunches—"

"True," she interrupted, whispering so Gabe wouldn't hear. "Then Lindy Lee had a change of heart and decided to give me a Christmas bonus, after all."

Mickey shrugged. "You didn't say anything to me. Not that it matters because *I* wanted to get this for Gabe."

"I didn't tell you I received my bonus?"

"You've done enough for the two of us," Mickey told her, his eyes warm with appreciation. "I didn't want to burden you with the added expense of Christmas."

"Hey, Holly, that means Finley's owes you two hundred and fifty dollars," Jake said. "Plus tax. By the way, Mickey, did you tell Mrs. Miracle who you were?" he asked, approaching the two of them. He slipped his arm around Holly's waist and she casually leaned against him.

Mickey shook his head. "Should I have?"

Jake and Holly exchanged a glance, but it was Jake who voiced their question. "How did she know?"

"Know what?" Mickey asked.

"That it was you," Holly said.

"Look, Dad!" Gabe cried out.

Mickey turned his attention to the robot, who walked smartly toward him, stopped and asked in a tinny voice, "When...do...you...go...back...to...Afghanistan?"

Mickey's eyes widened. "How'd you make him say that?"

J.R., who'd been working with Gabe, grinned at Mickey. "I programmed him," Gabe announced proudly. "Mr. Finley helped, but he said I can do it on my own now that I know how."

"You managed to get the robot to do that already?"

"He does all kinds of cool tricks, Dad. Watch."

While Mickey and Gabe were engaged in programming the robot, Jake and Holly stepped into the kitchen.

"She *couldn't* have known Mickey was Gabe's father." Jake's face was clouded with doubt. "Could she?"

Holly didn't have an answer.

Jake continued, still frowning. "I tried to reach her, but the phone number she listed with HR wasn't in service."

"Then ask her when you see her again," Holly said. Jake had mentioned that, as seasonal help, Emily Miracle would be working until after inventory had been completed in January.

"I won't be able to," Jake told her. "When I went to HR for her personal information, I discovered that she'd handed in her notice. Christmas Eve was her last day."

"But…" Holly wanted to argue. Surely Mrs. Miracle would've said *something* at dinner the night before. Things didn't quite add up…. And yet, this wonderful woman had done so much to brighten their Christmas.

Before she could comment, the doorbell rang again. Holly chuckled, not even daring to guess who it might be *this* time. Her apartment was turning into Grand Central Station. If she had to guess, the last person to cross her mind would've been…

"Lindy!" Her employer's name shot out of Holly's mouth the second she opened the door.

Lindy Lee smiled hesitantly. "I hope I'm not intruding."

"You came, you came." Gabe bounded up from the floor and raced to Lindy Lee's side, taking her hand.

Lindy gave Holly an apologetic look. "Gabe invited me and since I, uh, didn't have any commitments, I thought I'd stop by for a few minutes and wish you all a Merry Christmas." She glanced about the room. "I see you already have a houseful."

"I'm Gabe's father," Mickey said, stepping forward. "Holly's brother." He set his hands on Gabe's shoulders.

"She's the lady I wrote you about," Gabe said, twisting around and looking up at his father. "Isn't she pretty?"

"Yes, she is…." Mickey seemed unable to take his eyes off Lindy Lee.

Holly wouldn't have believed it possible, but Lindy actually blushed.

"Thank you," the designer murmured.

"Make yourself at home," Holly said. "I was just about to serve some eggnog. Would you like a glass?"

"Are you sure it won't be any bother?"

"She's sure," Gabe said, dragging Lindy Lee toward the couch. "Here, sit next to my dad." He patted an empty space on the sofa. "Dad, you sit here."

Mickey smiled at Lindy Lee. "I guess we've got our orders."

"Yes, sir," Lindy joked, winking at Gabe.

"You know what she said to me, Dad?"

"What?"

"I said," Lindy Lee supplied, "that I need a little boy in my life. A little boy just like Gabe."

Holly wondered if she'd heard correctly. This woman who looked identical to her employer sounded nothing like the Lindy Lee she knew. Gone was the dictatorial, demanding tyrant who ran her fashion-design business with military precision. She'd either been taken over by aliens or Lindy Lee had a gentle side that she kept hidden and revealed only on rare occasions. Like Christmas...

An hour later, during a private moment in the kitchen, Jake gave Holly a gift—a cameo that had once belonged to his mother. He said J.R. had given it to him for this very purpose the night before. Holly was thrilled, honored, humbled. She held her breath as he put the cameo on its gold chain around her neck. Holly didn't have anything for him, but Jake said all he wanted was a kiss, and she was happy to comply.

Two hours after that, the small group gathered around the table laden with Christmas fare, including several bottles of exceptional wine brought by Jake and his father. Gabe sat between Mickey and Lindy Lee and chatted nonstop, while J.R. and Jake sat with Holly between them. They took turns saying grace, then took turns again, passing serving dishes to one another.

Amid the clinking of silverware on china and the animated conversation and laughter, Gabe's voice suddenly rose.

"Mrs. Miracle was right," he declared after his first bite of turkey. "This is the *best* Christmas ever."

Emily Merkle reached for her suitcase and started down the long road. Her job in New York was finished, and it had gone even better than she'd expected. Holly and Jake were falling in love. J.R. had more interest in anticipating the future than reliving the pain of the past. Mickey had met Lindy Lee, and Gabe had settled in nicely with his aunt Holly.

Emily hadn't walked far when she was joined by two others, a beautiful woman and a ten-year-old girl. Kaitlyn skipped gracefully at her mother's side, holding Helene's hand.

"All is well," Emily told the other woman. "J.R. and Jake will celebrate Christmas from now on. It was a big leap for J.R., but once the grandchildren arrive, he will lavish them with love."

"Jake will marry Holly?" she asked.

Emily nodded. "They'll have many years together."

"You chose well for my son."

Emily nodded in agreement. Jake and Holly were a good match and they'd bring out the best in each other.

The other woman smiled contentedly. "Thank you," she whispered.

"It was my pleasure," Emily told her.

And it truly was.

* * * * *

The No.1 *New York Times* bestselling author

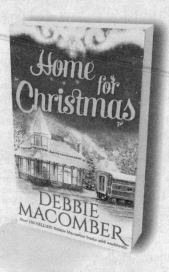

In New Hampshire a crowded train is taking holiday travellers home. But, when a snowstorm hits, this group of strangers ends up stranded at a deserted train station on Christmas Eve. Despite the bitter cold and longing for their loved ones, can they remind each other of what Christmas really means?

Make time for friends
Make time for Debbie Macomber

Spend Christmas with
DEBBIE MACOMBER

Make time for friends. Make time for
DEBBIE MACOMBER

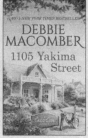

Loved this book?

Visit Debbie Macomber's fantastic website at
www.debbiemacomber.com for information
about Debbie, her latest books, news,
competitions, knitting tips, recipes,
Debbie's blog and much more…

 Find even more Debbie Macomber extras at
Facebook.com/DebbieMacomberWorld

www.debbiemacomber.com